DISCARD

THE IMMORTAL VON B.

A NOVEL

M. SCOTT CARTER

THE ROADRUNNER PRESS
OKLAHOMA CITY, OKLAHOMA

Published by The RoadRunner Press
Oklahoma City
www.TheRoadRunnerPress.com

Published October 16, 2012

Library of Congress Control Number: 2012939715

Publisher's Cataloging-in-Publication
(Prepared by The Donohue Group, Inc.)

Carter, M. Scott.
    The immortal Von B. : a novel / M. Scott Carter. -- 1st ed.

    p. ; cm.

    Summary: When Josie Brunswick has to move to Europe so her father can head a
secret genetics program for a mysterious global corporation, she thinks life couldn't
get any worse. Then her mother dies. Music becomes her reason to live, until an accident in her father's lab produces something that will send her on a mad adventure
throughout Vienna and through time.
    Interest age level: 14 and up.
    ISBN: 978-1-937054-30-4

    1. Teenage girls--Fiction. 2. Life change events--Fiction. 3. Cloning--Fiction. 4.
Time travel--Fiction. 5. Music--Fiction. 6. Beethoven, Ludwig van, 1770-1827--Fic-
tion. 7. Vienna (Austria)--Fiction. 8. Science fiction. I. Title.

PS3603.A784 Im 2012
813/.6   2012939715

For Paula,
… because I still remember the song

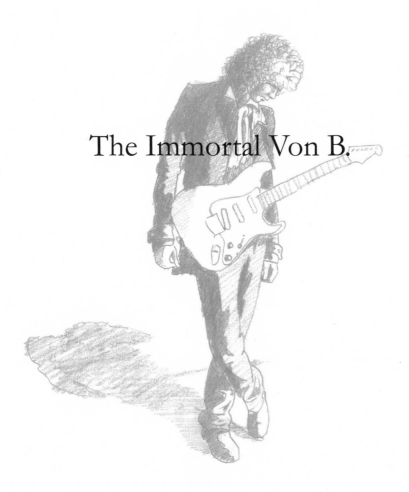

The Immortal Von B.

"What you are, you are by accident of birth;
what I am, I created myself. There are, and will be,
a thousand princes; there is only one Beethoven."

— Ludwig von Beethoven

Prologue

THE MUSIC WAS SCREAMING, but it was all wrong. I stood in the middle of the garage, surrounded by a huge, throbbing (off-key) guitar wail that rattled the windows and shook the stage. Behind me, a stack of Marshall amplifiers throbbed and pulsated every time I hit a chord — or every time Tria slid her fingers down the neck of her metallic purple Stratocaster.

The three of us — me, Tria, and Michelle — were practicing in the garage Dad had converted to a studio for me when we moved back to Oklahoma after the nightmare. He tacked up soundproof insulation, installed a recorder and a mixing board, and topped it all off with a ton of digital, high-tech equipment.

At one end, he had built a small stage. On it he stacked lights and a wall of amplifiers. There aren't too many garage bands that come this well equipped. But even with all the technology and the posh studio, my fingers wouldn't work. I tried a G chord and it came out sounding like a dying animal. I turned to Tria and made a slicing motion across my throat.

She scowled and stopped playing.

"What is it this time?"

Michelle threw her drumsticks to the floor. They rolled across the cement like small castanets. She wiped her face with her bandanna.

"Come on Josie, again? That sounded pretty good to me."

I shook my head, as Tria rolled her eyes and Michelle pouted.

The Immortal Von B.

They don't intimidate me. I know what I hear.

"Nope. It's still not balanced. It's not there yet. It needs more attitude, you know, more grit, more anger."

I pointed at Tria.

"You and that Strat have to snarl and growl. You have to play like you're going to rip out the throat of some hopeless guy in the front row and then stomp around in his blood."

Tria grimaced.

"Okay. Okay. More anger. I get it," she said. "But seriously, just how angry should you make Beethoven? I mean, *Ode to Joy* isn't known for its venom. It's a symphony about love and brotherhood."

I plugged my Flying V back into the amps.

"True, but the man who composed it was angry, very angry at the world when he wrote it. He poured every feeling, every emotion he had into these notes. This is my interpretation of that. You have to understand this isn't just another rock song. It's not three minutes of drum and a couple of guitars. This is pure emotion — raw, sensual, and angry."

Tria gave a nod.

"Okay, well, I usually don't think of classical music like that."

I pushed the Flying V's neck out of the way and put my hand over my heart, trying to still it so I could explain.

"Most folks don't. But understand I am not looking for something typically classical. This isn't about universal brotherhood. This is primal. This is about regret, about loss. This is new Beethoven. Metal and amplified with the top pulled down and the wind howling in your face like a wild animal. I want to feel music roll over me like a rogue wave. I want an eyes-roll-back-into-your-head sound. I want something so unchained that it makes you go numb."

Tria stepped towards me, flashed her perfect white teeth, and growled furiously, like a lioness taking down an antelope. She grinned.

"Something like that?"

I nodded with a big smile.

"Oh, yeah. Now do that with your guitar."

I slid my fingers down the strings.

"Let's try it again."

The chords weren't that difficult, pretty much G, D, B, A, and E.

The fingerpicking, however, wasn't easy. Not the way we were playing. We were two minutes deep in the chorus when my right index finger hit a stray guitar wire. It sliced my finger open in a long ragged gash; blood shot everywhere.

Tria dropped her Strat and rushed to help.

"Josie? You okay?"

I put my finger in my mouth to stop the bleeding. Michelle ripped off her headband, grabbed my cut hand, and wrapped the bandanna around the wound.

"I know you said you wanted to see blood, but I thought it was a metaphor," she said, with a grin.

I laughed, then winced. Michelle put my other hand on the bloody cloth and applied pressure.

"Hold that tight until it stops bleeding."

Blood coated my shirt and my hand. I looked at it, almost in shock. *I closed my eyes and the world spun out of control. I'm not sure what's wrong with me, but I know it's not about the blood or the pain. It's about the music. I can't seem to get it right. I've played guitar for years, but for some reason this piece — one that's so important to me — I just can't do it justice.*

Tears threatened. Everything — every feeling, every memory from that time, every regret — returned, leaving me stammering and helpless. I told myself it's because I still don't have the right sound. But it could as easily be because I still miss Mom. Or Fa8 or . . . him.

Whatever the reason, the tears not only spilled over, they wouldn't stop. Tria and Michelle stood in front of me a little in shock themselves: the Josie Brunswick they knew never cried.

Before they could ask, I took control.

"I . . . I'm sorry," I said, gulping for air. "Didn't mean to fall apart."

Tria put her arms around me.

"Josie, what's wrong? Why are you so upset? It's just a little cut."

I tried to answer her, really I did, but I choked instead. What words I managed to get out were garbled: "I . . . you see; it . . . ah . . ."

Michelle grabbed a chair, turned it backwards, and sat down in front of me. She put one finger on top of my hand. I looked up to see her more serious than I'd ever seen her before.

"Come on, Josie. We've played together for months and you act like we're strangers. Some days you're all fun and happy, but more days than I think you realize, you're a black cloud. And now you're freaking out. Seriously. I hate to tell you, but *Ode to Joy* is neither that hard nor that important in the big scheme of things. Even your angry-radical-ear-splitting version. Wanna fill us in on what's really going on?"

"I'm . . . I'm just a little emotional right now. That's all." Like a turtle, I could feel myself pulling into the safety of my shell.

Michelle would have none of it.

"Rubbish," she said. "I don't believe you. You've been this way a long time. And it makes no sense."

Her gaze ran from one end of the garage to the other.

"You have all this," she said, with a sweep of her arm, "but it's like you're still not happy. It's like you're somewhere else — somewhere far away. I swear, if my dad did this for me, I'd never ask him for another thing."

I wiped my eyes on my sleeve. "You guys wouldn't understand."

Tria pulled me close, wagging a finger at me like I could not be more wrong about them.

"Try us," Tria said. "We're friends. Heck, we're more than friends — we're bandmates, right? Can't get any tighter than that."

She had a point.

"It's just my life has been messed up for so long, and you guys are busy and have your own problems, and, well, we're just now getting our sound right and I don't want . . ."

Michelle stood up with an exasperated sigh.

"Josie. Stop. If something is bothering you, we want to know. Tell us. We're your friends. You don't have to deal with this alone!"

I so wanted to believe her.

I had been on my own for way too long. I wanted to talk to someone about what I had lost. I walked over to a small shelf by the door, grabbed a large leather notebook, and turned back to look at my two friends, who were staring at me like they didn't know what would come out of my mouth next.

"Are you sure? Cause it's pretty messed up," I said. "Look at me, I'm pretty messed up. The past few years of my life have been scary-movie strange. And you probably won't even believe me. This is your last chance to bail. I would understand if you did."

Tria's eyes grew big — she glanced over at Michelle.

"You . . . you didn't kill anyone, did you?"

"No, silly."

Michelle stepped towards me, a determined look on her face.

"Are . . . are you pregnant? I remember that one jerk . . . what's his name, Darren, drooling all over you the other night."

I stomped my foot in frustration.

"Come on guys. Get serious, will you? It's nothing like that."

I sat down and placed on the sofa a large, leather notebook, overflowing with newspaper clippings, notes, photographs, scraps of paper, cocktail napkins, and some torn (slightly burned) pages.

"It's all here. The story of my life before I met you."

Tria sniffed the air. "Smells like smoke. You must have had an exciting life if it involves fire."

I sat down on the edge of the stage and grinned sheepishly.

"You have no idea."

While Michelle and Tria drew closer, I opened the notebook and removed a small photograph, slightly torn on one end with colors beginning to fade.

"I . . . I guess it starts here," I said.

Michelle pointed at the woman in the photo.

"Who's that at the piano?"

I took a deep breath.

"My mother — the photo was taken in her studio."

"I didn't know your mom was a musician," Tria said. "A pianist?"

"Yeah. She was amazing. She toured all over the world."

Michelle took the photo from me, handling it as carefully as if it were a priceless artifact.

"She looks like she's smiling, happy. You said she was famous?"

"Yeah," I gulped more air. "Her name was Anna Heigle."

Michelle looked at me like I just told her Elvis was alive and working at the local Burger King.

"Anna Heigle. Your mom was Anna Heigle?"

"Yeah."

"Anna Heigle-Brunswick? The Anna Heigle-Brunswick?"

Tria shook her head apologetically. "I don't know who . . ."

Michelle jumped in before Tria could finish.

"Anna Heigle-Brunswick toured the world playing Beethoven in places like Vienna's Musikverein and the Boston Symphony Hall. She just might have been the most famous female pianist in the world. Jeez. I had no idea she was your mom. I saw her live in New York when I was eight — I'll never forget what she could do at the piano."

"She was pretty amazing," I said.

"I am so sorry, Josie," Michelle said. "I never realized, I mean, you said your mom died when you were young, but you never ever talk about her."

Tria reached for the faded photo and pointed at a small mound under the piano bench. "Is that you?"

I fought back tears at the sight of the small sleeping child.

"Yeah, it's me. I was three, I guess, maybe four. I used to sneak into her studio and listen to her practice. I guess that time I fell asleep."

Michelle smiled and now tears rimmed her eyes. "Now I understand. This piece, the Ninth, it's about your mom."

"Well, yes and no," I said.

Michelle and Tria exchanged looks. I smiled sadly at my two confused bandmates — I had told them it was complicated.

"Yes, I miss my mom," I said. "After she died I stopped playing the piano and started playing the guitar. But a couple of years ago, my whole world turned upside down again and only then did I realize just what she — and her music — meant to me."

Michelle flipped through the pages of the notebook, then looked up at me as if she had figured something out.

"Is all this stuff here about your mom?"

I shook my head. "No, remember how I told you I lived in Vienna for awhile? There's stuff about a boy I met there, too."

Tria handed me back the photograph, stood, and strapped her guitar back on. She looked at that moment like the most powerful woman on earth.

"A boy," Tria said, with a knowing grin. "It's always about a boy."

"He wasn't just any boy," I said, quietly.

Something in my voice brought both Tria and Michelle up short and left them speechless for a few seconds.

Finally, Michelle broke the silence. "Go on," she said.

"Let's just say I have to get this song right for him," I said. "It's important to me . . . and it would be important to him."

"Why didn't you just say so in the first place?" Michelle asked, walking back to her drums. "Let's play this song the way you hear it in your head. But after we get this right, you have to tell us the whole story. Okay?"

"Yeah," Tria added, grinning. "You want angry Beethoven; baby, you're gonna get angry Beethoven. We are your girls. We will give you a Beethoven that's furious and loud and all sorts of mean, but when we are done, you have to start at the very beginning and tell us everything. Promise?"

Her fingers ran up and down the frets on her guitar, releasing a raw rip of sound.

"And I do mean, *everything*," Tria said.

What could a girl say?

I nodded and slipped my Flying V around my neck.

"Okay," I said, "but it is not your typical boy-meets-girl story. Trust me."

Tria pulled me up on the stage. She cranked up the volume on the amps and strummed a perfect C chord — it echoed throughout the room and into the night.

"Josie, we never thought it would be."

Part I: Change

Chapter 1
Tulsa Time

AT FIRST, WE LIVED IN TULSA — Dad, Mom, and me — in a house west of town on Lookout Mountain, which isn't so much a mountain as a big hill. Our house sat near the top, halfway up the west side. It overlooked a train yard and some TV broadcast antennae.

My dad, Joseph, tall and slender with sandy brown hair and bright green eyes, was born in Tulsa. He always told Mom and me that he never wanted to leave. He said red dirt flowed through his blood. Every time he talked about Oklahoma, Mom would laugh. Mom was from Vienna and said she didn't care where we lived so long as we were always together.

My dad is a doctor by talent and choice. He has always wanted to help make sick people better. He went to medical school, and, when I was a baby, he did the doctor thing — you know, seeing patients and writing prescriptions — stuff like that. But in the end, being a family doctor wasn't enough for him.

Right after I finished the third grade, he gave up his practice and went into medical research. He became this genius scientist with specialties in microbiology and human genetics. He told me his research could help more sick people quicker than he ever could have being a regular doctor.

My mom, Anna, wasn't a scientist or a doctor, but she was in a creative field, like my dad: She was a classical pianist. As a girl, she studied music at Juilliard in New York City. Her father, my grandfather, was a famous musician, too. Before she married my father, my mom traveled the globe, playing concerts and performing for huge crowds. She was as beautiful as she was talented, with shiny golden hair and cornflower blue eyes. She brightened every place she went, and, after they met, she never went anywhere without my father.

And me? I'm Josie — short for Josephine. Josephine Brunswick, officially. I'm not very tall but blessed with my mom's eyes. Cursed with mousy brown hair, and, my Dad always said, slender as a blade of grass. I love music and I love to dance. My earliest memory is sitting next to my mom on the piano bench as she played her Steinway. Dad always liked to say that my mom and I were the musicians of the family. He was just our audience. He seemed to like it that way.

Anyway, that's my family: Dad, Mom, and me. At least it was my family before we moved to Vienna and everything got messed up.

I remember the year we moved overseas well, because I had just figured out how to ride my bike without killing myself and I'd kissed Jack Tolbert — a cute boy who lived down the hill from us.

I loved living in Oklahoma. Mom performed here and around the world, Dad worked in his lab, and I kept busy with school.

I know some folks wouldn't live anywhere but the beach or mountains, but I was born for wide, open spaces. I loved watching fiery orange sunsets set against a dark purple sky. I loved hearing thunderstorms roll over the plains late at night. And I loved sitting by an open window and listening to the semis cruise down old Route 66.

On the weekends, I'd walk down our hill, lie on my back, and watch the puffy clouds morph into animals, shapes, and magical beings.

We weren't rich. Nobody but mom was famous. But my world was storybook perfect.

Then everything changed.

. . . .

"Hey my girls, have I got a surprise for you."

Dad rushed through the front door and tossed his briefcase on the living room couch. He had the biggest smile on his face I'd ever seen.

"Where are my beautiful ladies?"

The Immortal Von B.

I ran into the living room and jumped into his arms; it was good to have him home. "Did you bring me something?"

Dad shook his head as if he had forgotten.

I pretended to pout, because I knew he was teasing. Our coming-home-from-a-work-trip-ritual demanded, however, that I play along.

"You didn't bring me a present?" I flopped down on the couch.

Dad frowned (more of the game) and tried his best to look remorseful. "No, honey. I didn't bring you anything. Guess you'll just have to wait until Christmas."

"But that's such a lonnnggg ways away."

"I trust you will endure. Now where's your mother?"

Dad never did anything — important or not — without Mom beside him. They were inseparable. A perfect stranger could have seen in five seconds how much he loved her.

I pointed upstairs.

"She's rehearsing *Für Elise* for, like, the billionth time."

Dad smiled again. "What? Again? I swear that woman loves Beethoven more than she loves me."

He cupped his hands to his mouth and shouted. "Anna, *mein schatz, vould* you please come down here, *ja?*"

Above us, the music trailed off. The floorboards creaked and Mom stepped into view. She wore jeans and a deep green T-shirt. Her hair was pulled back with a green ribbon. Her eyes sparkled like sapphires caught in the afternoon sun.

"*Gott in Himmel,*" she said in flawless German. "You'd never make it in the old country. Your accent is all wrong."

"True. But that's why I have you. My love, *mein schatz.*"

Mom blushed. She smiled and moved down the stairs.

"Even if I spend all my time at the piano?"

Dad nodded. Mom paused by Dad to give him a soft kiss.

"So tell me what is so important that you would interrupt my practice time? Beethoven, you know, doesn't abide interruptions."

A wide smile spread over Dad's face.

"Ludwig can wait, my dear. I have news, great news. News I wish I could wrap in a bow for you and Josie!"

"And this great news would be . . ."

Dad took her hands and pulled her down beside him.

"Well, let me put it this way: what is your favorite restaurant in Vienna?"

Mom cocked her head. "What did you say?"

"I said, 'What is your favorite restaurant in Vienna?' "

"Oh, Joseph, oh, my goodness . . . Do you mean?"

"Yes, I got the job. You might want to start packing, because come the first of the year, we're moving. We're shaking off this red dust for the cobbled streets of Europe. We're moving to Vienna."

Mom rolled into Dad's arms with a squeal of delight. For a few moments they twisted in the sun, then I watched as he cupped her face in his hands and kissed her.

In a movie, it would have been so romantic. But this was real life. We were moving. Not to a new neighborhood or a new city or even a new state, but halfway across the world. We were leaving Oklahoma, the only home I had ever known, and moving to Vienna, Austria.

How could Dad have ever thought this was a suitable coming-home gift?

. . . .

And sure enough, right after the holidays we said good-bye. I walked down our hill one last time to sit by the pond. I looked out over the rolling hills and pastures brown from winter's cold.

Nothing would ever be the same, I told myself.

But I could never have imagined what the future held.

. . . .

It took forever to get our belongings packed, the paperwork done, the boxes shipped, and the documents in order so we could leave one country and enter another. Seriously, moving was bad enough — new school, new people, new place to live — but moving to a different country on the other side of the ocean was the absolute worst.

Mom tried to tell me it would be okay. She talked so much about Vienna and Austria that I eventually became convinced the country was a magical place filled with wonderful food, beautiful people, and marvelous music — and that Vienna was its crown jewel.

Only too soon, I realized she had it all wrong.

. . . .

Our flight was long and bumpy, and my chicken was cold. Dad wouldn't let me watch the in-flight movie. He said it was too old for me. Instead, he loaned me his iPod. That would have been okay, except for my father's taste in music — everything from thrash metal to Gregorian chant but nothing I particularly liked.

I scrolled through his playlist. It was all old songs — the Who, Cream, the Rolling Stones, the Kinks. I even found some disco tunes. I counted more than thirty different numbers in Italian, some obscure numbers by classical composers, and an album by some guy named Spike Jones.

I clicked on Spike, hoping with a name like that that it was at least something recorded say, maybe in the twentieth century. Boy, was I left surprised. In between the burps, explosions, belches, and some strange sounds I'm convinced were not of this earth, was woven a strain of music I'd never heard before. You'd have thought this Spike guy was a distant cousin of Weird Al Yankovic.

I listened anyway. Spike might not be Beck, but he was better than Gregorian chant. Still, it made for a longer plane ride.

. . . .

Ten hours later we landed. The sky was gray, cold, and lifeless, and everyone seemed in a hurry.

Since Mom spoke fluent German — she was born in Vienna and reared in Heidelberg — she did all the talking for us. Sure, Dad could speak some German, and he understood a lot more, but somehow when he talked it always came out sounding like a weird cowboy with a cold. Trust me, Mom was the better choice.

We retrieved our luggage — which again took forever because we had shipped a million different bags and Mom could not remember, exactly, which ones were ours — and then headed to customs, where we were met by someone from Dad's new job.

Because he now worked for this big, important global research group, all our immigration papers and documents were ready and waiting when we got there. We spent a few minutes in customs, then took a taxi to the hotel.

I sat in the back and looked out the window at the gray Vienna sky. Deep inside, I wondered if I would ever see Oklahoma again.

From the Tulsa Daily Journal
Brunswick Assumes Leadership of Global Genetics Group

By Telluride Matheson
Science Correspondent

PARIS, France (AP) – A Tulsa man has been named chief scientist for the World Genetics Council, officials with the Vienna-based organization announced.

Speaking at a press conference in Paris, Dr. Igor Staniouski, chairman of the WGC, said Dr. Joseph Brunswick was chosen as the organization's chief scientist after an "exhaustive three-year search" to locate the world's top genetics researcher.

"We combed the world," Staniouski said. "In the end, we found exactly who we were looking for in the heartland of the United States."

Staniouski said Brunswick will lead the WGC's research efforts into human genetics, the human genome, and, specifically, the group's efforts to eradicate disease.

Since its founding in 1988 by billionaire software developer Hans Gottlieb, the WGC has led the industrialized world in human genetics research. In 2014, the organization announced it had developed a cure for AIDS, based on a mutated strand of human stem cells.

That cure remains controversial and is undergoing a third scientific review by officials with the United Nation's World Health Organization.

This week, Staniouski predicted the U.N. would endorse the WGC's AIDS efforts. He said Brunswick would travel to New York to address the WHO about the treatment later this month.

"Dr. Brunswick has reviewed our research and supports our efforts. We have the perfect man for the right job," he said. "Now it is time for us, and him, to get to work."

Brunswick, the former director of the University of Tulsa's genetics laboratory, said he was thrilled to start his new post. "Over the last 150 years medicine has made great progress, but I believe we are ready to take that research to the next level," he said.

Brunswick said he would focus his efforts on human tissue replication as it pertains to cancer. "I believe we now have the tools to eliminate cancer," he said. "We just need to understand how to use them."

At 37, Brunswick is the youngest scientist to head the WGC. He and his wife, Anna, have one child, a daughter. Brunswick replaces Dr. Matura Zuhdi, the South African Nobel laureate, who died earlier this summer in an automobile accident.

Chapter 2

Vienna Calling

OKAY, I LIED — not everything sucked. I liked the hotel. The Grand Wien was big and old and elegant. And if it had only been located in Tulsa, Oklahoma, it would have been perfect. I tried not to hold its address against it, because the place made me feel like that girl in *The Princess Diaries.*

Guys in dark suits rushed to our car upon our arrival, and an entire squad of bellhops loaded up our luggage and hurried it to our rooms. We didn't even have to ask. I was tempted to snap my fingers just to see what would happen.

At check-in, Mom blew away the manager — greeting him with a big wink. The poor guy just stood there and blushed. After he handed her the big brass key to our room, Mom thanked him in her own brand of Oklahoman-meets-German: *"Haben sie vielen danke,* ya'll."

At first, the man didn't seem sure how to respond; he just stood there with his mouth open. But the girl next to him laughed, gave him a nudge with her elbow, and graciously answered, *"Gern geschehen."*

Dad whispered to me: "Looks like we've gone native."

. . . .

For the first week we played tourist. Mom, who had traveled all over Austria when she was a girl and then later as a pianist, said it would be educational for me. She made a great guide. We toured the museums, ate beef salad at the Naschmarkt (Vienna's sixteenth-century food market), and tried *wiener schnitzel* at more than one *beisl* (Vienna's answer to the Parisian bistro). We also saw more castles and palaces than I could count. (Did you know there's a difference between palaces and castles? Me neither. Seems castles are fortified to withstand enemy attacks while palaces are made for relaxing.)

Anyway after three or four days and a dozen castles, it was all beginning to look the same. I could tell Dad was bored and ready to start his new job. At least we didn't have to worry about finding a house. Dad said the WGC would provide a place for us, and that it did.

"It's called Villa Theresa," Dad informed us, "and I'm told it's very old and beautiful. It's on an estate with a swimming pool and a tennis court and everything a worldly thirteen-year-old could want."

I had never lived in a villa before, so I wasn't sure what to expect. It sounded huge, and I wasn't sure if I wanted to sweep the floors of a house that big. But so far, things had been going okay, and I was willing to give it a try. Besides, if we didn't have to pay for a house, maybe Dad would buy me a pony.

"And this villa-place is ours?"

We were in a taxi on the way to see Villa Theresa for the first time. I still wasn't sure how everything worked. I mean if the people at the WGC got mad at Dad could they boot us out?

Dad turned and smiled at me.

"Don't worry, Josie. It's ours. It's your new home."

I gave him a thin smile. "Okay. If you say so."

Mom pulled me close. "You'll see, honey. You'll love it here."

I figured if Mom liked it, it must be okay, so I gave in and waited for the car to stop. We were outside of Vienna, traveling a long, twisty road that seemed to make another sharp turn every few feet. After what seemed like forever, we arrived at the estate. I swear as long as I live, I'll never forget seeing Villa Theresa for the first time. The car pulled in and stopped and some guy dressed in a formal, dark suit appeared out of nowhere and opened the back door of the car.

Dad smiled and took my hand. At first, I couldn't see because of the sun, but when my eyes finally focused, I just stood there with my mouth open. Villa Theresa was, well, a Vienna palace.

It was painted dark yellow and trimmed in white. The main house formed a "T" and stood in a courtyard filled with fountains and statues and miles of shrubs, so perfectly trimmed they looked plastic.

To the left sat a huge barn and stables; to the right, a pool and tennis court. The place was rimmed by a small forest of tall dark green pine trees. We followed the flower-lined path to the front door.

"The longest portion of the house is called the Great Hall," Dad explained. "It has quite a history. There's a dining room and two sitting rooms, a library, a study, a den, two kitchens, and a huge, glass conservatory, or sunroom."

While he reeled off the various rooms in the house, I found myself trying to figure out how I was going to keep from getting lost on any given day.

"Do we really need all this?" My voice squeaked as I posed the question to my parents, but the question had to be asked. I loved our house in Tulsa, and it only had a couple of bedrooms and a shower that leaked.

Dad laughed, as if I was joking and not asking a serious question, and continued reciting the features of our new home.

"Upstairs are several bedrooms — and a studio for your mother and her piano. Over here," he pointed to the left wing of the house, "is where I'll have my lab and office."

That caught my attention. "You'll be working from home?"

Dad nodded, with a pleased smile. "I thought you'd like that."

"This might not be so bad after all," I said.

We stopped before two huge oak doors — like the entrance to a dungeon. The guy in the dark suit set our bags down and pushed the doors open. His long, angular face was solemn and emotionless.

"Welcome *Herr Doktor* Brunswick," he said, slowly.

And we stepped inside.

I'm pretty sure a hundred people could have lived at Villa Theresa and never run into each other. It was that big: spotless and formal with big, heavy furniture; lots of paintings of stiff-looking people standing by more stiff-looking people; and miles and miles of Oriental rugs.

I went upstairs to see the bedrooms. They were perfect, too perfect. My bedroom was painted ice blue with white trim and held the largest bed I had ever seen. It would have been perfect in a museum.

Mom knocked on the door.

"Come on, honey," she said. "Let's go look at the stables."

I followed her downstairs. We toured the stables and the barn and the formal garden, though the latter was only a shadow of its summer self. I had to admit it was beautiful, but to me it also seemed rather stiff and proper — more like a fancy tourist destination than a home. We walked the grounds and talked until late into the afternoon, when more movers arrived.

I left Mom with one of the movers and a large, red truck (they were getting ready to bring in her Steinway) and ran back to my new room. People were everywhere, scurrying around like ants on a picnic blanket. I flung open my bedroom door: everything was unpacked and put away. My posters were already on the wall and my Starry Night bedspread had already been spread out on the bed.

It was creepy. I have this huge collection of old vinyl records and about a million CDs and tons of books. Whoever unpacked my stuff put all my music on one shelf and arranged it in alphabetical order. I always cataloged it by year and musical genre.

I was less and less sure that this move was going to work. It was like being caught in a weird dream — at any given moment I might wake up and be back in my old bedroom in Oklahoma.

I pinched my cheek.

Nope, I wasn't dreaming.

I sat down on the bed and looked around. I couldn't help how I felt about the place, but I knew I didn't have any choice but to try and make the best of the situation. Mom and Dad had said not to worry. I wanted to believe them, I did, but everything was a little too perfect and a little bit off.

And that was before we met the staff.

Seems along with a house the size of a luxury hotel comes built-in people. Yeah, again, just like in the movies. The full staff included a chauffeur, a chef, two assistant chefs, three maids, a head butler, and two footmen (*yes, footmen!*).

I tried to memorize each of their names, but everyone spoke so quickly and with a German lilt to their English that made it difficult to be sure what they had said. After a few awkward minutes, I managed to grasp the names of our chef, Andre; his sous chef, Leisel; and the line cook, Maria. With that, the rest of the staff scattered.

Andre seemed formal and a tad snotty to me, but Leisel and Maria had open faces with big smiles. They told me in English how happy they were we were going to be living there.

I grabbed my dad's arm, pulled him down to me, and whispered in his ear: "Does this mean that I can't go into the kitchen and make myself a sandwich?"

Dad smiled and shook his head.

"I'm sure that won't be a problem, honey. These people are here to help us get settled and fit in. They want to be helpful. Give them a chance."

. . . .

Come to find out Mom was not too sure about our new home, either. She didn't say anything at first. But after awhile, it became obvious she felt unsettled.

One afternoon on the veranda, she whispered to me that she was sure some mistake had landed us here. Later that night, eating dinner in the formal dining hall (it was the size of a football field) with Dad and me, she started to cry.

"Joseph, this isn't real." She pointed at the row of stuffed animal heads that lined the wall above us. "This isn't us. We don't have chauffeurs and maids and cooks. We don't hang a boar's head like a painting in the dining room, and we don't have a family crest. You're a scientist, not the Duke of Buckingham."

Dad laughed, but I don't think he realized she was not kidding.

"I know, I know, it's a little over the top," he said. "But honey, it's for a good cause. This is a company house and these people all work for the company. Believe it or not, I'll have to host dinners and meetings here. I'll bet you that's probably what these people will spend most of their time working on. They don't mean any harm. They're just here to help."

I focused on the work part of his explanation.

"But that sounds like you'll never ever be with just us." I slumped in my chair and crossed my arms over my chest. "You'll always be in your lab or meetings or working or away and you won't have time for us, and we'll be left to rattle around in this big old mausoleum that you call a house."

I couldn't believe it but Mom was nodding in agreement. She leaned across the table and whispered to Dad: "And there are all these strangers around. I swear, it's like they're always watching, keeping tabs on us."

Dad shook his head as if he didn't believe what he was hearing. I realized as I saw him scowl that I was a little scared, too. Mom and Dad never disagreed about anything. And this was a big something.

Just as I thought Dad was going to get mad, he got up from the table, walked over to me, and scooped me up in his arms, then he sat down next to Mom.

"Josie, honey, I adore you." He gave me a squeeze, then leaned over to caress Mom's cheek. "And Anna, you are the love of my life. Nothing will ever keep me from either of you. Nothing. You two are my whole world. My work is important, yes, but it comes second to you both. There will always be time for the three of us. I promise."

I buried my face in his shoulder.

"I just miss you," I said. "I liked our old little house. I miss Oklahoma. I wish it was just us three again."

"I know, honey. I liked our old house, too, and I do miss Oklahoma. But these people are just trying to help me do my job. And here I have a real chance to help people. Lots of people . . . lots of very sick people. And that's a good thing. Isn't it?"

Mom smiled, scooted nearer to me, and pulled me close, then she laid a hand on my father's arm.

"Well, all I know," she said, "is that wherever you are is where I want to be."

She pointed up at the stuffed wild boar.

"Even if it's here."

From the Tulsa Daily Journal
Brunswick Testifies at U.N. Health Group Meeting

NEW YORK, N.Y. — (AP) The new chief scientist of the World Genetics Council told the United Nation's World Health Organization today that his agency's mutated-gene-based treatment for AIDS was safe and represented "the first viable cure for this horrible plague of a disease."

Speaking at a hastily called meeting of the WHO, Dr. Joseph Brunswick, the WGC's new chief of scientific research, said mutated-gene therapy had been shown to have few side effects, and preliminary test results report an 84 percent success rate.

"We believe we're there," Brunswick said. "We believe this is it. This is the cure for AIDS."

Brunswick's testimony was greeted with skepticism by WHO delegates. However, after more than a week of briefings, intense questioning, and a last-minute peer review of recent results, several members of the WHO said they believed the treatment could represent a major breakthrough in AIDS research.

"I'm cautiously optimistic," said Dr. Raul Martinez, the American delegate to the conference. "I like what I've seen so far, but I still think we need more information. That said, this is the most positive step I've seen in AIDS research in years."

Brunswick, chosen by the WGC as its chief scientist earlier this year, said the AIDS treatment shows the commitment by his organization to improving world health.

"Our goal is to help the people of the world," he said. "It's that simple."

Chapter 3

Come Together

SATURDAY MORNING, EXACTLY three months and two days after we moved into Villa Theresa, a second fleet of black moving vans arrived. I had just stepped out of the shower when I heard the crunch of tires on the gravel below my window.

I looked out and beyond the hedges and the rows of yellow tulips, a dozen guys in gray-and-black uniforms hauled big boxes into the left wing of the villa. I threw my clothes on and ran outside. Dad was already there, standing and giving orders in a pair of running shorts and his favorite University of Tulsa sweatshirt.

"*Ja.*" He pointed to an open door to his left. "Those go in the lab. Everything marked with the green label."

I tugged on his sweatshirt sleeve. "What's going on?"

Dad turned and smiled. "Oh, hi, honey. They're moving in my lab equipment. Isn't that great?"

"But I thought you already had a lab."

"I do, but this equipment is for the new project I'm going to be working on. It's one of the reasons the WGC hired me. I showed them one of my ideas and they loved it. They're funding the development and the equipment I need for it."

I had never seen Dad like this before. His face was intense, and his eyes blazed. It was like he was reliving his favorite Christmas and he had gotten everything he wanted and then some.

I kicked some loose gravel with the toe of my shoe.

"Sure is a lot of stuff. What are you gonna do with all of it?"

"Honestly, honey, I'm going to try and make the world a better place. I'm going to cure disease. That's what I'm going to do."

The delivery guys remained all day. After they left, more people showed up at the villa, but this second wave of guys were different. They wore white lab coats and carried laptops and metal briefcases — techno-looking stuff. They didn't leave that day either. Instead, they hung around for almost two weeks.

One of the men was abnormally tall with bright yellow hair and dark eyes. He seemed to be the man in charge. He never smiled that I saw and he never actually spoke to anyone. He just grunted and pointed, and people scurried to do his bidding. I tried to talk to him once, but he looked at me as if I was sub-human. As uncomfortable as I felt around the villa staff, it was nothing compared to how weird this guy made me feel.

I tried to tell Dad, but he just kept saying everything would be okay.

"Don't worry, Josie. They simply have a deadline, and they are all very busy trying to meet it."

They didn't look all that busy to me; they looked like they were mad or mean or wanted by Interpol. I thought they would never leave. Mom kept asking if we should make them lunch or bring them something to drink, but Dad said to let them be. They never came near the rest of the house; they relayed items back and forth to the lab from their vehicles, and they didn't talk to anyone — except Dad.

Like I said, they all gave me the creeps, so I stayed in my room and watched them from my window.

. . . .

Dad had told the truth about working at home but not about being around for me and Mom. After the guys in the white coats finally left, he basically locked himself inside his lab. He would start in the wee hours of the morning before Mom and I woke up, work through lunch, and not turn out the lights until way past dinner.

Months passed and I hardly saw him — even though his lab was in a wing of the house.

The Immortal Von B.

One Sunday afternoon, I went outside to ride my bike. Usually I rode around the right wing of the villa to the swimming pool, past the tennis court, and up to the edge of the forest, but that day, I took a different route — around the other side of the house, near the stables. I didn't think about it at the time, but by riding that way, I ended up on the backside of Dad's lab.

I hadn't gone very far when I heard a familiar voice.

"Hey, beautiful girl, where you going?"

I looked over and saw Dad sitting on a small cement bench by a maple tree. I dropped my bike, ran over, and plopped down beside him. "Dad, it's you! Where have you been? I've missed you."

He pulled me close and patted my hair. "I've missed you, too, little one. Seems like a long time since I've had a hug from you."

I leaned back and shook a finger at him.

"Well, it's your fault. You never come home. You're always in your lab. Don't you love me anymore?"

Gently, Dad tilted my chin upwards. "Of course, I do. You know that. I love you very much. I've just been very busy with my research."

I pointed at the lab. "What are you doing in there?"

"I told you. Don't you remember?"

I scowled. "I remember, but why won't you let me or Mom see inside? That's not fair. We can't even come visit you. You lock yourself away . . . it's like you don't want us around."

He gave me a weak smile. "Tell you what. If you'll forgive me for being gone so much, I will take you on a tour now. Okay?"

A smile spread over my face. "Really!? Okay, I'll forgive you this time — just don't let it happen again."

Dad nodded with great seriousness, then took me by the hand and led me to a spot near the back of the lab. He said it was the side door. I had counted it off: it was exactly fifteen steps from the tree. I wanted to be able to find that door again, just in case my father went missing again.

"Well, here we are," Dad said. "This is the door."

I blinked and looked again. There wasn't a door. At least there wasn't a door that I could see. "Stop joking."

Dad grinned. "I'm not joking. This is the door."

He pointed to a spot on the wall directly in front of him. There was no door knob or hinges or handle. I didn't see anything except a small black square about three feet above the ground on the wall.

Dad touched the black square several times, like he was dialing a phone number. After a few seconds, I heard a click and sure enough a door-sized portion of the wall slid to the side.

"This is the lock," Dad pointed to the black square. "There are no keys, no numbers. To the untrained eye, it looks like a square of paint. But, it's actually a very sensitive numeric keypad. The numbers on the sensor are scrambled. And since no one but me knows the sequence, no one but me gets in. Keeps out the bad guys and, believe me, the bad guys would love to see what I'm doing in here."

"I don't understand. If you can't see the numbers how do you know if you have punched in the right code?"

"That's the trick," Dad said. "You don't, unless someone tells you the sequence of the numbers on the pad. And I'm not telling."

I looked down at the ground a little hurt. "Not even me?"

Dad smiled and tickled my nose. "Not even you."

"But I won't tell."

"I'm sure you wouldn't, honey, but this is top secret. Even my boss doesn't know the code."

I frowned. "So just what are you doing in here? Making a monster, like Frankenstein did?"

I had just finished reading the novel for school, so I had been thinking about Dr. Frankenstein a lot.

"No honey, I'm not playing Frankenstein. I'm trying to help doctors find a cure for cancer and other diseases."

"But if it's such a big secret how will doctors know how to do it?"

Dad laughed — a loud, silly laugh. "Oh Josie, you're amazing."

He started to say something else, but then frowned and fell quiet.

"Someday," he said, taking my hand and pulling me into the blackness. "Someday."

Chapter 4

Heart of Glass

I FOLLOWED DAD INSIDE the lab. At first, it was difficult to see anything but a wall of black. The whole room was dark. Dad held my hand tight. He leaned down and whispered: "Now, watch this."

Dad raised his voice: "WGC Alpha, lights on, please."

The instant he finished speaking, the room filled with a dim glow. I blinked, shocked by the sudden change in visibility.

"That's so cool. How? How did you —"

"Voice-recognition software. The computer hears my voice and responds to my commands."

"Like on those old *Star Trek* shows?"

Dad laughed and nodded. "Yes, just like on *Star Trek*."

"Can I try?"

"Sure." Dad leaned in and whispered: "Say, 'Lights off, please.' "

I nodded and cleared my throat.

"Okay. Lights, off, please," I requested in my most proper voice.

Nothing happened. The lights stayed on and I stood there puzzled, while Dad chuckled.

"I'm sorry, honey. Probably not my best joke; let me see if I can fix the problem." He dropped my hand and in a loud voice said: "Alpha Unit, this is Dr. Joseph Brunswick. Please respond."

From deep inside the lab, a voice that sounded a little like my mom and a lot like a machine answered: "Alpha Unit responding. Good afternoon, Dr. Joseph Brunswick. The time is now twelve hundred hours. All systems are go. How may I be of assistance?"

I grabbed my dad's hand and squeezed. A lab with lots of computers and stuff was one thing, but a lab that could talk to you was wonderfully creepy.

Dad pulled me close, then addressed the emptiness: "Reduce security to level two. Voice activation only. Scan and acknowledge new voice pattern."

After a few seconds, the computer responded. "Environmental adjustments via voice activation reduced to security level two."

Dad leaned close and whispered: "Now, Josie, try it again."

"Okay. Miss Computer . . ."

"No honey, say it this way: 'WGC Alpha . . .' "

"Oh, okay, WGC Alpha Unit. Lights off, please."

The room went dark.

"Responding. New voice noted. Analyzed. Encoded. Querying database. Match found. Voice is that of Brunswick, Josephine Marie. Female. Minor. Similarity of vocal patterns noted between female and administrator, Dr. Joseph Brunswick. Voice pattern also cross-references to Anna Heigle-Brunswick; data assumes maternal-paternal reference. Save file?"

Dad laughed and pulled me into the center of the room.

"Well done, Alpha Unit. Lights on, please. Oh, and yes, save file."

For the second time, the room glowed amber and the digital voice filled the air: "Responding. Decision noted. Executing. File saved."

The lab looked like the control room of a spaceship. Filled wall-to-wall with computers and huge monitors and lots of shiny stuff covered in metal and glass, it could have been something out of the future. To the right, a huge chrome and glass desk flanked by another bank of computers. Overhead, four immense high-definition monitors hung from the ceiling.

Underneath the monitors, in the center of the room, several computers ringed a long, large aluminum cylinder that looked like a metal coffin. One computer was wired to the cylinder. The cylinder sat atop a dark platform covered with cables and tubes and a jungle of hoses. I couldn't help it, flashbacks to the lab described in *Frankenstein* popped into my head.

I pointed to the center of the horseshoe.

"What's that big metal tube thingy?"

Dad looked at me and paused.

"It's . . . it's a tissue replicator. It's part of my research."

I walked towards it. "It's awful big. Looks like something for a high-tech funeral."

"It's for my research," Dad said abruptly.

For a second his face tensed, then he smiled and steered me away from the tube and to the back of the room, near his shiny desk.

"This is the master control area and this . . ."

As Dad described various features of his lab, I walked slowly around the room. If you had asked me at the time, I wouldn't have been able to explain it, but something about the place felt wrong.

It was like he was hiding something. And, I could tell by the way he had looked down at his feet when he answered my question about the aluminum tube, that he wasn't telling the whole truth about the big cylinder. But it had been so long since the two of us had spent time together, I didn't want to ruin it. I was just happy to be with him. Anyway, I was probably imagining things.

With that I tuned back to what he was saying about his recent research findings. I knew he was developing new treatments to help sick people by using mutated genes, and if I understood what he was saying correctly, it was going well.

But the longer he talked, the more I got the impression that he had something else going on in this lab, something he didn't want me to know about. And I couldn't help but notice that he sure worked hard to keep me far away from the tissue replicator.

By the time my tour ended, it was almost time for lunch. Dad suggested I go get Mom, which at first sounded like a great idea. Then I realized that he was trying to get me out of the lab, so I hesitated.

"What's that over there?" I asked, pointing to a small computer above the horseshoe.

Instead of a monitor, this computer was connected to a large square metal-and-glass box, with sliding clear doors, about the size of a small television set. Behind the glass was a clear tube about as long and thin as a pencil.

"That's how I scan the DNA sample," Dad said, giving me a nudge towards the door. "Now run and get your mother and we'll go get some lunch. Hurry now. I still have lots of work to finish today."

With that, Dad steered me by my shoulders out the front door of the lab and back into the courtyard.

"Hurry, Josie. I'll wait for you here."

I ran upstairs where Mom was practicing the piano. She was supposed to perform with the Vienna State Orchestra in a couple of weeks, and she'd been pushing herself hard to get concert-ready. I raced down the hall and pounded on her door. "Mom! Open up! Dad just showed me his lab. It's like a spaceship."

I threw open the door to her practice studio. Her piano — the big, beautiful white Steinway — filled the center of the room. I saw her sheet music. I saw the pen she used to make notations on the floor.

But I didn't see her.

"Mom? Dad wants to take us to lunch. Come on."

I started for the stairs. Mom was known to slip off to the kitchen to wheedle cookies out of the pastry chef. I'd just reached the landing when I heard a thump and something break. I turned and raced back into the studio. From the bathroom came a moan.

I ran towards the sound.

"Mom? Mom, are you in there? Are you okay?"

On the other side of the door a faint voice answered: "Josie . . . Josie, honey, is that you?"

I knelt in front of the door and tried to see through the keyhole.

"Yeah it's me. Are you okay? You sound sick."

"I'm fine honey. I just need . . ."

I heard something else topple. I shouldn't have, but I pushed open the door and stepped inside. I looked around and stopped.

"Mom? What's wrong?"

"Josie, you shouldn't be in here. I don't want you to see . . ."

Mom leaned over the tub. Her hair was pulled back in a ponytail. Her face, gray and twisted with pain.

The floor was covered in yellow vomit.

And the front of her sweater was covered in blood.

Chapter 5

Nights in White Satin

AT THE SIGHT OF THE BLOOD, I screamed and bolted. I had to get Dad and I had to get him fast. I raced down the stairs and out the front door of the villa, screaming for help all the way. Dad must have heard me, because he caught me before I could hit the ground. I was shaking and crying and trying not to freak out. Dad picked me up and carried me back into the house.

"Josie, what's wrong? Where's your mother?"

He stopped asking questions when he saw the look on my face.

I pointed up.

Dad dropped me and raced up the stairs.

. . . .

The doctor from the WGC refused to look at me. He just sighed and looked sad. I kept trying to hold Mom's hand, but the doctor kept getting in the way. He and my father kept speaking in German and all I could make out was "hospital" and "cancer" and "blood loss."

Dad looked like someone had kicked him in the stomach.

After the doctor left, Dad drove Mom like a madman to Vienna General Hospital. He wouldn't call an ambulance — said he could do it faster himself. Then he set out to prove it, throwing me in the back seat and bundling up Mom and putting her in the front, next to him.

Doctors were waiting for us when we arrived. A group of order-lies had a gurney ready. They put Mom on it and rolled her down to the Intensive Care Unit.

Dad never left her side. Just like we had moved into Villa Theresa, now we moved into the hospital.

For days, Dad didn't say much; he just sat next to Mom and held her hands. He called her *mein schatz* and told her over and over how much he loved her.

Mom only got worse. Every day she grew thinner and a little more fragile. She could barely lift her head off the pillow.

Late one Friday evening, the rain came. Thunder boomed and lightning slashed its way across the sky. I curled up in a chair by the window in Mom's hospital room. Dad thought I was asleep, but the rumble of the thunderstorm kept me on the cusp between sleep and consciousness.

A boom made me sit up. The room seemed to glow for a few seconds. I looked over at Dad. He had his back to me and he was crying. He held Mom's delicate hand to his face.

"Oh, Anna . . . I can't do this without you. I need a little more time. I'm so close. You can't leave me now. I'm doing all of this for you, for us. You are my whole life. I love you with every part of my being. Oh Anna . . ."

The thunder rolled again.

Dad's head dropped to his chest, and then, slowly he leaned over my mother and took her hands and placed them on top of the blanket.

And I knew Mom was dead.

From the Tulsa Daily Journal
Funeral Services Set for Famed Local Musician

TULSA, Okla. — Funeral services for the world-renowned American classical pianist Anna Heigle-Brunswick will be Tuesday at Saint Mark's Catholic Church in Tulsa.

Known internationally as a piano virtuoso, Mrs. Heigle-Brunswick, 35, died from a sudden illness while living in Vienna, Austria, with her husband, Dr. Joseph Brunswick, and their daughter, Josephine. The family previously called Tulsa home.

The daughter of composer and violinist Martin Heigle, Heigle-Brunswick made her professional debut at age 11. By age 13 she had performed in most of the world's major cities. In recent years, she has performed with such orchestras as the Vienna Philharmonic, the Berlin Philharmonic, The Cleveland Orchestra, The Chicago Symphony Orchestra, and the New York Philharmonic Orchestra.

Renowned for her ability to "play anything Beethoven," Heigle-Brunswick testified before the U.S. Congress in 2003 in an effort to encourage federal funding for the arts in rural areas.

In 2004, she shocked the musical world by announcing her retirement. At the same time, she told the Paris Match newspaper she was engaged to Dr. Joseph Brunswick, a geneticist based at the University of Tulsa in Tulsa.

In 2012 she emerged from retirement to serve as the featured pianist with the London Philharmonic for the 242nd anniversary of Beethoven's birth. That performance, broadcast across the globe, featured Heigle-Brunswick on piano, her father on violin, and the world famous cellist Yo Yo Ma, in a never heard-before orchestration by Beethoven of his *Symphony No. 9*, featuring piano, violin, cello, and a full orchestra.

Survivors include Heigle-Brunswick's mother, Annabeth Heigle of New York City; a sister, Celeste Norton of Boston; and her husband and daughter, both of Vienna.

A private memorial service will follow at the Heigle Foundation Nature Preserve in Tulsa.

Part II: The Machine

Chapter 6
Jive Talkin'

AFTER MOM DIED, THINGS got pretty messed up. I begged Dad to move us back to Oklahoma, but he refused. He said he had to continue his work — now more than ever. He said Mom would have wanted it that way.

All Vienna did was remind me of Mom and death and everything I had come to hate. For weeks after her funeral I sat in my room and cried. I couldn't even bring myself to listen to music.

Weeks became months, months became years.

Dad tried to be both parents, but in reality he was consumed by his work. We drifted apart. He stayed in his lab and I stayed in my room or at school. Family dinners became a thing of the past.

Somewhere along the way I fell into the darkness. All I wanted to do was stay in bed. It got so bad Dad made me go to a psychiatrist. That lasted until I threw a screaming fit one night and told him if he made me go back I'd run away and he'd never see me again.

I was lying, but Dad believed me.

The therapy sessions stopped.

. . . .

Not too long after that though I did try to run away. It was late, and the autumn sky was orange and clear and cold. I crawled through my bedroom window, grabbed my bike, and rode to the end of the drive. Twenty minutes later, I was walking down the road, with my backpack, trying to thumb a ride.

A nice Austrian man and his cute little wife stopped and offered to give me a lift. They looked okay, so I got inside their car. Ten minutes after that I was bawling my eyes out.

Then the nice Austrian couple took me home.

Dad was beyond mad.

He yelled at me and said things I'd never heard him say before. He called me stupid for getting into a car with strangers and said I could have been killed or worse.

I said that didn't sound too bad to me.

It was the second-worst night of my life.

It was like Dad didn't love me anymore.

Chapter 7

Purple Haze

FAST-FORWARD TWO YEARS, just before my sixteenth birthday. I was no longer in free fall, but Mom's death defined me. I no longer played the piano and I didn't dance anymore. It had been years since I felt like my Dad's beautiful little girl. I quit long ago pretending that we would ever move home to Oklahoma.

Music saved me.

One day I picked up an electric guitar and everything changed. I liked the way it felt in my hands — like a machine gun.

I liked the vibrations and the noise and reverb and the way the sounds went from intense and screaming to soft, like the breath of a whisper. I learned I could push all my anger and rage and frustration out through the strings and into the amplifier for all the world to hear.

Playing the guitar became my obsession.

For my birthday, Dad spent a ton of money and bought me a vintage 1967 Gibson Flying V. It was black with weird psychedelic graphics on the body. The guy at the music store — he looked like a cosmic toad with wild, neon-colored hair and huge round glasses — said this particular Flying V had been owned by Jimi Hendrix. He said Hendrix owed three Flying Vs and this last one was painted by Hendrix, himself.

I didn't believe the guy at first. Then late one afternoon, while I was polishing the neck of the guitar, I noticed scratches all along the bridge. I knew Hendrix had used right-handed guitars, turned them upside down, and restrung them because he was left-handed.

This guitar had been restrung the same way.

It was well used, too. There were scratches and marks where it had been handled and banged about. And the paint scheme was done by hand. I looked closer and inside the case the initials J.H. were stitched. I mean, it could have been Hendrix's guitar.

But whether or not it was owned by the famous guitarist, I loved it. I spent months learning to play it and late one rainy night when Dad was out of town and the staff was gone, the music and the electricity came together. I played for hours with the amplifiers cranked as loud as they could go.

That night I realized I'd finally found my purpose in life.

I was going to start my own band and play my own music.

Chapter 8

Yesterday

A YEAR LATER I TURNED seventeen. Dad took me to Steirereck to celebrate — just the two of us. The Reitbauers' family restaurant is supposedly one of the fifty best in the world, and Dad let me order whatever I wanted and I got to have wine with my meal.

He didn't say much during dinner, but I figured he was preoccupied with his work as usual. He'd talk for a few minutes then the conversation would drag.

Thank goodness, there's live music to fill in the lulls.

"So, honey, have you had a good birthday?"

I faked a smile. "Yeah, it's been nice."

"Good. I have a surprise for you."

I sighed. "Dad, I told you, I don't need anything."

"That's what you say, but . . ."

I started to protest again, but I realized he wasn't even listening. Again, as usual. Like so many other nights since Mom died, it was as if Dad were looking past me, like he wanted to be somewhere else, with someone else. After dinner we drove home in silence.

The next day, when I woke up, there was a note on my mirror. The note said to look out my window. I stumbled over and opened the curtains. The morning sun made the grass sparkle like a million scattered diamonds. Tethered outside was a beautiful Abyssinian colt. It was reddish-silver with huge, dark eyes: my birthday present.

How many times as a little girl had I begged for a pony? How many years?

But now I couldn't recall when I had last mentioned wanting a pony, much less a horse. *One year? Two?* I couldn't begin to imagine how much the colt had cost — much less what I would do with one.

I walked downstairs to look for Dad. Another note, this time on the refrigerator. He was in his lab, of course. I walked outside to see the colt. He nestled his long nose in my palm. For a moment I thought of Mom. I remember trying to convince her that I was responsible enough for a horse. Nothing had worked. But today, long after she's gone, I finally get one — and it's no big deal. *I don't feel a thing.* And for a moment, I miss that old Josie, the one who got excited about things like ponies.

The Abyssinian colt was a wonderful present. I knew Dad was trying, and I knew in his own way he was telling me that he still remembered what made me happy, but that was before. The only thing I still wanted now was to have my mom back.

Some days, honestly, I would have settled for one good, sharp memory. I was afraid I was beginning to forget what she looked like. It was becoming more difficult to remember moments we'd shared.

There was one memory, though, that I still held onto fiercely: I was two, maybe three. Her studio was yellow and the sun streamed through the windows. She held my hands and placed my fingers on each key. Then she gently pressed down each key, showing me which ones to play. That was how I learned to play the piano.

My first memories are of hearing her music. But when Mom wasn't playing, there was always one of Dad's old vinyl records spinning in the background or an old album from my grandpa. It was as if our lives had a soundtrack.

After Mom died, I moved all the music — everything, the entire collection — into my room. Dad didn't seem to care. I brought in more shelves and filled them with her records and CDs. I felt like all the world's music existed on the bookcases in my bedroom. Everywhere around me was a song waiting to be heard, or a musician waiting to be played. I told myself I could stay there and surround myself with music and never come out for the rest of my life.

I told myself that the music would take away the pain.

Chapter 9
Got My Mojo Working

From: Fa8@wildplace.com
Subject: Muddy Waters, Life, etc.
To: JosieBgirl@viennanet.net

Josie, my luv, I am in desperate, and I do mean desperate, need of the Muddy Waters album you recently procured through our on-line friends in Germany. I realize this particular album has become your pride and joy-joy — for the moment. But do remember our friend Karma says sharing is a good thing.

And, furthermore, if I don't get this second riff correct on my new song (which, if you listen closely, is similar to Muddy's best work) then I fear Karma — and the tall bass player at the Killer Rabbit (my new favorite pub) — will become somewhat unpleasant.

Of course you could bring your Flying V along and jam along with us. The world always needs another angst-ridden female guitar player, however weird she may be.

I am forever yours — at least until someone newer comes along.

Fa8

The Immortal Von B.

From: JosieBgirl@viennanet.net
Subject: Purchasing your own music
To: Fa8@wildplace.com

Fa8:

How is it that I am your sole source for music? At
some point you are going to have to pay for the occasional
song — those of us who want to make a living by performing
would appreciate it. Besides, when I loan you my records —
especially my rare vinyl albums — they always comes back
sporting scratches, smelling like beer, or, worse yet, bearing
the smears of your greasy fingerprints.

Come by after ten, tomorrow night and you may borrow Muddy. But if anything happens to this one your fate
will be, most assuredly, unpleasant. Remember Vivaldi
and the potato chips?

Musically,

Josie

P.S. I have no desire to jam with you if you remain
insistent that I dress like a cheap streetwalker. Seriously, I
don't wear dresses. And I refuse to be mistaken for one of
Vienna's less expensive hookers.

. . . .

Okay, understand that I had exactly one friend.

One.

His name was Fa8. And, yes, he thought I was weird, as in awkward and strange and messed up. But how could you take offense with
a fellow who can't even spell his name right.

Fa8's real name was Fredrick Bartholomew Rosenguild.

He hailed from Liverpool and claimed to be a political prisoner (he
wasn't, he was my age and we went to the same international school).
Fa8 is seventeen. He was tall, mouthy, and skinny (think toothpick)

— and a computer-hacker-wanna-be-thrash-metal-guitar-player with big dark gray eyes, long fingers, and thin lips that always seemed to be twisted into sort of a weird grin.

I don't think he ever combed his hair (but he changed the color frequently). Fa8 wore clothes that . . . well, let's just call them different: skinny jeans, Wellington boots, and a slashed T-shirt along with chains, bandannas, or various stray pieces of cloth wrapped around his upper arm.

He pushed his British accent to the extreme, and added weird endings to words. He also changed his name — and decided to become a musician — after he survived a car wreck several years ago. He told me once a piece of plastic shaped like a guitar kept the seat belt locked when the convertible he was riding in flipped.

Ever since he had called himself "Fate," only he spelled it F-a-8 (I blame his computer-geek side for that). I know he sounds strange. But Fa8 was my friend: funny, a true computer genius, and loyal. He was also the only person on the planet who could still make me laugh. He may also have been the only person at my school who understood me. Our relationship wasn't boyfriend-girlfriend. Fa8 was more like a weird brother (the one who escaped from prison). I couldn't imagine ever kissing him, but I told him more of my secrets than I told anyone else and I cried a million tears on his shoulders.

He had been there for me when no one else would listen.

And, so you might say I had my Fa8.

He could be moody and, at times, cynical. He talked strange, but he also rocked a serious rhythm guitar, and he could break into any computer system on the planet. And I knew he cared about me.

And right now that was enough.

. . . .

Okay, so I lost Mom when I was fourteen. Which meant for the next three years (not counting the months we were fighting or ignoring each other) Dad had to be both father and mother to me. And though he is a good man and a good father, being reared by a scientist (a man who sets the standard for obsessive-compulsive behavior) wasn't easy.

The Immortal Von B.

Honestly, it's not every girl's father who read steampunk novels, loves old Sherlock Holmes movies, had a secret thing for peanut butter and mustard sandwiches, and seriously believed that disco was just a misunderstood musical genre.

But my dad was not every girl's father.

Fa8 was right: I was weird. I was seventeen and I had no idea how to be a girl. Sure, I had all the right parts. And yes, they worked. But I sucked at the female stuff: flirting or putting on makeup. The last time I had tried the eyeliner-lipstick-blush thing I ended up looking like a raccoon that flunked out of clown school.

It was so bad Fa8 laughed out loud — and I mean he literally laughed out loud — at me, to my face, in my room. That's not all, either. Most of the time I wore T-shirts and jeans or maybe cargo pants — you know, something baggy. I had never, ever worn a pair of heels in my life — I was clumsy even in tennis shoes. I couldn't make my hair behave — and I got so tired of trying that I cut it super short. Problem solved? Wrong. Now it did all this funky stuff. Fa8 had suggested a solution of gel, hair spray, and egg whites. But eggs make me gag. So I gave up.

How else did I fall short? Let me count the ways: I chewed my fingernails, and once in a while I liked to belch song lyrics. Dad said I was rebelling against my femininity. But when you don't have a Mom, is there really anything to rebel against? Besides, being an asexual nongirl made life so much easier. Or so I told myself.

Still I remembered when I was little watching Mom get dressed and it was like magic. She'd throw on one of Dad's shirts and a pair of jeans, pull her hair back, and in five minutes she looked like a fashion model. If I tried that, I'd end up looking like one of those guys who scavenged through the dumpsters in the dark alleys of Vienna.

I didn't even know if I wa pretty. Last year Fa8 told me I "looked okay and I didn't stink," but I think he was just being nice, because when I looked in the mirror all I saw was a skinny, weird girl with tiny little boobs, short hair, and chewed-to-the-nub fingernails.

Dad always said I was beautiful. *But doesn't every father tell his daughter that?* I mean I guess I wasn't horrible, but I was certainly not pretty. I wasn't good at things girls my age were supposed to be good at either. I wasn't good at kissing or even holding hands. The best kiss I ever had was years ago (and the boy wasn't looking when I did it).

I had never been in love.

I had never had a real boyfriend. I spent way more time reading and writing and playing my music than a normal girl.

So it probably isn't a shock that I didn't get phone calls from anyone at school — except Fa8. I rarely went to the movies, and most of the time I tried to avoid anything social. I did like to go to concerts — any music was fine — but most of the time I went alone, or I dragged Fa8 with me.

Oh yeah, my feet were also too big and my nose was slightly crooked. It wan't that I wouldn't have liked to have a boyfriend, because I would have — even if only for a little while — but I was not playing with a deck that was likely to attract one anytime soon.

Good points? Well, Dad said I was smart — as in geek smart. I rocked at anything mathematical, and, for me, algebra, trig, and all that hard-core science stuff came as easy as the ABCs.

And, yeah, like my mom and my dad and my grandpa, I grooved on music. I could spend years talking about music — rock, classical, punk, industrial, trash, country, jazz, rap, urban, ethnic — any of it. You name it and I would listen to it.

For me, music was like a drug — and I needed a fix every day.

I'd been in orchestra since I was ten. I played violin at school, like my grandfather, but at home I studied piano. . . . or I did until Mom died. Dad once said I could play as well as she could, but he was just trying to make me feel good. Nobody could play like Mom. She was a true artist — music was like air for her. She just breathed and the music came out. I loved watching her; it was like she and the piano were connected. Dad always said part of her soul was fused with the wood. I only know her fingers danced across the keys like prima ballerinas.

My favorite memory of her? I have one more I held tight to, which hadn't faded like the rest. I was four. I was in my room playing with finger paint. My hands were bright purple. I was sleepy. I walked down the hall to find Mom. She was practicing. I listened at the door for a while, then the music stopped. I opened the door just a little and peeked inside. Mom was gone.

I walked in the room and crawled up onto the bench of her huge, white Steinway and started to play. I remember watching the purple drip onto the white keys. I thought it looked so pretty.

When Mom came in, she stood quietly and listened. Then she told me what keys to press. I tried to play the way she showed me, but my fingers kept slipping and smearing purple paint.

Mom just smiled.

Purple paint was everywhere — on the bench, the keys, and all over me. Mom never said a word. She simply cleaned me up, wiped down her piano, and finished practicing.

I remember falling asleep under her piano bench that day.

Not long ago, I sat down at her Steinway. Everything was the same. The big piano looked just like it did that day years ago. I glanced at the keys. On the middle and on the low C keys, there were several faint small purple fingerprints. I sat there for a long time, just looking at them. Then I heard something move.

Dad stood by the door. I guess he knew what I was thinking.

"Your mother loved you with everything she had, Josie," he said. "She left the paint there because it reminded her of you and those sunny afternoons you both spent at the piano."

I looked down at my feet, so he wouldn't see me cry.

"I think that was her favorite part of each day," he said. "She would sit you down next to her and teach you. She loved having you beside her. That was, for her, bliss."

I stood, walked past Dad, and didn't say a thing.

I don't go in Mom's studio anymore.

And I haven't touched her piano since that day. The maid dusts it and, occasionally, she'll polish the wood. And the big white Steinway is still as beautiful as the day Dad bought it.

But like my mom, the big white Steinway is silent.

Chapter 10

Rave On

From: JosieBgirl@viennanet.net
Subject: Stark RAVEing Mad
To: Fa8@wildplace.com

Fa8:

Why do I keep hearing I'm hosting a rave? I told you "no" several million times. Enough. Plan your own sick, drunken fertility rites. But leave me, and my music, out.

Do not tell anyone else I am hosting anything or I will post your real name (and that photograph of you in your Union Jack underwear) on every guitar-related blog throughout western Europe. Trust me! After I get through with you, you'll never play in this town again.

Josie

P.S. You're a jerk, in case you're wondering.

. . . .

The party was Fa8's idea. He called it "a rave." I had made the mistake of whining about being lonely and complaining about not having any friends. I guess you could say Fa8 got tired of it and took matters into his own hands.

"You know, luv, you're not very social," he said.

"I am so."

"Liar."

I glared at him. "I'm social. I participate. I'm in orchestra. That's social."

"Or-ches-tra, Josie, is not social. Very few of the members of the or-ches-tra talk to anyone else. They play music written by a bunch of old, dead wankers and, for the record, I have never seen an or-ches-tra person at a rave."

"But they're my friends."

Fa8 cocked his head. "Really, luv? Friends? I thinketh not."

"They are good people. I like them."

Fa8 looked at me with a crooked smile. "Alrighty then, tell me, what's the name of the first-chair violinist? Who is the tall chappie with the dark hair?"

"Ahhh, that's easy," I lied.

"Yeah?"

"Sure, his name is . . ." I stalled for time. "It's Eric. That's it."

Fa8 laughed. He put a finger on his nose and made a sound like a buzzer.

"Sorry, luv, that's not the correct answer, but thanks for playing. The first chair violinist is not Eric. Eric is a very tall boy with flaming orange hair; he plays the drums, likes boys, and has been suspended from school on not one but two separate occasions."

"But I was . . ."

"You don't even know the difference between the bloke who stands five feet away from you in class and the first violinist?"

I looked at my feet and mumbled. "Is it Ian?"

Fa8 shook his head in disgust. "I'm sorry Miss Brunswick. But once again that is an incorrect answer. The correct name is Ethan. Say it with me, E-t-h-a-n."

I rolled my eyes. "Okay, so I don't know everyone. That doesn't make me a troll."

Fa8 leaned in. "You're right, luv. It doesn't. You are not a troll. But you are weird, most assuredly weird, and truly, you are anti-social.

All these noble students at the Inter-Global Academic Center would certainly agree with me: you are the weirdest of the weird."

Fa8 cupped his hand and whispered in my ear: "They also think you don't like guys."

I slugged Fa8 in the arm. "That's not fair. I like guys."

Fa8 laughed. He held up his hands as if surrendering. "How do we know? Have you kissed a bloke? What exactly are your intentions? What type of documentation do you have? I, for one, have no evidence of which gender you prefer. It's all yet to be decided, I'd say."

I buried my face in my hands.

"Just stop, Fa8, okay? It's not my fault no one asks me out."

Fa8 put an arm around me and squeezed.

"It's all right, my luv. See, you are right about one thing . . ."

I wiped my face and turned towards him.

"Yeah?"

"Other than me you don't have any friends."

. . . .

After Mom died, Dad made me go to this exclusive private school — the Inter-Global Academic Center. It was supposed to be a school that brought students from all across the globe together to learn and study. The teachers called it "United Nations High."

But I can assure you, no one there was concerned with world peace.

It wasn't that the people, as in the teachers and instructors, were lame, because they were actually pretty smart. But it was everything else. All the kids were from these uber-rich families. They formed these little cliques and clubs and if you weren't in the right one, then you were considered the total loser of total losers. And at the Inter-Global Academic Center, I had become the poster child for the total losers.

Fa8, however, somehow had managed to assemble a huge collection of friends. Most of the time, though, he could be found with the emo-Goth musicians and this strange collection of Japanese guys he called "the Samurai Wannabes."

The musicians usually sat around and snarled as you walked by, and the Samurai Wannabes spend weeks practicing kicks, writing code, and trying to bring down big computer networks. Every time I tried to talk to Fa8 in their presence, they pointed at me and jabbered in Japanese.

And Fa8 called *me* weird.

There were other groups to contend with, too. Several of the junior girls were the daughters of British royalty, and the president of the student council was the oldest son of the Canadian prime minister.

I had become known simply as "the American."

. . . .

Today it was another field trip. Most of the time I used field trips to catch up on sleep or as an excuse to slip away from school early. Last month my class spent three hours at a World War II museum. Before that, we went to a big conference center for a lecture on ancient Rome by some wheezing, almost-dead historian who urged us to "embrace the past."

I haven't even been embraced in the present.

Whatever.

Still, this trip was supposed to be different. For several days now, it had been a big hush-hush secret that no one at the school would talk about. Then this morning word leaked out: we're going to the Haus der Musik.

"Big dealy-oh." Fa8 scratched his head. "What's so special about the bloomin' Haus der Musik? I do believe you and I have traipsed its marble steps many times."

I watched the blocks go by through the van's rain-splatted window as we weaved through the streets of Vienna.

"Yeah, that was one of the first places Mom took me to when we moved here. It's pretty cool, but, you're right, I've been there before. No big deal."

Fa8 slipped down in his seat. "True enough, luv. But I do believe whatever the big secret is — and I don't think it's our destination — we shall know soon enough. The van just stoppie-stopped."

Honestly, even on a non-school day the Haus der Musik is a pretty cool place. It is located between Saint Stephen's Cathedral and the Vienna State Opera House. It used to be the palace of Archduke

Charles. Now it's a museum and center for the performing arts. It is open all the time and, occasionally, it hosts live performances.

A couple of years ago, Fa8 and I snuck out on a Friday night to see this South African jazz fusion band play there. The acoustics of the place were amazing. The Haus der Musik is also a big tourist draw and so it's always busy. But it's certainly no secret.

"This way, students, please." An usher dressed like Wolfgang Amadeus Mozart pointed to the back entrance. "Please enter quietly."

I stepped out of the van and looked around. Most of the kids in line looked as bored as I felt. The girl behind me — the British snob who claims to be a princess — kept pushing people and whining about the weather.

"Could you please hurry?" she said. "This queue is long and the damp weather is doing horrible things to my hair."

Fa8 whispered to me. "How, exactly, does one improve on the wet poodle look?"

I couldn't help but laugh.

Mozart led us through the back entrance, while another usher — could he possibly be a young Elvis? — shoved us onto a freight elevator. He plugged a small flash drive into the elevator's control panel and pushed a button for the top floor.

"So what's the big deal? What's with all the secrety goings-on?" Fa8 asked. "How come we didn't come through the front door like the rest of Vienna's elite?"

Elvis' face went blank and he answered in a thick German accent. "I am not allowed to say. But you *vill* know soon."

A few seconds later, the elevator door opened. Elvis moved us into a large yellow-and-white room with arched windows and overstuffed couches. The walls were covered with massive paintings. At one end of the room, squatting on top of a mammoth rug stood a dark wooden desk. Near that stood a large bust of Beethoven.

Elvis pointed to the sofas.

"Please, you sit," he said. "*Frau Direktor vill* be along shortly."

With that, Elvis bowed slightly and stepped to the back of the room. I watched him get on the elevator and disappear.

Fa8 chuckled: "Looks like Elvis has, once again, left the building."

Before I could respond, *Frau Direktor* arrived. A slender woman, about thirty-five years old, she was pretty with bright green eyes and sandy-colored hair.

"Welcome students," she said in flawless English. "Welcome to the Haus der Musik. My name is Theresa Malfatti and I am the director here. I know you have questions about all the secrecy, but if you will please be patient, I will explain everything."

Riding over I was sure this would be another typical boring field trip, but now I wasn't so sure. At least she had my attention.

Theresa moved in closer. "First I want you all to know that I am an alumnae of your school. I attended some years ago and continue to have strong ties with the faculty and administrators. That's why you are here today."

The Japanese wonder-boy three seats over waved his hand. "Please now, inform us. What are us doing here?"

Theresa smiled. " 'What are *we* doing here,' " she corrected. "And we'll be doing a great deal — in just a few moments. One of the missions of your school is to expose you to new and important cultural discoveries. And, today, with the help of several private European and American foundations, we are going to do just that."

As she spoke, she moved by the bust of Beethoven. "A few weeks from now the Haus der Musik will premiere a new, never-before-seen historical retrospective of Ludwig von Beethoven's life and work. This will include three newly discovered musical works and personal artifacts that were believed to have been destroyed. Because of the importance of this retrospective, access to the entire center will be limited for all of next year."

Fa8 stood and waved his arms like a cop directing traffic.

"Excuse me, luv. But I'm not sure I understand you. Ol' Beethoven has been singing with the choir invisible for quite some timey-time. It's not like we don't know his stuff."

The director made an attempt at a smile.

"You are correct, young man. But this is a major historical discovery and, already, requests are pouring in from around the globe. These particular arrangements, as well as some of the artifacts, were previously thought to no longer exist. Now, because of my connection to your school we wanted to give you an opportunity to explore the retrospective before it opened and . . ."

"Cool," I said quietly. "New Beethoven."

One of the British snobs interrupted the director.

"So, you ferried us over here just to look at a bunch of Beethoven's moldy old castoffs? Seriously? That's what the secrecy is about?"

The director's face turned red. I had the feeling she recognized the girl asking the question.

"Well, you see," the director said. "We felt, in light of the historical significance of the exhibition that you, as students, would benefit from being allowed early access and a chance to question our archivists."

The eyes of the British princess narrowed like those of a large, fashionably dressed snake.

"Who cares about a dead composer and his old arrangements? I hardly find either worth the secrecy and the inconvenience this trip has caused me."

Her pals tittered.

The young Brit sniffed.

"I'm sure my father would not approve."

"But we thought . . ." The director stood with her hands on her hips. "And no one has ever seen or heard . . ."

"An absolute waste of my time." The British girl tossed her hair. "I mean, Beethoven. Not much of a composer, really."

I don't know where the anger came from, but at that moment, my whole body went tense and rigid. *A waste of time? Beethoven was inconvenient? Not much of a composer? Who the hell was this person? What gave her to the right to decide for the rest of us?* I leaned forward, ready to hear the director put the princess in her place, but the director, shocked by the unexpected attack, stood silent.

"Well, I, for one," said the princess, "am not going to waste my time here. I have other, much more important things to do than listen to the plinkings of an old dead man."

"Plinkings? Are you kidding me?" I jumped to my feet. "Why, you uppity twit! Do you have any idea who Ludwig von Beethoven was?"

I stepped towards her. The princess turned slowly. Her face was that of a red cobra — slits for eyes and a thin, sharp line for a mouth.

"Oh, I should have suspected, it's the American."

"Well, sweetie, 'the American' knows far more about Beethoven than you obviously do. Do you have any idea how important Beethoven is to the history of the world? To music? Could you possibly be that shallow and ignorant?"

Behind me, Fa8 gasped. And the room went still.

The director stepped forward, trying to smooth things over.

"Now girls, there's no need to fight." She pointed to an elevator and a set of stairs in the corner. "Let's get started, shall we?"

"I don't think so," the princess hissed. "Josie has insulted me and that is something I shall not tolerate. I was merely expressing my opinion. But this person is reacting as if she wishes me harm."

She waved a perfectly manicured hand in my direction. "She should be removed."

"You haven't answered my question," I said.

The princess snarled. "Question? And what question was that?"

"Do you even know who Beethoven was? Can you name one piece he composed?"

Her majesty tossed her hair a second time. "Of course, I can. The Ninth Symphony, *Ode to Joy*, anyone knows that."

"And when did he write it?"

"When isn't important." She stomped her foot. "I have answered your question."

"You mean you don't know?"

"Of course I do."

"Okay, so when was it written?" I took another step towards her. Every eye in the room — including the director's — was locked on the princess and me.

"Please, your majesty, tell us. Because I don't think you know anything about Beethoven at all. I think you're just a spoiled brat who whines when she doesn't get her way."

Fa8 stood and leaned forward, flexing his long fingers. He glanced around the room and in a perfect Cockney accent said, "Yer 'ey-ness, tell us. If you're so bloomin' smart. When did this ol' bloke, Beethoven, write his *Ninth Sym-pho-nee*?"

Several of the kids sitting with Fa8 laughed. The princess's face turned bright red. "Well, I . . . believe it was . . . I think, I mean . . . some people believe . . ."

"You don't know." I snarled. "You are ignorant and arrogant and absolutely useless."

"I refuse to be spoken to like that," the princess protested, taking a step away from me.

I stepped directly in front of her; this chick wasn't going anywhere until she got a little music history lesson.

"Beethoven started writing musical sketches for the *Ode to Joy* in 1817. He was ill at the time, and writing in what many scholars call his Late Period. He wrote five piano sonatas, plus the *Diabelli Variations* and the *Missa Solemnis* during that same time."

I took a step back. "But, of course, you already knew that."

The princess's face turned a deep crimson.

"You tell 'er, Josie. I do believe her 'ey-ness has insulted the wrong composer."

I pointed to the bust behind her. "Oh, did I forget to mention that since he first composed them, none of Beethoven's works has ever been out of publication? That's more than two hundred and forty years, your highness. And Beethoven's music is still played today and has influenced thousands of musicians and their musical styles through the centuries. He is not just some old dead guy; he's . . ."

"He wrote very goodly," a Japanese wonder-boy said. "Very goodly indeed."

Fa8 nodded with a wicked grin. "Yeah, ol' Ludwig rocked and rolled. Name another bloke who was stone deaf and could still write and play."

The mouth of the British princess dropped open. "Deaf? You're lying," she said. "That's a myth. No one could do that."

The director opened her mouth to respond, but I was quicker.

"Fa8's right. By the time Beethoven began writing his *Ninth Symphony* he couldn't hear anything. He was completely deaf. He lost his hearing, yet managed to compose hundreds of incredible pieces."

"I don't believe you. You're lying."

"No, she's not." The director pointed to me. "This young woman is absolutely correct. Ludwig von Beethoven lost his hearing, yet he continued to compose and . . ."

"How?" the princess asked. "How does a deaf man compose?"

I leaned towards the princess. Every muscle in my body felt like a taut bowstring. I pushed my face into hers until our noses were only inches apart.

"It's called passion. The music filled his mind, his soul. To get it out, he cut the legs off his piano. Then he lay on the floor and pounded on the keys until his fingers bled. He pounded so he could feel the vibrations of the strings. That's how he wrote."

The princess rolled her eyes.

But there was no stopping me now: "He bled and sweated and cried and wrote until all the music came out. He heard the sounds in his mind and felt the music in his body. It was his passion, his love. He needed to write. He had to write; there was no other way. He could not hear a whisper and, yet, he wrote amazing, beautiful music."

"Enough," the British princess stammered. "I care nothing about this Beethoven. And I refuse to be spoken to this way anymore."

Fa8 grandly motioned for her to leave.

Several others followed her. Then Fa8 slipped back through the crowd to stand by me.

"Impressive, luv," he whispered. "I believe game, set, and matchie-match goes to the young woman from the colonies."

"All hail the victorious American," he said, holding my right arm up like a victorious boxer.

I jerked my arm down.

"I didn't mean to get so mad, but she . . ."

Fa8 put his forehead against mine. The sweetness of the gesture caught me off guard, but no more so than what he said next.

"Look Josie, ole girl, I knew Beethoven was deaf, but I didn't know ol' Ludwig took the legs off his piano-machine. You have to love music to do something like that. I do believe I shall endeavor to listen to Mr. Beet-hoven more often."

I gave him a weak smile. For so long, I had been upset about Mom dying. And today, when the princess started to trash Beethoven, well, it felt like she was insulting my mom.

"I guess I got a little emotional. Sorry."

Fa8 patted me on the back.

"You don't have to apologize to me, luv." He pointed across the room. "But you might want to talk to *Frau Direktor*, she doesn't look much like a terribly happy-chappie."

Chapter 11

Moonlight Sonata

MY FRIEND RARELY READS social occasions right, but he looked to have called it this time. Theresa, the director, was not happy. Her face had twisted into a scowl and she stood stiffly. She pointed to me.

"Young woman, may I please speak with you alone."

The director motioned to a small door, near the back of the room. I nodded and followed her.

"It's okay luv." Fa8 called after me. "You didn't do anything wrong. I'll wait right here for you."

I walked through the door and swiped my eyes. If I was going to get yelled at I didn't want anyone to think I was crying about a fight with some princess.

The director shut the door behind me and motioned towards a large yellow sofa. We were inside another office; this one, smaller with no windows. In one corner were propped several tubes of concert posters. On the wall hung a modern-looking sketch of Beethoven in a large ornate frame. Behind the desk, a shelf sagged with the weight of hundreds of compact discs.

"Please. I will only be a second."

She stepped into another smaller adjacent room then returned with two small cups of coffee.

"I thought this might help." She handed me a cup. "Would you care for cream or sugar?"

"No. Black is fine." I gave her a sheepish smile.

She nodded and sat down behind the desk. After adding a little sugar to her coffee, she leaned back in her chair.

"I take it you don't like our British friends?"

"Not really. For royalty, they don't seem very noble."

Theresa smiled and nodded.

"Agreed. Keep in mind she is related to George III. I believe some branches of the monarchy still have a great deal to learn."

"That's an understatement."

Theresa paused for a moment to stir her coffee, then looked up.

"I must say I was impressed by your knowledge of *Herr* Beethoven."

I set my cup on the edge of the desk.

"My mother was a pianist. Beethoven was her favorite composer."

"Ahhh, that explains many things. And your name is . . ."

"I'm sorry, I'm Josie. Josie Brunswick."

For a second, Theresa looked as if she'd been slapped.

Her face turned pale.

"You are Josephine Brunswick? The daughter of Anna Heigle-Brunswick?"

I looked at my feet. The mention of Mom's name had made my eyes fill with tears again. "Yes ma'am," I said.

"*Mein Gott,*" Theresa slapped her own forehead. "I am so stupid. I should have realized you were a student at the school. I believe I had been told this. Your mother, she was, she was like no other pianist before or since. She was . . ."

". . . amazing," I said, choking on emotion. "She was absolutely amazing. And I guess I'm a little sensitive about her and her music and, well, maybe Beethoven, too."

"I can certainly understand why. Your mother inspired me. I first heard her play in London. She was one of the finest classical pianists the world has known, possibly the finest when it came to interpreting Beethoven's works."

I smiled. Hearing someone else talk about my mom and hearing them tell me they loved to hear her play made me feel a little better.

"I'm sorry, *Frau Direktor.* I did not mean to cause a scene. I love this place and it was important to my mother. But maybe because my mom loved playing Beethoven so much, I kinda feel like he's part of the family."

Theresa smiled. "But of course you do. You might like to know that it was your mother who inspired this retrospective."

She opened a drawer and rummaged through the contents, before pulling out a compact disc. The jewel case was cracked and had yellowed, but the disc inside appeared in perfect condition.

"This is the original digital recording of your grandfather and your mother playing a little-known arrangement of Beethoven's *Ninth* in London many years ago. We're featuring the same arrangement during the retrospective."

I leaned forward and touched the disc.

"You have the CD of my mom and grandpa playing? I've wanted a copy of this for years; Dad said the recording was lost."

"The others were, but this is the original. I believe it is the only one in existence," Theresa said, pausing as if afraid that what followed might open a wound. "This retrospective has been in the works for several years, Josie. Originally, it was to be your mother who was to perform the new arrangements we found."

I felt the tears threaten again. For a few seconds everything came back — the times my mom practiced, her study, her piano, and always the music she played.

"She would have loved that," I said quietly.

Theresa reached across the table and laid her hand on mine. "Josie, I must apologize. I didn't mean to reopen a wound. I understand how hard this must be for you."

"It's okay. It's nice knowing that at least some people like the music that my mom loved so much."

Theresa gave a soft smile. "Oh, don't worry about the princess. Her only claim to fame is as breeding stock. Your grandfather and your mother, well, you come from a family of giants."

She took another sip of coffee, then abruptly, stood. "Come with me and I'll show you something I think you will like."

We walked back into the meeting room. Everyone — including Fa8 — was gone.

"Where'd everybody go?"

Theresa pointed at the elevator.

"They're probably in the auditorium by now." She looked at her watch. "And I believe they should have just started listening to your mother's Stockholm performance of *Für Elise*."

This time the elevator went to the basement. When the doors opened, Theresa pointed at what looked like the inside of an underground warehouse.

"Come this way, and watch your step."

We walked through the dim light to a huge polished metal door. It stood flat against the wall, without hinges or handles or knobs.

"This is our vault."

"How do you get in?"

"This way." She placed her hand in the center of the door and waited. After a few seconds, there was a click and the door swung inward. "It's a thermal scan. The sensors read my hand size, shape, and temperature. The sensors recognize the data from my hand and activate the lock."

"But couldn't someone else . . .?"

Theresa stepped inside the vault. I followed her and watched, eyes wide, as she shut the door behind us.

"No, and I'll show you why. Put your hand here."

I placed my hand in the center of the door. I heard a faint purr; the area behind my palm grew warm.

"It's reading your data," she said.

Nothing happened. The door remained closed.

"See, even though you are female and our hands are similar in size, the measurements are not exact. Nor is the shape of your fingerprints, or the temperature of your body."

"Wow, that's cool."

"Technology can be miraculous. But come, let's spend a few moments in the past."

Theresa turned and flipped a small switch on the wall. Around me, the room began to glow. When it was finally illuminated, I thought I'd stepped into a different time. The entire room was decorated like a nineteenth-century sitting room. The chairs were high-backed and gilded. A writing desk, painted in garish colors, sat in one corner. In the center stood a magnificent fortepiano. The wood was dark cherry with fine, thin scrollwork along the base. The legs of the fortepiano were elegant and slender and inlaid with tiny ribbons of gold. Theresa pointed to the instrument.

"You know what a fortepiano is, yes?"

"Oh yes. It's an early version of the piano, developed by Bartholomew Cristofori, the Italian instrument maker, probably around the late 1790s. Haydn, Mozart, and Beethoven all had them. During Beethoven's time, they began to change, but they were in use until after his death. The grand piano of the late twentieth century is a direct descendent."

I ran my fingers across the fine wood.

"This one is beautiful, absolutely beautiful."

"Amazing, Josie. If you should ever want a job at the Haus der Musik, please call. You would be a welcome addition to our staff. And you are right also, about the date of this particular fortepiano. This one was owned by *Herr* Beethoven. It will be part of our exhibit."

I touched the middle C key. The fortepiano responded with a perfectly tuned note.

"Yes, it's in tune," Theresa said. "It's to be played during the opening night of the exhibit — of course, that will require tuning it again once it's been moved to the hall."

"I wish my mom could be there; she would have loved this."

"Josie, your mother would have been the one to play this instrument. She is why we had it restored."

I wanted to say more, but again, emotion got the better of me.

"I don't know what . . ."

Theresa hugged me. "It's okay." She pointed to the back of the room. "Come look at this."

We stepped through a doorway into another room; this one was filled floor to ceiling with shelves and large high-tech-looking metal boxes. Theresa touched the numbers on a keypad of one of the metal containers and it opened with a hiss.

"You have to see this. These were recently discovered in an antique shop in a somewhat questionable part of Vienna."

She reached into a cubby for two pairs of white gloves and indicated I should put one pair on, while donning the other herself. Then she removed an antique amber pen from a small wooden box.

"This ink pen belonged to a young Beethoven," she said. "As you can see it is worn and the nib has also been damaged."

"He probably threw it against the wall or something, when he was angry," I said. "I read a biography that suggested he was bipolar."

"Some scholars would agree with you," Theresa said, "and it would not surprise me."

She set the box back on the shelf and reached again inside the container. This time, she removed a short, red scarf. The material looked to be wool.

"We think this was a scarf he wore as a young man. We tested it and the skin and hair samples belong to Beethoven."

I reached for the scarf. It felt thin and fragile. I held it against my face and inhaled.

"I can't believe I'm holding something Beethoven once wore."

Theresa smiled. "I still get a thrill when I think about it, too."

"How did you find it?"

"We didn't, a collector did," Theresa said, gently taking the scarf from my hand. "Before it was loaned to us for the retrospective, it was in someone's private collection. It is fragile, and it's in line to be cleaned so that it can be exhibited."

"It smelled sort of musty."

"Yes, there are many things here like that. We've discovered clothes, more conversation books, and several unfinished manuscripts. Sometimes the pages have just a few notes. Others are more . . . complete."

"My mom would have so loved this. You would have never gotten her out of here."

Theresa placed the scarf back into the wood box and then the metal container. She tapped the top; the lid and the container sealed with a click. She removed her gloves and looked at her watch.

"Oh, my, how the time has flown. I must get you back upstairs with your classmates. They will be leaving in just a few minutes."

I gave her my gloves, and we walked back to the vault-like door. Theresa touched the center and it opened again. She stepped out.

I started to follow, but hesitated. "Thank you, *Frau Direktor*. You have no idea how much this meant to me. To have the chance to see this and to know that my mom was going to be a part of it, well, I'm so glad I came today."

"First Josie, please call me Theresa. I feel like we are destined to be great friends. And second, I am sure your mother would have been proud at how you stood up for her favorite composer today. She was an amazing musician. She brought joy to millions of people. I am so very sorry for your loss."

I turned my head. I didn't want her to see me tear up again.

Theresa gave me a weak smile.

"It's okay. Even after this much time has passed. I understand why you still grieve." She stood quietly for a second. "Tell you what, why don't you come back for the exhibit's opening day as my personal guest? I would absolutely love to have you here, and you could meet many of your mother's friends. She had many, many fans. Would you like that?"

I wiped my eyes and nodded. "Oh yes, I'd love to."

Theresa motioned towards the elevator.

"Then, come with me," she winked. "Let's see if the princess has learned anything."

Chapter 12

Long Cool Woman

From: Fa8@wildplace.com
Subject: Life, Raves, etc.
To: everyone@anonmaildrop5.com

All right blokes, time for another rave-y-rave. Our own Josie
Brunswick has offered to host our little e-vent Friday. Josie is
pixie-haired guitarist with vintage Flying V. Her place is Villa
Theresa manse off twisty-turny Grand Boulevard (look for yellow and miles of shrubbery). Liquid entertainment provided.
Music courtesy Josie's sterling music library. Bring anyone
in need of a good frolic. Apologies for a-non-y-mous way of
shooting this to your in-box, but thanks to my reputation for
hackery Vienna's finer Internet providers no longer allow my
little missives through. Alas. Until Friday.

Fa8

. . . .

Sometimes a girl just needs her space, but Fa8 wouldn't leave me
alone. On the ride back to school, he kept yammering about the rave.

It was like being trapped next to a scratched CD stuck on repeat.

"Come on Josie, you ab-so-lute-ly must do it. Now is the perfect time. All these people, they now know who you are — there is already a video of you and the princess on YouTube . . . you can thank the Japanese wonder-boy for that. I'm telling you it would be huge. A great ravey-rave."

"But I told you I don't want to have a party. Why won't you listen?"

Fa8 rolled his eyes. He reminded me of the British princess.

"Because, luv, you don't have a good reason. You're just scared. Raves and music, well, they're connected, see, and you, Josie, are standing in the way of progress."

I pushed myself against the window. Outside, dark clouds hung heavy and pregnant against the sky.

"But I don't know any of these people. We never talk. Remember? And when by chance we do, it rarely goes well. Weren't you watching in there?"

"Josie, they don't talk to you because you don't talk to them. You walk around all wrapped up in yourself. You don't even smile. You're just, well, you are just there. It's like all these people are in your way."

"That's not fair. I'm not like that. I'm not mean."

"You're not intentionally mean. You just don't try," Fa8 said. "You act like you don't care about them. So, luv, they return the favor."

I pushed myself down in the seat. I didn't like where the conversation was going. "But my dad's gone to London. He won't be back for weeks. He'd be really mad if he found out."

Fa8 pushed a hand through his hair. He leaned in so close to me I could count the freckles on his cheeks. "Who the 'F' cares? Do you do everything daddy-o says to do?"

I gave him a push. "You don't understand. You don't know what it's like. I'm so tired of trying to explain."

Fa8 patted my leg. "Josie, luv, I do understand. I know you're terribly unhappy. And you're brilliant and beautiful and sweet and, yes, amazing. But you're also wrapped up and walled off from everyone else, so no one but me sees how amazing you are."

"I'm not like that."

Fa8 gave me a weak smile. "Yes, yes luv, you are. And all your distance from everyone else, my dear, is not going to bring your mum back. You're just shutting yourself off from the ole human race, which pretty much guarantees you being lonely."

I looked at my hands. Fa8 had never said anything like that to me before. He'd never said I was beautiful and I had never heard him tell anyone they were sweet. It was all so confusing.

"But I have never thrown a rave. I don't know what to do. Let's talk about doing it later in the semester, okay?"

"Sorry, luv. We're through talking. Rave starts at your place at ten. We'll need that fab stereo of yours and several million pieces of music, too. And, well, plan on about thirty or forty souls."

He pointed to the crowd of students in the van.

"Cause I've already invited most of the class."

. . . .

Fa8 lied.

By eleven, there were a hundred people in my living room alone. After I had gotten home from school, I found Leisel and warned her about the party. She didn't ask if there'd be alcohol, and I didn't volunteer. She did offer to make food, but I told her I had it covered.

Well, actually, Fa8 said he had it covered.

Around nine, Fa8 arrived with about fifteen of the Samurai Wannabes. They'd brought a couple of kegs of beer and a mountain of chips and junk food.

"I told you luv, our raves come self-contained." He elbowed his way past me. "Where do I, ahh, where shall I put the liquid refreshments?"

I pointed to the den. "In there. Try not to break anything. And please, no puking on the rugs."

Fa8 walked around the room looking at the walls. "Righty-o. No *vomitus extremus.*" He pushed one of the beer kegs into the empty hearth. "You've done well for yourself, luv. I do believe ye old fireplace will work nicely. Keeps the spilly-spills off your fancy rugs."

I rolled my eyes. "Just don't get me arrested. Okay?"

Fa8 laughed and pointed to a painting of a stern-looking man sitting on a horse. "Who's the elderly geezer-looking gentleman?"

"I don't know. That painting was here when we moved in; it's not any of my relatives."

Fa8 tapped the keg. "Well, if you asked me, I don't think he ever attended a rave. Doesn't look like the musical type."

"I just hope I don't end up hanging next to him," I said.

By midnight the rave was in full swing. Besides the kids from our school, Fa8 had invited loads of other people, none of whom I knew.

"Don't worry, luv," he said. "You're in for a treat. Now, where is your disc of the Dropkick Murphys? I feel the need to *Go Out in Style*."

I sipped my beer and sat down on one of the couches. Next to me a Samurai Wannabe flirted unmercifully with a pretty girl in a short pink dress. He kept fumbling the words, but I had to give him credit, the girl laughed — and she didn't leave. Still I didn't want to hang around for what would surely end in a good face slap.

"I'll give you two some time alone," I mumbled as I left.

I walked over to one of the large beveled glass windows that lined the north side of the room. Outside, the moon was full and heavy. I felt strange. I wanted to have fun, I really did, and I knew Fa8, despite everything, was trying to help make that happen. It was just that everything was still so painful. For some reason, going to the Haus der Musik that morning and hearing the recording of my mom playing had made me sad once again. It was like the trip had re-opened all the wounds caused by her death.

I would have probably stood there looking out the window for the rest of the party, but Fa8 had other plans.

"Why so glum, luv?" Fa8 grabbed my arm and pulled me towards the center of the room. "When you throw a rave you have to participate. You know, do the hostess-thingy."

"I thought you were the hostess?"

"Not hardly, I'm more like your able-bodied assistant. Remember my goal is to undo skirts. Not wear them." Fa8 pulled on my arm. "Now, come this way. There are some blokes I want you to meet."

With that Fa8 pulled me — literally — to a strange-looking group of boys hovering in front of the tapped keg.

Behind me, a song started. It was an oldie — played in a minor key with a single guitar followed by two loud drumbeats. I was just about to stick out my hand and introduce myself when Fa8 pulled me into his arms and twirled me around the center of the room.

"Alright luv, let's play name that tune."

"Why? You'll lose. You always lose."

Fa8 put his hand in the small of my back and pulled me closer. "I'm not so sure about that. Try me."

I pushed him away and pirouetted in the center of the rug.

"Okay, I know what song it is. Do you?"

"Give me a minute. I think, I do believe . . ."

I laughed and danced by him. "I'll give you a hint: The band is British. Late 1960s."

Fa8 gave me a blank look.

"Would it be our friends, The Rolling Stones?"

I laughed. Loud. "Listen to the words, doofus: 'She was a long cool woman in a black dress.' I taught you the chord progression last year."

Fa8 stopped. His eyes twinkled, like someone inside his head had turned on a light. "Oh yes. I have it, luv. I do believe that song is called *Long Cool Woman*? Is your Fa8 correct?"

"Okay. You know the song. Now tell me who's performing it. If you're gonna play Name That Tune you have to know the band, too."

"Josie, my dear. You do not play fair." He took me in his arms again and whirled me around. "You do not play fair at all."

With that he pulled me over to a new crowd of boys that had gathered around the beer keg and then took a bow.

"I shall have to think. But first, I do believe we have been most impolite to our guests, so I shall correct that situation post-haste." Fa8 pointed at a tall, red-headed boy in a dark sweater. "That's Tony, an absolute genius coder. He drinks way too much; he's the laziest bloke you've ever met. But if you're looking for someone to get into all sorts of trouble with, Tony is, most assuredly, your man."

I rolled my eyes. "You still haven't told me who's playing the song."

"I thinking, I'm thinking," Fa8 said.

I stopped dancing. "You lose. You only get half credit."

Fa8 frowned. "I told you, you don't play fair. Now, I'm going to have to re-in-tro-duce you to a few chaps who might like a weird, crop-headed, angst-ridden, female axe player."

"Gee, thanks."

Fa8 pointed to a boy standing next to Tony. Max, a short, stumpy troll-type, glared at me, grunted a "hi," then returned to his beer.

"He's quite the talker," I said, with a grin.

Fa8 laughed. "Okay, let's try this one." Fa8 walked me over to a guy by the front window. "This is Chaz. You might remember him."

Chaz stood about six feet tall with sandy-brown hair and gorgeous blue eyes. He looked as if he had been chiseled out of solid granite. He stuck out his hand and smiled a perfect white smile.

"Hi, the name is actually Charles William, but as Fa8 would have it, I've been dubbed Chaz. Pleased to meet you."

I paused for a second, then reached over, and grabbed Fa8 by the ear. "Hey, skinny boy. You still haven't told me who wrote the song."

Fa8 turned his head, trying to break my hold. "Was it The Hollies?"

"You are correct. Of course, I'm sure you cheated, but I'll give you a half-point for finally getting one right."

Fa8 laughed a fake, high-pitched laugh. "Well, thanks, luv. Thanks for making me look like Lord High Wanker in front of me mates."

"You didn't need my help," I said. "You are the textbook definition of 'wanker.'"

Chaz laughed. He introduced himself a second time.

"Ah, hi," I stammered back. "I'm Josie. Josie Brunswick."

Chaz face reddened, then, almost instantly, the smile returned.

"Are you Dr. Joseph Brunswick's daughter?"

"That's me."

"Brilliant — your dad's quite the scientist."

"How do you know my father?"

"I follow his research."

I felt myself blush. "Really? Not your typical teen hobby."

Chaz pointed to a small leather sofa. We sat down. He looked at me as if he was trying to read my mind.

"Is your father still with the World Genetics Council?"

"Yes. Right now he's in London at a conference. He's supposed to be delivering an address on curing AIDS."

"Didn't mean to eavesdrop, but you'll have to excuse Chaz, Josie," said Fa8, suddenly hanging over the back of the couch. "His father is Canada's prime minister. You know how those poly-itical typey-types are; they are always asking their ever-so probing questions."

I turned back to Chaz. "So why are you in Vienna?"

"I'm still in school, a senior at the Inter-Global Academic Center. You know, the same school you attend," he said.

I felt the blood rush to my face.

"Oh, sorry, I guess I haven't paid a whole lot of attention to anyone for a while."

Chaz laughed. This time the laugh seemed real. "Perfectly understandable after losing your mom so young. A great loss. Tragic, really."

For a second I felt my stomach in my throat.

"How did you know about my mother?"

"Your mother was famous. She played all over the world. She played in Canada several years ago."

Now I felt stupid.

"Yeah, I remember. I went with her on that trip."

"It's okay. I'm the one who should apologize. I caught you completely off guard."

"You're the second person today who has told me a story about my mom. It's surreal."

Across the room, the music changed — a song by The Beatles.

"I'm sure I would feel the same way," Chaz said. "Your mother was amazing. But, I'd really like to know more about your father."

"Huh?"

Chaz scooted closer to me. His blue eyes seemed to glow.

"He's the top geneticist in the world. But I have reservations about his employer, the WGC. I mean, did you know it's under investigation by authorities in several countries? A rather controversial group, don't you think?"

"I don't know anything about that," I said. "And my dad is very private about his work. I'm afraid I don't know anything about the doings of the WGC."

"Oh come on, Josie. You don't know anything? Seriously? Wouldn't you agree that the WGC, well, that sometimes its scientists have been known to push the boundaries between morals and science?"

"I don't know. I told you . . ."

"Don't you think it's wrong to use stem cells that have been mutated? Isn't that like, well, isn't that like playing God?"

Okay, this was the second time today someone had complained about one of my parents. First I had to deal with the British princess, now it was the Canadian prime minister's son. I was beginning to get ticked on a global scale.

"I don't think you understand," I said. "Not long ago, my dad introduced me to an eleven-year-old boy who had been treated for AIDS with the gene therapy Dad developed. The boy was going to die. But after the treatment, he is perfectly healthy."

"I read about that case," he said. "Did your father tell you the cost of those three months of therapy was more than six hundred thousand dollars? More than half a million dollars for a few months of treatment. Very expensive cure seems to me."

"Actually, the boy and his family didn't have to pay anything. The cost was covered by the WGC."

"Oh, well, that's good, but you have to wonder if they'll do that for everyone who gets the disease."

"That's not fair and you know it." I scooted to the edge of the couch. "The treatment was experimental; eventually as it becomes more accepted or the norm, the cost of treatment should drop."

"This house reminds me of the WGC's offices," Chaz said, looking around. "Rather stuffy, don't you think?"

"I hadn't noticed."

I wanted to leave. I was tired of playing twenty questions about my parents with the Canadian prime minister's knuckleheaded son. I looked around the room. Fa8 was flirting with group of girls by the stereo. I glanced towards the door — a huge crowd of Samurai Wannabes blocked my exit.

"Isn't that music rather annoying?"

The record had changed to an early punk song — a simple guitar, some slightly off-key singing, and a heavy drum line. The music was loud and primitive, the perfect expression of how I felt.

"That's actually a classic punk song from the early 1970s called *Love Comes in Spurts*," I said. "And, for the record, it was written by a gentleman named Richard Hell. This particular version is being performed by the Voidoids."

"Obviously you know your music."

"Got that from my mom," I said. "And, besides, the album they're playing is mine."

"Touché," Chaz said.

I rose to leave. I'd had my fill of Chaz and his why-is-your-father-trying-to-destroy-the-world questions. The music changed again.

"Well, it was nice talking to you — but next time I want a lecture, I'll go to school. Mr. Richards does a great talk on ancient Rome."

Chaz's face reddened. He stood and his face softened.

"Josie, I apologize. I didn't mean to insult your family, but I hope to make a career of public service and issues like advances in genetics interest me. And you getting mad at me doesn't change the fact that the corporation your father works for could be exploiting people."

Now I felt my face grow hot.

"You don't know a thing about my father or anything about his work. You have no idea what he's trying to accomplish. What you are is rude. And the questions you're asking seem more about damaging my father's reputation than gaining any insight into his work. So please excuse me, but right now I don't have the time for that, or you."

AnonInstantMessaging

> **To:** Fa8
>
> **From:** JosieBGirl
>
> **Message:** Dear Mr. Fa8: You suck. Loud. And in stereo. Chaz is a total douche and this rave sucks as much as you do. People have been sick on the floor and I'm going to have to be the one to clean it up. I'm watching you. I'm going to tell the girl standing next to you — the one in pink — that you date sheep and that you wet the bed. Rescue me now and fast or die a horrible death, my bed-wetting sheep-boy.
>
> Josie

AnonInstantMessaging

> **To:** JosieBGirl
>
> **From:** Fa8
>
> **Message:** As you wish. But might I inquire as to when you have observed my nocturnal activities? Yes, luv, that's a joke.
>
> Fa8

Chapter 13

Games People Play

I STOOD BY MYSELF IN THE hall trying to escape the thumping rhythm of the song *Disco Inferno*. It's not that I didn't like the group, The Trammps, but it was Dad's CD and he played it at least once a day when he was home. Why, I'll never understand.

I slipped down the hall to find some quiet. I'd only been there a few minutes when I heard voices near the indoor entrance to my dad's lab. I walked towards the sound.

"I think this is the place," one voice said. "She told me her father has a lab here and works from home."

Another voice answered in a whisper — I couldn't make it out.

"Shhhh," the first voice (I'm pretty sure it belonged to Chaz) said. "Be quiet. I just want to get a glance inside. If you keep making noise she'll hear us."

"With that crap playing down the hall? Sounds like a sick cat."

Obviously some people don't get old Rod Stewart songs. *Gasoline Alley* was one of Rod's better albums and I loved the song that had just come on, *Cut Across Shorty*. I stood still until the song faded, then stepped into a small pool of light.

"Perhaps, next time you should ask before you try and break into someone's private office," I said.

The trio of boys jerked around like they'd been slapped. I didn't recognize two of them — maybe they were Chaz's security detail posing as teens, but I knew who the tall, handsome one in the center was.

Overhead, the music changed again; this time, the speakers throbbed with *I Never Told You What I Do For a Living*.

"Do you sneak into people's rooms often, Chaz? Because I do believe it's still a crime. Not very smart for a young politician in the making."

Chaz stammered a weak apology then pointed at the door.

"In my defense, I merely wanted a look inside. I don't think that's breaking and entering; as you can see, the door is still closed." He motioned at the ceiling. "My Chemical Romance? I prefer something a little less intense myself."

"Don't be a killjoy."

I pushed the other boys out of the way and stood in front of Chaz.

"Well, your lack of taste and skill at burglary obviously makes everything okay. I mean, since you had been invited to go into my dad's lab and all . . ."

Chaz shuffled his feet and hung his head.

"I, well, I didn't mean . . ."

"Yes?" I said.

He flashed me his best fake look of sincerity.

"Ah, Josie, I must apologize for my boorish behavior and for overstepping my welcome. I do hope you will forgive me."

I smiled. Chaz was amazingly good looking, but I suspected he shared the same DNA as the British princess.

"Certainly, but if you're that interested in my father's work, maybe you should talk to him instead of trying to break into his lab."

"I would jump at the opportunity to speak with him. I'm very eager to learn about his work." He moved towards the door. "Is this where your father does his research for the WGC? I've been to the WGC's offices in Vienna and they are far too small. There's no lab there."

I pointed to the door.

"He works in there. And it's off-limits."

Chaz smiled. "Really — couldn't we just take a peek?"

"My father is very private about his research. He never lets anyone in there. And I don't appreciate you trying to push your way in without permission."

Chaz suddenly looked at me like a detective interrogating a crime suspect. "Have you ever been inside?"

"Yes. Many times. After my mom died Dad stayed very busy with his research. He spends most of his time in there. If I want to see him, this is where I go."

"I would love to see inside. I promise I won't touch anything."

"I don't think that's a good idea." I pointed down the hall. "Why don't we go back to the party?"

Chaz stepped closer to me. "Josie, I have to be honest. I like you. You're very pretty and very, very smart. But I have another reason for wanting to meet you. Right now my father's government is considering proposals that would regulate and limit the WGC's work in Canada. Part of the reason for that is that your father and the rest of the WGC administrative team won't talk."

I rolled my eyes; more politics, boring. "So what does that have to do with me or my father's lab?"

Chaz attempted another little smile.

"Well, if I had the chance to take back some first-hand knowledge to my father, then it might make things go easier for your dad. Besides, if he is as serious and dedicated to his research as you say he is, then I might be in a position to help him and you."

I wasn't sure what to think. Part of me wanted to turn, say no, and tell everyone to go home. But the other part really wanted to believe Chaz. I was so tired of being an outsider and misunderstood. It would be nice, for once, to shut people up with some facts.

"I don't know. Like I said, my dad would be mad if he knew people were even in our house, much less his lab."

Chaz whispered: "He doesn't have to know. Does he?"

"Trust me, he'd find out." I pointed to the hall. "Now, let's go."

Slowly, people began to leave. I stood at the front door and tried to shoo them on their way. The wind was so cold it stung. It was beginning to feel like winter. Behind me, I heard the faint sounds of Ultimate Spinach's masterpiece, *Fragmentary March of Green*.

After seeing a particularly irritating gaggle of girls out the door, I felt a tap on my shoulder. It was Chaz again.

"What are you doing?" he asked.

"Trying to get people to go home," I said.

"It was a very impressive rave," Chaz said.

I closed the front door and turned. Chaz followed me down the long hall. In front of the door to the lab, he stopped again.

"I hate to bug you, but I would love to see inside."

"It's locked and I don't have the key," I said. "Besides, I've already told you. My father doesn't let anyone in there."

Chaz touched the door.

"Are you sure?"

I pointed to the keypad. It was the same kind of lock that Dad had on the side door — the small black square.

"It's a type of numeric keypad. My dad showed me once. You have to know the sequence the numbers are in, then you have to know the passcode, and I don't know either."

"Oh, now I understand. Maybe I can help," Chaz reached into his pocket and pulled out his car keys. He fingered the keys until he found a slender metal tube.

"This is a small, high-tech laser. The technology your father is using is normally invisible. But many times the numbers on that type of keypad are visible under a certain type of light. It's based on the chemicals in the keypad."

Chaz moved the laser back and forth over the black square. For a few seconds I couldn't see anything, then he turned a small dial on the light, which made it dim and then dim some more, until, slowly, the keypad began to glow; the numbers seemed to float off the door.

"Thought so," he said. "This particular pad is made in China. Very high-end stuff."

I looked at the black square. Dad had taken all the even numbers out of normal sequence and placed them at the end. Instead of 1,2,3,4,5,6, the keypad read 1,3,5,7,9,2,4,6,8. I thought it would be something much more complicated.

"Okay, so we know the sequence. My problem is I don't know the access code."

Chaz peered at the door. "If you look very closely, you might see faint smudges on some of the numbers."

I leaned over and looked hard at the black square. In the black light the numbers seemed to glow and float. It took a second for my eyes to adjust, but, slowly, I thought I could make out smudges on the numbers nine, seven, one, and two.

"That's the oil in your father's fingers reacting with the chemicals,"

Chaz explained. "It is the one flaw with this type of unit."

I leaned closer to the square. "So what do I do now?"

Chaz snorted. "I suggest you write down the numbers and see if we can figure out your father's code."

I paused. I knew that Dad would be furious. And I didn't want to let Chaz inside; I didn't like his attitude and I didn't trust him. But once, just once, I wanted someone to understand my world.

I put my face close to the keypad. "Okay. Remember this: seven, one, nine, and two."

"That's only four numbers, Josie." Chaz moved the light closer to the keypad. "This is probably a six-digit unit. We'll need two more numbers."

"I can't find them," I said, pulling my sweater tighter. "Let's go. It's cold and I don't like this. It's like I'm telling my Dad a lie or something. I feel like I'm trespassing."

Chaz knelt down beside me. "Please? I just want to see the inside. I promise I'm not trying to hurt you or your father."

I felt myself shiver.

"Okay. Hold the light still; you're moving it too much."

I stared back at the square. Every other number was clean. The only prints were on seven, one, nine, and two.

"Chaz, there's not any more, just those four. Maybe he's cleaned it or it wore off or something." I stopped, took a step back, and shook my head.

"No, it couldn't be that easy. It just couldn't . . ." I said, softly.

Chaz looked at me like I needed therapy.

"Huh? What are you talking about?"

I grabbed his hand. "Hold the light there. Let me try this."

I stood and slowly pushed the number one twice. I pushed one again, then two, then seven twice. Nothing happened for a second. Suddenly, a sharp click and the door slid open.

"How'd you . . . I thought you didn't know the passcode."

"I didn't. But then I recognized those numbers."

"What do you mean?"

"My dad is sentimental. Eleven, twelve, seventy-seven is my mom's birthdate. She was born on November 12, 1977."

Chaz and I stepped into the darkness. The room was pitch black except for a faint purple light at the opposite end from us. That light, I knew, was from the central computer. I pulled Chaz over to me.

"Stand still and don't say anything," I whispered.

Chaz nodded. I stepped to the center of the room and addressed the ceiling. "WGC Alpha, lights on please."

Instantly, the room was filled with a soft, blue glow. From above I heard the electronic version of my mom's voice. "Responding. Good evening Josephine Marie Brunswick. The time is one forty-three a.m. and the outside temperature is negative two degrees Celsius. How may I be of assistance?"

"We're just looking," I said.

"Perimeter scan notes unauthorized visitor. Unauthorized entry is not permitted. Do you have a passcode?"

I looked at Chaz. I wasn't sure what to do. I had no idea that we would need another passcode once we were inside.

Chaz stepped closer and put his lips to my ear. The moist heat from his breath sent shivers down my spine.

"Try the code you used outside," he whispered.

I nodded. "WGC Alpha?"

"Responding. Unauthorized entry is not permitted. A passcode is required. Do you have a passcode?"

"Yes," I said. "Eleven, twelve, one nine seven-seven."

Slowly the lights changed from pale blue to light purple. In the back the light of the central computer grew brighter.

"Responding. Secondary passcode accepted. How may I be of assistance, Miss Brunswick?"

"Show me my father's last data entry. Main computer. Overhead."

"Responding. Central display." Overhead a large flat-screen monitor flashed on. Several images spun onto the screen in what looked like a video presentation. "Some data is encrypted. A separate passcode is required. Do you wish to proceed?"

"No," I said. I looked at Chaz. "Like I said, my father is pretty protective of his work."

Chaz moved towards the center of the lab. He walked to the semicircle of computers and stopped.

"What's this?" He pointed to the large metal tube in the center.

"That's a tissue replicator. According to what my dad told me, it creates the samples of flesh and tissue from DNA sequences."

"Wow. It's huge. That's the largest replicator I've ever seen."

I cocked my head. "Really?"

Chaz nodded. "Yeah. The biggest one in the world has been at CERN in Switzerland, and it's only the size of shoebox. This unit is amazing."

I moved by the large tube. It was as wide as a coffin and about three-feet deep. A thin glowing band wrapped all the way around the sides.

"It's not being used right now," I said. "I was in here the other day and Dad was talking about the replicator to someone on the telephone. He said something about the nitrogen seal being weak and it needing to be fixed."

Chaz looked at me. "Do you know how it works? How your father creates tissue from a DNA sample?"

I pointed to the center of the horseshoe.

"That's easy." I pointed to the large monitor above the coffin-shaped replicator. "See the computer there? And the unit above it?"

"The one that looks like a silver television set?"

"Yeah. The top unit is where the DNA sample is placed. A laser reads the sample, and those banks of computers over there crunch the code, and generate the proper genetic sequence."

"Amazing," he said. "But I don't understand how it actually determines the DNA."

I walked over to the scanning computer and moved my hand in front of the glass doors. The doors opened with a quiet swish.

"You need something that contains a strand of DNA. It could be liquid, like saliva or urine, or a piece of tissue, skin, or something similar. Or it can be hair. This scanner will read them all."

Chaz pointed to glass cylinder. "So the sample goes in there?"

"Yes. You place it inside, then it's scanned by the laser. From that, you get the sample's DNA sequence. It's cool to watch. Last year, I helped Dad scan some tissue samples of a Siberian tiger. It was amazing, but Dad has never let me in the lab when the replicator was on. It requires a sterile environment and you have to wear gowns and gloves when it's running."

"Does it take long to do a scan?"

"No, the initial scan takes only a few seconds. But I think it takes the computer much longer to verify the DNA, encode it, and prepare it for replication."

I looked around the lab. It was sleek and clean, like a hospital operating room.

"I would show you how it works, but I don't see any of Dad's samples; he usually doesn't leave stray biological matter floating around."

"Darn, it would be . . ."

"Wait, I have an idea." I looked down at my sweater and pulled a long, stray hair off my left shoulder. "This will work. It's just a single strand of hair so the scan won't take long."

Chaz smiled. "Well, if you're sure."

"Yeah, give me just a second." I took the hair and placed it in the center of the scanner. The scanner's glass doors closed. Inside the small tube glowed bright red.

"That's a type of radioactive vacuum cleaner," I said. "It's making sure no stray particles are attached to the sample. Once it's clean, the sample can be properly scanned."

Chaz moved next to me. His breathing quickened.

"Astounding," he said. "Absolutely astounding. I know my father would be very interested in this."

I pointed to the scanner. "Now watch. See those numbers?"

Chaz nodded.

"When they reach one hundred, the scanning starts. The laser will move slowly from the bottom to the top of the sample and then back again. Once it's done that five times, the scan is complete."

I looked at Chaz as the laser moved slowly across the strand of hair. The small box pulsated and behind me, faintly, I heard a hard drive whirl, as the information was written to the disc.

In a few moments, the scanner stopped glowing.

"WGC Alpha," the computer said. "Scanning process complete. Sample is filamentous biomaterial, protein-keratin composition."

I smiled at Chaz.

"See I told you. Now watch. WGC Alpha display sample."

The center flat screen glowed again. An image of the hair appeared. Next to it the computer displayed the hair's genetic code as a double helix. The computer answered. "Responding. Visual display present."

I walked to the center of the room.

"WGC Alpha, determine origin of sample."

"Responding. Sample is human biological material. DNA data currently being sequenced. Full genetic outline available at eleven p.m., Greenwich Mean Time. Stand by for replication."

Chaz slipped his arm around my waist.

"Josie, this is mind-boggling. I could stand here and watch this for hours. Do you think your father would let me come back, sometime?"

I pushed his arm away.

"I'd have to ask him," I said. "But we need to get . . ."

"There you two are."

I jerked around, startled by the voice behind me. Fa8 stood just outside the door, a strange look on his face.

"Been lookin' for you two. Josie, luv, almost all of the tribe has left your little rave and now, I see you here, doing the late-night-squeeze with me friend, Chaz."

I blushed. Luckily, in the dim light, no one could see.

"Sorry Fa8. I was just showing Chaz Dad's lab."

Fa8 laughed.

"Right-o. Looks more like a little bit of snogging to me."

He grabbed me by the arm. "Come on you two, time to say nighty-night. Your little Fa8 has just wasted the last hour or so trying to explain to several Samurai the finer points of industrial rock and why one shouldn't deposit the contents of one's stomach on a late eighteenth-century Oriental rug."

Fa8 waved his hands like he was trying to erase the sky.

"Can you believe these kids have never heard of, or for that matter listened to, Chrome or Killing Joke? I do believe they haven't even lent an ear to Shinedown or Edgar Winter or even Bob Marley." Fa8 shook his head sadly. "And some of these blokes are so young they can't even keep a pint down. This makes me deeply concerned for the future of our species."

In the dim light I saw Chaz frown.

"Come on, luv," Fa8 said. "Your Fa8 likes his raves, but he likes sleepin' in on a Saturday, too."

Chaz stepped towards the door, too. "Thanks Josie. That was amazing. Maybe next time, we could hang out or something?"

"You're welcome." I didn't bother to answer his second question. Not now, anyway.

"And I really would like to come back and meet your father. His lab is impressive. Very impressive."

I walked towards the doorway, then stopped.

"Oh, wait. I need to shut things down. But . . ."

"What's wrong?" Chaz said.

"I'm trying to remember what stage the computer was at. If you shut the process down too early, it crashes the mainframe. That would really cheese my dad off."

"I remember. It was something about . . . ending sequence."

I took a deep breath. "Good. I was afraid it still might be crunching data. All I have to do is tell it to finish the sequence and execute shutdown. Give me a second."

Fa8 waved his arms to get my attention.

"Hurry up, luv. It's colder than a well-digger's bloomers out here."

I stepped back inside the lab.

"WCG Alpha execute final command, then terminate operation."

I turned back towards the door as the computer answered:

"Responding. Decision noted. Executing."

I stepped outside and touched the door a second time. Slowly the wall began to close. As it did, I watched the small screen on the coffin-shaped replicator start to pulsate and the lab's blue lights fade to black.

Part III: Rebirth

From an AP News Bulletin
Authorities Uncover Network of Human Organ Smugglers

MONTREAL (AP) — French and Canadian authorities, working with Israeli military police, raided a Montreal medical supply warehouse this week, confiscating millions of dollars in laboratory equipment and what one official described as something out of a horror story.

Investigators refused to comment on what was taken in the raid, but an unnamed source told the Associated Press authorities discovered "canister after canister of human organs."

According to the source, the organs were less than 24 hours old and were being shipped through a global network of black-market traders.

"These groups are smuggling human organs in and out of the country and selling them on an underground black market," said the source. "This raid will be the first of several."

Canadian law enforcement officials confirmed several employees of the warehouse were arrested but refused to identify those taken into custody.

Chapter 14

500 Miles

OKAY, I THOUGHT, THAT MAY well be both my first and last rave. It was well after four in the morning before everyone left. I spent the next hour cleaning up beer stains off various rugs.

Around five, Leisel found me on my knees.

"I *vill* finish that for you Mistress Josie," she said softly.

"It's okay, Leisel. I can do it. I was the idiot who agreed to host this stupid party."

Two hours later I stumbled to bed. Through my window I could see the first pinkish-yellow rays of the sun. I crawled under the covers and nestled deep into the thick, soft mattress.

I'd just dozed off when my phone buzzed. I looked at the screen; it was Dad. His voice was way too chipper.

"Hey, beautiful girl. How are you?"

"Hi, Dad."

"You sound tired."

"I am. Didn't get much sleep."

"Ohhhh." Dad stretched out the "oh" until it was almost painful, like he knew something I didn't want him to know. "Sooo, how's the weekend starting off? Do anything special?"

I sighed. *He's looking for a confession.*

"Oh, not much. Just hung out with friends. Same old routine."

"Try not to get vomit on the rugs next time, okay?"

I sat straight up in bed.

"Ah, ah, I didn't . . ." I could feel the blood draining from my face. "I don't know what you're talking about, Dad."

More laughing. "Josie. I know about your little party. What was it called? Oh yeah, 'The Rave.' Now, don't lie to me. We've been through that before and it never ended well. Remember?"

"Yeah." I leaned forward and put my head between my knees. "Sorry."

"Just be a little more careful next time. Okay? I'm not that mad. Actually I'm glad that you've found some friends to hang out with besides Fa8, but I'm not thrilled about the vomit or what I suspect was beer. You know better than that."

"Yes, sir. But honestly, in my defense, the beer wasn't my idea. It just sort of appeared."

"Ah, so Fa8 brought it?"

My dad was a thousand miles away and thankfully he couldn't see me. I was embarrassed at being caught and mad at Fa8 for getting me in trouble over something I didn't want to do to begin with.

"Yeah, he brought it. Sorry. Won't happen again."

"It's okay, sweetie," Dad's voice was soft, like when he used to talk to me when I was little. "I just don't want you to go back to that dark time. I was afraid I'd lost you then."

"Dad you're never going to lose me again. I love you too much for that. We may not always agree. But I think you're the best dad in the world."

"I love you, too, honey."

Through the phone I could feel him smile.

"So when are you coming home?"

"I'm not sure. I still have several meetings with the head of the British Science Academy, and I have to prepare for another round of hearings in front of the United Nations."

"Doesn't sound like much fun."

"It's not. Believe me."

I started to tell him about meeting Chaz, but something stopped me. If he was having that much trouble with the British I figured he didn't want to know about troubles with Canada.

"Dad?"

"Yes, sweetie?" In the background I could hear him clicking keys on his laptop, and before I could say anything I heard his voice back on the line. "Say Josie, when you get a minute, please stick your head in my lab and see if the mainframe has crashed."

Suddenly, I felt cold. "Ahhh, okay. What's wrong?"

"Well, the Alpha Unit sent me a status alert today, and it's a weird one, from what I can tell."

"What do you mean?"

"It says it's sequencing a huge sample of DNA, but the last sequence I processed was a small strand of a rare avian for a friend in Moscow."

"You think it's an error?"

"I'm not sure," Dad said. "But this isn't the Moscow sequence. In fact, it says it's human."

My chest started thumping. "Are you sure?"

"Well, actually, no, I'm not. Once before that unit crashed and it did the exact same thing. It showed it was sequencing a huge strand of DNA, when it just had a serious software problem. That's why I want you check and see. All you have to do is look at the unit above the tissue replicator. If it has crashed, there should be a flashing yellow message and an error code."

"Okay, I'll check it," I said. "What do I do if it's off-line?"

"Simple," Dad said. "Just type W-G-C-1-A-2-6-Z on the keyboard and hit Enter twice. That should force it to reboot."

"Okay, Dad. I'll go check it as soon as we hang up."

"Thanks, honey. You will have to enter from the outside door. Remember, the one by the bench?"

"Yeah, I remember."

"The sequence on the keypad, I think, is even-odd to zero. The code is one-one-one, two-one-nine-seven-seven." Dad paused. "But do not repeat that to anyone. I'm trusting you, okay?"

"Got it." I paused a few seconds to let him think I was writing the number down. I didn't want him to know I already knew it.

"That number looks familiar."

"It should," Dad said. "It's your mother's birthday."

"Oh, my gosh, it is," I said. "Well, that will make it easier for me to remember. I'll go do it right now, Dad."

Of course, the machine hadn't crashed. I knew that. But I didn't say anything to Dad. Instead I went to the lab — for some reason I felt like I should — and stood in front of the coffin-shaped replicator.

The screen was dark. I turned to the right and addressed the main computer. "WGC Alpha acknowledge."

"Responding. Good morning, Josephine Marie Brunswick. The time is seven forty-seven a.m. and the temperature is twelve degrees Celsius. How may I be of assistance?"

I stood still. Even though I knew I was the last person in Dad's lab, for some weird reason I felt like I should do what he asked me to do.

"Status report," I said.

"Responding. Awaiting command."

"Perform self-test. Determine status of primary mainframe."

"Responding. Testing in process."

I stood quiet and listened. In the dim light I heard the large mainframe's disc drives spin. The noise was faint, almost like a distant purr from an unseen cat.

"Testing complete. All systems normal."

I walked to the door.

"WGC Alpha lights off, please."

Behind me, as I stepped into the sunlight, the room went dark.

Chapter 15

Don't Cry

TWO DAYS LATER, Dad called again. This time it was to tell me he would not be home for three more months.

"I'm sorry, sweetie," he said. "But it's a critical time, and these meetings could mean whether our project goes forward or not. I won't finish at the U.N. until the end of the month, and after that I have to meet with the Vatican's chief science officer."

"You're going to Rome?"

Dad paused for a moment. I had always wanted to go to Rome and he knew it. In fact, he had promised me that the next time he went to Italy I could go. At least, that's what he had said then.

"Well, Vatican City. I'm sorry, Josie. I really am. This just came up. For several years now the Vatican has criticized the WGC, and this is the first time the pope has offered to meet with us. It could be a major breakthrough. I can't afford to not go."

"I understand." But my voice betrayed my disappointment.

"Don't sound so sad. I will take you to Italy, soon, and we'll spend as much time in Rome as you want."

"You've said that before."

"I know I have, but I give you my word this time I won't forget. I just can't afford the time off right now."

"Will you be home for Christmas?"

"You bet, sweetie. I'll be home sooner than you think."

Through the phone I heard Dad sigh. I didn't have the heart to guilt him anymore. But before I could tell him I understood, I heard him catch his breath and then the click, clack of his fingers on his laptop.

"Say Josie, did you ever check the Alpha Unit like I asked?"

"Yes, sir."

"And what did you find?"

"Nothing was wrong. I even asked the computer to perform a self-test, like you told me to do. Everything was fine. I didn't even have to use the reboot sequence."

"Interesting," Dad said. "Very interesting. I may have to call Chris and have him take a look at that drive unit. I cannot afford to have it off-line, and something does *not* look right from here."

"Dad, nothing is wrong. Like I said, I checked."

"Okay, honey. Thank you. Listen, I have to go. They're waiting for me. Will you call me later? I miss you."

"I miss you, too, Dad."

I touched the End button on my phone.

More than you'll ever know.

Chapter 16

Sister Golden Hair

IT HAS BEEN EIGHT WEEKS since my last phone call with Dad. Okay, it's not like I haven't heard from him. I get a text message every morning and, when he can, a few texts throughout the day. But I haven't talked to him in real time in weeks.

And it seems like forever since I last saw him.

I want my father back. Mom's gone and Dad is always away.

I feel like an orphan.

. . . .

At school, Chaz has been all but invisible and Fa8 won't leave me alone. Yesterday in the school computer lab I was trying to get ahead on a report that's due next week, but Fa8 kept trying to convince me to ditch it to go to Sass. The pub is in Wien and Fa8 loves the place, but all I could remember was that the last time I hung out in a pub, some drunken college boy kept putting his hands on my rear.

So just like I told that drunken college boy, I told Fa8 to get lost. I was getting ready to flip him off to emphasize my point — he'd been bugging me a lot, lately — when my phone buzzed. I looked at the display. It wasn't a number I recognized.

"That's weird."

Fa8 cocked his head. "What's wrong, luv?"

I turned the phone towards him. "That's the second time someone has called from this number. No one but you and Dad ever calls me. Now I'm getting calls from numbers I don't recognize."

"So answer it," Fa8 said.

"Why?"

"Might be a bloke wantin' to hire you for your ab-so-lute-lee smashing guitar skills."

I rolled my eyes. "Yeah right. Or it could be one of those perverts you hang out with. The ones who have my number because of you."

Fa8 blushed and stepped away from me. We'd been through this before, and I was pretty sure he didn't want an encore.

"Well, about that, luv. Those blokes are truly harmless and . . ."

My phone buzzed again.

Fa8 scowled. "Perhaps these chaps, whoever they are, left you a little mess-age." He pointed at the screen. "You know that modern invention thingy we call, ye ole voice mail?"

I glanced at the small screen. "Nope. No message."

Another buzz. I started to put the phone back in my pocket, but before I could Fa8 grabbed it and, with a laugh, tapped Talk.

" 'Eh-low? 'Eh-low? This is Miss Josephine Brunswick's British lackey. And whom, might I ask, is interrupting our little confab?"

I tried to grab the phone back, but Fa8 sidestepped me.

"I'm sorry, luv, but I'm having' a bit o' trouble 'earin' your voice. Must be some type of celestial interference. Mars is in the seventh house, you know. Would you kindly re-peat your last statement?"

I reached for the phone again. Fa8 pushed me away and kept the phone tight to his ear. Suddenly he went quiet. Then he turned pale.

"Ahhh, Josie, luv, I do believe you might want to take this call."

Fa8 handed me the phone. I looked at the screen as if the number would make sense if I just stared long enough at it.

"Is it my dad?"

Fa8 shook his head and whispered. "No, luv, I believe it's that woman from the Haus der Musik. *Frau Direktor.*"

I smiled. "Oh, you mean Theresa?"

"That would be her, but I'm afraid I'm not a hundred percent certain as to her sense of humor in such telephone matters as these."

With that, Fa8 gave me a weak smile and handed me the phone.

I didn't hesitate; it wasn't me who had been caught in the act of being a moron.

"Hello, Josie speaking."

"Josie? Josephine Brunswick? This is Theresa. Theresa Malfatti."

"Oh hi, Theresa. Sorry about my friend . . . too much caffeine."

Theresa chuckled. "Well, that explains a lot. I was beginning to think I had the wrong number. I've tried calling you several times."

"I'm so sorry *Frau Direktor*. I didn't recognize your number."

"It's okay," Theresa said. "And what did I say about calling me Theresa? Please, I consider us friends. It was my fault anyway; I should have left a message, but things have been so hectic here I haven't had much time to do anything but deal with the next crisis."

"That's okay," I said, "but why have you been calling me?"

"Forgive me," Theresa said. "I'm calling about our Beethoven retrospective. It opens in a week, and I wanted to know if you would still like to come as my guest on opening night?"

I felt myself smile. "I'd love to. I'd forgotten all about that."

"I meant to call you earlier," Theresa said, "but again we have been so busy. We had several staff issues at the last minute, which made things more difficult with the deadline we face."

The idea flashed though my head so quickly I spoke before my natural shyness could stop me.

"Could I be of help? I'm not busy right now, and my dad's out of town again, and, well, if you needed some extra help I'm available."

Fa8 tugged on my arm. I pushed him away.

"Are you serious?" Theresa asked.

"Oh, yes. I'd love to volunteer. I was so impressed with what you're planning for the exhibition. And, well, my mom was to have been a part of everything. It would be nice, I think, to be a part of things."

"I think that would be wonderful. Could you come tomorrow? After school?"

"Sure, I can catch a ride after my last class."

"Outstanding," Theresa said. "Oh, Josie, you have solved several of my problems in one call. *Danke*."

"No, thank *you*. I have been so bored. It will be great to have something new to focus on besides school and my guitar. I'll see you tomorrow then."

I touched the End button and glared at Fa8.

"You make it difficult to have a regular conversation."

Fa8 shrugged his shoulders.

"I'm not that bad, truly I'm not. Remember those handsy-handsy boys just want you for your body. I, however, prefer your smashing guitar skills and your effervescent personality."

He pointed at my phone.

"Now, what was all that about? Sounds like you've landed yourself a little jobbie-job. Have we decided to join the gainfully employed and contribute to the global e-con-o-me?"

"I'm just going to help out with the Beethoven retrospective."

"Can't resist hanging out with old Ludwig, eh?"

I couldn't help but laugh.

"What can I say. He was a good friend of my mom's."

From an AP News Bulletin
World Genetics Council Under Investigation

MONTREAL (AP) — Canadian authorities today launched an investiga-tion into the operations of the World Genetics Council, a source close to the government confirmed this week.

The investigation was triggered by a recent anonymous tip that a WGC-owned warehouse in Montreal was being used by a multi-national organ smuggling network.

The tip led to a raid on the warehouse, with more arrests to come, according to the source.

A spokesman for the WGC could not be reached for comment.

Chapter 17

Für Elise

AFTER SCHOOL, I CAUGHT UP with Fa8 in the parking lot. He didn't know it yet, but he was my ride to the Haus der Musik. I slipped onto the back of his motorcycle.

"I need to get to the Haus der Musik quickly, but safely. Think you can handle that?"

Fa8 rolled his eyes.

"You do realize I was supposed to instruct a certain young woman this afternoon in, err, a rather private music lesson?"

"She will have to wait," I said, thumping the top of his helmet. "Remember I know your real name, and I've seen you in your skivvies."

Fa8 shrugged and twisted the key in the ignition. The motorcycle rumbled to life.

"All right luv, you win. The Haus der Musik it is. I suppose you'll need a ride home, too?"

"I'm not sure. I'll call and let you know."

"Ab-so-lute-ly wonderful. I have nothing better to do than be on stan-dy-by, until I hear from you. It's what I live for, dear Josie; oh, you do make my life diff-o-cult. You do know that?"

I smiled wickedly. "Yes, yes I do."

Twenty minutes later I stood in the main gallery of the Haus der Musik. The place had been transformed since our field trip. The whole building had gone nineteenth century — authentic nineteenth century. Several gilded fortepianos graced the hall and a massive portrait of

Beethoven in his prime covered most of the gallery's north wall.

"Do you like it?" Theresa asked, turning in a circle to take it all in. "We just finished decorating this final gallery."

"Wow, it's like we've stepped back in time. I didn't realize the retrospective would include the entire museum."

Theresa nodded. "*Herr* Beethoven had an extensive career over such a long period of time — not to mention how his music has endured and influenced others. I felt we couldn't cover it with a couple of paintings and a fortepiano or two."

"Well, I think even Beethoven would be impressed." I walked over to a large window at the south end of the gallery. "Is this the fortepiano I saw last time?"

"Yes," Theresa said. "We're having a reception on Saturday. Eric Smack is going to play."

I spun around. "Did you say Eric Smack? Lead guitarist of the Fallen Angels. That Eric Smack?"

"Yes. In addition to his rock career, he happens to be a piano virtuoso. Few people realize Eric is classically trained. On Saturday, he'll be playing Beethoven's *Piano Sonata in D major, Opus 28.*"

"The Pastoral?" I wrapped my arms around myself and twirled in a circle. "I love that piece. It was one of my mom's favorites."

"I thought you'd approve." Theresa laughed. "And, this Saturday you'll get to meet him. Eric's a dear old friend. You'll love him. And you'll also get to hear this fortepiano played publicly for the first time in two centuries."

"I can't wait," I said, and I realized I meant those words more than anything I had said in a long time.

For the next two days, Theresa and I were kept busy. It was as if she had a billion tasks to check off her to-do list and I was the only one who could help her get them done. By Friday, I was exhausted. I'd skipped school and spent all morning helping the new staff finish up the last details for Saturday's reception.

Late that afternoon I realized I had a problem, a big problem.

I had just finished explaining chord progressions to one of the volunteers when a thought flashed through my brain: The reception was less than twenty-four hours away and I didn't have a thing to wear.

Instantly, I felt fear. This fear wasn't about how I would or would not fare at the event itself. And it wasn't sadness masquerading as fear because my mom couldn't be there. No, this was fear on a much more basic level; this was sheer panic over having to go tomorrow to a huge, formal reception without a thing to wear. Literally.

I didn't own a dress.

Not a single one.

And I had nothing that could stand in. I had no jacket with ruffles or lace, or even a long skirt. All I owned was a collection of T-shirts, jeans, sweat pants, and tons and tons of sweatshirts.

No dress. Nada. Not a one.

I had no business attending a black-tie reception. I had to tell Theresa. I rushed to her office and banged on the door.

"Theresa. I have to talk to you!"

Theresa flung open the door, panic on her face.

"What's wrong Josie? What's happened?"

I gulped for air. "I have a huge problem. And I'm so sorry to let you down. But . . ."

Theresa's eyes grew large. "What is it? You look as if you have seen a ghost. Are you okay?"

"Oh, I'm fine. Well, not fine, but, well, it's that I just realized the reception is tomorrow night."

"Yes, dear. That's right. That's why we've all been working so hard this past week. Remember?"

"Yes, and I'm supposed to be there tomorrow night, right?"

"Of course you are. But Josie, you're shaking. What's wrong?"

"You said it's a formal reception. All black-tie and everything."

Theresa smiled, wanly. I could tell she was beginning to think I'd gone insane. "Yes, that's pretty normal for a VIP event. You know, Vienna's very important people."

I gulped and looked at my feet. "Well, I hate to tell you at this late date, but I will not be able to attend."

Theresa looked shocked.

"After all your hard work and given what this night would have meant to your mother. Josie, I don't understand. What's going on?"

I wrung my hands, too embarrassed to say.

But Theresa stood there looking expectantly at me.

I had to come clean.

"I don't have anything to wear."

Theresa laughed, and her relief was palpable. "Oh, Josie. It will be fine. Any nice dress suitable for church will work."

I had twisted my body into a knot.

"No, you don't understand, *Frau Direktor*. I . . . don't . . . own . . . a dress. Not one. I never wear them. I wear shorts and sweats. Stuff like this." I pointed to my jeans. "This is what I wear all the time. I don't have a dress and I don't have a pair of heels."

Theresa shook her head, then clucked her tongue. "Hmmm. You don't have anything? Nothing at all?"

"The cupboard is bare."

She looked at me closely for a moment, then nodded with conviction. "Well you might not have a dress to your name, but I do. We look about the same size. Only you are a little smaller in the bust. But I have hundreds of dresses." She patted my arm. "Trust me. We'll find something for you."

Relief washed over me. For a moment, all felt right with the world, just like when my mom was alive. Theresa knew what to do. This was one girl problem I wouldn't have to figure out all on my own.

"Thank you, Theresa. I didn't want to miss tomorrow night, but I didn't want to look like a moron either. These people all knew my mom. I didn't want to embarrass you or her."

Theresa gave me a big hug. As she took a step back, I could see tears in her eyes.

"Josie, I am absolutely sure that you could never embarrass your mother and you certainly could never embarrass me. I think you are one amazing young woman. Consider the problem solved. After work tonight, we'll go to my flat and we'll find you something to wear. You can borrow anything you need: heels, hose, makeup. Okay?"

I wiped my eyes on my sleeve. "You sure it won't be too much of an imposition?"

"An imposition? Are you kidding? This is like getting to dress my own little girl for the ball. By the time I'm finished with you they will think you're a countess. I promise."

I sat down on a small bench — relieved but worried. *I'm about as far from a countess as they come. Oh, if Fa8 could see this.*

We worked frantically for a few more hours then called it a night. I had already rung Fa8 and told him Theresa would be taking me home. He knew from the tone of my voice not to ask any questions. I was smiling as I slipped into Theresa's car — European and expensive — and we took off.

Through the windows the streets of Vienna faded in and out like scenes from an old movie.

. . . .

Theresa lived on the top floor of a luxurious apartment in the First District. It's where all the big software developers and foreign millionaires buy homes and buildings to show how rich and important they are. And yeah, even though I live in a huge villa, her exquisitely furnished apartment made me feel poor.

"Make yourself at home," she said as we walked through the door. Theresa pointed to a small room to the left of the living room, then walked down a long hallway and disappeared. "That's the kitchen. There's water and soda in the fridge."

I was nervous. Not only was I in a stranger's house without my parents, but I was about to borrow clothes from said stranger because none of mine were suitable. I know it wasn't as bad as it sounded, but it sounded pretty bad and it made me feel cheap.

"Are you sure you don't mind loaning me a dress?"

It bothered me how weak my voice sounded.

Theresa didn't appear to notice. "Josie, it's my pleasure. Now, give me a few minutes and I believe I can come up with something."

I found a place on the sofa and ran my hands through my hair. For the first time in my life I was embarrassed to be wearing tennis shoes.

"Here, try this."

I whirled around. Theresa stood behind me with several dresses over one arm. With her other hand she raised a short yellow dress.

"This might look great on you. Try it."

I took the dress and held it up against me.

"It's really short."

"Yes, I get lots of attention in it, which is why I don't wear it all that often. But you have the legs for it. I bet you would look stunning in it." She pointed to a bedroom across from the living room. "You can change in there, Josie. And don't forget these pumps."

I took the dress and heels and headed for the bedroom. It took several minutes to negotiate the change. When I was done, I took a long look at myself in the mirror.

"I look a lot like a lemon in a short skirt," I said. "Theresa, are you sure about this one?"

"Come out and show me."

I opened the door and walked into the living room.

"Well, what do you think?"

Theresa looked at me critically for several moments as if studying a painting. It felt unnatural being on display.

"I'm not sure," she said. "You definitely could carry off the length, but you may be right about all the yellow. Let's make that one a possibility but keep looking."

An hour later we were still looking.

"I thought this would be easier," Theresa said. "It's not that you don't look great in a lot of these; it's just that none of them seem to fit your personality. They're not . . . they're just not you."

I looked at the pile of frothy dresses on the floor.

"I think we've gone through your entire closet."

Theresa smiled and shook her head.

"Nope. I have other closets, several other closets. Trust me. We just have to keep looking — to the persistent goes the spoils."

She turned and walked back down the hall. From the den I could hear the sound of hangers scraping against metal as Theresa continued her search.

I had given up. I'd gone from no dress to wear to a pile of discarded dresses — and I knew the old saying that beggers can't be choosers. Maybe we couldn't find the perfect dress, but I had no doubt I would have a dress for the gala. That had been settled, at least in my mind. Now Theresa's couch — deep and soft and very comfortable — called to me. I closed my eyes for only a second, when I heard her shout.

"Oh, Josie. Come quickly."

"Huh? What's wrong?"

"I think I have found the perfect dress for you."

I followed her voice down the hall and to the left. It must have been a spare bedroom, because the furniture was simple and several dress boxes were piled in one corner.

"Take a look at this."

At first I wasn't sure what she'd found. Then I saw it. It was soft and frilly in a shade of blue only seen in mountain rivers. I'd never seen anything so beautiful in my life.

"You must try this one," Theresa said. "This is it. I know it."

"It's so beautiful," I said.

Theresa pushed the dress into my hands. "Go! Change! I can't wait to see how you look."

The dress was short but not too short. The rest of it was all lacy and gauzy and, if I do say so myself, stunning.

"But Theresa, this dress hasn't ever been worn. It still has the tags."

"You're right. I bought it last year; it's been hanging in my closet."

"I have a Grateful Dead T-shirt like that," I said.

"Then you know," Theresa said with a grin. "Okay, now, let's see how you look in it — try it on."

I rubbed my thumb across the price tag. I gasped when I saw the price had four zeroes.

"Uh Theresa, it seems awfully expensive. Are you sure you want me to try this one on? I'm warning you, I'm pretty much a klutz. What if I spill cocktail sauce on it or worse?"

"Don't be silly. It's just a dress. It's a little small for me anyway."

Theresa's definition of "just a dress" didn't match mine, but who was I to argue with my fairy godmother. I slipped out of my jeans and T-shirt and pulled the blue concoction over my head. Theresa zipped up the back then pulled me towards the floor-length mirror.

"This is definitely the one," she said.

I stood quietly and looked in the mirror. I wasn't sure what to say. I couldn't argue that the dress was beautiful, because it so was. It was shiny and soft and reminded me of clear water. Everything about it screamed feminine. And it fit well. But I wasn't so sure how I felt about the girl wearing it. I'd always hoped I would have a moment like this with my mom. Standing here with someone else picking out my first formal made the fact that I didn't even own one dress all the more painful.

Theresa smoothed a wrinkle on the skirt.

"Look," she said, smiling, "the color almost matches your eyes."

Theresa stood there so pleased and proud at having found the perfect choice. I couldn't bust her bubble with my ghosts. *Take the gracious route*, I told myself. *She's done you a huge favor and she hardly knows you. And it does make you look like someone else . . . that has to be a good thing.*

"If it's okay, I think I'd like to wear this one," I said. "But only if it's okay with you."

"Oh yes. In fact, I insist on it. You will be the prettiest woman at the party."

I was saying, Thanks, when my phone buzzed. It was Fa8. I tapped the Talk button.

"Don't you have something better to do at this time of night?"

" 'Ello, luv. Have you been missing your Fa8?"

"Not really."

"Oh, Josie, you are impossible. I spend all me time worrying about you and those blokes you hang with and you kick Fa8ie-boy to the curb when he's already down."

I rolled my eyes. Most of the time Fa8 was great — except when he whined. And lately he whined a lot.

"I take it tonight's 'private lesson' fell through?"

Long pause. "Something like that, luv. So I thought I'd live all vicariously-like through you. Which is why I am now ringing your digital telly at this very moment."

"I can't talk. I'm trying on dresses."

"No, luv, seriously. What are you doing?"

"I told you. Trying on dresses."

Another long pause. "You're not serious."

"Totally. I'm going to a black-tie reception tomorrow night and I needed a dress. Theresa said I could borrow one of hers. So I'm trying some on."

The laughter came so hard and so loud, it hurt my ears.

"Josie, Josie, Josie, you are always good for a surprise. Might I get the chance to see you in this new at-tire? Send us a photo. Pretty please."

"No. Why should I? All you'll do is laugh at me."

The phone went quiet. "Ahhh, sorry. It's just that the idea of you and a dress in the same room is so unlike you. You've caught Fa8 off his guardy-guard. I shall cease all unnecessary jocularity immediately. Allow me to ask again in a more subdued tone, might I get the chance to see you in your new ac-cout-tre-ments? I'm thinking just one little photograph . . ."

"Maybe."

"When would this maybe be?" Fa8 asked.

"Tomorrow. Before I leave for the reception. Now I have to go. You're interrupting me and I'm very busy."

Fa8 laughed again. This time it didn't sound mean.

"Alrighty luv, we shall play by your rules. Give us a ringy-ring when you get done exploring your feminine side."

"Good-bye, Fa8."

I touched the End button.

Maybe Fa8 was right. Maybe it was laughable to think that I would look pretty in a dress. No matter, I held my phone up to the mirror and took a picture.

Chapter 18

Piano Concerto No. 5 in E-Flat

ERIC SMACK HAD the longest, most beautiful hair I had ever seen on a man. It was raven black and reached all the way down his back, like a river of dark velvet against the bright gold of his jacket.

I leaned over to Theresa and whispered in her ear.

"He's so beautiful. I could watch him play forever."

Theresa smiled and squeezed my hand. "I don't think you are listening to his music. You are reacting to something and it has nothing to do with music or Beethoven."

I felt myself blush. "Well, maybe."

"I'm pretty sure Eric has that effect on lots of women."

I wanted to stay put and watch him warm up, but Theresa pulled me towards the center of the gallery, where she pointed out a tall, muscular man with brown hair and green eyes.

"That's Telluride Matheson, a correspondent for the London Times. Do you know him? I believe he knows your father."

"He and my dad are pretty good friends. He's originally from Tulsa. Some of the state newspapers carry his articles. Dad calls him 'Tel.'"

"So you know him well, then?"

I cocked my head. "I was introduced to him once, but I wouldn't say I know him all that well. He's friends with my dad."

"I see," Theresa said, as someone across the room caught her eye. "Could you excuse me for a moment, Josie. There's someone I need to speak with . . ."

"Sure," I said, as Theresa gave a little wave and headed towards a tall woman in an expensive beaded gown.

Left to my own devices, I turned to a table filled with hors d'oeuvres, filled a small plate, and tried not to spill anything on my dress. I'd just taken a tiny crab cake when I heard a voice behind me.

"Excuse me, please." A burly man in a black-velvet evening coat reached for a tray of shrimp. "I was seeking more shrimp."

I stepped out of his way and watched as he piled several shrimp on a small plate, then licked his fingers.

"But I have lost my manners. I am Hans, Hans Gottlieb."

I shook his hand (yes, the shrimp hand, but at that moment I didn't have much of a choice).

"Hello, I'm Josie."

"Enchanting." He didn't say anything else for awhile, but instead, looked me over like he was inspecting a package. It made me feel, well, it made me feel dirty. I think he was trying to look through my dress.

"Yes, enchanting," he said, with a mouth full of shrimp.

I faked a smile and scanned the crowd for Theresa. For some reason I felt frightened. I didn't want to be alone with this man.

"Ahhh, there you are." Theresa touched me on the shoulder. "I see you have met *Herr* Gottlieb."

"Ah, yes," I said. "We were just talking."

Hans extended another chubby hand. "How are you Theresa? You remain beautiful, as always."

Theresa smiled and shook his hand. She then placed herself between us, as if she were a lioness guarding a cub.

"So, *Herr* Gottlieb, what do you think of our little party?"

Hans gave Theresa a watery smile.

"Wonderful," he said, as he turned towards me. "Especially the beautiful guests."

I felt a chubby paw on my arm.

"Tell me, Theresa, where did you find this charming young woman?"

Theresa stepped back, knocking Hans' arm away and blocking him from me for a second time.

"She is helping me at the museum."

Hans turned back to me. I could tell he was trying to figure out exactly who I was, and the fact that he could not quite place me was bothering him somewhat, though he tried not to show it.

"Absolutely, charming."

I watched him chew the last of his shrimp and lick his fingers once more. Theresa smiled as if she'd seen him do this a million times.

"Are you in town long?" she asked.

"No, I leave tomorrow for New York. Yet another meeting." He looked at his watch. "In fact, if you'll excuse me, I must bid you a reluctant *adieu*."

Theresa smiled and, gracefully, extended her hand.

"It was wonderful to see you again," she said.

Hans nodded. He kissed the top of Theresa's hand, then straightened his tie and nodded slightly.

"Well, I must be going. It was a pleasure to meet you, Josie. I do hope I will have the honor of seeing you again soon."

I gave him my best, fake smile. "Oh, me, too."

Theresa tried to hide a smile as we watched Hans walk away.

"He's creepy," I said, after he disappeared into a sea of people.

"Hans?"

"Yes. It was like he was trying to look through my dress or something. I felt like a trapped deer."

Theresa stood quietly for a second, then whispered: "Never, ever be caught alone with him. He has a thing for young girls and he has a violent temper."

Suddenly I wasn't sure if I ever wanted to attend another reception. Theresa stayed near me the rest of the evening, circling the room looking for people she wanted me to meet. I felt a little like a trophy, but, at the same time, I thought it was sweet she would go to so much effort to help me mingle. I must have met or talked to about twenty or thirty different people, though I'd be hard-pressed to give you even one name. Theresa could tell I was pretty well wiped out, but she begged me to stay a little longer.

"You must say hello to Countess Fiona," she said. "She would never forgive me if I didn't give you two a chance to chat."

I couldn't imagine why a countess would want to talk with me, but who was I to argue with Theresa. Thirty minutes later, we had just found our way back to the main gallery from Eric's performance of the *Pastoral*, when Theresa spied an elderly woman in a long dress and strands of pearls. Even from across the room, I could tell this was no ordinary woman. She held herself like a head of state, a former queen, or some fabulously wealthy widow.

"Come with me," Theresa said.

She took me by the hand, and we headed for the woman. I found out quickly enough that she was no queen, but she was a widow, and she was fabulously wealthy. She was about my height, with ash blonde hair, and deep bluish-gray eyes. I figured she was in her late sixties. Theresa told me later she was eighty-four.

"Josephine, I'd like to introduce you to the Countess Fiona von Waldstein," Theresa said. "The Countess Waldstein is a great champion of the arts and one of the Haus der Musik's main benefactors."

Since I didn't know exactly what one was supposed to say when speaking to a countess, I simply tried to do what my mom would have done in such a situation. I nodded politely, shook the countess's hand, and said how pleased I was to meet her.

"Countess, Josephine comes from quite a musical heritage herself," Theresa said, with a twinkle in her eye. "She is the daughter of Anna Heigle-Brunswick."

At the mention of my mom's name, Countess Waldstein blanched. Then a huge smile spread over her face, causing her eyes to crinkle and her dimples to show.

"This is little Josie?"

Little Josie? I wasn't sure how to respond to the endearment.

"Ah, yes ma'am," I said. "I'm Josephine."

"Oh, child. Forgive me. Your mother and I were old, old friends. And the last time I saw you . . ." she held her hand down near my knees. "You were only about that big."

"I didn't know you knew my mom."

The countess nodded. "Knew her? Josephine, your mother was one of my treasured artists. I remember her as a child, when she played the church organ and your grandfather accompanied her on violin."

I stepped closer to her. "You knew my grandfather, too?"

"*Ja*," she said. "Your mother was just a tiny baby the first time I saw her. She was so beautiful. So, so beautiful."

A lump caught in my throat. Mom never talked much about her childhood and my grandfather died before I was old enough to know much about him. Hearing someone else, someone so important, praise my family was overwhelming. I wanted to thank her or ask about her memories of these two people I so loved and missed, but the words wouldn't come.

"Th-hanks," I stammered.

Countess Waldstein touched my hand and dabbed at her eyes with a cocktail napkin. "I am sorry for your loss, Little Josie. I cried all day at the news of your mother's passing. Please, forgive me. I do not mean to cause you pain. But you look so much like her. Even more beautiful, I believe. Don't you think so Theresa."

Theresa smiled and nodded.

I shook my head. "Oh no, I'm not pretty like my mom."

The countess waved my words off. "Do not say that. Why, you're stunning. Now, please tell me that you are a musician, too. What instrument do you play?"

"Piano and a little violin. But I stopped piano after mom died."

She looked as if someone had slapped her. "But why? Why would you do such a thing?"

"It was just too painful to keep playing her Steinway. It was like I was taking something from her."

Countess Waldstein nodded and dabbed her eyes again.

"I understand," she said. "Grief doesn't recognize time."

Theresa nodded at me. "Josie has taken a different musical path," she said. "She is an outstanding musical scholar."

The countess looked at me, her face a question mark.

"So you study music?"

"Sort of," I said. "You could say I've grown up with it."

The countess scowled and shook a long, withered finger at me. "Young woman, you are trying very hard to be coy. That won't do. I am an old woman and I don't have time for such nonsense."

"I'm so sorry. I didn't mean to be disrespectful."

The countess smiled. "Child, you are wonderful. Sometimes I can be rather abrupt — I'm afraid it comes from too many years of people jumping when you call." She took my hands in hers. "But enough of this, I can tell a guitar player when I see one."

She turned my hands over. "It's in the fingertips. Calloused. Short nails. And from the looks of it, you've been playing for quite a while."

Theresa seemed confused, but I just smiled. This countess was nobody's fool. "Several years now," I said. "Guitar was a much better fit for me than the piano."

"I see. Please tell me you favor more than one musical style."

I scratched my head. "I'm not sure I follow you."

Countess Waldstein laughed. "I'm assuming you play rock 'n' roll, but I am hoping that you also play something more, something with depth. And not just this electronic, computer-generated noise that is foisted on the public today."

"I like all kinds of music. Muddy Waters, Hendrix, old Johnny Cash, and tons of others."

"Excellent," the countess said. "As do I. Have you mastered Mr. Chuck Berry's duckwalk?"

This time I was the one who laughed. "The duckwalk? I've tried that — once. I'm not very good, though."

"Well," she said, "you will have to let me teach you. I have been known to duckwalk with the best of them."

I couldn't help but giggle at the idea of this elegant woman walking backwards playing an electric guitar. And my giggles proved contagious, because in a matter of seconds, all three of us were laughing.

"I don't see what's so funny." The countess tossed her hair. "I am, in truth, an excellent duckwalker, but I can see I shall have to prove it to you." She looked at me as if she was angry, then slowly, a huge smile spread across her face. "Oh, Josephine, you are a gem. You do me good. We must see each other again."

"Thank you, Countess Waldstein. I'm glad I got to meet you, too. It makes me feel, well, it makes me feel closer to my mom."

With that, the countess pulled me into her arms. "If you ever decide to turn professional, let me know. I have backed some of the finest rock 'n' roll bands in the world, including Mr. Berry's."

She pointed to the now-vacant fortepiano. "And the Fallen Angels. My musical tastes run deep and broad. You might say I am everywhere."

I pointed up at the portrait of Beethoven. "Even to Beethoven?"

Countess Waldstein smiled and nodded. "Oh, my yes. Beethoven is like an old lover. We visit frequently. He takes me places only the two of us know about."

"I think my mom had similar feelings about him," I said.

The countess gave me a wry smile.

"Josephine, Beethoven is unique. But he was at his best when he was played by your mother. She knew Beethoven better than he knew himself."

This time I couldn't stop the tears.

Tissues were shared and backs were patted, and then the countess and Theresa and I talked for a few more minutes before the crowd began to thin, and it was time for her to go. We waved good-bye, and Theresa pointed to the almost-empty gallery.

"I think this is it. I need to give the staff some last-minute instructions, and we'll be off, too."

"I don't mind waiting, but do you need me to do anything?"

Theresa shook her head. "No, Josie, you've already done plenty tonight. I haven't seen Countess Waldstein so happy in a long time."

I started for the door but stopped — Hans was across the room, talking to a tall, yellow-haired man. This time he didn't look quite as happy as he had during our first encounter.

"I thought he had left," Theresa said.

"Doesn't look like it."

I stepped behind her. For some reason I felt better with her blocking me from view.

"We'll have to a wait a moment before we leave."

I looked around. Occasionally, Hans would point in Theresa's direction, then return to his conversation with the tall fellow.

"I wonder who he's speaking with," she said.

Something about the man was familiar to me. I closed my eyes. I knew I'd seen that yellow blonde hair before, several years ago.

An image flashed through my head.

"I know," I whispered. "That's the guy who helped Dad install all the computer equipment in his lab right after we moved here. He works for the WGC."

"Interesting," Theresa said.

"I knew I'd seen him somewhere. It was right after we moved into Villa Theresa. He came with a group of men after Dad's computers were delivered. They spent a long time installing everything."

"Do you know his name? He doesn't look all that friendly — in fact, he looks more than a little out of place."

"No," I said. "He never spoke to me, just Dad. I wonder why he's here and talking to Hans? And why does he keep pointing over here?"

I felt Theresa grow tense.

"I think I can answer both of your questions," she said. "First, they keep pointing over here because of you. And second, he's talking to Hans, because Hans is Hans Gottlieb, the billionaire who founded the WGC."

Suddenly, I was so cold.

"Oh, no, you mean, my dad works for . . . him?"

Theresa nodded slightly. "Yes, I'm sorry to say Hans is the man who founded the organization your father now works for, and this other man, well, I'm afraid he probably knows a lot more than you would want him to about your family and your father's research."

Both men spoke for a few minutes more, then we watched the tall man leave. Hans turned, looked at Theresa for a long moment, then with a little dismissive nod, he, too, left.

"Oh, Hans, what are you up to?" Theresa said quietly.

. . . .

I waited at the front entrance of the Haus der Musik while Theresa went to get her car. Even though I could see her from the sidewalk, I felt vulnerable standing outside at night, alone. The air was damp and cold. Around me slender, ancient street lamps spilled pools of light onto the pavement.

I was just about to run after her when I felt a hand on my shoulder. "Josephine?"

I turned. Countess Waldstein stepped from the shadows into the circle of light. She was wrapped in a fur coat and turban.

I jumped. "Oh, I didn't realize you were there."

"Child, I apologize for frightening you. Forgive me."

I took a deep breath of relief. The countess didn't scare me; it was those two men from the WGC that had me rattled.

"Are you waiting for a taxi? Do you need a ride?" I pointed across the street. "I'm sure Theresa would be happy to give you a lift."

"Oh, no. Terrance will be here shortly for me." The countess reached inside her coat and removed a sparkling handbag. "I didn't mean to startle you. I only noticed you standing all alone and I wanted to tell you again how delightful it was to meet you tonight. And I wanted to give you this."

The countess opened her handbag, pulled out a slender wallet, removed a small square photograph, and handed it to me. The picture was old and faded, but I knew instantly that the blonde woman seated at the grand piano was my mother.

"That's my mom."

"Yes, child, it is."

"But how do you come to have this? My mother refused to let anyone, even my dad, take her photo. Hundreds of photographers tried and she always told them 'no.' "

"Your mother was not one who could be easily photographed, and not only because she disliked the camera so much."

I held the photograph up to the light of the street lamp.

"Where did you get it? And why do you carry it with you?"

"Well, first questions first. I have it, actually, because of a small white lie," the countess said. "I loved your mother dearly. And we were great friends, but she would no more let me take her picture than she would the many photographers I hired to do so. Until this one."

"I don't understand."

The countess drew closer as if about to share a secret.

"I told her that day that I didn't want to take a photo of her but rather of her lovely daughter."

I looked at the image again.

"But I'm not in this picture; it's just Mom at her Steinway."

The countess pointed to the photograph again and whispered: "Keep looking. You are there. Don't you see? Under the bench."

I turned the picture into the lamplight and gasped. She was right. There, under the piano bench in the shadows was a child, curled into a ball, fast asleep.

"Is that really me?"

The countess smiled. "Yes, my dear, that's you. You were only about four years old and you refused to let your mother practice without you. Even if it mean napping under her bench."

Tears rimmed my eyes. "Thank you, Countess Waldstein. Until tonight, most of my memories have been vague ones of being little and watching her play, and those memories fade a little more with each passing year."

"Yes, well, I've held onto that photo for far too long. I always meant to send it to your father, but I had forgotten where I last put it — until tonight. I happened to bring this purse and it was inside. I found it a little while ago, after meeting you. It was like it was meant to be discovered tonight, like it had somewhere else to be. And now I have answered your second question."

I wanted to say something else or at least thank her, but once again words failed. So much had happened to me over the past few days, that I felt like all I'd done was cry. Fa8 would not recognize this Josephine and not just because I was wearing a dress and heels.

I slipped the photo in my coat pocket as a long, gray Rolls Royce pulled up in front of us.

"Why do I suspect this is your ride?"

The countess gave a throaty chuckle.

"Yes, my dear. That would be Terrance, with my car. I don't take the Rolls often, but when I do, he likes to make a show of it."

The countess stood regally, while her chauffeur exited the car, walked around to the side, and opened the back door.

"Madam," he said, stiffly.

The countess turned to me, with a little smile both sad and warm.

"Come see me soon," she said. "And remember my promise to you: if you should ever need anything, anything at all, all you have to do is call."

"Yes ma'am. I'll remember."

Gracefully, the countess gathered the folds of her skirt and fur and slipped into the car. A few seconds later, the Rolls disappeared into the night.

Chapter 19

Frankenstein

THE COUNTESS HAD BEEN gone only minutes when Theresa pulled her sedan up to the sidewalk. I walked around the car, opened the front passenger door, and hopped inside. It didn't take her long to realize I was crying.

"What is wrong, Josie?"

I handed her the photograph. "The countess gave me this while you were bringing around the car."

Theresa looked at the picture. In the dim light, I saw her smile.

"It's a beautiful photo of your mother," Theresa said. "Why would that make you sad?"

"I guess because it's one of the only photographs ever taken of her," I said. "I don't know if you remember this, but she refused to have photos taken even of her performing. It was written in her contract. This photo is of just me and her. Can you see me under the piano bench?"

Theresa peered closer at the photo and nodded.

"Until tonight, I didn't even know such a picture of us existed," I said. "My dad used to say I was Mom's little practice shadow, but those were words. I thought he said them to make me feel better after she died. But this photo makes those words real to me."

Theresa remained mum, as if she knew I had more on my mind.

"It's so weird meeting all these people who knew my mom and, I guess, also knew me as a child. When I don't remember any of you."

Theresa nodded with understanding.

"I had hoped it would make you feel better knowing how much your mother was beloved and meeting her friends . . . your childhood friends. As a toddler, you literally adored the countess."

"I guess I feel better, but it also makes Mom real again, when I've spent so long trying to put the pain of losing her behind me."

Theresa handed me back the photo.

"Keep this close. I have a feeling you rekindled quite a friendship tonight. The countess may have adored little Josie, but she seemed quite taken with the guitar-playing Josephine."

I smiled.

"Can she really duckwalk?"

Theresa nodded and grinned.

"Indeed, to the point that nothing the countess does surprises me anymore. She's quite a woman. She is fearless and, trust me, you do not want to get on her bad side."

"That I would believe," I said.

. . . .

It was three twenty-one in the morning when I crawled into bed. Of course, I couldn't sleep. Instead I stared at the ceiling for what seemed like hours. Sleep eluded me. I plugged in my iPod and made a random selection. That didn't work either, so I closed my eyes and tried to imagine a peaceful, far-off place . . .

The buzz of my iPhone sounded before I could drift off. It was Fa8 and the message was short: "Love the digital of you in the dressy-dress. Your Fa8 would welcome the opportunity to escort you to any one of Vienna's finer pubs."

Yeah, right. I'd be the world's best dressed wingman.

I tapped the End button and set the phone on the nightstand. The clock said four-eighteen. I got out of bed and stood in front of the window. A round full moon hung low in the sky. I relived the evening — chatting with that weird Gottlieb guy; watching Eric Smack play; meeting the countess, and talking to all the other people who knew my mom as a young musician. Part of me wanted to dance and the other part wanted to cry. Every day it seemed like I missed my mom more and more. And, with Dad gone so much, I felt so alone it hurt.

I grabbed my phone and tapped Dad's number.

All I got was a recording: "Hi, you've reached Dr. Joseph Brunswick. I'm sorry I can't take your call right now. Please leave your number, and I'll return your call as soon as I can."

"Dad, this is your daughter, Josie. Remember me? I'm the one you promised to call. And love. And stay in touch with. Well, I just wanted to let you know I'm going to go get pregnant by the entire Austrian rugby team, then move to the mountains and live in a dirt hut with my brood of twelve kids. Hope that's okay. Josie."

I figured that'd warrant a fast return call.

It didn't.

At five twenty-seven I pulled on my sweats and a hoodie and went outside. The frosted grass crunched under my feet. Since Dad was gone, several of the staff had taken off, too. Being lonely is one thing. Being lonely in a huge, empty house during the Christmas season is something else again. I walked around the villa until I found the bench by Dad's lab. I plopped down and pulled my hoodie tight around me. This was not what I thought my life would be like at seventeen.

I wanted more. I deserved more. I was tired of being alone.

I stood and walked to the hidden door. I'm not sure why I did it. Maybe I just needed to see Dad's picture or touch something he had touched. Whatever the reason, I tapped in the access code, and the door opened with a hiss.

The lab was cloaked in a deep, black velvet. No ambient light, not even the small yellow lights on the sequencing computers. I stepped into the center of the room.

"WGC Alpha lights on, please."

Nothing. The mainframe didn't answer. I tried a second and a third time. The computer remained silent. After a few moments more I tried the backup unit.

"WGC Delta, acknowledge voice command. Lights on, please."

A whirl sounded and a faint glow appeared near Dad's desk. I followed the light and sat down. The backup CPU threw a small circle of yellow on the floor. Through the glass of the desk, it was like looking down a huge, dark tunnel lit by a single bulb.

Above me, the computerized voice of my mother answered.

"Delta unit responding. Good evening, Josephine Marie Bruns-wick. The time is five thirty-one and the temperature is nine point nine degrees Celsius. Alpha unit non-functioning. Mainframe failure detected; all sequencing units off-line. Replication unit on auxiliary power. Restoration sequence loaded. Activate?"

Mainframe failure? Restoration sequence? I scratched my head then spoke to the computer: "WGC Delta status report."

"Mainframe failure caused by completion of full genetic sequence and tissue replication. Power to subunits terminated and rerouted. Replication unit online. Replication complete. Theta and Gamma units off-line."

I took a deep breath. For some reason the computer had crashed and taken almost every other computer in the lab down with it. Dad was going to be so mad he'd scream for week. *And what was that about crashing during a tissue replication? What replication?*

I needed more information.

"WGC Delta, restore regular lighting."

After a few seconds the room filled with a faint blue glow.

"Responding. Auxiliary power online, lighting available at eleven percent of capacity. Diverting power for Gamma and Theta units."

I turned in a circle. It was still difficult to see. I heard the hum of the mainframe; over by the door, several of the sequencing computers began to beep and chirp. The rest of the room remained silent and in shadow.

I felt my way back to the center of the lab. I had to find out if I'd destroyed everything Dad had been working on. I had thought being a sometime orphan was the worst thing that could happen to me, but I now realized being the bane of my father's scientific research would be even worse.

"WGC Delta, full report on cause of system failure."

"Responding. Adapted replication complete. System failure caused by incomplete genetic sequencing in sectors five, seven, eleven, and nineteen of sample. Sample indexed and interpolated using preexist-ing code. Replication complete. Alpha unit restoration at sixty-two percent. Continue?"

Replication? What replication?

It looked to be a while before every single computer in the lab was back online, but meanwhile I didn't understand why the computer kept saying it had completed a replication or why it was asking to continue replicating.

Unless . . .

I walked over to the coffin-shaped cylinder. I hadn't noticed it before, but the top of the unit was covered in frost. In fact, the entire replicator was coated with a thin film of ice.

I touched the lid, tracing a small line with my finger. Something was wrong. The replicator was on and functioning but for some reason it was ice-cold. I looked down at my feet. The cylinder vented a thick purple fog across the floor.

"WGC Delta, analyze replicated tissue."

"Responding. Tissue replication and analysis complete: replicated tissue is human genetic material. Complete sequence?"

"Complete sequence?" I echoed.

"Responding. Executing last command. Replication complete."

I stood still and tried to imagine what I didn't dare imagine. *Dad was not going to be happy.*

Okay, I told myself, breathe, then find a phone.

I turned and started for the door. Behind me, the replicator began to hiss, like a dying animal breathing its last breath. I turned just as it vented again, filling the room with purple-colored steam.

What the . . .

The fog was so thick I could barely see. Beyond me, I heard the sound of gears turning and metal sliding.

I squinted, trying to see through the vapor. In front of me, tracer lights around the edge of the lid pulsated and stopped. Lights blinked. Off to the right, something beeped.

"Omega unit open. Replication complete."

Slowly, the top of the cylinder began to open. I stepped forward. My heart felt as if it would leap through my chest at any moment. Thick fog swirled around me.

There — I thought I saw something on the edge of the replicator but I couldn't be sure. Don't be stupid, I told myself, this is not real. It's just a computer malfunction. There's nothing there; it's my mind playing tricks. All that's happening is a large metal cylinder in my dad's lab is venting steam. I took another step towards the silver vessel. The replicator spilled more fog into the room.

Something inhaled.

"Ahhhhh."

In the stillness, I jumped.

Something was gasping for breath.

I moved through the fog, closer to the replicator. The top was open. Along the edge, a thin semi-transparent film stretched like a paper-thin curtain. The film was crisscrossed with strands of liquid that sparkled and formed long, cascading lines like a glittering spider's web.

I stood, transfixed. I watched as something — something alive — pushed against the delicate membrane. In the dim twilight of the lab, the film pulsated and flexed and moved as if ready to give birth.

To my right, on the floor, another vent opened; more steam filled the room. In front of me the membrane-like film stretched and pushed. Whatever was inside the replicator was trying to paw its way out.

I felt the hairs on the back of my neck stand up. Fear washed over me. I tried to move my feet, to run. I might as well have been bolted to the floor. My legs wouldn't work. Part of me was frightened beyond all reason and the other part of me was awe-struck — like someone present at the moment of creation.

I wanted to turn and race through the door and keep running and never look back, but I could no more move than I could tell you what was going to happen next. I could only stand and wait, my brain on overload, watching, as the glittering, moist film pulsated and flexed.

The fog swirled and eddied around me.

And then . . .

Oh, God, no.

I watched in horror as three fingers of a perfectly formed human hand tore a large hole in the membrane.

Whatever was inside had hands.

Human hands.

The fingers flexed, opening and closing, then balled themselves into a fist.

My heart raced. I covered my face.

The light grew brighter.

I dropped my hands and slowly opened my eyes. Whatever this

was, it was no computer malfunction. Something — something with hands and fingers — was crawling out of the replicator.

I whirled around and ran to the back door. I raced outside and fell to my knees on the cold, hard ground.

And in the icy cold of the Vienna night, I started to scream.

Chapter 20

Bad Moon Rising

I RAN BLINDLY IN THE opposite direction of what I feared. The cold stung my face. I was sure whatever had just been born in Dad's lab was following me. I ran to the front door of the villa and jerked the handles. The hinges rattled with a loud clang. The door was locked.

"No! Please no, please," I screamed, though there was no one around to hear me.

I jerked the handles again. The huge oak doors clanked and stuttered. There was no way in and everything I had — my keys, my phone, my computer — was inside. I leaned against the door and forced myself to breathe. The world was quiet. Slowly, my head cleared. I took several more breaths and turned around. There was nothing in front of me. All was still, just a large winter moon and the occasional goose making an early morning flight. Peering into the cold, I turned and scanned the landscape, trying to see what might be approaching.

My breath frosted. I squinted, trying to see beyond the shrubs.

Nothing.

I slipped off the landing and walked to the right side of the villa towards the library. About halfway down a large window opened onto the lawn like a pair of French doors.

I twisted the handle. The latch clicked. I slipped inside the library, shut the window, and pushed the lock in place. Whoever was out there — whatever was out there — was going to have to come inside to get me. I told myself not to panic and crept down the hall to the stairs.

I raced upstairs, found my room, ducked inside, and bolted the door and the windows.

Everything seemed normal.

But somewhere, outside, something was alive, and waiting.

. . . .

I called Dad about fifty times. No answer. Once again, I couldn't help but think, we really need an emergency signal for, well, emergencies like this. I had to settle for sending him about ninety million texts marked "urgent" saying I needed to talk to him. Obviously, I did not make myself clear, because my phone remained silent.

I even tried calling Fa8.

Again, no answer. *Since when does Fa8 not pick up when I call?* I threw the phone across the room and pulled the covers over my head.

. . . .

Daylight.

The sun sparkled through my window. I rolled over and looked at the clock: nine twenty-three. I felt like crap. My legs ached and my head throbbed. Being scared enough to pee yourself is never a good thing.

I crawled out of bed and peeked through the curtains. The morning looked clear and normal. I was still frightened, still convinced something was wrong, but somehow, the bright sun and blue sky made my Frankenstein fears seem a tad silly.

I slipped on some clean clothes. I needed caffeine and food.

Whatever was lurking outside could wait.

. . . .

Leisel had made coffee, and she'd left me fruit and bagels for breakfast. The rest of the staff was gone. I filled a cup, snagged a bagel, and picked up an apple. I wanted to go outside, but I was petrified of what I might find. It also only seemed polite to warn Leisel and anyone else who might show up that I'd unleashed a monster accidentally on the grounds. But then again, I couldn't recall Emily Post ever specifically addressing this situation.

Truth be told, I didn't want someone to get hurt because of me.

I tried Dad again. Still no answer. I could feel the panic inside me surging. Things were way out of control. I needed my Dad, this was over my pay grade.

I called a third time and left another frantic message: "Dad it's me. Call me now! Something horrible has happened and there is something loose in your lab. I'm scared, Daddy. Please call."

I pushed the End button. If Dad had any doubt as to the urgency of the situation it would be erased the moment he heard "Daddy." I hadn't called him that since I was a grade-schooler and accidentally lit the barn on fire with a stray sparkler.

I found a spot on the large sofa in the library, tried to sip my coffee, and curled into a tight ball. I was scared and angry and, as always, alone. They don't send seventeen-year-olds off to war for a reason, I thought. *So why do I seem to always be taking on the world by myself?*

Please, Daddy, please call.

Five minutes later my phone buzzed.

"Josie? Josie, honey, what's wrong?"

I exploded into the phone.

"Please, please come home right now, it was a hand, a human hand! Something alive! Purple! I'm so scared! I-locked-the-windows-and-it's-out-there-and-it's-alive-and-has-a-hand-and-it-was-in-your-lab-coming-out-of-the . . ."

"Josephine!" My dad's voice was firm, but I had too much pent-up fear to be stopped easily.

"Daddy-it-was-coming. It-was-going-to-get-me. And-I'm-scared-and-alone-and-you're-not-here. And-I-ran-inside. And . . ."

"Josephine! Hush!"

I pushed myself deeper into the sofa corner.

"I'm so scared, Dad, really scared. I need you."

"Now calm down, honey. Take a deep breath. Everything is going to be just fine." Dad's voice was calm, reassuring. "Josie, listen to me carefully. First, I need to know exactly where you are?"

Slowly, I let the air out of my lungs.

"I'm in the library in the villa."

"And you're okay?"

"Yes. For the moment."

"Are you hurt?"

I put my hand on my chest. My heart felt like it was playing Verdi's *Anvil Chorus*.

"No, I'm fine. Just scared."

"Good. I want you to do exactly as I tell you: Go to your room. Stay on the phone with me. Move now! Quickly!"

"Okay, I'm going." I slipped off the sofa and scurried down the hall to the big staircase by the front door. I ran up the stairs and into my bedroom.

"I'm inside."

"Lock the door behind you," Dad said.

I twisted the lock. "Done."

"Now, look around. Check the armoire, under the bed, and in the closet. Are you alone?"

I flung open the doors — nothing. I lay on the floor and raised the bed skirt — nothing but my guitar case and a couple of sleepy dust bunnies.

"Nothing here."

"Check your bathroom."

More doors opening and closing. "Nothing. It's just me."

"Good. Bolt the windows and draw the shades."

"I already did that."

"Excellent," Dad said. "Now I need you to focus, okay? I want you to sit down and calmly tell me exactly what has happened and why you are so frightened. Take it slow — do not leave anything out. Think in sequence. Can you do that?"

I forced myself to take another deep breath. "Yes, sir."

"Good," Dad said. "Now start at the beginning."

I talked, non-stop, for most of the next hour. Dad didn't say much. Once in a while he asked a question, but mostly, he listened. He didn't even comment when I told him I had taken Chaz into his lab.

After I finished, there was a long silence.

"Josephine?"

"Yes, sir?"

"I want you to listen very closely now." Dad's voice was calm, but tense, as if he was trying to control his anger but worried, too.

"I'm listening."

"First, do not leave the villa. I want you to stay up in your room and only go downstairs to grab food and bring it right back. Is Andre there?"

"No. I think he went to his mother's for the weekend."

"You're alone?" I could hear the tension rising in Dad's voice. "No one else is there?"

"It's just me, I think," I said. "Leisel was here this morning. She left me breakfast. But I don't know where she went."

"Okay," Dad said. "Then it looks like you are going to be on your own until I track someone down or get back. Can you manage a little while longer?"

The thought of being alone made my stomach hurt.

"I think so."

"You're going to have to be strong."

"Okay. I'm trying."

"I want you to go through the villa and lock all the doors and windows — I'll stay on the line while you do this. You can get something to eat at the same time. Then I want you to go back to your room."

"But what about —"

"Josie, you need to do what I say. Have you been back to my lab?"

"No," I lied.

Dad sighed, as if he didn't believe me.

Could I blame him?

"Do not go back there. I want you to stay out of my lab until I return. Do you understand?"

"Yeah, but stuff is still on and what if . . .?"

Dad's voice rose. "Do as you are told; this is for your own safety. Do not go in my lab. Stay out. I can lock it down remotely."

"Okay, please don't yell at me."

Dad's voice softened. "I'm sorry, honey, but I am several hundred miles away and all hell has broken loose there and you are alone. And this is not the kind of situation that we can dial up 9-1-1."

"So there is something alive in the lab, Dad."

"Josie, let's not get into that right now. Just know everything is going to be okay. Now, do you have my old laptop handy?"

I glanced at my desk. Dad's old Mac was buried under a stack of CDs and piles of music magazines.

"Yeah. It's on my desk."

"Excellent. Fire it up and use the secure video link the next time you call. I'm not sure I want to use the cell phone to talk."

"Okay, but what about what's . . ."

"Honey, if you stay in your room you'll be fine. Nothing is going to come grab you, I promise."

"But what if it got out . . ."

Dad's voice rose again.

Even hundreds of miles away, I knew he was livid.

"I said I'd take care of it, Josie. Didn't I make myself clear?"

"Okay, okay, I heard you the first time."

Again, his voice softened.

"Josie, everything will be okay. But I want you to stay in your room and far away from the lab. I don't want you hurt. Understood?"

"Okay. What are you going to do?"

"I have several things I need to do," Dad said. "This changes everything. Josie?"

"Yes, Dad?"

"I want you to know how much I love you. I am sorry that I'm not there. I know you're frightened, but I need you to do what I ask and to be strong."

"I'm trying."

"I know you are. Now, I want you to try and get in touch with Andre or Leisel and have them contact the rest of the staff. Tell them there's a problem with the lab and you need an adult or two there immediately. See if one or more of them can come. If they have questions have them call me."

"I have Leisel's number. I'll call her."

"Excellent. Meanwhile, could you go and stay with a friend until I can get back to Vienna?" he asked.

"I don't know Dad, that's a pretty long time."

"Huh?"

"Well, you won't be back for awhile."

"It won't be that long," Dad said.

"I don't understand."

"Josie, I can't stay here when all this is going on with you there. I have messaged the airport. I should be back no later than Friday."

I couldn't believe it. *Dad was coming home.*

"Really? You're coming home?"

"Yes, honey. I'll get home as fast as I can, but it may take me a day or two. Is there a friend you could go stay with until then? Or is there someone who could come and stay with you until I get home?"

"I could call Fa8."

"Ahh, Fa8?" Dad's voice betrayed his hesitation. "Isn't there anyone else? Maybe one of the girls from orchestra?"

Dad wasn't real fond of Fa8. I was pretty sure he was remembering all the weird things Fa8 had done in the past, not to mention how he dressed or the recent kegger. And I knew he hadn't forgotten the time Fa8 introduced him as the Upper Extreme Most Exalted Grand Poobah of the Genetical Worldly-World.

"Fa8 would come; he's my friend." I lowered my voice. "I don't have many of those, Dad."

But Dad didn't hear my confession; he was too fixated on the idea of the British wanker possibly spending time under his roof alone with his only daughter.

"He's a very strange young man. Very strange."

I tried one more time.

"But he cares about me and he would defend me. I know he's a little different, but he's a good guy."

Dad sighed. "I just don't know."

"Dad, hear me out. Fa8 is not only the best friend I have; he's my only friend at school, and right now I would say my options are kinda limited to bodies in Vienna, ya know."

"Okay, honey." I could tell by his voice that while Dad was not happy, he was resigned to the inevitable. "Give him a call."

"I will. I'll call him next."

"Good," Dad said. "Now, there's one more thing."

"Yes, sir?"

"Do not, under any circumstances, go looking for whatever it is you think was in the lab. Do you understand me, young lady?"

"But Dad, I think something has happened and . . ."

"I'm serious, Josephine. I have no idea why, or really how, but something biological was replicated there, and I don't want you to go running around trying to find it. There is no telling if this being is in pain or its right mind or what. We can't risk that and I most certainly won't risk losing you. Do you understand me?"

"Yes, sir. Dad?"

"Yes, honey?"

"Are you really coming home? Really?"

"Yes, sweetie. I'll be home by Friday. But I insist that you do exactly as I have told you until then. Now let's make that tour of the house and get you something to eat."

It took almost an hour to check all the entrances and windows in the villa and for me to raid the kitchen for sustenance. But Dad stayed on the line with me the whole time.

Finally, I made it back to my bedroom.

It was time to sever the lifeline.

"Dad?"

"Yes, Josie?"

I took a deep breath.

"I'm not so scared now."

"I'm glad, sweetie. Remember you are more important to me than anything in the world. I love you very much. Now, be safe, stay in your room, call Fa8, and don't talk to anyone else. Understood."

"Understood. I love you, Dad."

"I love you too, Josie. Very much."

I tapped the End button. I felt better now that Dad was coming home. But I knew he was right, everything I knew had changed.

Only even I didn't know yet how much.

Chapter 21

Born to be Wild

From: HansG@wgcalpha.com
Subject: Vienna
To: security@wgctheta.com

Klaus:

It is my belief the replicator has been activated; the remote monitor shows the unit came online exactly 24 hours ago.

The material appears to be biological — as in human. The DNA is unknown. Because of this, you must proceed with your plan — but stealthily. We want no additional problems with the Canadians.

Tell the staff to clear the area.

Meanwhile, I shall pursue another avenue for information.

H.G.

. . . .

I did everything that Dad asked of me — except the not-going-outside part, the calling Leisel and the staff part, and the getting Fa8 to come stay at the house part. But in my defense, by the time I finished securing the villa, I couldn't wait to get back to the safety of my own bedroom — and Dad had told me to hole up there. Safely behind a locked door, I curled up in my big soft bed under the big fluffy comforter and promptly passed out . . . yes, before I could call or text Fa8 or telephone Leisel.

It was a textbook response to an adrenaline rush in a crisis, and I must have slept for several hours, because when I woke, the sun was low in the sky. My first thought was pure fear. Whatever had been in the lab was still there and I was still alone.

It was way past time to call in reinforcements.

I dressed and tried to call Leisel, leaving her a message that there was trouble at the villa and asking her to call the rest of the staff to see if anyone was available to come stay with me.

She called me back an hour later.

She apologized for leaving me alone, but said she had been called home to care for a sick child. She had left me a note to that effect in the kitchen. Maybe she had; I hadn't thought to look. She promised me she would call later to check on me and that she would do her best to locate someone else on the staff who might be free to come be with me, but she also didn't sound too optimistic. Then she told me she didn't know when she'd be back.

So that was it, something horrible had crawled out of my dad's lab, the holidays were almost here, my mom was dead, and I was officially home alone sans adult supervision . . . for God only knew how long.

My head ached and my body felt like it had been twisted in two. I needed more sleep. Instead, I grabbed a soda and proceeded to do another search of the villa, checking closets and storage areas, looking for places where someone — or something — could hide.

That done, I returned to my room and collapsed again in bed.

It was early evening when I surfaced. The last of an orange sun had faded to purple. I crawled out from under the covers and rubbed my face. I needed more food. I went downstairs and grabbed the rest of the bagels and a bag of chips out of a kitchen cabinet.

I started back upstairs, only to change course and head for the library, where I was careful to look in each of the closets and cupboards another time. It was strange exploring a place — one you have lived in for years — and feeling nervous about looking in a closet.

The Immortal Von B.

I didn't find much, except a few boxes of books and papers from the guy dad replaced — I think his name was Zuhdi. I also found Andre's stash of dirty movies buried under several boxes of Christmas decorations. Seriously, you'd have thought he would have found at least some movies with cute girls in them, but from the look of the covers, these girls — well, let's just say they made me look beautiful.

I finished my closet check and started back down the hall. For some unexplained reason, and even today, I still couldn't tell you why, I turned to the left — towards the lab.

I know, I know: Dad had told me to stay away, but I couldn't help myself. Maybe it was a twist on that classic belief that death couldn't happen to me, but I couldn't resist checking to make sure everything was okay in his lab.

Look, it wasn't like I was seeking out who or what was in there, but I couldn't help but feel a little guilty about the whole mess. And because I knew Dad would be really mad when he got the whole story, I wanted to make sure the lab was clean before he did. I needed to put some stuff back in its proper place and, at the very least, sweep the floor.

The lab was just like I had left it: door locked and everything inside bathed in dim light. Entering, I had to wait for awhile for my eyes to adjust; I tried to force my heart not to thump its way out of my chest.

Several of the sequencing computers were still online — I could tell by the lights. But the units around the replicator — and the replicator, itself — were off.

A cold chill worked its way down my spine.

I touched the replicator again. Most of the ice had melted but the metal still felt cold. Around the edges of the lid, small traces of purple goo clung to the metal.

Whatever had been inside was slimy . . . and it was gone.

Maybe there'd be some clues in my dad's desk.

I took a step and fell flat on my face. I rolled over and reached for the corner of the desk and pulled myself up. Purple goo — thick like grape jelly — covered my shirt. It smelled like unwashed socks.

I followed the trail across the floor; slimy purple footprints in the shape of human feet started in front of the replicator and led to the back door.

My heart was beating like a well-played rhythm guitar. Dad's voice ran on a loop in my head: *Do not, under any circumstance, go looking for whatever was in the lab. Do not, under any circumstance . . .*

I pushed the door open and followed the purple footprints down the sidewalk until they disappeared at the edge of a long row of shrubs. About a hundred yards away, the grass — now faded and brown — ended at the edge of a large row of skyscraper pines. To my left, the large barn stood silent and menacing; on the other side, the tennis court.

Around me the grass remained untouched. I sank to my knees and moved my hands in a large circle, trying to feel if more of the smelly, purple goo had fallen nearby.

Nothing.

No footprints.

No slime.

For a second I felt panic. Even though it was still early evening, the sun was almost over the horizon. I had no desire to be caught outside in the dark with whatever-it-was loose. I looked at the shrubs again.

Nothing.

Above me bold stripes of crimson yellow and purple crossed the sky. The wind whined and whipped my hoodie over my head. One part of me knew I needed to get back inside; the other part of me wanted to keep looking . . . *but for what?*

As usual, the other part won.

Overhead, the first star of the evening appeared in the sky. Every step across the lawn brought both fear and want. I was afraid of what I might find, but I wanted to look.

I walked towards the tall pines that lined the road. The wind pushed against me. To my left, I heard the thump of the barn door. Leisel had said earlier in the week that she had called a workman to fix it — obviously he hadn't shown up yet.

I took a few more steps.

From inside the barn, my colt snorted.

And, suddenly, everything made sense.

The barn.

Why hadn't I thought of it earlier? Of course, if I was cold and didn't know where I was, I would look for shelter.

The Immortal Von B.

I pulled my hoodie a little tighter and started for the barn. My heart raced. I had never been this frightened — and excited — at the same time. Something pulled me to the stables.

Dry, frost-covered grass crunched under my feet. The cold seeped its way into my skin. A gust of wind pushed hard against my back. The large wooden door quivered, then banged shut.

Slowly, I reached out and touched the door.

Purple goo covered the wood.

I grabbed the edge of the door and pulled it towards me.

Then I heard someone scream.

Chapter 22

Roll Over Beethoven

OKAY, SO IT WAS NOT SO MUCH a scream, but more like someone shouting my name.

"Josephine!"

I turned and squinted in the twilight.

"Josephine Marie Brunswick. Do not move! Stay right there!"

A figure ran towards me. In the dark I couldn't be sure . . .

"Dad?"

"Honey, what in the hell are you doing out here?"

"Dad? Is that you?"

His arms went around me. He picked me up and hugged me
against his chest.

"Oh, honey."

"Dad — what are you doing here?"

"What am I doing here? What are you doing *out here?* I told you to
stay in your room."

I pointed at the barn. "I heard the pony whinny. I thought on the
phone you said you couldn't get back until Friday."

Dad frowned. "I left right after we hung up — you sounded scared.
I got here as fast as I could."

Deep, angry wrinkles formed on his forehead.

"I should be furious with you, young lady. You lied to me. You said
you would stay inside and you didn't. I've been looking all over the villa
for you."

I buried my face in his neck. "I mean, well, I heard the pony and I wanted to help make things right."

Dad looked me in the eye, before setting me back on my own two feet. I smiled a faint smile.

"I'm okay. But I think whatever came out of the lab is in the barn."

"Okay, but now you have to go back inside the house."

I shook my head. "No! There's something in there. Something alive. We have to find out what it is. You can't just let it roam around out here. What if it's sick or hurt?"

Dad's face softened. The scientist-part of his brain started working. He put his hands on my shoulders and turned me back towards the villa.

"Well, then, as I said, you go back to the house and I'll go check."

I whipped around. "I'm not going anywhere. Don't you remember? I'm involved, too. You wouldn't be here if I hadn't called."

Dad frowned — scientist or not, I could tell he was this side of furious. "Young lady, I told you to —"

The crash of breaking boards and the tinkle of broken glass interrupted him. Dad handed me a flashlight. There wasn't time to argue.

"Stay behind me and promise me, if I tell you to run you'll run."

"Okay."

He still looked doubtful, and who could blame him with my track record, but together we pushed the barn door open. I pointed my flashlight into the dark interior.

"My horse is in the second stall to the right."

Dad stepped inside. "Stay behind me. Keep the light steady."

We crept towards the second stall. In the dim light, I saw the outline of the horse's head, hanging over the stall. Nearby a lantern lay broken in the dirt.

Dad grabbed my upper arm. "Hold up. Shine your light there."

I pointed the flashlight at the horse. He didn't seem hurt, just restless. I moved the beam across the floor. About three feet from the stall's entrance I stopped.

"There, on the floor," I whispered. "More slime."

Dad leaned close and whispered.

"Whatever it is, it's probably in the stall. That's why your colt is nervous. Don't make any sudden moves. Keep your light low."

Dad waved me behind him, then silently crept to the edge of the stall. The colt's long nose appeared just over the rail. I watched his breath frost in the dim light of the flashlight.

"Shhh." Dad stroked the colt's mane. "Easy, boy."

He whinnied uneasily. Dad stepped into the opening. I stood still, willing my heart to slow down.

"There's something here. Shine your light towards the back."

I pointed my flashlight just below the colt's flanks. At first I couldn't make out anything but a large mound of hay and a wooden trough. I moved the flashlight to the right — just as the hay lump moved.

"Dad, there's something . . ."

"*Gott im Himmel!*"

I screamed and dropped the flashlight.

Everything went dark.

Then something — or someone — pushed me to the ground.

From: security@wgcalpha.com

Subject: Our new friend

To: Hans@wgctheta.com

Your information was correct. We have a subject, alive and, apparently, viable. Preliminary reports show subject to be male, approximately 19 years of age. I have contacted the extraction team and notified the facility in Syria.

Dr. Brunswick, however, has not accessed his computer. Awaiting your instructions.

Chapter 23

I'm a Believer

I FELT A TOUCH ON MY shoulder, and I froze, not sure at first who it was, but something seemed familiar about the clasp.

"Dad?"

"Josephine, are you okay?"

Dad pulled me up off the ground.

"Sorry, honey, I tripped. Are you hurt?"

"No, I'm fine."

"Where's the flashlight?"

"Dropped it. Give me a sec." I knelt down and ran my hands through the hay until I found it.

"Is it broken?"

I clicked the button. A bright spear of light answered Dad's question. He froze in place.

"There," he said and pointed.

I turned the light towards the stall. To the left, curled into a ball, a figure quivered in the hay.

"It's a person. Isn't it?"

"Oh, God," Dad said. "It is indeed."

I pointed the light at the mound on the floor. Whoever — or whatever — it was had covered its head with hay.

"It looks like it's scared," I said quietly.

"Stay back," Dad ordered. "We've no idea if it's in pain or crazed."

"But what if it needs . . ."

"Back!" Dad hissed at me.

I stepped behind him, knelt down, and peeked around him. The figure on the ground shook with cold or fear. In the light, I saw a large puddle of purple near the trough.

"Dad, can it hear or speak?"

"I don't know, Josephine. Now quiet. I'm trying to think."

The figure shivered again, pulling more hay over its head.

I stood up.

"Dad, I think it's cold." I pointed at the ever-growing mound of hay. "See, it's shaking."

I took another step closer to the figure. In front of me, the colt snorted and shifted from leg to leg, frightened by the stranger and the strange smells, and skittish about the strange vibes he was picking up.

I held my hand out to the figure in the hay.

"It's okay," I said. "We're not going to hurt you."

Dad motioned me back, but I ignored him. I took another step forward. The figure's teeth were chattering.

"Are you cold? Can you understand me?"

In front of me, the figure cowered; then, slowly, as if it were some long, strange creature being born, it began to unfold. I stood, amazed, as it reached up, gripped a leather strap hanging from the wall, and pulled itself up from the hay.

My eyes moved slowly across the naked human in front of me.

"Why it's . . . it's a boy."

Dad snorted. "Well, it certainly looks like a boy."

The figure looked about eighteen, maybe nineteen. He was a head taller than I was, with broad shoulders, dark olive skin, and curly hair. He had an intelligent face and a strong, square jaw. His eyes were large, intense, and they seemed to glow with an internal fire.

He was also naked and covered in purple slime.

I looked back at my dad.

"Obviously, Dad, it's a boy. You can see his pen . . ."

"Josephine!" Dad shouted. "I see that it's a male. What I don't know is what or who this male is."

"I am me," the boy answered.

I jerked my head back to the boy in the hay.

"What did you say?"

The boy tilted his head to one side. He shivered, pointed to his chest, and said in German, "I said, 'I am me.'"

"Oh my, God," Dad said. "He can talk."

I stood with my mouth open, dumbfounded. Standing in front of me, a naked teenage boy, translucent in purple slime, shivered in the frigid air. Dad stood next to me, breathing heavily and repeating, "My God, my God, my . . ."

The boy shivered again.

"Cold, it is so cold."

And with that, the boy swayed and collapsed.

I looked at Dad.

"We have to do something."

"You're right. There's no telling how long he's been out here. He's freezing — he has all the signs of hyperthermia."

I looked around the stall for a horse blanket. All I could find was a sheepskin pad used with the saddles. I pulled on the sleeve of Dad's coat.

"Your coat," I said. "Give him your coat."

"Yes. Of course." He took off his coat and started for the boy, only to have the boy cringe and push himself back deeper into the far recess of the stall.

I grabbed the coat. "Let me try."

I draped the coat over one arm and crouched down in the hay.

"Here. This will make you warm."

I laid the coat over the boy's back. Slowly, he worked his arms through the sleeves.

"Can you stand?" I prayed my schoolbook German made sense.

The boy nodded and looked at me curiously while I tightened the belt around his waist.

I turned to Dad.

"We have to get him out of here . . . and inside."

Dad shook his head.

"I don't know if that's a good idea. What if . . ."

"Dad, he can't say out here in the barn. He'll freeze to death."

"You're right. Okay. Let's take him inside."

I stepped towards the boy and slipped my arm about his waist.

"It's okay," I said. "I'm going to help you."

The boy seemed to understand. He nodded and leaned unsteadily on me. Dad stepped to his right and, together, we moved him out of the barn.

"Do you know your name?" I asked.

The boy's head lolled back and forth.

"I . . . I am Lud . . ." he tried to say. "I am . . . "

He never finished.

He had passed out.

Chapter 24

Bridge Over Troubled Water

IT IS NOT EASY TO DRAG one hundred and seventy-five pounds of teenager two hundred feet across frost-covered grass.

But somehow, we managed.

Dad and I took the boy inside the villa and stretched him out on the big leather sofa in the den. Dad got his old medical bag from the lab. Then he built a huge fire in the fireplace and sent me off in search of blankets and water.

Dad said we needed to make sure the boy stayed warm and hydrated, so I piled several thick wool blankets on top of him and draped another, larger blanket across the back of the sofa. I filled a carafe with water and brought a glass for him from the kitchen.

Dad pushed the sofa closer to the fire.

"That should keep him for now. But we have to watch him. His core temperature is way too low."

Dad knelt by the boy and scanned his blood pressure with a small, hand-held monitor.

"They've just started using these in Japan," he said, pointing to the mini scanner. "What a wonderful tool."

I shook my head. Part of me wanted to hug my father, but the other part wanted to scream. Dad could have been studying a tissue sample, he was so matter-of-fact. He didn't speak at all to the boy, but instead, stuck him with probes, swabbed his mouth, and scraped tissue off his palms and the soles of his feet.

Finally I'd had enough. "Dad, what are you doing?"

"What do you mean?"

"I mean, what are you doing? It's like you're in your lab running an experiment. He's a sample to you, not a person."

Dad turned, put the scanner on the end table, and scowled.

"I'm trying to help this boy." He pointed to the figure asleep on our couch. "Remember. I didn't do this. You did."

I felt my face grow warm.

"What do you mean, 'I'? 'I' did this! You're blaming me?"

"I wasn't here, Josephine," Dad hissed. "I didn't put a sample in the scanner. I didn't tell the computer to replicate a human. That wasn't me. That was all you."

"You think I did this on purpose?"

Dad stood and walked to the door of the den.

"Josie, I don't know what to think. But the issues here are huge — as in global as in historic as in biblical. I don't believe you realize that."

"I was simply defending you. I wasn't trying to create anything."

Dad pointed in the direction of his lab. "I told you to stay out of there more than once. You didn't listen. Not only were you in my lab, you also took strangers in there, again without my permission. How many times have I told you the lab was off-limits?"

"I was trying to get people out of your lab and away from your equipment. I was trying to protect you and defend your reputation."

Dad's face grew dark.

"That is beside the point now. You disobeyed me." He pointed to the sleeping boy. "You . . . did . . . this."

I spun on my heels. He was being so unfair. This was not my fault; well, at least not *all* my fault. I'd been left on my own for so long, and then he blames me when something goes awry? *I don't think so.*

"You weren't here. You don't know what happened." I pointed to the boy on the sofa. "And even if I did push the button, I am not the one who started the whole thing. That machine down the hall didn't just appear; it was made by you!"

Dad shook his head sadly. "You don't understand."

"I don't understand what? About wanting to cure disease? About all your talk about wanting to help humanity? Come on, this has nothing to do with any of that. What exactly have you been up to, Dad?"

I could see my words shocked him.

"What do you mean by that, Josie?"

I stepped forward. My fists clenched at my sides.

"You lied. You said you were trying to cure disease. You said you were fighting AIDS, trying to decipher the virus behind it, but you're not. You made a machine that replicates things . . . animals . . . birds . . . and people."

I glowered at him, trying to put into words what I had begun to suspect.

"You have lied to the whole world, Dad. You've traveled across the globe saying you were 'trying to help humanity' but you aren't. You're making monsters . . . you're like Dr. Frankenstein."

For a moment Dad didn't say a word. Maybe I'd gone too far. He stepped away from me, his face blank and expressionless. When he finally spoke, his voice was dead and cold.

"That's not fair, Josie. I've spent years, many long years, trying to cure a horrible, wasting disease. What have you done besides throw beer parties, play your guitar, and lie to me? I'll put my record up against yours any day, young lady."

What he said hurt, partly because it was true, but also because I felt he was more intent on trying to distract than insult me — there was something he wasn't telling me. I could feel it.

"Dad, you want me to believe that you're curing disease with a replicator the size of a coffin?"

Dad's eyes narrowed. "You would never understand."

"What's there to understand? Chaz said your replicator is the largest he'd ever seen. He said the world's biggest replicator is supposed to be at CERN in Switzerland, and it's the size of a shoebox."

Dad closed his eyes tight. "I wouldn't know anything about that."

I balled my fists tighter.

"I don't believe you. That replicator in your lab isn't for copying organs or tissue; it's for creating something — someone, something human."

Dad's faced turned pale. "It is for my research. It's . . ."

"It's designed to make humans!" I screamed.

Dad turned away and headed for the hall.

"That's preposterous," he shouted over his shoulder.

I was so angry I wanted to scream. Instead, I followed him, peppering him with questions and accusations.

"Is that what you're doing? Making humans? Trying to play God? That's what it seems like to me. You say I'm to blame for all this, but you're the one who invented that machine."

Dad waved me off, like he didn't want to hear what I was saying.

I caught up with him, grabbed one of his hands, and pulled until he was facing me again.

"You're the one who started all this, Dad. It's your lab, your replicator, your vision. I may have pushed the wrong button, but it was the button on *your* machine."

I could tell my words infuriated him, but I couldn't stop. I had to make him see what I saw.

"That's not fair, Josie. All we have, all this," he said, "is because of my work. You're living here because of the research I've done. You have a wonderful life and go to a wonderful school because of the work I do. At least your mother understood that."

"Mom?" The blood drain from my face. "What does Mom have to do with any of this?"

Dad shook his head.

I leaned forward and spoke very slowly. "You have not answered my question. What does Mom have to do with this?"

"I told you, nothing . . . I misspoke. I'm frustrated, because you won't listen to reason."

"I don't believe you."

The fuse was lit; it burned for a moment, then exploded. Dad's face turned beet red and he slammed a fist against the wall.

"You don't believe me?" He enunciated each word like it was a slap. "How dare you!"

He pointed at me like a prosecutor might a recalcitrant defendant on trial for murder.

"You're the one who's been doing the lying. You have no idea what you've done. I rushed back to make sure you were okay and to clean up your mess, and all I get is attitude. I am your father. You will not talk to me like this!"

"I don't know who you are either." I pointed down the hall, towards the lab. "All I know is that my father, Joseph Brunswick, has spent his life trying to help people. Not trying to play God!"

When Dad spoke next, it was through clenched teeth.

"I told you I'm doing research — cutting-edge research. I am on the cusp of a breakthrough that could change the world, yet I have to waste my time answering questions about my work from everyone: the Vatican, those idiots in Canada, the FBI, the French — everyone, including it would seem my own daughter.

"Nothing has gone right since your mom got sick. She would not have died if I had simply had more time . . ."

The hairs on my arms bristled. Suddenly, it was all so clear. I understood. Cold logic flowed through my veins like liquid nitrogen.

"Dad, exactly what does all this have to do with Mom?"

Dad looked at me as if he'd just met me.

"What? What did you say?"

I stepped towards him. "This is *all* about Mom. Isn't it?"

"No, no, you don't understand."

"Yes, yes I do. I think I understand everything now." I looked around the lab. "This, all of this, it's *all* about Mom."

Dad's eyes narrowed and he raised his hand.

"You have no idea what you're taking about, young lady. And I will not listen to any more of your speculation."

"Dad, you're lying. This is *all* about Mom. My mother. Your wife. You know, the love of your life."

"Josephine, stop. Stop now before you say something you will regret. You have no idea what you're talking about."

"Yes, I do," I said. "If this has nothing to do with Mom, then why do you keep mentioning her name?"

Dad looked confused for a moment. "I miss her; that's all. She was the only one who understood my work, what I am trying to do. With all the doubting Thomases, I need her now more than ever."

"I know how much you loved her, Dad. I loved her, too. And I miss Mom, Dad, just like you do. Sometimes so bad it hurts."

Slowly, Dad looked at me. The pain in his eyes made me flinch.

"I told her, if she could just . . ."

"Just what, Dad?"

It was like watching a building topple. Dad covered his face with his hands and began to sob.

"I couldn't save her," he cried. He fell to his knees, almost like he was praying. "I tried. God knows I tried, but I couldn't save her. All my research, all the high-tech equipment, none of it did any good. I had all of this marvelous technology, but I was too late. I couldn't save her. I promised her. I promised her I would make her better.

"And I couldn't."

Dad's faced twisted in pain.

Dry heaves moved across his body in waves.

Softly, I touched his shoulder.

I knelt beside him.

"Daddy, what were you trying to do?"

"I had computations that showed that if a mutated gene was inserted into the cancer cells, it could replace them. It worked in theory, but she died before the procedure could be perfected. I had the key to saving her, but I lost her anyway."

Chapter 25

I Never Told You What I Do For a Living

IN THAT MOMENT, all the memories of that day I found Mom on the floor of the bathroom and all those horrible days and nights at the hospital by her side washed over me. I felt terrible.

"Dad, it was not your fault. You did everything you could."

"You don't understand. I gave her my word. I told her that she would be okay. I never lied to your mother. Never."

"Why didn't you tell me?"

"You were too young, and your mom didn't want to scare you. We'd known for a while that it was cancer — before we left Oklahoma. That's why she retired. But she couldn't bring herself to completely stop playing or performing. And at first I thought she would be okay. The cancer appeared treatable, then, after we arrived in Vienna, we realized it was more serious."

"Did you think about going home?"

"No, I thought I could help her better here. The lab had all the equipment I needed to replicate the tissue. Her tissue. I told her those cells wouldn't be cancerous. But it didn't work. I didn't want to believe that. But the procedure didn't work."

Dad took a seat at his desk. I could tell he was wiped out, but something was nagging at me.

"Your research is on a cellular level, Dad. So why a replicator the size of a coffin?"

Dad looked at me and sighed. His face told me he was tired of keeping secrets. "I took samples. I thought afterwards that I could replicate . . ."

"What, Dad, what? I am your daughter. Tell me the truth!"

Dad buried his head in his hands. "Her — your mother. I was going to replicate her! I had the tissue samples. I had the DNA sequenced. All the data was there, but the damned computers kept crashing!"

I couldn't believe what I was hearing.

"You . . . you were going to clone Mom?"

"No," Dad said. "I was going to replicate her."

It sounded like semantics to me. My brain was officially on overload. Listening to Dad was like listening to the narrator of a sci-fi flick — only what was unfolding in the here and now was real and it involved both of my parents.

"Dad, that doesn't make sense. Even if you managed to copy her, she might have looked like Mom, but she wouldn't have been Mom. She wouldn't have known either of us. She wouldn't have had Mom's experiences, beliefs, personality . . . or musical ability. She would have been a child that could only grow into a beautiful shell."

Slowly, Dad stood and took several deep breaths.

"Not exactly, Josie. There's more. So much more that you don't know about our discovery."

"Okay, so tell me. I'm listening."

Dad gazed into the fire for what seemed an eternity, before slowly, he began to speak.

"It was late one evening several years ago, back when I was at T.U." He looked at me. "Remember my lab there?"

I nodded. I loved his lab at the University of Tulsa. It took up a whole corner of the life sciences building. It was open and airy with tall ceilings. Right next to the door that led into the main hallway one of his students had placed a skeleton with a big mustache and glasses, and from the ceiling hung a display of a double helix wrapped in tiny twinkle lights. I loved going there as a kid. Dad was always happy, and everyone who worked with him was always smiling.

I smiled. "Yeah, you worked with that goofy guy, Clay."

"Correct, my graduate assistant. Clay loved research and English football. Remember him singing the Manchester United fight song at the slightest excuse? 'We're the boys in red and we're on our way to

Wem-ble-y.' He was a little outside the norm, but he was also a certifi-able genius. Anyway, that night we had stayed late, trying to decode a series of what appeared to be new kind of genetic marker."

I swallowed hard. Every time I listened to my father talk about his research I found myself feeling both amazed and stupid.

"Not sure I follow, Dad."

"Look, genetic markers can be used to study the relationship be-tween an inherited disease and its genetic cause," he said. "And that evening I stumbled on something by accident. It changed the entire course of my research. Clay called it the 'EM gene.' "

Now I was lost again. "What's an 'EM gene'?"

"Embedded memories."

I pointed to my head. "Memories? Like in your brain?"

Dad smiled, faintly. "Yes. Clay discovered that certain genes not only dictate characteristics such as height and eye color, but they can also act as a backup hard drive. We found genes that functioned like memory storage scattered throughout the body."

"I'm not sure I understand."

"Well, most people think that your emotions and thoughts and feelings — your personality — all those things that make you, you, are stored in your brain."

"But you're saying my feelings and emotions are stored throughout my entire body?"

This time Dad nodded.

"Yes. Remember the discussion Fa8 and I had a couple of years ago about computers and storage and hard drives?"

I grimaced. Remembering any discussion between Fa8 and my fa-ther was normally terrifying. That exchange had been unusual, because it had ended in laughter; I remembered that even Dad had ended up with a case of the giggles.

"You guys were arguing about rain arrays or something like that."

Dad smiled. "We were talking about how labs had stopped using RAID arrays, or a redundant array of independent discs, for storage."

"A pretty funny discussion if I recall," I said. "Remember Fa8's RAID dance?"

"The image still haunts me," Dad said with a chuckle. "Anyway, while computer technology may have progressed beyond the RAID system, our bodies haven't. Everything we hear, see, feel, and think is stored not only in our brain but also throughout our entire body.

"It makes sense when you think about it. Imagine all the data you are exposed to in a lifetime. Mammoth, massive amounts. That's why it takes your entire body to preserve the record of your life."

I closed my eyes, trying to absorb everything I'd just heard.

"Every feeling, too?"

"Yes, most certainly your feelings. Feelings and emotions are basically information — or data. And so they, too, are stored throughout the body. I think it lends credence to why so many people believe your soul is near your heart and not in your head."

I sat lost in thought. I'd never imagined my body that way. But then, I thought about how I felt — deep inside — when I played my guitar. Those feels weren't in my head. They were, well, they were everywhere, even in the tips of my fingers.

"So if you replicated Mom, and used this marker . . ."

Dad finished my sentence for me: ". . . she wouldn't have been just a shell. She would have had all her original experiences and feelings. She would be human, an exact copy."

"But wouldn't replicating something as complex as a person take forever, or at least nine months," I asked, "and wouldn't you still have ended up with Mom as a baby, not as a woman?"

"That's where Clay comes in again," Dad said. "He developed a way to speed up the replication. That large replicator in my lab was his design. It houses an artificial womb that uses a super-synthesized form of amniotic fluid. Clay was able to reduce gestation from nine months to about nine weeks and the replicant emerges the same age as the donor that gave the DNA sample."

I opened the door to the den and pointed at the boy still slumbering in the glow of the fireplace.

"That explains why he was born so fast . . ."

"And why he was born fully grown," Dad said. "The secret is the amniotic fluid and the age of the DNA sample. Clay eliminated certain chemicals, reducing the chance of disease. Then he changed the ratio of proteins, carbs, and phospholipids. That sped up the process and allowed the replicant to be birthed well beyond infancy. Our results on lab animals were encouraging."

"You're getting a little over my head. But I think I get it. Is the amniotic fluid that stinky purple slimy stuff?"

"Yes," Dad said, with a little smile. "I'm sorry, honey. I did not mean to yell at you and then give you a lecture to boot, but this is radical stuff with world-changing implications."

"Even I can see that," I said.

Dad's face suddenly changed and he seemed uneasy.

"I just wish Clay was around to finish it."

"What do you mean?"

Dad's face grew grim. "Clay died in a car wreck right after we announced the results. It was a hit-and-run. The other driver was never found. Clay died at the scene."

"How horrible," I said, with a shiver.

"Agreed. It happened right before we moved here. Your mom knew about the accident, but we agreed not to tell you. You were dealing with enough changes at the time, if I recall, what with the move and all."

Dad turned as if to go. But I had another question that needed to be asked; I just wasn't quite sure how to ask it.

"Dad?"

"Yes, honey?"

"Did you *really* try to replicate Mom?"

Dad stopped, turned, and looked at me. His eyes were red and bloodshot. He looked like he'd been on the wrong end of a fight.

"I never planned to, but after she got so sick and the gene therapy failed to work . . ."

I asked him again, my voice edgy and raw.

"Dad, answer me. Did you copy her?"

I could almost see my father will himself to say the words.

"I tried, but a few weeks afterward we lost her."

Bile rose in the back of my throat. "What do you mean?"

Dad looked so forlorn. "She, the replicant, wasn't viable. Her brain didn't fully develop."

Dad's face turned to ash. "And she died."

"She died?"

"Yes," he said. "Not long after the sequence completed. She was in severe pain. I gave her a sedative and she died peacefully, but it was like losing your mother all over again. I suspect it's why I turned inward and buried myself in my work, why I haven't been here for you like I should have been. Losing her twice was simply more than I could bear. There was a spell when I wasn't sure if I would recover from it."

I covered my face with my hands, stunned. In a matter of hours, I'd learned my mom knew she was dying of cancer and didn't tell me, that my dad was treating her with an unorthodox gene therapy, and, when that failed to save her, he'd tried to make . . . a copy of my mother that he had ultimately had to bury.

My stomach turned over. "Where did you . . .?"

"She's buried on your grandfather's farm, in the family plot. For the record, she was listed as your mom's sister, Helen."

"Mom didn't have a sister named Helen."

"True," Dad said. "But only a few people know that. I couldn't just put her in a bag and dump her in a ditch. She was human. She was my wife. She deserved a proper burial."

This was all so far removed from the father I knew that I wasn't sure how to respond. I tried to put myself in his place: a grieving husband who thought science could give him a second chance.

"Did you really think she could replace Mom? Did you think I wouldn't notice?"

Dad gave me a weak smile. "I don't know, Josephine. I really don't know. I was in pain, overwhelmed with guilt and loss. I would have done anything to have my wife back. And I wanted to give you your mother back."

I stepped next to him and took his hand.

"I'm sorry that I yelled at you," I said softly. "I know how much you loved Mom and . . . and I know how much you love me."

Dad pulled me into his arms. "I do love you, Josie, with all my heart. And I want to make this all up to you. But much as I hate to say it, that is the least of our problems right now."

He moved to the doorway and pointed to the boy on the sofa.

"We know that he is a replicant of someone. What we don't know is who that someone is."

I took Dad by the hand and pulled him into the den.

"Well I guess we're just going to have to ask him," I said.

Chapter 26

Forever Young

I SAT IN THE DARKNESS and stared at the fire, while Dad checked the boy's pulse and, slowly, ran the scanner across his forehead.

"His temperature is almost normal," he said.

Dad took the boy's right hand and examined his fingertips.

"Blue — his blood oxygen level is still low," he said.

Bathed in the glow of the fire, the boy's face was strong and peaceful. His olive skin looked like rich cream, and his long hair poured across the pillow in dark waves. I watched the blankets slowly rise and fall with his breathing as he slept.

"He looks so familiar to me. It's like an image from my past."

Dad nodded. "I had the same feeling."

Dad sat quietly for a few moments, then turned and looked at me. "Josephine. It is imperative that we figure out who this is, and we have to do it sooner rather than later."

"Couldn't we just ask him?"

Dad smiled, weakly. "We could, but we'd have to wake him up first. And even if we could wake him — and I'm not so sure we could — I don't think we should do that. Right now, he's like an infant. After babies are born they need long hours of sleep while their body adjusts to the stress of life outside the womb."

Dad pointed to the boy. "His body needs time to do that, too. He's been outside and exposed to harsh temperatures. He's suffering from exposure. And I don't want to lose him, too."

"Okay, but then how do you suggest we figure out who he is without asking him?"

"We apply logic," Dad said. He put the scanner back into his bag and looked at me. "We know he is not a clone of you. That's obvious."

I smiled. "Yeah, well, that kinda goes without saying."

"And we also know you provided the DNA material. Right?"

I felt my face grow warm. "Right. But I . . ."

Dad touched my arm. "Josie, relax, we're beyond allotting blame. But the fact remains that you were in possession of the genetic material. That's what you said, right?"

"Right. I think it was a hair from my sweater. At least that's what I put in the scanner, a hair."

"Okay," Dad said. "We know it was a hair. And we're pretty sure when you started the replication. Right?"

I gulped and looked down at my feet. Now I felt guilty again. "Yes sir. It was the night of the rave. I was with Chaz, in your lab."

Dad sat on the floor and pulled a tablet from his bag and tapped the screen. "Okay, that was exactly nine weeks and four days ago."

Dad leaned back against the edge of the couch. "So, we know what material was used. And we know when the process started. And we have some knowledge of where the material came from. Right?"

"I guess . . ."

"Okay, honey, what we need to know is where you came by the strand of hair. Think back. When did you last wear that sweater?"

I closed my eyes. Since I wasn't that big on clothes, I never worried about what I wore each day. Usually I just grabbed something out of the closet, or off the floor.

"Oh, man, I have no — no wait."

"What?"

"I hadn't worn that sweater in a while. It was in my closet. It had been cleaned. I remember taking the plastic bag off the hanger the morning of the rave."

Dad gave me a huge smile. "Are you sure?"

I nodded. "I'm positive. It was in the back of the closet."

"Okay, then we know you must have picked up the sample that day. Now, what about school? You went that day, didn't you?"

I rolled my eyes. "Of course, Dad. I'm no juvenile delinquent."

Dad scowled. "I didn't mean anything by my question, Josie; I wasn't here, remember?"

I bit my lip, trying to think. "Okay. Okay. I don't remember much. We had orchestra, then my Latin class, and, later, lunch."

Dad's face fell. "You could have picked it up anyplace. It could be any one of a thousand people you encountered at school or brushed against in the hallway. Damn."

But what Dad didn't know, and I did, was that I usually kept to myself at school. And unless the air that day was filled with stray, falling hairs, I don't think the sample would have come from anyone at school — except maybe Fa8, and anyone could take one look at our sleeping beauty and know he was not born of that Brit's DNA.

"I don't think I got it at school, Dad. I usually avoid people."

Dad frowned. "Well, that's nice to know, but then where did it come from, Josie?"

I closed my eyes and tried to remember the images from that day.

"I . . . we . . . ah, we went on a field trip."

Dad sat up straighter. "You did what?"

"I said, I went on a field trip that day."

"Where?"

"The Haus der Musik."

Dad couldn't help but smile. "Your mother loved that place. She became friends with a lady named, oh, I can't think of her name, but it's on the tip of my tongue . . ."

"You mean Theresa?"

Dad snapped his fingers. "Yes, that's it. Theresa Malfatti. She and your mom really hit it off."

"I know, I know. The director. I met her, too. I got into an argument with this British snob and she, Theresa, broke it up. Then she took me to her office and then down to the basement and then . . . "

For the second time that night, the little light in my brain clicked on.

"Daddy?"

"Yes, honey."

"I think I know why the boy looks so familiar. I think I know where the sample came from."

Dad's eyes bulged. "Are you serious? You really think you know?"

I nodded, but as I did I felt myself break into a cold sweat.

"Yeah Dad, I'm pretty sure." I grimaced.

Dad leaned in. "So who is it?"

I wiped the sweat off my face. "That day we went to the Haus der Musik. Theresa, Mom's friend, broke up an argument between me and a British princess."

Dad rolled his eyes. "Okay, but what does that have to do . . .?"

"Mom. It has to do with Mom," I said. "The princess was being a little bitch. She was talking crap about Beethoven and his music and I was missing Mom and, well, I guess I lost it."

"It's okay, Josie. I understand. Your mother could be defensive about Beethoven, too."

"Yeah. Well, anyway afterwards Theresa took me into her office, like I said. Then she told me about this big retrospective the museum was planning about Beethoven, and she took me down into the museum's basement to see some of the . . ."

Dad frowned. "Josie, I still don't understand. What has this got to do with who . . .?"

"I'm getting there," I said, interrupting him.

I took another deep breath. "Theresa wanted to show me some of the new artifacts they'd found."

"Artifacts?"

"Yeah. Stuff from Beethoven's life."

Dad's face turned white. "You mean?"

I nodded. "Yep. Theresa showed me a wool scarf, a red one, that once belonged to Beethoven. She said it had been found at an old thrift shop or antique store and the owner had lent it to the museum."

"And did you touch this scarf?"

I nodded again, feeling a little light-headed. "I wasn't supposed to, but before Theresa could stop me, I put it to my face. It might have touched my sweater."

Dad closed his eyes and swallowed, the expression on his face was a new one to me.

"It can't be."

"Yeah, Dad, it can. That's why he looks so familiar; there's a painting of him in Mom's studio — not to mention all the images we've seen of him through the years, thanks to Mom."

I pointed at the boy. "That hair is a few hundred years old."

"Oh my, God, no," Dad said.

The idea was almost too bizarre to imagine, but nothing else fit. I closed my eyes. My heart pounded. This could change everything. I opened my eyes and looked at Dad. His face was a ghostly white. I could tell he wanted to say something, but words failed.

"Dad?"

"Yes, honey?" he said in a shaky voice.

"I, ahh, think, ahh, I sorta by accident, kinda replicated Ludwig von Beethoven."

Dad's head dropped into his hands.

"I was afraid you were going to say that."

At that instant, the boy on the sofa sat straight up and screamed.

"*Gott im Himmel!* Where is that bastard Mozart? He said he would be here and he's late again!"

Chapter 27

Simply Irresistible

I ANSWERED THE BOY'S yell with a scream of my own, one that landed me on the floor. I had just picked myself up, when he yelled again. This time, I landed against the mantle, breaking a vase and scattering a collection of eighteenth-century knickknacks all over the Oriental rug in front of the fireplace.

The boy leaped off the sofa and stood over me, waving his arms, like a mad man. He looked frightened and wild. And he was still naked.

"You!" He pointed at me. "You! Where is *Herr* Mozart?"

I backed up against the wall.

Dad grabbed a poker from the fireplace and waved it like a sword at the advancing composer.

"Back!" Dad cried. "Back I say."

The boy looked at me. Then he looked at Dad. He stepped back, yielding if only for the moment.

"Who are you?" the boy demanded in a thick, but flawless German accent. He glanced quickly around the room. "What is this place?"

Cautiously, Dad stepped towards him and in German said: "You are in my home. You have undergone an intense physical experience. We are not here to hurt you but to help you. Please take a step back. We mean you no harm. Do you understand me?"

The boy looked at Dad and then at me again. He seemed hesitant to surrender his ground, but after a moment gave a little nod.

"*Ja*," he said. He glanced down and realized he was naked. His face turned white. He grabbed one of the blankets off the sofa to cover himself.

"Where are my clothes?"

"We have some for you. Please sit." Dad smiled and motioned towards the sofa. "Please, you need to stay warm."

Slowly, with his eyes locked on Dad, the boy settled back on the sofa. He pulled his knees up under his chin and wrapped himself in another blanket.

"Who are you?" he asked quietly.

Dad pointed to me and back to himself. "I am Dr. Joseph Brunswick. This is my daughter, Josephine."

The boy's eyes opened wide as saucers. He looked at me, then back at my father.

"You are *Herr Doktor* Brunswick?"

Dad nodded.

Shaking, the boy pointed to me. "And she is *Fraulein* Josephine Brunswick. Your daughter?"

Dad smiled. "Yes. Yes, you are correct."

The boy looked at me for several minutes then leaned back and looked around the den.

"I recognize this room. This is Villa Theresa, *ja?*"

Dad scooted closer to the boy. "Yes, this is Villa Theresa."

The boy cocked his head and pulled the blanket tighter around him. "Is *Herr* Mozart here?"

"No, I am afraid Mozart is long gone. But you are welcome to stay. We have plenty of food and drink if you are hungry."

The boy sat quietly for a moment. He settled deeper in the sofa. "What has happened to my clothes?" he asked. "Why am I naked?"

Dad sat on the edge of the sofa and offered the boy the last of the stale bagels. "I will explain everything in a moment. Right now you should eat. Then we will help you clean up and find you some clothes."

Like a puppy unsure of its new master, the boy sniffed the bagel. After considering it for a moment, he took a bite, then another. I took up a place on the floor and, in the glow of the fire, tried to grasp this latest turn in my life.

"*Zis* is stale," the boy said, frowning. "Stale but good. The old man in the market makes them better. Lots of butter."

"We'll find some fresher ones for you," Dad said. "Would you like something to drink?"

The boy shook his head. He finished his bagel, then began to take stock of his condition. He seemed particularly concerned about the slime that caked his arms and legs. His face grew alarmed.

"I want to know where I am and why I am without clothes!" he shouted. "Who has taken them and why am I purple?"

Dad nodded. "That's completely understandable. I shall explain, but first, please, we need to find you something to wear."

The boy glared at Dad only to sigh in surrender. He turned and looked over at me.

"It's okay," I said. "I promise. No one is going to hurt you. You were inside a lab . . ."

"No, I was inside a barn." He picked at some of the dried purple slime on his blanket. "I do not remember how I came to be here."

"We brought you," I said.

The boy seemed to accept my explanation. He sniffed the air and frowned for a second time.

"The air in here is foul," he said.

I smiled, waving, trying to clear away the smell of stinky socks.

"Yes, it could certainly be improved."

I pointed at the dried slime on his blanket. The boy nodded.

"*Ja*. I see. I am the one. This is not good." He held his arms out from his sides as if he wanted to get as far away from them as possible. "Where may I?"

Dad stood up.

"Come with me. I'll show you."

I smiled as the boy, still wrapped in his blanket, pattered after Dad down the hall. Come to find out he had never seen a shower before. He wasn't that used to bathing with hot water, either.

The combination of these new experiences had him laughing and shouting so loudly I could hear him all the way in the den. I knew there would be a billion things that would surprise him in the coming hours and days ahead . . . *if he survived*, but I would never have guessed that he would be amazed by something as simple as a shower and limitless hot water.

"Amazing! All the hot water I want!" he kept saying over and over again. Something about his laugh made me smile, and I could tell it touched Dad, too, because occasionally I heard him chuckle.

After an hour or so, Dad and the boy returned to the den. The shower had wrought a dramatic change in our guest. He had pulled his long hair back in a ponytail. He was wearing a pair of Dad's old jeans and a University of Tulsa Golden Hurricane sweatshirt (you could tell he was a little bemused by both).

Still he walked slowly across the floor, carrying himself much like a soldier, proud and unflinching. I knew he was frightened and out of his element, but he didn't show it. I had to admire such self-control. I was pretty sure I'd be a raving lunatic if caught in a similar situation.

He had a square, firm chin and that long, glorious wavy hair. His eyes sparkled as they caught mine. The realization of just who was standing there before me slowly dawned on me. My pulse raced and, suddenly, I was quite warm. In all my wildest dreams I had never imagined meeting Ludwig von Beethoven much less him ever standing in my home.

For a second, I imagined touching his face.

And, for the first time in years, I blushed.

Luckily, no one seemed to notice — not Beethoven, not my father.

Maybe that's because they were by then deep in conversation. Beethoven asked questions and listened patiently while my Dad answered them. More than once, I noticed Beethoven put his hands up to his ears and pull them away.

It seemed strange, until I remembered . . . I was about to comment on it, when Beethoven returned to his favorite topic of conversation.

"You said *Herr* Mozart is gone. Will he be back soon?"

Dad shook his head. "No, I'm afraid he won't."

"It's strange," the boy said. "One moment I am sleepy from too much wine and the next I am here."

Dad pulled a chair up to the sofa. "Perhaps I had better explain exactly what has happened to you. You may not believe what I say at first, but several years ago . . ."

I faked coughed to stop him; Dad looked over at me puzzled.

"Ahh, Dad, I don't think you need to go back that far. How about just starting with the machine — maybe the night of the rave? We don't want data overload."

"Good point, this is going to be hard enough to explain."

With that Dad turned his chair to face the boy and looked him square in the eyes. He spoke slowly and deliberately.

"Do you know who you are?"

"Of course, I am Ludwig von Beethoven. I am the son of Johann van Beethoven and Maria Magdalena Keverich. I was born eighteen years ago on December 16, 1770."

Dad turned to me and winked. "That's what we thought you'd say."

Beethoven cocked his head. "I don't understand. How could you know that? Neither of you are familiar to me. Your names are familiar, but your faces are those of strangers."

"Yes, we are strangers to you." He patted the sofa. "But you are no stranger to us. Now, if you'll sit back I'll explain what has happened to you and why you are wearing — as you so aptly described them earlier — such strange garments."

For the next two hours, Dad walked Beethoven through how he came to be sitting in our den, wearing jeans and a sweatshirt. It was all going pretty well, too, until he told Beethoven that he had actually been dead for going on two hundred years.

That little fact propelled Beethoven up and off the sofa as he back-pedaled away from us as fast as he could until the wall brought him up short. Horror filled his face.

"This is a lie!" Beethoven cried. He patted his stomach. "I am here. I am Ludwig von Beethoven! I am not dead. I am right here! I am speaking with you and your daughter. How could I be dead?"

Dad plucked a hair from his own head.

"You are, indeed, alive now, but you were dead."

Dad held the strand of hair up to the light.

"It has to do with the chemicals that make up your body, down to a single strand of hair; a laboratory of very powerful modern-day machines; and some scientific discoveries that happened generations after your first time here on earth. In effect, you have been, literally, born again. You have been given a chance to see everything that came after the end of your first life.

"You have been given a second chance, son."

"This can't be. This is unholy. It is witchcraft!" Beethoven shouted as he circled the room, shaking . . . but I could not tell if it was from anger or outrage. "You are both witches! Please, I beg you, stop. Return to the hell from whence you came! Torment me no more!"

Dad stood and tried, unsuccessfully, to calm Beethoven. I could tell he was getting frustrated and feeling helpless. Trying to get someone from the eighteenth century to realize he'd come some two hundred years forward in time was not the easiest thing in the world.

The boy looked so unhappy and frightened, I couldn't stand it anymore. I walked to Beethoven and took his hand. He jerked it away from me as if he had touched something evil.

"I promise you, Ludwig, we are telling you the truth, and I promise you we are *not* witches."

I reached for his hand again; this time he didn't pull away.

"My father is not lying to you. You have been given a second life. It's my fault, actually, and I am so very sorry to have done it. But for whatever reason: a technological glitch, fate, God, whatever — you are here now. And you have been given a chance that no other human in existence has ever been given. You have the chance to live your life for a second time."

For the longest time, Beethoven looked into my eyes. After several awkward moments, he finally spoke.

"My friends? My family?" He struggled to speak the name of his friend. "*Herr* Mozart? Are they?"

I lowered my eyes and nodded.

"I'm sorry, but yes. They've all been dead for a long time."

Beethoven buried his face in his hands.

"They are all I've ever known."

He walked back to the sofa and sank into its cushions. He sat quietly for several minutes. In front of him, the fire crackled.

Dad motioned to me to follow the boy. I walked around and sat on the arm of the sofa near him. None of us spoke.

We simply sat in the amber glow of a dying fire and listened to the world's greatest composer cry.

Chapter 28

Canon in D

FOR THE REST OF THE night, Beethoven seemed a lost soul. He walked in circles around the den, occasionally humming softly to himself, and avoided looking at either of us. He didn't accuse us of being witches anymore, but his silence said everything. His face was twisted with fear and dread. I couldn't remember the last time I had felt so horrible. I had never wanted to hurt anyone, let alone someone who was so important to my family. I wanted to go to him, to comfort him, to tell him things would be okay, but Dad said, No.

"Give him time to take it all in," Dad whispered. "He's just trying to get his head around everything."

So I wedged myself into a corner of the sofa and tried to escape my guilt. Though the Beethoven standing in my den was born of a machine, he was a human. And it broke my heart to see him in such pain. I pulled one of the blankets tight around me and waited.

Finally, Beethoven walked to the far side of the room, knelt in front of the large window, and there, silhouetted against a full winter moon, he prayed.

. . . .

Morning found us sprawled about the room, like children who had keeled over where they stood after a long day of play. Dad had fallen asleep at the desk. I had stayed awake most of the night. Beethoven brooded in a large winged-back chair near the fireplace. Exhausted, I pulled my blanket tighter around me, snuggled down in the couch, and closed my eyes. I had almost fallen back asleep when Beethoven jostled my shoulder.

"Please, if you have a moment," he said.

I smiled sleepily. "Sure. Are you okay?"

Beethoven gave me a weak smile.

"*Ja.* I would like to speak with you," he said, as he found a place beside me on the sofa. "This is almost too much to understand. I am not sure what to do or where to go. How am I to live? Or will I even live? Is this a temporary state of being?"

I sat up straighter on the sofa; I didn't know if my dad even had the answers to all his questions. But I did know one thing for sure, and so I went with it.

"I know you are frightened." I pointed to Dad. "But my father and I will help you — you won't have to do this on your own."

Beethoven seemed reassured. He put his hands to his ears again, like I had seen him do the evening before.

"And this, this is not what I expected."

"I don't understand."

He pointed to his ears. "My ears. They were useless before. Since I was a young boy, I have had trouble hearing. God made me a composer, but he made me a composer who could not hear."

I felt my eyes bulge. "I knew you lost your hearing. I mean, that's what your biography says, but I don't know a lot about your life as a teenager. I guess I always thought your hearing loss was just an old age thing."

Beethoven gave me a weak smile. "Few people outside my family knew I was deaf or why or when it happened, but I lost my hearing when I was a young boy."

He was deaf as a boy?

"I thought you lost your hearing much later. You were going deaf even as a child? How did you manage? I'm pretty sure most people didn't think you were deaf until much later."

"This is true," he said. "For many years I was a frail child. Much sickness. Much time spent in a sick bed. My father was a talented man, and a good man, but he was not a good father. He was . . . quick . . . with the fist."

I felt myself gulp. "I . . . we didn't know."

"It is fine." He stuck out his chin and squared his shoulders. "People did not know. I did not tell them. I did not want their sympathy. Instead I watched them. I watched their mouths and the way they moved their lips and their bodies. And when I didn't want to talk I waved people away."

I laughed. Beethoven smiled in return.

"Is that why people thought you were aloof and arrogant?"

"*Ja.* I said I was busy and they left me alone."

I scooted closer to him on the sofa. "And now . . .?"

Another smile, bigger this time, as Beethoven put his hands to both of his ears.

"It is amazing. I hear perfectly, both ears. There is no ringing; there is no muffled noise. The sound is pure and beautiful."

Overcome, I stood and thought about a piano that sat above us, silent since the passing of my mother.

"I cannot imagine trying to write music and not being able to hear it. It seems impossible, but it would also be so, so heartbreaking."

Beethoven shook his head.

"Music is not in your ears, Josephine Brunswick. Music is in here." He pointed to his chest. "You must feel it. It must consume you. To play without passion is inexcusable. The heart is where the music comes from. Not the ears. Even if you cannot hear anything, you can feel music. This is how I became Beethoven."

His words entranced. And, without even realizing it, I reached out and touched his hand.

"My mother always said there was no one else like you. And she was right; your music always touched me like no one else's."

"Thank you." With that, Beethoven smiled and fell silent, but his eyes never left mine. And then, he reached over and touched my cheek.

"You are most beautiful, Josephine, and kind and frank — so unusual in a woman."

I looked away. My face felt warm. Being here with Beethoven and having him tell me I was beautiful, well, it was all a little hard to take in. Before I could respond, the moment was gone.

Beethoven smiled. "Is there something more to eat? To drink?"

This I could handle. I stood up, grabbed his hand, and pulled him up off the sofa.

"Yes, there is. I know I can help you there."

Together we walked to the villa's big kitchen.

. . . .

Beethoven stood in the kitchen, turned in a circle, and stared.

And stared.

And stared.

"What is this place?" He spun in a circle, first pointing to the iron-gray commercial-grade oven and then to the stainless steel Subzero refrigerator. "Is this the laboratory your father spoke about?"

I laughed.

"No, this is our kitchen, our, how would you say it, our *küche*." I opened the refrigerator door and grabbed two sodas. "It's bigger than most even by today's standards. But all kitchens are pretty much the same. This big box keeps food cold, you know, to preserve it."

"I see," Beethoven touched the refrigerator. "No rotted meat?"

"Nope. Here, try this." I handed him a cold can of soda. "It has a little more kick than water."

Beethoven held the can to the light.

"What is this?" He turned it round and round and upside down looking for an opening.

I took the soda back and pulled the tab. The can opened with a click and a hiss.

"It's called Coca-Cola. Try it, you'll like it."

I opened my soda and took a sip. Beethoven watched me then put his can to his lips.

"Sweet," he said, with a smile. "Bubbly."

"Sugar, water, and carbonation," I said.

"Car-bon-ation?"

"Bubbles," I said.

While Beethoven worked on his soda, I rummaged through the refrigerator until I found a large pizza box from earlier in the week. If memory served, it held most of a pizza that I had never gotten around to eating, what with all the excitement.

I opened the box, slid the pizza on a pan, and popped it into the big oven.

"You have to try pizza," I said. "I'm pretty sure you'll love it."

Beethoven belched and rubbed his belly.

"Does it go with Coke?" he asked.

Chapter 29

Circle of Steel

THE PIZZA WAS A HIT. Beethoven ate four slices. Then he had another soda and some bread and cheese. He also became a fan of peanut butter and jelly.

"You have fed me well," he said, with a contended sigh.

"It's easier to deal with the world on a full stomach."

"*Ja*," he said, but his face fell.

The world had inserted itself back in the room.

I could tell by his expression.

"I still do not know what will become of me," Beethoven said.

"I don't know what to tell you. All I know is my father is a very, very smart man. And I promise you that we will both help you."

"Thank you," he said. "Is it permissible to see the rest of Villa Theresa? I am curious as to how it has changed since I saw it last. Could we see the grounds perhaps?"

"Sure, I guess. Just give me a second." I finished the last of my pop, rinsed out the empty cans, and dropped them into the recycling bin. "I should probably tell my Dad that I'm going to show you around, though."

"*Ja*," he said. "That would be wise."

"No need," a voice behind me said.

I turned, as Dad stepped into the kitchen.

"I smelled the pizza. I figured you were feeding our guest."

I pointed to the empty pizza box.

"He said he was hungry, but I saved two pieces for you."

Dad laughed and picked up both slices. He folded them together, like a sandwich, and stuck the end in his mouth.

"Mmmm. Hey, do we have any peanut butter and mustard?"

I rolled my eyes. "Dad, please just eat your pizza, okay?"

I took Beethoven by the hand and gave him a tour of the rest of the kitchen and pantry.

"It's pretty big," I said, "but everything in this place is big."

Beethoven took in each appliance, scratching his head when we came to the microwave. I tried several times to explain how it worked, but I could tell Beethoven was lost.

"Think of it as a small oven with a sun inside," I said.

"To warm food?"

"Something like that."

"Good pizza," Dad said as he wiped his hands on his jeans. "It's been a long time."

Dad perched himself on a tall wooden stool and motioned me to come closer.

"We need," he said, pointing to Beethoven, "well, actually, he needs a thorough examination. A physical. I need to do it as soon as possible. I need to make sure there were no problems with his replication. I suspect at some point he is going to want to know if this second life will be like the first. Will he live to a nice old age. Right now, I don't know if I could answer that if he were to ask."

"You should also check his hearing, Dad."

"What do you mean?"

"He can hear," I said. "He's not deaf."

"You're kidding, right?"

"Nope. Right before we came looking for something to eat, he told me how wonderful it was to be able to hear. He said in his first life he'd started going deaf about the age of twelve."

Dad sat quietly for a moment.

"That means the replication wasn't pure."

"I don't understand."

"Well," he said. "If Beethoven was deaf when the sample was taken, then he should be deaf now."

"But he's not, Dad. I'm sure of it."

"My point exactly. The computer must have interpolated the sample," my father said, a frown on his face.

I felt the hair stand on my neck. "Oh my gosh, I remember now. When I went in your lab, all the computers were down, and the Delta unit said the replication was completed, but it also said that several sectors were, what did you call it?"

"Interpolated?"

I snapped my fingers.

"Yeah. It said they had been 'interpolated.' " I looked at Dad. "Is that bad? What does it mean? 'Interpolated'?"

Dad looked at me like I'd just ask him to explain the Big Bang Theory. "Are you sure you want to know?"

I nodded, and as I did, Beethoven joined us.

"I, too, would like to know about this inter-pol-a-tion," said Beethoven, who had finished checking the villa's wine vintages while we were talking.

"Okay, let me see if I can explain," Dad said. "Interpolation is a way of sampling data. For example, in digital signal processing, interpolation is the process of converting a sample of a signal to a higher level by using a filter."

I rolled my eyes. "Okay, I still don't understand."

Dad tapped his forehead with a finger as if in deep thought. He walked out of the kitchen only to return with his tablet computer.

"Think of it as adding a few more notes, *Herr* Beethoven," my dad said, as he tapped the screen of his tablet. "Josie, do you remember this picture? The one your mom took of you, when you were seven. The one in your swimsuit."

For the second time in twenty-four hours, I blushed.

"You mean, the one where my bottoms are falling off, like the baby on the suntan lotion bottle?"

Dad laughed. "Yes, that one."

I covered my face with my hands. "I hate that photo."

Dad tapped the screen of his computer again.

"I know, but your mother and I loved it." He turned the computer towards me. The display showed me walking away from the camera. We were at a swimming pool in Tulsa and my swimsuit was a tad large, so large and sagging that half of my bottom showed.

"So what does my naked little butt have to do with interpolation?" Dad tapped the display again, enlarging the photo.

"Like I said, your mother loved that photo. I thought we'd lost the original when we moved, but she found it buried in a box of shoes. Since it was taken with film, there was no digital file of it."

"Okay, but you still haven't answered my question."

Dad turned the display back to me. "I'm getting there. Basically, I scanned the print of the photo, but because I wanted to end up with a larger print of it than I began I scanned it larger than the original. And because the photo was damaged and so small, to end up with a complete picture, the computer had to interpolate some of the image. It sampled portions of data on each side of the damaged areas, averaged it, and filled in the rest."

"So it sort of filled in the holes in the photo with its best guess."

"Exactly."

"And that's what the replicator did?"

"Basically," Dad said. "It took data from other genetic samples that were close to the original and interpolated them where *Herr* Beethoven's data was missing."

"Okay, I follow you," I said.

"I do not know what a scanner is," Beethoven said.

Dad sighed. "I'll explain that later. For now I'm not sure what it all means. Because we don't know what other sample was used and because the computer crashed, we don't know what sectors were interpolated."

I smiled. "Yes, we do."

This time, Dad looked at me like I was the smart one.

"We do?"

"Yes, we do. When the Delta Unit was rebooting, I thought it would be smart to save all the logs, so I backed them up on that big external optical drive. Remember? That's what you did the time we did that sample of the tiger."

Dad pulled me in his arms. "Josie, I think you've saved the day."

From across the room, Beethoven smiled.

"And her pizza is good, too."

Chapter 30

I Am . . . I Said

AN HOUR LATER, we were back in Dad's lab. It looked like an army of slime men had marched through it: dried goo — okay, amniotic fluid — covered the floor and crusted the surfaces of several of the computers. The air smelled foul and stale, and dirt and the residue from the fog covered the room like a fine mist.

"Well, this does not look promising," Dad said.

"Sorry, Dad. I promise I was going to come back and clean everything, but you said stay out. Remember?"

Dad smiled. "Since when do you listen to me."

Beethoven stood in the center of the room and hummed.

"I have seen worse," he said. "You should see my residence."

Dad and I spent an hour cleaning. Then I mopped, while Dad hooked Beethoven up to several monitors to start his physical.

"I'm checking your vital signs," Dad told him.

"This is much less painful than the old ways," he said, with a smile. "I never did like the leeches."

I felt my stomach turn. "Leeches?"

Beethoven nodded.

"I am not sure you would want to discuss it. It was not pleasant."

I swallowed and faked a smile. "I think I've already heard enough."

It was late afternoon when I finished cleaning the lab. I sat down on a chair by the bank of computers.

"How's the physical going?" I asked.

Dad pointed to Beethoven, who had quietly found himself a nice large open spot on the sofa by my dad's desk to crash.

"I still need to do a neurological scan, an MRI, and a few other lab tests that will require me taking blood. It may scare him, but we can't let him run around not knowing the state of his health." Dad clasped his hands. "Especially after last time . . ."

"Do you want me to talk to him?"

"No, I'm responsible. He should hear this from his doctor."

"There is no need, *Herr* Brunswick." Beethoven stood, stretched, then walked over to Dad. "I have never liked doctors. They have always brought me bad news."

Beethoven pulled up a small chair and positioned himself in front of Dad like a schoolboy waiting for a lesson. "But you, *Doktor*, have been very kind. I will take your other tests."

"I just want to make sure you're okay. You had a difficult rebirth."

Beethoven shook his head. He still looked frightened and, almost, well, almost sad. "I am not sure why I am here," he said. "But the fact is that I am here. I do not believe you would try to harm me. And I do believe you are an honest man."

Dad gave Beethoven a weak smile. "I . . . we never meant for any of this to happen. But this is where we are. My concern, right now, is making sure you are healthy. After that, we'll worry about the rest."

"*Ja*. That is a good plan. What do we need to do?"

Dad grabbed his medical bag, opened it, and took out the scanner he had used earlier.

"Well, we've already done some tests. We have your heart rate, and we have a full set of x-rays. So let's start by taking your temperature."

. . . .

I had chewed my nails to the nub by the time Dad finished the last lab. But I shouldn't have worried. Everything came back normal, and over and over, Beethoven assured my dad that he felt fine.

"This is good, *ja?*" he asked, as Dad closed his medical bag.

Dad smiled. "Yes, I believe you are fine. I'll check your heart and your blood oxygen levels again tomorrow, but everything shows you to be as healthy as any normal nineteen-year-old."

Beethoven nodded with a pleased grin, then yawned and stretched like an old tomcat. "You would excuse me, then please? I believe I would like to sleep again."

Dad nodded and smiled. He motioned to me where I had hunkered down at his desk during the last battery of tests.

"Josie, why don't you take *Herr* Beethoven to one of the extra bedrooms on the second floor? It will be much warmer there. His body is still trying to regulate his core temperature, so he's going to sleep a lot for the next few days."

I smiled and gestured for Beethoven to follow me. He looked uncertain, but I figured that just had to do with him being an old-fashioned fellow.

Was he shocked at a single woman offering to take him to his bedroom?

"Come on. It's quite proper, I assure you. I'm only going to show you to your room so you can get some rest."

We climbed the stairs to the second floor, and I led him into one of the bedrooms in the right wing of the house. The room was decorated in period pieces, so I thought he would feel at home. I pointed to the massive armoire.

"There are extra blankets in there. And, through that door is your bathroom."

Beethoven looked confused. "Bath-room?"

"Ahh, the toilet?"

"Ahh, yes. Where the shower bath place is, correct?"

"Yes. That's right. Where the shower bath is. We now call it 'the bathroom' or 'toilet.' "

Beethoven nodded as if he understood. He walked around the room, taking in the full-length mirror and the electric lights.

At that moment, I noticed I felt a little strange. Part of me wanted to take this darling boy in my arms and kiss him. But, at the same time, another part of me felt like a mother putting her sleepy child to bed; all I wanted to do was make sure he was safe and warm.

I paused as Beethoven perched on the edge of the big, canopy bed.

"This place," he said, "and you, are unlike anything I have known."

I turned to him. "What do you mean?"

"You are direct and strong and so very, very beautiful. And this place — I know I have been here in my past, and some things look familiar, but other things are so different from my home and from the Vienna of old."

I felt my face grow warm. "I don't know what to say."

Beethoven patted the edge of the bed. He no longer seemed tired. "Please, sit. Tell me of your life and . . ." He pointed around the room. ". . . your world."

We talked a good while. I told him how we had come to be in Vienna and about my school and a little about Dad's work. I told him about some of the marvelous inventions that had occurred since his days in Vienna, about automobiles and jet planes and ships that took men to the moon.

Beethoven was bug-eyed through much of my talk, but I could see he had decided to believe what I said, and so he asked good questions and expressed an interest in seeing these things for himself.

Eventually, simple biology took over. He began to yawn, and his eyelids grew heavy as sleep overcame him.

"We could talk again tomorrow, if you'd like," I said.

"*Ja*," he said. "That would be nice."

When I returned to the lab, I found Dad at his desk. His face was dark and frightened. He stared intently at a small black rectangle about the size of my iPhone.

"Dad, Beethoven's asleep; he was pretty tired," I said.

Dad nodded absentmindedly. "Fine, thank you, Josie."

"Dad?" I walked to the desk, but he didn't even look up. "Dad?"

"Sorry, I'm a little preoccupied."

I pointed at the box. "What's that? It looks sorta like my phone."

"I'm not sure," Dad said. He pointed to the tall chrome-and-glass shelf behind his desk. "I found this under the bottom shelf. It was taped to the back wall and a USB cable stretched from it to the main Alpha unit."

I picked up the small box and ran my fingers along its edges.

"It's heavy, Dad, but there's no screen or visible power source. There is, however, a USB port and some other type of jack."

I set the box back on Dad's desk.

"Is it like a backup drive?"

"I have no idea, but I've never seen it before in my life," he said. "And that's what worries me."

I sat down in a chair next to his desk. "What do you think it is?"

"I don't know if I'm ready to say yet," he said. "But let's say it makes me suspicious. I need more information. Actually, what I really need is an expert."

Slowly, a smile filled my face. "I think I know a way to help you."

Dad tilted his head. "Yes?"

I nodded. "I think I know someone we can call."

Fa8 answered on the second ring. " 'Ello, 'ello. Why Josie, I see your lovely face on my digital telly. And what does your Fa8 owe the pleasure of this call, my luv? Especially, after you have so obviously been ignoring your dear Fa8 these last few days."

I rolled my eyes. I had to give Fa8 credit — he's consistently a pain in the butt.

"Fa8, I, well, I . . ."

"I do believe the last time we spoke I had been promised a show-ing to see you in your new accoutrements," he said. "Are we still ex-amining dresses?"

"No, silly, that was days ago. The reception is long over and you have seen the dress. I sent you a photo. Remember?"

Fa8 sighed. "Hence your Fa8's disappointment," he said. "I was most certain that I would get the opportunity to witness the new Josie a second time in person, but, alas, it's all no-no-a-go-go for poor Fa8. I must confine myself to a single digital image. Though I must say such a second-hand viewing seems in poor taste to Fa8."

Knowing that Fa8 could go on this merry tear for hours if so al-lowed, I cut it short. I did not need a Fa8 pity-party right now. I have a formerly dead composer sleeping in a guest room at my house and my dad has discovered something sinister in his lab that isn't supposed to be there. The last thing I needed was my best friend whining because he didn't get to see me twirl in a friggin' dress.

"Fa8, stop your whining, and I'll explain. Or I can hang up. It's your choice, but, honestly, I am in need of your help."

Silence. Time for a little reverse psychology and a dose of the of-ten ever-so-effective guilt trip.

"I need you, Fa8, and yet you don't seem to care," I said. "That's fine, really it is. I'm sure that new cello player in orchestra with the major computer skills would be happy to help me in my time of need."

Before I could say another word, Fa8 mounted his metaphorical white horse and began riding to my rescue.

"And what, my luv, is of such concern that it has caused you to cry?" he said. "I shall slay the beast. Perhaps I should contact the Samurai Wannabes and our friends at the Killer Rabbit? We shall all run-run-run to your aid with loins girded and swords drawn."

"No," I said, trying hard to stifle a laugh. "I just need you."

"Well then," Fa8 said. "What can your Fa8 do to help?"

"Dad and I found something in his lab. It's a small black box about the size of an iPhone. I need you to come over and look at it."

Fa8 coughed, like he'd just swallowed a black widow spider.

"Your father, Doctor B., is home? May I assume that he is aware of your contact with me?"

I rolled my eyes. "Yes, Fa8. He is. In fact, he was the one who asked me to call you."

A very long pause. I wasn't sure if Fa8 believed me or had keeled over in shock. Behind me, Dad rolled his eyes and mouthed, "Moron."

"The grand poobah of the ge-ne-ti-cal world has requested my presence? I am honored," Fa8 said, "and I shall rise to the occasion. I shall endeavor to persevere."

"Just get over here quickly," I said. "And bring your laptop."

"Oh my, my, my," Fa8 said. "Sounds like some skullduggery-do is needed. Shall I assume this is an operation that one shouldn't tweet about? You know, keep it off the Internety griddy-grid? No posting of photos on the ole blog?"

"Duh, doofus. That's the last thing I need. Now get your skinny British butt over here and hurry."

I tapped the End button and sat down next to Dad.

"When he gets here, Dad, please try to remember that you are the one who wanted him to come over, okay? Promise me."

Dad looked offended. "I didn't ask you to invite him. I thought he was *your* friend in need. Isn't Fa8 supposed to be the only person at school who understands you, the one ready to help at a moment's notice? So why the lie?"

"No, he *is* the only person who understands me," I said. "Unlike my father. And right now, he's on the way to help. And though Fa8 is his own special kind of weird, I want him to feel extra important.

Besides, he really wants you to like him. So, if he thinks you need his help, he will get over here all the faster, not to mention he'll bring his best game. See?"

Dad just laughed.

I tried not to be offended.

As my dad walked out of the room, I heard him say quietly: "Okay, Josephine, but this has nothing to do with me. For all his silliness, Fa8 is in love with you.

"And he would do anything you asked him to do."

Chapter 31

Triple Concerto

COULD MY FATHER BE MORE wrong? There is no way that Fa8 is in love with me. I refuse to believe that. Nope. Not hardly. I don't think so. Someone is living in an alternate universe, and it's sure not me. My dad might be one of the world's best research scientists, but he knows squat about love.

Fa8 doesn't love me. Fa8 is the one who is always Mr. Johnny-on-the-Spot when a new girl shows up in English. Fa8's the one who is always hooking up with girls at the latest blues bar or writing bad love songs to some leggy blonde fresh off the Paris runway.

In love with me?

I don't think so.

. . . .

Yet whether out of love for me or adoration for my father, Fa8 got there in a hurry. The rumble of his motorcycle announced his arrival. And before I could get to the front door, he was pounding on it. The massive hinges moaned as I let him in.

"There you are."

Fa8 bowed. "Ah, Josie, my luv, you look absolutely smashing. Is that by chance a new shirt?"

"You've seen this before," I said. "The Ramones? Remember? *Rock 'n' Roll High School?*"

"I am aware of the band and its music, but I was unaware until now that the band had launched a clothing line." He pointed to his own pairing of yellow, blue, and green bandannas tied to the upper arm of his plaid lumberjack workshirt. "Perhaps I should obtain a similar shirt. I do believe it would blendy-blend with me yellow sash."

Enough, there was no time for Fa8 to be, well, Fa8. I grabbed him by the arm and pulled him down the hallway.

"We can talk clothes later," I said. "Right now I need you to look at something in my dad's lab. Okay?"

"I am at your service, luv. Show your Fa8 the problem."

Usually, I can't get Fa8 to shut up. The world could be ending, and he'd be rambling on about something and, more often than not, that something would be inappropriate. Don't get me started on the time he wanted to discuss the finer points of girls' panties.

But that evening in Dad's lab, Fa8 was speechless. He stood there rooted inside the lab doorway with huge eyes and an expression of absolute bliss. Finally after, I guess, the shock had worn off, he spoke.

"All this is Doctor B.'s?"

"Yeah, this is it. By the way, he's over there by his desk."

Fa8 grinned. "Didn't get to see all this the night of the rave. Now I know why Chaz was itching to get inside. Never seen such an array of tech-nol-o-gee. And I've owned me share of tech-nol-o-gee."

Dad stepped out from behind the shelf where I could tell he had been studying something.

"Didn't realize you'd never been in here before, Fa8."

" 'Ello Doctor B.," Fa8 said. "Well, let's just say this is me first good look."

"Good to see you again, young man. I appreciate your coming so quickly to help us." Dad threw a glance at me. "We, uh, I am in great need of your expertise."

Fa8 bowed with a flourish; his smiled almost filled the room.

"Most happy to serve, Doctor B."

I pulled two chairs over to Dad's desk and plopped down in one.

"I don't understand the theatrics, Fa8. You've been in here at least once before."

Fa8 shook his head.

"Not really. The night of the rave, I did step in to find you. But in the poor light I didn't have the chance to give the place a good lookie-see-see."

"Well, now you can look all you want. But first, we need you to look at this." Dad rolled his chair over beside Fa8's and handed my pal the small, black box. "Can you tell me what this is and why in the hell it would be in my lab?"

Fa8 turned the box over in his hands for several seconds. Then he put it up to his ear and shook. A few seconds later, his eyes folded into narrow slits and a frown settled on his face.

"Josie, would please you hand me that letter-opener?"

I reached across Dad's desk for a slender opener shaped like a sword. "You mean this?"

"That's it." He placed the black box down on its side, so the small, circular port at the bottom faced up. Holding the box with one hand, Fa8 pushed the letter-opener inside the circle and pushed down. A second later, the side of the box popped off.

"Just what I thought." Fa8 turned the inside of the box to the light until it shone on a small red button. He tapped the button twice. "Now we can talk and we won't be heard."

Dad's face turned pale. He looked like someone had punched him right in the guts.

"What do you mean, 'now we won't be heard'?"

Fa8 sat the box before Dad.

"What you have here is a very sophisticated monitoring device," Fa8 said. "I believe they call them buggie-bugs. This one, however, is a little more powerful. It can transmit sound, video, and data. And it's designed to send to a remote service, then make a backup copy, and log everything it uploads."

Dad picked up the box and looked at it more closely.

"What? What are you talking about?"

Fa8 reached for the box. "May I?"

My dad handed it over to him.

Fa8 held the box up to the light. "Dr. Brunswick, the bottom line is that this is a bug of the highest James Bond order. You're not only being listened to but whatever you do is being recorded, whoever comes in or out of this lab is being monitored, and, it would not surprisey-prise me if you were being watched, too.

"Somewhere, probably miles and miles away from here, possibly in a different country altogether, maybe on a different continent, some computer has a copy of every keystroke that's ever been made and every word that's ever been spoken in this lab."

I felt my stomach turn over.

"But how? When?" I asked.

"I can't answer that question until I know what's been sent." Fa8 turned the box over in his hands. "I shall have to see if I can get our little friend here to tell me its secrets."

Dad dropped his head into his hands. He looked shell-shocked.

"Who would . . .? Why would they . . .?"

I touched his arm. "Dad, you said yourself your research is one of a kind, and that usually means big bucks to come in patents for new medicines or applied applications. And with all the traveling you've done and all the places you've gone, well, there's no telling who has caught wind of what you're trying to do here."

"But how could they get in?" Dad asked. "How did anyone access my lab? I told no one the code to the entrance of the lab."

I felt my face grow hot. "Ahhh, that might be my fault, Dad, re-member, the night of the rave?"

Fa8 shook his head. "I don't think so. If the door was locked when you got down here . . ."

"When I found Chaz, he was standing outside the door and it was closed . . . but later I remember seeing light inside the lab."

"Who is Chaz?" Dad asked.

"He's the son of . . ."

"He's the son of the Canadian prime minister," Fa8 said, interrupt-ing me. "But Chaz is an okay bloke. I don't think he would buggie-bug your lab. And even if he was so inclined, poor Chaz wouldn't have access to this kind of technology. This little buggy-bug is state-of-the-friggin'-art. No, I would bet this little unit has been in place for a while. Was it, by chance, connected to your computer?"

Dad sighed.

"Yes. There was a small clear USB cable that connected it to the Alpha Unit."

"I thought so," Fa8 said.

"So what do we do next?"

"Well, Doctor B., I believe we shall see what secrets this little box holds. Please direct me to a flat area with several electrical-like outlets, and I shall be able to discover more."

Dad gestured for Fa8 to take his place at his desk. I moved stacks of books and files to another table and cleared a large spot where Fa8 could work. Dad found a power strip and plugged it in.

"Okay, Fa8, you now have power and a flat space." I pointed at the door. "I'm going to get us something to drink and something to snack on. I have a feeling we're going to be here for a while."

I was right. It took two six-packs of cola, another bag of chips, and one slightly aged Italian sub (I found it in the back of the refrigerator and had no idea how long it had been there, but Fa8 ate it anyway) before my hacker friend managed to break inside the inner workings of the bug.

" 'Ello, 'ello. What's this, then?" he said. "I do believe we have a pathway."

Fa8 motioned me over to his laptop. With a finger, he pointed to an index of files displayed on the screen.

"This is our friend's most recent index," he said. "After it intercepts a file, it transmits it off-site. This shows the file name, the date it was transmitted, and the time of the transmission."

I scanned the list.

"Why, this shows the last transmission was only a few days ago."

"That's correct, luv. Now my next step is to find where it was transmitted. That should tell us a great deal about the sneaky-Pete-rat-faced types who are stealing Doctor B.'s confidential information."

I set another cola in front of him.

"Keep going," I said. "I have access to plenty more caffeine."

For more than an hour, Fa8 quietly worked. Occasionally, one of his long slender hands would reach out and nab a pop or a handful of chips, but he never said anything and his eyes never left the computer screen. His fingers, however, were in constant movement, scrolling and clicking.

Dad paced back and forth.

I didn't know what was driving me more nuts — Fa8's silence or my dad's pacing. Eventually, Dad broke the quiet.

"I can't believe someone would do this," Dad said, circling the sequencing computers. "I wonder if it was an industrial spy or some foreign agent. I mean, I've been pretty visible lately, ever since that blowup at the Vatican."

"Dad, stop. You're driving me crazy." I pointed to Fa8. "Give him a little time."

Dad stopped and dropped into a chair.

"It's all so overwhelming. I mean, you, Bee . . ."

Silently, I waved my arms. Fa8 didn't know anything about Beethoven and I didn't want to tell him — just yet.

Dad gulped. ". . . ahh, the problem with the replicator, and now this bug."

"It's going to be okay, Dad. We're here, and now we have help. We just need to . . ."

Before I could finish my sentence, Fa8 stopped and stood up so quickly the chair he was sitting in fell over with a loud crash.

"Well if that isn't the most nasty-wasty thing I've ever seen." He pointed at his laptop. "Just who are these blokes? I don't believe I like them very much."

"What do you mean?" My father's voice was all nerves as he asked the question.

Fa8 righted his chair then sat down with a loud thump. He turned to Dad and me, a scowl on his face.

"Doctor B., you don't have any Mafia-type friends do you?"

"What in heaven's name are you talking about?"

Fa8 looked at me and then at Dad. "The Mafia, you know, the gunny-gun boys? Dark suits. Accents. Lots of nasty-wasty types with their il-le-gal-a-tee?"

Dad looked irritated. "No. I'm not involved in the Mafia. Why would you ask me that?"

Fa8 turned his laptop so the screen faced us.

He pointed to an e-mail file.

"This is a file that was sent from someone in the 'security department' at the WGC. It references moving 'a new shipment to Syria and having the payment made to Bank Gutenberg, an offshore account in the Cayman Islands.' It all sounds rather Mafia-like."

Dad rolled his chair next to Fa8's and looked over his shoulder. "We don't have an office in Syria, and I'm pretty sure we don't have an account at Bank Gutenberg. At least, I've never heard of it."

I watched Fa8's fingers dance across the keyboard. A few seconds later, he clicked on another file.

"Well, I hate to differ with you sir, but there are several accounts at this Bank Gutenberg — all private — and, if me zero-counting ability is still good, there is lots and lots of money in them, about three billion Euros."

Dad leaned back in his chair and sighed.

"This can't be happening. Why would that much money be parked in a private, offshore bank?"

Behind me, I heard Fa8 speak.

"Well, well, well, well, well," he said. "We'll just tappy-tap a little bit more and find out."

I sat quietly and closed my eyes.

Something told me things were about to get a lot worse.

Chapter 32

Know Your Enemy

ABOUT TWO HOURS — and seven Coca-Colas later — Fa8 stopped what he was doing and turned and looked at me like he had never seen me before in his life. "Josie, luv," he said quietly. "I need to ask you something. And I need an honest answer."

"Fa8, what's wrong?"

Dad had stretched out on the sofa in his office and slept quietly. I'd stayed awake to help Fa8. But, at this point, I was beginning to second-guess my decision. I had never seen such a weird expression on my friend's face.

Fa8 pointed to the screen and whispered: "I downloaded a huge portion of the WGC's mainframe. And, well, reading these documents, it looks an awful lot like your father is working for some type of nasty-boy crime syndicate."

I wanted to laugh. Really, I did. *My dad a criminal? I don't think so. Goofy? Yes. Weird taste in movies and food? Oh, yeah. But a criminal? Never.*

"Fa8, I don't know what you've found, but I swear to you on my Flying V that my father is not a criminal. He's such a bleeding-heart he could never hurt another person."

The tension on Fa8's face eased for a moment, only to return as he pointed to his computer. "Well then, luv, according to all this, your father is in way over his head and you are both in danger."

I pulled my chair next to Fa8's. "What do you mean danger?"

"All this," Fa8 said. "All this stuff, it's not for the faint of heart."

I took a deep breath. I knew I needed to stay calm. For the past few days, I'd felt like I'd been running away from something. Part of me wanted to bolt and never look back, but the rest of me wanted to understand what was going on . . . if only to save my only remaining parent. Calm Josephine won.

"Okay," I said. "Tell me what you know and start at the beginning."

Fa8 nodded, clicked open a couple of files and folders, and turned the laptop screen towards me.

"Okay, luv, first look at this. This is an e-mail from some bloke named Dieter, who works in security for your World Genetics Whatever. You know, your father's place of work."

"Yeah. Go on."

"Well, this was written right after you and your lovely family came to Vienna. See the date?"

On the screen, dated three months after we'd moved to Vienna, was a short message. It read: "The American and his family are in the villa. Monitoring system in place and active."

I pointed to the small black box next to Fa8's computer.

"Is that what they're talking about?"

Fa8 gave me a weak smile.

"Believe so, luv. Keep reading; there's more." Fa8 clicked on another file; it, too, was written by Dieter: "Dr. Brunswick's system is up. Data feed working in real time, as expected. No complications."

I couldn't believe what I was reading. Since we'd lived in Vienna the WGC had been spying on us. I wanted to scream.

"This is like something from a bad spy movie."

Fa8 put a long arm around my shoulder. "Yeah, but I've now copied their entire server. At least we know what they know."

"We just don't know why." I pointed to another file on the screen, named Syria. "What's that?"

"I don't know," Fa8 said. "I thought we could take a lookie-see-see together on this one — it was protected by some extra special security, so it must be good."

"Click away," I said.

The contents of the file jumped on the screen. It was a spreadsheet filled with a list of cities across the globe. Each city had a ten-digit number next to it. Next to the numbers were lists of names, following each name was another number — an amount listed in Euros.

"It looks like they are recording payments," Fa8 said.

"Did this come off my dad's computer?"

"No luv," Fa8 said. "I found this in a separate file on the WGC server." He pointed to the long code following the name of one city. "I do believe that's a wire transfer code. One of me mates used to work in a bank's I.T. department. He told me stories of all these blokes who would move money all over the world via the old wire transfer routine so they wouldn't have to pay taxes."

"Great." I pointed to the bottom of the page. "Why no total?"

Fa8 chuckled. "This is just the first page, my luv. There are thirty-six more to go."

"You're kidding."

Fa8 put his hand over his heart. "I sweary-swear. The total comes to a little more than eight billion Euros."

"Holy crap! What in the world are they selling?"

Fa8 scrolled back to the top page. "I do believe that little five-digit number there could tell us, if we just knew what to ask it. That's what I've been trying to crack."

"Okay, keep looking," I said, "though I'm not sure I want to know."

"Your instincts are good," said Fa8. "Far as I can tell we have some kind of black-ops thingy going, wouldn't you agree?"

"Yeah. How much more is there?"

Fa8 waved his hands like the conductor of an orchestra.

"Tons, I'm afraid. There are thousands of pages here."

I felt my stomach sour. I did not want to believe this was happening. And there was more. "That could take weeks to comb through."

"Yes, it could, but I intend to ex-pee-dite our little examination. I shall use a piece of software of my own creation — something one of the Samurai Wannabes and I developed. I believe it shall nicely shorten our search. If the kinks have finally been banished."

I was scared to ask how it worked.

Fa8 tapped on a few more keys and then turned towards me.

"Sit back and try to relax. This should only take a few minutes."

I leaned back in the chair and closed my eyes. Everything was crashing in on me. And even though Dad was home, I felt cold and frightened and very, very lost.

By the time Fa8 looked up again, it was late. What was supposed to have taken a few more minutes had turned into more than an hour. While Fa8 hunched over his keyboard, I walked out of the lab and down the hall. The moon sparkled through the big windows. Icicles, glistening like silver daggers, hung from the eves of the roof.

Surrounded by the cold beauty of winter I felt alone and more frightened than I had ever felt, save for the day Mom died. I walked back to the lab: Dad covered the couch like a blanket, while Fa8 slaved over his laptop like a giant colorfully dressed bug. And upstairs, just down the hall from my bedroom, Ludwig von Beethoven slept.

· · · · · · · · · ·

Outside, the keen of the wind was so loud it sounded as if a pack of wolves had circled the villa. I bounced back and forth between trying to help Fa8, checking on Dad, and, once in a while, slipping upstairs to look in on Beethoven.

I was tired and jealous of the men in my life, who either had something worthwhile to do or who at least got to sleep. I dragged Dad's big overstuffed "thinking chair" to an open spot near his desk and poured myself into the soft, leather cushions.

I was just about to drift off when . . .

"Josie, luv, are you awake?"

"I am now."

I opened one eye. Fa8 was standing over me holding several pieces of paper. His face fluctuated between a frown and a nervous smile.

"I do believe I have determined what those nasty-wasty boys and the World Genetical Emporium are up to," he said. "You might want to wake Doctor B. He should probably hear this, too."

"You don't have to," a voice behind me said. "I'm already awake."

· · · · · · · · · ·

"The Sultana Razi? Who is the Sultana Razi?" I scowled, wondering if Fa8 has been staring at his computer screen too long.

Fa8's expression said I had to be the dumbest person on earth.

"For your information, Sultana Razi is a very important woman. You can't click on the old Intery-net, pick up a newspaper, or turn on a cable news show and not see her photo or read a story about her."

"He's right. The WGC has been trying to get her attention for years. She's huge, a major donor to medical and scientific research."

Fa8 spread a handful of pages out on Dad's desk.

"Well, sir, I believe they have succeeded. It took me a while to figure all this out, but I traced this bank account, the one that shows a seven-hundred-thousand-Euro payment to the WGC. And I believe the money came from the sultana."

"I don't ever remember seeing, or hearing about, a donation from her. I was positive that she had never contributed. Like I said, the development guys have been trying to woo her for years."

"Well sir, they have long since con-sum-mated the relationship, be-cause this is the third payment the sultana has made to the WGC in the last two years. And, by the way, they are not donations."

"If it's not a gift, what is it?" Dad asked.

"I'm not sure yet," Fa8 said, "but the memo on the payment says 'medical services,' and then there's this."

He handed me an article from the New York Time's website. The story was about Sultana Razi. It said doctors were struggling to find a donor heart for her and that the sultana had offered to make a mil-lion-Euro gift to any family who could supply her with a genetically matched heart.

"She sounds desperate, but I don't see the connection," Dad said.

"Well, Doctor B. That story was posted about a year and a half ago." Fa8 pointed to the payments listing the sultana. "And if you look here, you'll see she made her first payment to the WGC about three months after that."

"That's not that unusual," Dad said. "Perhaps she wanted a full genetic workup. Those can get very expensive, especially when family history is involved."

"But wouldn't you be aware of something like that?" I asked. "Wouldn't you know if that was being done?"

"Most of the time I would, but not every time. Especially if it was some VIP, like the sultana, who wanted to stay anonymous."

Fa8 laid another piece of paper on the desk.

"This might help."

The paper was a copy of several e-mail messages from the sultana thanking the WGC's medical team for her successful surgery.

"Now that is unusual," Dad said. "As chief scientist and medical officer I should have been included in that."

Fa8 leaned back and stretched. "Doctor B., they didn't want you to know for a reason. Read this . . ."

And Fa8 handed Dad several more sheets of paper.

I watched Dad's face turn gray as he scanned the pages.

"Oh, my God," he said. "It can't be."

"I'm afraid it is, sir. I couldn't believe it me-self at first, so I didn't say anything until I could find plenty of collaboration. And find it I did. I am afraid it's the truth."

"What is so awful?" I asked.

Dad handed me the papers. He looked like he had killed a man.

"This cannot be happening."

It took me a few minutes to read everything. There were several pages of e-mails, a list of files, and page after page of shipping invoices, copies of wire transfers, inventories of medical supplies, and receipts for organ bank donations.

"I'm confused," I said. "I thought organ donations were free."

"They are," Dad said quietly. "Except, it would appear, at the WGC."

Dad pointed to the pages in my hands. "When you put together all the documents Fa8 has found, it shows that the WGC has, for the past several years, been selling human organs to the highest bidder. The person with the winning bid — such as our friend the sultana — purchases the organ and the operation is then 'donated.' "

"The WGC is auctioning off organs to the highest bidder?" I felt like I was going to puke. "That can't be right."

I grabbed the papers again and, slowly, read each line.

"But that's so wrong . . . so immoral. Isn't it also illegal?"

Dad covered his face with his hands.

"That's not the worst part. Look at the last page. In the case of the sultana's heart, it shows the WGC made 'payments' to orphanages in Iraq, Lebanon, and Syria. The orphanages supplied the children —

for a price — and those children were the organ donors."

I closed my eyes. I didn't want to even imagine how an orphan could be sold off to become an organ donor.

"You mean they are taking these children and . . . ?"

"Yes, the WGC is buying orphans, killing them, and harvesting their organs." Dad waved a printout of one of the invoices in front of my face. "Their organs are listed here, just like machine parts. A nine-year-old male lung, a sixteen-year-old female pair of kidneys, oh my God, this is a nightmare."

"No, it can't be," I said. "Are you sure you're reading that right?"

"Josie, luv, your father is reading it exactly right."

"But . . ."

"It's like this, luv, your father is the chief medical officer for a global group that buys children, kills them, cuts them up, and sells their insides to the highest bidder."

"But I don't understand why," I all but cried.

"They had been pushing me to perfect the replication of organs," my dad said. "That was what my research was originally focused on. We would recruit donors to obtain the best possible DNA and sample it. Then we would replicate healthy organs that could be used to re-place diseased ones."

"That doesn't sound much better." I spun around and faced Dad. "And you were helping find innocent boys and girls to do this, Dad? I thought you said you didn't know anything about this."

Dad slumped over his chair.

"I didn't know. I swear, I didn't," he said.

He could see the skepticism on my face, and he rushed to explain.

"I was working to perfect organ replication. That's how this . . ." he pointed around the room. "That's how all this came about, but my work was solely focused on replicating healthy organs. You have to believe that. I knew nothing about the children."

Anger surged through me. Part of me wanted to comfort Dad and the other part wanted to slap him for being so naive.

"Then how come they're not replicating organs?" I asked. "I thought this damned machine was such cutting-edge technology."

When my dad finally spoke, it was quietly, in almost a whisper: "Josie, honey, I was trying to make everything perfect. I thought if we had a huge database of DNA, organ replication would become commonplace. It would completely change medicine — not to mention people's lives."

He reached for me. I pulled back. I didn't want him to touch me.

"You have to understand, Josie, I was trying to help. I knew nothing about any of this other business."

"Then how did it happen, Dad? When did the WGC start selling little kids?"

"I don't know. We had some successful trial runs with replicated organs. Everything seemed okay, but there was a huge amount of pressure to do more. Then the Canadians began questioning our AIDS treatment. The pressure became overwhelming."

Fa8 stepped towards me and gave a nod in my father's direction.

"Josie luv, don't be so hard on him. I do believe he is telling you the truth."

Fa8 turned his laptop to show me.

"Look at this. It's a memo from the WGC's security guru, and he talks about your father being 'too soft' and how he would 'never accept the idea of the Syrian project.' I believe they knew your father would freak out so they simply didn't tell him. Besides, if you look here . . ."

Fate pointed to a date on an invoice. "This shows they were making donations to orphanages three years before your father ever went to work for them."

"Please honey, you have to believe me. I would never do anything like that," my dad said.

"You've said that before. Remember? And then I watched something come out of that replicator right over there."

Fa8 looked at me, confusion on his face.

"I don't believe I follow you, luv."

I scowled. I still wanted to hit Dad, but part of me also wanted to believe him.

"I said, that something came out of . . ."

Dad stepped between Fa8 and me and pointed to the hallway.

"Frederick, err, Fa8. I haven't been totally honest with you either."

Fa8's eyes grew huge. He pulled himself back as if he was worried what my dad would say next.

"You, you don't have any orphans here, do you, Doctor B.?"

"No, son, I don't. But, well, there is someone you should meet. He is deeply involved in all this and, well, since you've put yourself in danger on my behalf. I feel you should know the whole truth of what we're dealing with here."

Fa8 turned to me.

"Josie, luv. Is your father feeling okay? Might he be in need of medical assistance?"

"No," I said. "I believe he's trying to do the right thing. Just listen to what he has to say."

Dad walked Fa8 over to the replicator in the center of his lab.

"That machine, there, is capable of replicating — cloning, if you will — a human being, a living, breathing, human being. It only takes about nine weeks, and, if it's done properly, it will create an exact replica, down to the same memories, emotions, and feelings of the person up to the moment the DNA sample was taken."

Dad paused then mouthed each word slowly: "An exact replica."

"So you're telling me, you can make another person from a little bit of this DNA-genetical-stuffy-stuff?"

I had never before seen the look I was seeing now on Fa8's face.

"Yes, son, it sounds like you are familiar with the technology. You know how powerful it can be — scientists have successfully cloned sheep, carp, goats, and horses, among other creatures. It was only a matter of time, really, until a person was cloned, and, yes, it has now been done successfully. I have done it successfully."

"Well, there's something a bloke doesn't hear every day," Fa8 said. "Am I right to assume that this successful cloning was done here? And if so, might I get the opportunity to met this artificially created man-and-or-woman-type-person?"

Dad smiled. I could see he was impressed with how well Fa8 was taking the news.

"I think that can be arranged."

Dad pointed to the doorway.

"In fact, he's standing right behind you."

Chapter 33

Exile

MY FRIEND JUMPED OUT OF his chair like he had been shocked with a cattle prod. I couldn't remember when I had ever seen Fa8 move so quickly. Like my dad, I had been amazed at how calmly he had taken the news of human cloning . . . in this very lab. But knowing Fa8 as I did, I just wrote it off as typical for a guy who lived on the edge of all things technological.

This freaked-out Fa8 was much more what I had expected.

"What! What? Doctor B., you're kidding me, right? Trying to get even with good ole Fa8, are ya?"

Dad walked over to Beethoven, who gave a little bow.

"Good evening," he said to Fa8. "I am Ludwig von Beethoven."

Fa8's eyes bulged. Dad stepped in to save the moment.

"Fredrick Bartholomew Rosenguild, I would like to introduce you to Ludwig von Beethoven, late of nineteenth-century Vienna; composer extraordinaire; musician to kings and emperors; and, as of three days ago, now enjoying his second life."

Beethoven bowed again, though the U.T. sweatshirt and jeans did undermine the gesture a bit.

"It is a pleasure to meet you, sir," Beethoven said.

And for the first time since I've known him, Fa8 said nothing. He just stood looking at Beethoven as if he were from another planet.

"Righhhht," Fa8 said. "Am I supposed to believe that you are not an attempt by Doctor B. to punish me for some past indiscretion, possibly a recent rave that went bad? That you are *the* Ludwig von Beethoven? Mister Ode to Joy-Joy? The *Für Elise* boy and master of all that Moonlight work. That Beethoven?"

Beethoven scrunched his nose uncertainly.

"I'm am not sure about these other people and things you mention, but I am Ludwig von Beethoven, *the* Ludwig von Beethoven."

Fa8 dropped into the nearest chair. He ran his fingers through his hair, then turned to Dad.

"So, Doctor B., you would have me believe that this bloke, right here, in this room, this is old Beethoven, himself? Brought back to life by your genetical-computer gadget and birthed in that rather large aluminum cigar case?"

"I know it's hard to believe. But, yes, the young man standing here before you is Beethoven." Dad pointed to the replicator. "And that 'cigar case' is about seventy million Euros' worth of technology, just in case you're wondering."

Fa8 then proceeded to face me. "And you think he's Beethoven?"

"Yes. You have to trust me. I don't just believe it, I *know* he's Beethoven."

"And just how do you know this?" Fa8 asked. "What makes you so sure? Did you ask his mum and dad? Have him play a quick piece on the ole piano?"

I leaned down until my nose was just inches from Fa8's.

"I was there when he was born," I said. "I watched him crawl out of the cigar case, ahhhh, the replicator. And I believe he is who he says he is. He has no reason to lie."

Fa8 looked at me, then Dad, then turned and eyeballed Beethoven. Finally, after what seemed an eternity, Fa8 turned to Dad.

"I have just one question," he said. "Could you bring back Elvis, Ritchie Valens, and Buddy Holly, too? With those three blokes I would have the world's greatest rock band."

Okay, even Dad laughed. For a brief moment, Fa8's little joke broke the tension and reminded me why I couldn't help but adore him despite his eccentric ways.

Dad motioned to Beethoven to follow him.

"Think I'll introduce *Herr* Beethoven to the modern coffeemaker," he said. "Nothing quite like grinding a few beans to calm one's nerves."

"I have always appreciated a good cup of coffee," Beethoven said.

With that, I watched two of the three men in my life walk out of the lab, which left me free to do something I really needed to do.

"Ouch!" Fa8 rubbed his upper arm, where I had just slugged him. "Buddy Holly? Really, Fa8?"

Fa8 flashed a toothy grin then sat back in his chair.

"Well, luv, I just thought since ol' Beethoven is here anyway, while I'd prefer to play, I could be talked into managing a band like . . ."

I started to say something snarky, but before I could open my mouth Fa8's laptop started banging and burping like it was going to explode before our very eyes.

"What's going on, Fa8?" I hollered.

Fa8 whirled his chair around and flipped open his laptop.

"Just a minute, luv," he said, staring intently at the screen. "I do believe someone — or something — has set off me alarm. I shall have to continue our confabie-fab in a minute."

Thirty minutes later, his face ashen, Fa8 spoke.

"Josie, luv, go find your father and our late composer friend and hurry back here posthaste, pronto-tonto. I do believe we need to speak with them immediately."

"What's wrong? You look like you just lost your last friend."

"Please, just go get your father and *Herr* Beethoven, now hurry."

"Okay, okay."

I ran down the hall. Our little light exchange was already history.

By the time I returned with Dad and Beethoven, Fa8 was pacing the floor, his face still wearing the same pained look.

"There you are. I do believe we have a problem. A serious, serious problem," Fa8 said.

"It wouldn't be the first time," my dad said. "I must say that problems have become our daily fare around here. What is it now? Has the WGC declared war on the Vatican? Or Canada, perhaps?"

"I believe that would be easier, sir." Fa8 pointed to the screen. "Whilst I was rummaging through the WGC's files I uploaded a few choice pieces of spyware. I thought it would help keep an eye on these global meanies."

One glance at my dad, and I could tell he wasn't happy about Fa8's computer tampering.

"Why would you do that?" Dad said. "We're already in deep trouble and now, you could have made it even worse."

Fa8 stopped his pacing and looked Dad square in the eye.

"Doctor B., with all due regard, I do believe we are a little beyond that. I do realize you might think I'm just some weird nerdy-nerd who likes strange clothes and is smitten with your daughter. But there's a little more to me than that. Maybe I did not earlier make myself clear as to the danger-danger you and yours are now involved in."

Dad wasn't used to being challenged, and he didn't seem to know which accusation to address first.

"Well, I never said . . . didn't mean, what I meant, was, well . . ."

Fa8 waved him off.

"I don't believe you, sir. But that's all righty-right. Because I just might be all those things you think." Fa8 glanced at me then turned back to my father. "And, yes, I am quite taken with Josie, but right now I believe we have more pressing matters. Along with me modest guitar skills I am known to do a little hackery and writing code and all such computer nonsense. Some might even say, my mathematical skills rival your own."

Now my dad looked positively surly. "Well, I don't know about that, young man, but I would hazard to say that you will find . . ."

Fa8 interrupted.

"The point is, Doctor B., I've got this." Fa8 pointed to his laptop. "And the little piece of software I left for your WGC friends will not only inform us of any of their future activities, but, as I suspected, act as a warning if they should be lurking out there in cyberspace."

Now Fa8 had his attention.

"What do you mean, a warning?" Dad asked.

Fa8 ran his fingers through his hair.

"They are hunting you, sir." Fa8 said. "Just like a little kitty cat does a mouse. That noise Josie heard was me laptop's alarm sounding. I have intercepted several e-mails between our friends in WGC security and someone simply called 'Hans.' "

"*Herr* Gottlieb," he said quietly. "The WGC's founder."

"If you say so," Fa8 said. "The message doesn't list a last name. But whoever this Hans person is, he knows that an err, human, has been created by your aluminum machine. And he is returning to Vienna to personally oversee the 'collection and analysis of the specimen.' "

Dad pointed at Beethoven. "He's coming here? To get *Herr* Beethoven? The last I heard, Hans was in Turkey, something about a meeting with the ambassador."

"I do believe you are correct as to his whereabouts. But our *Herr* Hans has cut that meeting short and now, according to his previously encrypted e-mail — which I was able to peeky-peek into — he is sending the WGC security team here to extract *Herr* Beethoven."

Dad's face turned bright red.

"Security team? What the hell?" Dad drove his right fist into the palm of his left hand. "Why of all the lowdown, cheap tricks, I can't believe they would stoop to —"

"There's a little bit more," Fa8 whispered.

"What do you mean?"

"Well, sir, the WGC security boys aren't only coming for *Herr* Beethoven. They want you and Josie, too."

"What? What do they want with us?"

Fa8 took a deep breath. "I believe they discovered that our Josie was the one who started the, err, 'successful replication.' At least that's what they called it."

"That makes sense. They knew I was out of the country. She would be the only one who knew the process and who the computer would respond to." Dad pointed to Beethoven. "Do they know who he is?"

"No," Fa8 said. "They know a male human was replicated. And they have an estimate of his age, but they don't know where the DNA came from. At least that's what our friend Hans said in his e-mail."

Dad was angry and going all Alpha male.

"Well, I'll just have to explain to them that neither Josephine nor *Herr* Beethoven is going anywhere. The WGC and *Herr* Hans will just have to get over it."

"I don't think that will work sir," Fa8 said. "You see, I don't believe they are coming here to do any talking."

"What do you mean?"

"Well, Doctor B. The team has been ordered to 'take possession' of *Herr* Beethoven and then 'eliminate' you and your daughter."

"What did you say?" Dad looked as if he'd seen a ghost.

Fa8 grabbed his laptop and pushed it into Dad's face.

"It's all right-y here," he said, the crack in his accent betraying his fear. "They have been ordered to kidnap Beethoven and then kill you and Josie."

"Are you kidding me! Kill us? Someone is being sent to assassinate me and my dad?"

Fa8's head bobbed up and down.

"Yes, luv, the exact wording was 'eliminate Brunswick and the girl, then return to the safe house in Stuttgart.'"

"This is insane," my dad said. "This can't be happening."

With that, Beethoven walked to the center of the lab.

"*Herr* Brunswick, I believe we must accept the facts," he said. "I do not believe Mr. Fa8 is trying to be humorous."

"You are most correct, Louie. And there is very little about this that is funny."

"Then we must act and quickly," Beethoven said, "To arms."

Fa8 smiled.

"I think Beethoven has it right," he said, "especially about the quickly, because according to this, the WGC boys will be making us a little visit in less than three days' time."

Chapter 34

That'll Be the Day

FOR THE THIRD TIME in my life, the world turned upside down. Dad went from Alpha Male to panic-mode in a matter of seconds, and Beethoven ran through the villa looking for weapons so we could "smash the imperial dogs who would do us harm." (He couldn't understand why so many of our spears and swords were hanging on the walls with the tapestries; I didn't have time to explain.)

I fought the alternating desire to either throw up or curl into the fetal position on my dad's couch.

Fa8, of all people, remained calm — weirdly, strangely calm.

I hadn't noticed this, being busy having a personal meltdown, until I happened onto him and Beethoven in the hall. Fa8 was trying to talk Beethoven out of a pitchfork.

"Really, I don't think you want to be running across the grounds with that," Fa8 said.

Beethoven scowled. "But we must defend ourselves. These men, they will be here soon, sooner than we think."

"True, but I don't think a supposed-to-be-long-dead composer waving a rusty pitchfork is going to stop the boys from Vienna."

"They have not met Ludwig von Beethoven," he said, waving the pitchfork about like a martial artist would a kali stick. "I have been given a second life. It is hard to fight a man who has already been dead."

Fa8 couldn't help but smile. "You could be right there, Louie, but, I suspect these blokes will have guns. Your pitchfork would be like bringing a knife to a gunfight — destined to end badly."

"Then we will fight them with our fists," Beethoven said.

I touched Beethoven's arm and quietly shook my head.

Slowly he lowered the pitchfork.

"No, we need to outsmart them. I'm afraid Fa8 is right; a pitchfork won't do the job. We need a plan."

"I agree," Dad said, stepping into the room. He tapped the screen of his phone, making a call. "I'm working on it right now."

· · · · · · · · · ·

"What do you mean, leave? Leave and go exactly where?"

Dad gave me his I-Am-Your-Father look. For the past three minutes he had been on the phone deep in conversation with someone — someone whose name he wouldn't say — about me and Beethoven.

"Why won't you answer the question?" I asked.

"It wasn't much of a question, dear," Dad said. "It was more of a snarky comment. I'm trying to keep you safe despite the situation in which we find ourselves. But your attitude isn't helping."

I took a deep breath. "Sorry. Everything is happening so quickly."

I flinched as Fa8 touched my shoulder. "Josie, luv, perhaps if you gave your father a chance to explain."

"Thank you, Fa8." With that my dad proceeded to give me a big wink and commenced to talk in a dialect unique to one whiny British wanker. "Josie, luv, I shall endeavor to explainy-splain me thoughts right now."

I rolled my eyes.

"Okay, okay. I give. No more questions. So what's the plan?" (Dad and Fa8 were kind enough not to mention that that was a question.)

Dad put his phone away. "I want you and Beethoven to go to London. I have friends there. They can keep you safe."

Beethoven looked like he understood my dad's reasoning, but he wasn't sold on the idea.

"Leave Vienna? But this is my home," Beethoven said. "Vienna and Austria, why, they are all I have ever known."

Dad nodded and his features softened with sympathy.

"I realize that, son. But right now, the biggest danger is here in Vienna, and for your own safety, and that of my daughter, we have to get you both as far away from here as possible and among those who can protect you." Dad pointed in the direction of his lab. "All of this right now is about my research, my work. But it could quickly become about you, if the bad guys find out who you are and how you came to be here."

I stepped in front of Dad. "What about you? Are you coming?"

"Not at first," Dad said. "I want to get you two out of the country right now. Then I'll join you."

"No, I won't go without you!"

Dad's face turned bright red. "Josephine! Do not argue with me. You're going. You're going to take Beethoven and you're going to get out of here. These people want to kill you . . . and Beethoven. I'm not going to let that happen on my watch. It's my job to keep you safe. I lost your mother . . . I won't lose you, too."

Big, round tears rolled down my cheeks.

"But Dad, I don't want to leave you. You're all the family I have."

"It's only temporary. I'll be fine, but we have to move now. I talked to Telluride. You remember Telluride, don't you?"

"He's the newspaper guy, right?"

"Correct. He's in London. Tel and I have been friends for years, even before I married your mom. He has all sorts of connections with British security. If I can get you and Beethoven to London, he can keep you both safe."

"But Dad, he's a reporter. What if he writes about Beethoven?"

"Tel is my friend first, Josie. He's my Fa8, the one person who would do anything for me."

Fa8 grinned. "Well, he sounds like a good bloke to me. Let's pack our undies and go meet mister newspaper man."

. . . .

There was no way to pack up six years' worth of living, all my music, Mom's massive Steinway, and all Dad's research from his lab in a day or two. The very thought was overwhelming. To make matters worse, even if we could get it all packed, I had no idea where it would be going — since I didn't know where we were going to end up. Dad wanted us to go to London, but given that both planes and trains were off the table, it looked like London would have to be by way of Germany and France. That, of course, depended on our being able to get out of Vienna and across the Austrian border.

"Dad, all this is going to cost money, and I don't have much and what I have isn't in ready cash. We know Beethoven is broke, because, well, he literally came into this world naked. And, believe me, Fa8 lives on the edge."

"I like to think of me-self as frugal," Fa8 said.

"Josephine. I have this covered." Dad reached inside a file cabinet and pulled out a small safe. "When you travel as much as I do you learn things." He took out a large, yellow envelope. "Your passport and identification are all here."

"But what about Beethoven and Fa8?"

"I have a passport at the ready," Fa8 said. "And I know where we can get papers for Beethoven, if you don't ask too many questions."

I could tell my face must have a stunned look on it, because Fa8 couldn't resist a smirk.

"Anyway, Dad, we'll still need money and if the WGC isn't going to trace it, it's going to have to be in cash. I watched those James Bond movies. With its global connections and high-tech lackies, it won't take long before the WGC starts making things difficult for us."

"Oh, they will," Dad said. "In fact, I'm counting on it."

"Huh? I don't follow you."

Dad reached inside the safe and pull out several bundles of bills.

"I have currency from countries around the globe," he said, "but since we're only going from Europe to Britain or the United States via Britain, most of it won't be necessary."

Dad placed a large stack of Euros in front of me. He set a second stack in front of Fa8 and a third in front of Beethoven. "Each of you now has ten thousand Euros— more than eleven thousand U.S. each."

Fa8's eyes bulged. "That's a fair amount of traveling money, Doctor B. Quite a helluva lot of cash-ola."

"Yes, it is Frederick, but you have to understand the WGC is a powerful entity in Europe and especially here in Vienna. Josie is right;

it would be far too easy for the WGC to convince the authorities to track credit-card purchases and the like, in hopes of locating you. You have to go off the grid. And that means cash . . . and a lot of it."

"*Herr* Doctor, I do not believe I have ever seen so much money," Beethoven said. "At least not in my first life."

Dad sat down by the young composer. "I am afraid, my friend, that you will see many things you've never seen before in the hours and days to come. The world, as you knew it, is no more. The Vienna of your previous life is no more. Few things from your past remain as they were."

Beethoven lowered his head and stared at the floor for several moments, then he looked up at Dad and spoke.

"This does not surprise me. After seeing how Villa Theresa has changed, I knew the world of my first life was gone. But I take solace in the fact that I have been given another life."

Beethoven stood and shook his long hair back, like a lion shaking its mane. He looked magnificent. He slowly looked each of us in the eyes, before settling a direct gaze upon my father.

"No one, in all of history has been given the chance I have been given. I intend to make the most of it," Beethoven said. "But for now, my first duty is to those who have brought me this far safely: you, your lovely daughter, and her helpful friend, *Herr* Fa8. They will not be harmed by those security men you say are coming for them. I, Ludwig von Beethoven, will make sure of that."

Fa8 walked over and threw an arm around Beethoven's shoulders.

"I'm with our composer friend, here, Doctor B. Those ge-ne-ti-cal blokes, well, they can kiss me arse if they think I'll let them harm ole Louie here or the lovely Josie."

Dad smiled — a huge, toothy smile.

"I knew I could count on the both of you," he said, putting his own arms around Beethoven and then Fa8. "There is far more at stake than just my work. This is a fight for humanity, science, and . . ."

"And music," I said. "And we don't have much time. Let's rock."

Part V: The Underground

Chapter 35

Don't Let the Sun Go Down on Me

I PACKED AS QUICKLY as I could, filling two suitcases and several plastic tubs with clothes. It took two more tubs to handle my CDs, laptop, and books. I took my guitar, too. I wasn't leaving anything that was once owned by Jimi Hendrix to a bunch of weirdos with guns.

Dad packed a duffle with clothes and things for Beethoven. Fa8 said he would wait until nightfall, then slip home and pack.

"Frederick, you don't have to do this," my dad said. "All this, my work and what I've done, could put you in great danger. I don't think your parents would understand."

"It's okay, Doctor B." Fa8 folded up his laptop and took a sip of flat soda. "I haven't seen me mum in years. She lit out right after I was born. For years, it was just me and Pop. He worked in the Liverpool shipyards. One day he and a two other blokes went in together on a lottery ticket. And, well, believe it or not they won. After that, Pop and I and were set up right nicely: new digs, new car, you know, the whole thingy-thing-thing. Then about six months later, one of the other blokes up and died and left Pop his share of the money, too. Now we had a true fortune."

Fa8's eyes turned watery. For a moment I thought he was crying, but he was standing in the window and I couldn't tell for sure because of the backlight.

"Ol' Pop, well, the extra zeroes changed him. I guess too much money does something to a person. He stopped talking and going round to his favorite pub. He up and sold our flat, moved to the country and assumed the life of a country gentleman."

"That doesn't sound so bad," I said.

"I guess not," Fa8 said. "But he wasn't the same Pop anymore. He became consumed with owning things and comparing it to what others had. He quit talking to any of his old mates . . . and to me. Set me up with a big trust fund, then sent me out into the world. All but locked the door behind me."

"I'm sorry, son," Dad said.

"Pop died about six years ago. Last couple of years I've been on me own, really on me own. The whole estate is tied up in court — all those legal types fighting over crumbs — so I've lived on the interest from me trust fund and hoped things would get better."

I felt a little piece of my heart break. Fa8 had never told me of his father's death, but it explained why he always seemed to understand me when no one else did after Mom died.

"I didn't. . . . You didn't. . . . How come you never told me your father died, Fa8?" I asked.

"It wasn't that important, luv," he said. "You had other problems, and I, well, I don't do that sad lonely boy thing very well."

"But I could have . . ."

"Josie, luv, it's all right. I'm still standing and I'm making me own way. I've me music, a few good friends, and, if I say so myself, me hacking skills have come in rather handy. Wouldn't you agree?"

"Yes, they have. You are quite right." I kissed him on the cheek. "That's for all your help and for being my friend."

Fa8 touched his cheek and smiled. "Now, if you'll excuse me, luv, I must depart to pack and to secure a passport for Louie. Don't wait up. It could be several hours before my return. Lots to do, you know."

By the time Fa8 returned it was well after one in the morning, and I had actually slept for a few hours; Beethoven was still crashed on the couch. Dad had never gone to bed.

Fa8 arrived in a beat-up Volkswagen van that looked as if it had been parked on the bottom of the sea for the past decade. Dull, rust-colored brown with several dents and a broken taillight, its doors were sprayed different colors, and near the back someone had painted "The Clash" in a spidery scrawl.

"This looks like a piece of crap-on-wheels," I said. "It's the ugliest thing I've ever seen."

"I thought we needed something less conspicuous," Fa8 said. "Besides, The Clash is one of me favorite groups."

"It's perfect," Dad said, nodding. "Absolutely perfect."

"You're kidding, right? You're going to send me off to who-knows-where in that?"

Dad pointed out the window at the crap under discussion.

"That van," he said, "will allow you to hide in plain sight."

"Whatever do you mean, Dad?"

"Josephine, really, you should read Sherlock Holmes. I think you'd enjoy it."

"Dad, you're not making any sense. What the heck does Sherlock Holmes have to do with Fa8's crappy old van?"

"Josie, for a smart girl, you are so blind. In the story *The Adventure of the Naval Treaty*, a document is stolen and hidden by the thief in the last place one would think to look. It takes Holmes and Watson the whole story to discover the document is hidden in plain sight. Fa8's van, as ugly as it is, will allow you all to move about in plain sight and not be suspected."

"But wouldn't we be much safer in your Jag, Dad? I'm thinking this van has never known the words 'air bags.'"

"Yes, probably so," Dad said, "and you'd probably be warmer, too. And at any other time, I'd probably ban you from such a ride, but today is not any day. Today, any cop within a ten-mile radius would have you out of my Jaguar and in cuffs before you reached the end of the drive."

Dad pointed to the boxes piled in his lab.

"There's also no place in the Jag for all your stuff. Would you like to leave your Flying V behind?"

Okay, that changed things. I wasn't going anywhere without my guitar.

"Now I understand."

"Good," Dad said, "because we need to get started."

Beethoven grabbed a box. "We should move these things, *ja?*"

Fa8 picked up a blue plastic tub, this one filled with some of my clothes and a small mountain of vinyl and old photo albums.

"That's correct, Louie. Follow me."

Fa8, who at times can be so much socially smarter than he lets on, had cleaned out the back cargo area of the van; he had also brought plenty of ropes and bungee cords, some packing tape, and a few blankets and a tarp. I noticed he had brought his guitar, too, a beautiful dark-hued Fender. There was also a small box filled with his laptop, USB cords, some computer stuff, and one other bag.

"Those are me clothes, luv," he said, when I asked him about the tiny canvas tote. "A few jeans, favorite concert tee shirts, and me unmentionables."

"But we could be on the run for a while. You sure that's enough?"

Fa8 laughed and put his arm around me.

"Josie, I am a little inclined to believe that you have never spent any time at a public laun-dro-mat," he said. "Perhaps, later, we could meet up at one."

I'm running for my life and Fa8's talking laundry.

. . . .

The van was packed. Everything that I valued, including the two strange men I would be riding with, were ready to leave. A bitter north wind had begun to blow, pelting sleet and making me, for some reason, more frightened than I already was. I looked at Dad. He was trying to smile and be strong, but his face betrayed him.

"I don't want to leave you," I said, fighting back the tears. "I feel like I just got you back."

"I know, sweetie, but you can't stay here. Not with what I think is going to go down. These people will spare no expense; they will stop at nothing. I want you far away before they realize you're gone."

"But what will you do? Fa8 says they want to hurt you, too."

"I have a plan," Dad said. "I have more friends than you know. Many more. Smart friends in strategic places. Things are already being put in motion."

"But Dad, what about our stuff? Your research? Mom's Steinway?"

Dad waved me off.

"That can all be replaced. You, cannot. It will all be okay, Josie. You have to trust me. I'm not just going to sit here with a pitchfork — no offense, Louie."

Okay, that did make me chuckle. I glanced over at Beethoven. It was hard to tell but in the dark, I thought I saw him grin.

"Josie, luv, we need to go. This weather is getting worse, and traveling whilst it is dark would benefit us greatly," Fa8 said.

I crawled inside the van and slid the door closed behind me. The van shuddered. I was sure it was going to collapse.

"At least it's warm," I said. "I'm just scared. I'm sorry."

In the dark, Beethoven place a comforting hand on my shoulder.

"Josephine. I make few promises, but you must believe me when I say that I will do everything in my power to protect you and Mister Fa8 from these rascals. *Ja?* You will see. I know many places in Vienna. Many places few would think to go. You will see."

"But this isn't the same Vienna, remember? You're working off memories from two-hundred-odd years ago."

"We Europeans hold onto our past, we do not chase the modern or readily give up the old. Granted some things have changed but not all things. You must trust me," Beethoven said.

With that, Fa8 slid in the driver's seat, shut the door, and started the motor.

"Actually, Josie, luv, you would be surprised how little some places in Vienna have changed," Fa8 said.

With that, Fa8 shoved the van in gear and headed out the gate.

I looked back out my window and watched Dad until the darkness covered him like a black shroud.

Chapter 36

Time for Me to Fly

THE FLAT WAS dirty and cold. After living in one of Vienna's largest villas the last few years, I had grown accustomed to more space than a girl should ever need. I was ashamed to admit it even to myself, but it made me anxious to think about staying in such a tiny place, with stains on the walls, no carpet, and insects scuttling across the wood floor.

Of course, I didn't say anything. We'd driven for hours, wandering the streets of old Vienna trying to find this particular place. It was Fa8's idea, and, though it made my skin crawl, I had to admit, it was a pretty good one.

"I know it's not really your kind of place, luv," he said. "But we know that the police are on the lookie-see for us, and I have no desire to end up in jail after I told your father I would protect you."

"I understand, but isn't there anyplace else we could go?"

"Not at the moment. This is actually one of me friend's flats," Fa8 said. "And while it's not much to look at, there are two rooms, heat, and our own loo. Pretty luxurious for two blokes and a girl on the run. I figured Louie and I can share one room whilst you occupy the other."

Fa8 pointed down a dark hallway, where I was sure a large, girl-eating insect awaited my arrival.

"I guess you're right, Fa8; goodness knows I don't have that much on-the-run experience."

I ran a finger across the wall; it left a trail in the dust. "You sure this place is safe, Fa8? It kinda looks like a dive."

"Yes, it's a dive and yes, I believe it to be a safe dive. It's quite out of the way, and downstairs, a nice Chinese chap runs a rather good resty-raunt. We are also within walking distance of several of Vienna's better beer gardens."

"This will be fine," Beethoven said. "I would like some beer."

I shook my finger at the both of them.

"Oh, I bet you two would, but we're not here on a pub-crawl. We're trying to avoid some nasty people who want to kill us. Remember?"

"True, true," Fa8 said. "But I don't believe those nasty WGC boys will be waiting at The Tombs, do you? Not quite their scene."

Located underground near St. Michael's, The Tombs was a kind of music mecca. Any musician of any note who has ever toured Vienna has played at The Tombs. A few years back, when I was fourteen, Fa8 snuck me inside for a late birthday present. That night, X-Japan dropped by for a few cold ones and a jam session.

"Didn't realize we were so close," I said.

Fa8 pointed out the soot-stained window.

"Right across the street, luv. That's why me mates like the address."

Across the room, Beethoven shuddered. "I am not sure that I want to go back to the tomb," he said. "I have already been there. Granted my memories of it are dim, but I have no desire to return."

Fa8 slapped Beethoven on the back. "Louie, old boy, it's not that kind of tomb. It's a pub, a pub with music that will make you want to trade your piano in for an instrument with strings. I should think a chap, such as yourself, would appreciate good music. Am I right?"

Beethoven smiled like a child who's been promised a trip to the candy shop. "It's been a very long time since I have heard live music."

"Exactly two hundred and forty-seven years," I said, with a grin.

. . . .

We slept through most of the day — spent, I'm sure, from the adrenaline surge that had carried us through our escape. I sent Dad an encrypted e-mail via Fa8's computer saying we were okay and lying low. He messaged back: Calm here; contacted by Igor; he asked about you several times; told him you were in Japan with friends. Not sure he believed me but didn't want him to suspect we knew their plans.

I replied with three words: I love you.

By six that evening I was starving and pretty sure Fa8 and Beethoven would be hungry when they woke, so while they slept I crept down the stairs and visited the little café in the lobby. It wasn't much more than a get-it-to-go place, but the little Chinese man seemed friendly enough. He filled my order silently, handed the bags to the boy at the register, and turned back to watch his TV show.

"You want more egg rolls?" the boy — he looked to be about my age — asked. He pushed three small bags filled with chicken and rice towards me. I smiled, said No, and turned to climb back up the stairs.

A news report on the television made me stop.

"Viennese police are investigating a computer break-in at the headquarters of the World Genetics Council," the anchor said. "Authorities say several million Euros worth of computer equipment was rendered worthless after hackers uploaded a computer virus that crippled the organization's network. WGC spokesman Dr. Igor Staniouski said the break-in looked like the work of highly trained cyber-terrorists."

Quietly, I took the stairs back to the apartment. In a matter of days, I'd gone from being the daughter of an internationally beloved musician and world-famous scientist to a terrorist.

But somehow I couldn't drum up the energy to feel too sorry for myself. My world may have been upended, but it was nothing like what we'd done to Beethoven. If he could handle being brought back to life with such aplomb, surely I could survive this.

Interestingly, my introspection did nothing to take the edge off my appetite. An hour later, my dinner of cheap Chinese food digested, I attempted to turn our dive into something akin to home: I moved my guitar, suitcases, and a box full of CDs into the smaller of the two bedrooms. Compared to the rest of the apartment, it was pretty clean. It held a nightstand, a chest of drawers, and a closet, and the twin bed's only offense was a layer of dust.

"I can live with this," I said, as I set my Strat on the bed.

"I told you that you would grow to love it," Fa8 hollered from the other bedroom.

The inmates had arisen. I pulled the bedspread off the bed, opened the window, and shook the bedspread out over the street, hard. The sleet had stopped, and the night was clear but bitterly cold.

Fa8 popped in the doorway, wrapped in a thin blanket.

"Josie, luv, I don't think you want to leave those windows open. It's a tad coldy-cold outside, if you hadn't noticed."

"I'm not going to sleep on that much dirt," I said. "You could grow corn in here."

"Well, luv, tonight I don't think you're going to get that much sleep anyway. If you'll look across the street, you'll notice a river of people moving down the sidewalk. A signal, I do believe, that The Tombs is open for business."

"I'm not sure I want to go," I said. "What if they're out there?"

"They are out there, luv, but they are most certainly not at The Tombs. First, a group of stuck-up sticky-beats like the WGC boys wouldn't get past Rolf, the bouncer, any more than the Mafia or the right-wingers at the Wiener Korporationsring would."

"If he is that tough, then how are we going to get in?"

Fa8 smiled, grabbed his Fender, and waved Beethoven and me towards the door.

"That's very simple. Rolfie is me friend. He likes me music and if you will flash him three seconds of that killer smile of yours, I do believe his imagination should do the rest. Now, no more talk. Off we go."

It wasn't that I didn't want to go — I loved The Tombs; what I wasn't so sure about was stepping out in public, any public, with people out there looking for us in hopes of, well, offing us. But Fa8 had a point: No one knew we were here. And Beethoven seemed excited. He kept asking Fa8 questions about his guitar.

"You say this stringed instrument is a guitar?"

"Yes, Louie, it is. This particular model was made by our friends at the Fender Company. It is quite the instrument."

"It looks much different than the lyre-guitar I played as a child," Beethoven said. "And, this word, 'chords.' Does it mean what I think it means?"

Fa8 ignored the question, jerked the door shut, and faced Beethoven squarely. "You played the guitar, Louie?"

"*Ja.* Only it looked nothing like this one. And it was not, how do you said it, a Fender."

"But a stringed instrument, just the same, correct?"

"*Ja.* That is correct." Beethoven pointed to Fa8's guitar. "But I think that I should like to try this instrument."

"And I think you shall, Louie, my friend. I think you shall."

Chapter 37

Crimson and Clover

WE MADE IT PAST ROLF WITH no questions asked. I even smiled for less than three seconds. Although I don't think Fa8 or Beethoven appreciated it when I waved good-bye and blew Rolf a kiss.

We navigated a long flight of ice-covered stairs until we were deep underground. True to its name, The Tombs is a dark, cavernous oval carved out of solid rock. A stage with lights and enough sound equipment to fill the entire Vienna Opera House took up one end, while the other housed a kitchen, bar, several couches, and some big overstuffed chairs. In the center were clustered tables, each lit by a tiny candle. There was an absence of natural light. Instead, overhead, small strands of yellow lights glowed; they reminded me of tiny suns shining against an ebony sky.

We found a small table near the south end of the stage. Fa8 waved to a curvy waitress who took one look at him and quickly signaled a gorilla-sized man behind the bar.

The gorilla-sized man did not seem happy to see us — well, he didn't seem too happy to see Fa8. He stomped his way over to us, shaking his fist.

"You have a lot of nerve showing up here," he said in broken English. "Do you have any idea what you cost me?"

Fa8 gave him a crooked smile and waved him to a chair.

"Billy, me boy, I understand why you might be perturbed with me, but I swear that I have come to make amends. Honest I have, guv."

Billy snarled, revealing several crooked broken teeth.

"And how do you plan to do that? You still owe me three hundred Euros. Or have you forgotten?"

"No, my friend, I have not forgotten. And I am here to pay me tab in full." Fa8 counted out three hundred Euros and placed them on the table. "There is all I owe you, plus . . ." He laid another hundred Euros next to the stack. "A little interest since you've been such a swell bloke about my could-not-be avoided delay."

Billy's snarl morphed instantly into a twisted smile.

"Well, I'll be damned," he said. "You're a good Joe after all. Thought you had skipped out. But you didn't. Saved yourself a lot of trouble, you did."

"I agree. Never keep a friend wanting," he said, winking at me. "Now, this is me friends, Louie and the lovely Miss Josie. We came for a little liquid refreshment — three pints of your best ale — and some smokin' hot tunes."

"Can do," Billy said. "You came on a good night."

"Why is this a 'good night'?" Beethoven asked.

"Because Joan Jett just plugged in her guitar," Billy said.

Fa8 leaned over to Beethoven.

"Welcome to the twenty-first century, Louie. Tonight you're going to hear music like you've never imagined."

A few minutes later, Joan Jett walked to the front of the stage. Dressed in skin-tight black leather, she let her presence silence the crowd. Then the room went dark, save for the beam from a single spotlight that ricocheted off her white guitar. Bathed in the glow of the spotlight, she prowled the stage, a predator claiming her territory. When she finally stopped, she did so with her back to the audience.

Fa8 scooted his chair closer to me and whispered: "I'll bet you a pint she turns around packing a beat-up Gibson Melody Maker that looks like it's been dragged down a flight of stairs."

Beethoven leaned over. "This woman, she is a musician?"

"Yes. I'd try to describe her style, but it's better if you experience it. Give her a second, I think she's about to start."

I had no more settled back in my chair than the spotlight clicked off and the room went black. For a moment, perfect silence hung over the room, then the strum of a single chord, throbbing, loud, and intense, then four more notes, each lower than the last . . .

Then the graveled voice: ". . . I don't hardly know her . . . but I think I could love her . . ."

The progression was simple, angry, and loud. Beethoven leaned forward, as if trying to get closer to the stage, his eyes focused on the hands on the white guitar.

"This instrument she plays, this is the electric guitar?"

"Yeah," I said. "And, as you can see, Fa8 called it. That's her original Gibson. Look at all the stickers."

Beethoven squinted. "What does 'girls kick ass' mean?"

I sipped my pint and laughed.

"It's a statement about the power of women," I said.

"Crimson and clover, over and over . . ." The song filled the room. The music was throbbing and powerful and, at the same time, lonely.

Beethoven sat silently watching every move Jett made. He didn't say another word until the last chord, and then he turned back to us his face filled with emotion.

"This guitar, this instrument, it is like a weapon," he said. "It is powerful, sweeping and cutting; it pushes the sound into you."

Fa8 tapped me on the shoulder.

"I do believe our friend, Louie, is a fan," he said, with a wink.

I looked at Beethoven. He had slid the empty glasses to each side of the table and leaned forward with his face cupped in his hands, mesmerized by the music and the woman on the stage.

"Well, it's either the music or Joan Jett and her black leather," I said.

Fa8 laughed. "I bet it's a little bit of both, luv. Madam Jett has always had the same effect on me."

We closed The Tombs down that night. By four-twenty-two in the morning, the last of the musicians had finished, and the big, ugly bartender had called for a last round.

It had been a classic night at The Tombs. Fa8 had sat stone-like through Joan Jett's performance, but after she finished, he flittered about like a butterfly, moving from table to table shaking hands, laughing, and hoisting a pint with some very unsavory characters.

Throughout the evening, Beethoven had stayed close to me, his thigh touching mine under the table. In the dim, smoky room, I watched him close his eyes in ecstasy as wave after wave of music swept over him. Talking to him in such a state was impossible. Every time I tried, he waved me off. Instead, he sat, rock-like, tapping his fingers on the tabletop, and though it was clear he was most taken with Joan Jett, he stayed equally focused on whichever musician was playing on stage.

When the lights finally came back up. Beethoven stirred slowly, stretching as if emerging from a long, sensuous dream.

"What powerful music," he said.

"I guess we did come on a good night," I said with a smile.

Beethoven returned the smile, then looked at me like a schoolboy would his teacher. "But I have many questions."

"Such as?"

"What is a Sex Pistol and why is *Herr* Johnny so rotten? And *Herr* Sid so vicious? Were they raised by bad families?"

I tried hard not to laugh. Really I did. I could see that Beethoven was in need of an in-depth lesson in rock 'n' roll. So I tried to answer his questions, but each answer only sparked more questions and, between that, and his constant tapping on the table, I was exhausted. The sound of last call had been welcome.

"Let's go," I said. "We can talk on the way home."

Beethoven nodded. "This music has such intensity. Such passion."

"I'm glad you liked it. Joan Jett is an icon in the world we call rock 'n' roll. Her music is, well, almost primal. And the Sex Pistols, oh man, that band was cutting-edge punk; it created a whole new style of music."

Beethoven looked at me so intensely I blushed.

"I have never heard anything like this rock 'n' roll. Is there more?"

"Oh, yes. Tons of it. Joan Jett is one among thousands. Although I do have to say she has few equals."

Beethoven leaned closer to me and whispered.

"I must say I have never seen a woman dress in such a manner, but as far as her musical skill, she is a virtuoso."

"You still know talent when you hear it. She's considered one of the ten best female guitar players in the world."

Beethoven stared at me; disbelief written on his face.

"There are more female players of this electric guitar?"

I laughed and nodded. "Oh, yes. Joan is one of many. I mean she's a billion times better than me and most of the others out there."

Beethoven looked at me like he was seeing me for the very first time. "You, Josephine? You play this instrument, too?"

"Well, yeah," I said. "But trust me, I'm no Joan Jett."

"I understand," he said. "I have also doubted myself at times. But this, this music, this instrument, I must learn it. I must know how to make music with it. Could . . . would you teach me?"

Suddenly the pub disappeared and the din of closing faded away. I felt very warm. One of the greatest composers the world has ever known had just asked me to teach him to play guitar. If only my mother could have been here to hear it: *Ludwig von Beethoven just asked me to teach him the electric guitar.*

I shook my head to make sure I wasn't dreaming. I looked up into his eyes. Between the surreal fact that he was, indeed, standing next to me, asking me to show him how to play theguitar, like some bloke on the street asking directions to the Alps, and the reality of who he was, I could feel myself being drawn closer and closer to him.

A glance from him was like a bolt of electricity racing through my body. I'd never really been in love with anyone, but this feeling had to approach what it was like. It took everything I had not to lean forward and kiss him.

Instead, I coughed and waved him off.

"I'm still learning, myself," I said. "There are better players out there. Fa8 is so much better than I am; he'd be a much better choice."

"Please," he said, softly. "You must teach me. I am a good student. I would learn quickly. I must learn this electric guitar, and it would be unpleasant to think of learning it from anyone other than you."

Who was I to argue?

"I'd be happy to," I stammered.

. . . .

We found Fa8 and, over the noise of the thinning crowd, I told him it was time to go. He was at a table of shady-looking girls near a dark corner by the stage. He appeared to be having a great time.

"What's up, luv?"

"Who's this?" one of the girls said. "I thought you said you was unattached?"

Fa8 looked at me and squirmed.

"I am, dearie." His eyes darted from me back to the table of girls. "This is just me bandmate, Josie." Fa8 moved his arm in a large, exaggerated circle. "And Josie, luv, these are me new friends: Brigitte, Doreen, and Ursula."

I acknowledged the table with a little nod, then turned to Fa8.

"I'm worn out and ready to go."

Fa8 scowled and looked at his watch, then back at me.

"What? So early?"

"Fa8 it's after four in the morning. Didn't you hear last call?"

Fa8 looked at me, then back to the table full of giggling, barely dressed bimbos, then back at me again. He sighed, reached inside his pocket, and pushed a key in my hand.

"Tell you what, luv, you go on ahead." He moved his head in the direction of the table. "Let me tell these birds by-the-bye-bye and not long from now, I shall meet you at the flat."

"But I do not want to walk home alone."

Fa8 pointed back at our table. "You won't be walking alone. You've got Louie, there. And from what your Fa8 has witnessed, it did look like you two were getting rather chummy."

I felt myself blush.

Fa8 closed my hand over the key.

"I shall see you later, luv. Don't wait up."

When Beethoven and I stepped up to the street from The Tombs, the snow was heavy. In the warm yellow lamplight, the narrow, twisting streets were glazed with frost; giant heavy snowflakes drifted to the ground. Beethoven walked close to me. I hooked my arm through his, mainly because I wanted to be near him, but also just in case we met some of Dad's friends from the WGC.

I found myself wanting to say something, but Beethoven seemed lost in thought. He walked quietly, tapping his fingers against his wrist and humming softly to himself. Maybe Fa8 was right. Maybe my desire to get chummy with him had been too obvious.

Honestly, I suck at flirting. I refused to be one of those girls who dresses like a hooker to get a boy's attention, but I wasn't sure what to do instead. Oh, well, maybe Beethoven hadn't even noticed. Just enjoy being with him, I told myself.

And so for a few seconds it was, almost, a perfect night. I was simply a girl out with a boy for a walk. Everything was normal, and I felt happy . . . more happy than I could remember feeling in years. It was almost too good to be true . . .

The thought no more than flitted across my mind then everything that had happened over the past few days came rushing back. The boy beside me was someone whom I had "accidently created," and he just happened to be a famous dead composer, and we were both running for our lives from some bad guys who wanted to kill us.

The only thought stranger was the realization that I had just spent the night listening to rock 'n' roll with Ludwig von Beethoven, and now he wanted me to teach him to play guitar.

I couldn't wait for the lessons to begin.

Chapter 38

Rock and Roll Music

SIX-THIRTY IN THE MORNING. Outside, a hard wind piled deep mountains of snow on the streets. In the small flat, ice formed on the inside of the windows and the cold crept into my skin. I should have been still asleep, but too many thoughts danced in my head for me to get any real rest.

I sat up in bed, shivering. Whoever Fa8's mysterious friends were, they did not believe in comforters or, for that matter, heat. I slid off the bed, wrapped the thin blanket around me, and went in search of the control box for the furnace. I found it in a corner of the main room and turned it to High. After some grinding and smoke blowing, the heater kicked on, and the small vent in the ceiling puffed warm air. Okay, not so warm, or the ice on the windows would have melted.

In the kitchen, I found a small kettle and a tin about half-full of coffee. Using a paper towel for a filter, I added cold water, and put the kettle on a burner. Soon the comforting smell of hot coffee brewing wafted across the room. I took my cup and a seat at the small table in the kitchen. Through the window, a gray sun rose and the storm howled, covering the city in a heavy blanket of white.

I opened Fa8's laptop and typed Dad a message. I knew he would want to know what was going on, and I didn't want him to worry any more than he surely already was.

I hit the Send button, just as the front door opened. I figured it was Fa8 finally coming home, but Beethoven walked in the room.

The Immortal Von B.

"L.B.! Where have you been?" I tried to keep my voice calm.

Beethoven looked apologetic. "I am truly sorry, Josephine. I did not mean to worry you. I am quite safe; I was not followed by any of those rascals. I'm afraid our outing last night left me thinking about my home, about the Vienna of old. I did not want to leave you alone, but I had to see what of my Vienna remained, if only for a moment."

I should have been furious. But I understood.

Given a chance to see Oklahoma again, I would have grabbed it in a New York minute. I couldn't begin to imagine how much stronger that impulse would be if I had not seen my wild red dirt state for more than two centuries.

I nodded and offered him a seat at the table as a peace offering.

He looked so vulnerable.

"What did you find?" I asked.

"My childhood home remains," he said, "as do the imperial landmarks. But the pace of the Vienna I loved is gone, lost to these motorized contraptions you drive — I did not have time to visit my beloved woods. I used to spend hours walking in the forest."

Before I could commiserate, he grinned.

"One particularly good thing did remain," he said.

"And what would that be?"

"My favorite sweet shop."

I had to laugh — the look on his face was that of a little boy.

"My only regret," said Beethoven, "is, of course, it wasn't open, but maybe someday I will take you there. You would like it. Their sweets are like tiny bursts of joy in your mouth. It was one of my very favorite places in the world. It is good that time does not take everything."

With that, Beethoven yawned, stood up, and headed to bed.

I took my cup to the sink, rinsed it out, and put it up.

Then I went to the window, looking out over Vienna.

Where are you, Fa8?

. . . .

Seven twenty-three. I had had far too much bad coffee and not enough sleep. The bed beckoned, but the north-facing windows left the room just too cold. I turned the oven on, opened the door, and sat back down at the table.

I'd finally dozed off, when . . .

"I smell *kaffee*," a voice said.

I rubbed my eyes. Beethoven stood in the doorway of the kitchen dressed in Dad's U.T. sweats and the ugliest pair of green hunting socks I'd ever seen.

"Well, at least you look warm," I said.

"I am now," he said.

"Would you like some coffee?" I asked, walking over to the stove.

"*Ja*. It smells wonderful."

"I'm not sure what brand this is, but at least it's hot." I found another cup, wiped the grime off, and filled it. "Here, this should help fend off the chill."

Beethoven slid a chair up to the table.

"*Danke*." He sat quietly for a moment, then took a long sip of coffee with a loud slurp. "Not bad, though it could use some rum."

I smiled and poured myself another cup.

"Fresh out — believe me I was lucky to find this."

"Understood," he said, tapping his fingers on the table.

I watched him tap and sip his coffee for several moments, before my curiosity finally got the better of me.

"Could I ask you a question?"

"Certainly."

I pointed to his tapping fingers. "What in the heck are you doing?"

"I do not understand."

"The tapping. For several days now, all you've done is tap, tap, tap — long pause — tap. What are you doing?"

Beethoven smiled.

"I am composing, dear Josephine. I am composing."

Chapter 39

Fifth Symphony

THE REALIZATION OF WHAT he had said hit me like ice-cold water to the face. I felt like a dolt and a genius all at the same time. I grabbed Beethoven's hand and pulled him up and away from the table.

"Composing. As in writing music?" I asked as I dragged him down the hall to my room.

"*Ja,*" he said. "Ah, Josephine, where are you taking me?"

"To my bedroom. Now hurry."

Beethoven stopped dead in his tracks, looking both confused and a little scandalized. "I thought you and *Herr* Fa8 were . . ."

"Gosh, no! No! Jeez. You boys literally do only have one thing on your mind."

Beethoven winced in embarrassment. I slugged him in the arm.

"It's okay, silly." I pulled open my bedroom door and pushed him inside. "Now sit there on the bed and give me a minute."

Okay, it was several minutes. I dove into my closet and pulled out a small clock radio-CD player. I shoved the player in Beethoven's hands.

"Here, plug this in."

"I do not understand. Plug what?"

"Oh, honestly. For a genius you can be a little dense, you know?"

Beethoven smiled. "My father always said the same thing."

"Funny, funny."

I took the CD player and set it on the small nightstand by my bed, then pointed at the socket in the wall.

"You plug the cord in there. That's what provides the electricity to make it work."

Beethoven looked at me as if I spoke a different language. "Electricity?"

I rolled my eyes. "L.B., it's electric, like Joan Jett's guitar."

Beethoven smiled, then nodded.

"*Ja*, now I understand. But this is much smaller than a guitar. How do you play it?"

"No, no, it's not an instrument. It's more like a music box, an electric music box."

"Hmmm," he said, but I could tell he still wasn't sure what the box did. Still after several tries, he pushed the plug into the socket. "Okay. It is in. Now how do we get music?"

"Hang on. I need to find the right CD." I flung open the closet door again and starting throwing clothes behind me. "I know it's in here somewhere."

"Josephine. You are making quite the mess."

"Yeah, I know. Just hang on." I pulled a big battered plastic tub off the top shelf. It was heavy and scratched and stained and smelled faintly of beer. "Oh, I think this is it."

I put the tub on the bed. Inside were dozens and dozens of CDs — a tiny portion of my entire collection, but the portion that I could not bear to be without.

"These are my favorites," I said. "They contain the music of many composers."

Beethoven's eyes grew large. "That is an impressive number. You brought this the night we left the villa?"

"Wouldn't leave home without it. I may be running for my life, but I'm not running without my music."

Beethoven reached inside the box. He pulled out a black CD in a badly cracked jewel case.

"Who is this *Herr* Johnny Cash, this man in black?"

I smiled and took the CD from him.

"We'll listen to him in a minute, but first I want you to hear this."

With that I opened a green-and-yellow case and pulled a CD out. Holding the disc by the center hole, I placed it in the player, selected track three, and adjusted the volume.

"I'm sorry it took me so long to think of this," I said. "I didn't understand what was going on until you said you were composing."

"*Ja*. Rhythms fill my brain. All the time. It is almost maddening." He tap-tap-tap-long-pause-tapped on the nightstand, then frowned. "You see? I am still trying to work it out. It is my fate."

I cranked the volume to high.

"Well, if you want to know where it is going, listen to this."

Suddenly the room was filled with sound. Bows sawed on bold brassy violins, each playing four very well known notes: da, da, da, dum; da, da, da, dum.

"This is your music," I said, "the rhythm you've been tapping for days becomes this. It's the opening of your Fifth Symphony."

"You mean?"

"Yes. You wrote this. In your first life. Of course, you were in your thirties when you did it. But this, this four-note motif, is known throughout the world. It's probably the most famous piece of music ever written."

Beethoven listened for a little longer, then turned towards me.

"You say I wrote this exact work?"

"Yes. My mother said you wrote it because you were angry or upset about something. I read one historian who said you wrote it for Napoleon."

"Napoleon?" Beethoven rolled his eyes. "Napoleon is a useless mercenary. Why would I write music for such a man?"

"Well, actually, like I said, you haven't written it yet. You didn't finish it until you were thirty-four. It's still in your future."

Beethoven's face grew pale. He listened to the music for a few moments more, then as if he had been jolted by lightning, he jumped off the bed and jerked the cord to the CD player out of the wall.

"My future? My future is also my past, a past that I no longer have," he cried. "Please, Josephine, I beg you, show me no more of my past future. Until this life, music for me has been painful. I could imagine it, I could birth it, but I could not hear it. For so many years, I was close to insanity, the music filled my mind, but the sounds my ears heard were still like the grave."

Beethoven covered his ears with his hands. He stood shaking, as if he were recalling every moment of unwanted silence in his life.

"The music is here, always here," he cried, pointing to his head. "Yet I could not hear it anywhere else."

The anguish in his voice brought tears to my eyes.

"I'm so very sorry, Beethoven. I didn't mean to upset you. I only wanted you to know how amazing you were . . . you are."

The room went silent. I wondered if he would forgive me.

Slowly, Beethoven turned back and faced me. He sighed and gave me a weak smile. The storm had passed. Seemingly at peace now, he walked over to me and, like he would hold a frightened bird, he gently took my hands.

"Josephine, please. I reproach myself for causing you tears. But I have been given a second life by God. I wish to live that life in the here and now. I wish to share it with people, such as yourself; please, I beg you, show me no more the ghosts of my past."

"But your music is not a ghost," I said. "It is as alive and thrilling and powerful as the day you wrote it. It's part of you, part of your soul. It will always be with you."

"What you say is true, but that music . . ." He pointed to the CD player. "That music is the music of my first life. If I am to write it, then allow me to experience it as it would come in this life. If it is not to be, so be it. I must come to terms with my fate."

His face turned stoic, a profile engraved on a Roman coin.

I felt tears drift down my face.

"I'm so, so, sorry. I should have asked before I played it for you. I never meant to upset you. I wanted to share your music with you, to give you something that I thought you hadn't had the chance to experience before."

"Of course, you did not know." He pulled me into his arms. "All that is today, that is here with you, is now my world. I seek to know about that future. I wish to learn of you, instead. Your father told me my time — from my first life — has passed. So I ask you, instead, please share this time, your time with me."

Softly he touched my face.

I closed my eyes, shivering from the electricity that raced through my body. Then, without seeing, I felt him lean into me until his lips brushed mine.

The kiss was soft and slow, like the snow falling outside.

"Share with me your music, Josephine. Tell me of your passion," he said, kissing me again. "Make me a part of your world."

And with that Beethoven smiled, reached behind me, and picked up the black CD that we had set aside earlier.

"And please, please, tell me who this man, this Johnny Cash, is."

Chapter 40

Take Five

WE LISTENED TO MUSIC the rest of the morning. At his insistence, I played the Johnny Cash CD and made a lame attempt to teach him the words to *Ring of Fire*. I have to give him credit, he tried really hard to capture Johnny Cash's tone, but come to find out *Ring of Fire* does not translate well into German.

After that, I played him several songs by the Doors, a couple of ballads from Cream, Eric Clapton's *Layla*, and Sam Cooke's *A Change is Gonna Come*. We listened to old jazz and some rhythm and blues.

I couldn't help but smile when Beethoven closed his eyes and swayed to the soulful vocals of Bessie Smith. And I almost laughed out loud when he danced around the room to Little Eva's *Locomotion*.

Watching him experience new music for the very first time filled my soul with joy. I took him in my arms and slowly, we danced.

"What is this song?" he asked.

I leaned over and pushed the play button on a new CD. "Well, you just heard ABBA's *Dancing Queen*. But this song is a little different."

Beethoven pulled me closer and smiled. "Oh, how so?"

"This song," I said, "is an oldie by Barry White."

As the first slow notes of *Let's Get It On* filled the room, we adjusted our dancing to its beat, holding each other and trying to reach beyond the centuries that divided us. I swayed against him, tracing the lines of his face with my fingers. I thought about kissing him, but the music had taken him a million miles away.

I wanted to say something to capture the moment, but words failed me. Then Bob Dylan's *Mr. Tambourine Man* came on. Beethoven had already listened to that song about fifty times.

"You know, Dylan did tons of other songs, besides *Tambourine Man*," I said, realizing I sounded a little cranky, like a parent who started out wanting to read to her child until the child asked to be read *Where the Wild Things Are* twenty times in a row. I pushed the track selector on the CD player. "Here, try this one: *Subterranean Homesick Blues*."

"*Herr* Tambourine Man," Beethoven sang, reverting to German.

"Come on, L.B., be serious."

"Ahh, Josephine, I am sorry. But this man . . ." he pointed to the CD cover of Bob Dylan's face. "This man's music is so simple, so winsome."

"Yeah, Dylan is amazing," I said. "But this song isn't my favorite."

"Oh? You have another?"

"Yes, try this." I selected track eight on the player. The room went silent for a moment, then began: How many roads . . .

"*Herr* Dylan is a poet," he said. "His words are simple, but his message is universal."

"I'm glad you like that song," I said. "It's one of my favorites."

"I can see that you like it; the joy is spread across your face."

I touched my fingers to his lips. "In just a few days you have completely stolen my heart. I have never met anyone like you."

For a second he didn't say anything.

Then, he pulled me close and kissed me.

"I have lived two lifetimes," he said. "And in both, you are the most beautiful thing I have ever seen."

I turned away from him. "Don't tease me. I was serious."

Beethoven turned me back to him.

"As was I," he said.

. . . .

I have never been that good at kissing. Seriously, I haven't had many opportunities to practice. Still, Beethoven didn't seem to notice.

"Kissing you is like beautiful music," he said, touching my cheek.

For the second time I felt myself blush. It was all so overwhelming: the sense of fear from being on the run, my feelings for L.B., and the weird tension that I felt between Fa8 and me. Honestly, it wasn't that I wanted Fa8 to myself, because, obviously, I didn't. But I couldn't shake the pang of jealousy I felt when I saw him with those bimbos at the pub.

I kissed Beethoven back. *What a crazy idea to get my head around. I am kissing Ludwig von Beethoven . . . and doing a pretty good job of it, if I do say so myself.*

Beethoven looked at me like he sensed something was up.

"Sorry if I'm acting weird," I said. "I'm still getting used to all this." I pointed to the CDs scattered all over my bed. "We've listened to almost everything I brought, at least from this tub."

Beethoven smiled. "Your music is most inspiring, Josephine. It is quite different from the music of my past."

"Agreed. During your first lifetime, there was no Grand Funk Railroad or Bob Seger or Bill Haley or Green Day or Steely Dan."

"Music has changed greatly since my first life. I especially like the way the blend of ..." He paused and looked at me as if he were searching for a word. "What did you call this type of music?"

Beethoven pointed to a CD of pianist Dave Brubeck.

"That's purely American," I said. "It's called jazz. You heard the third track, *Take Five*."

"*Ja*, it was most inspiring. But I don't just want to listen," he said. "I wish to learn."

"I thought that was what you were doing."

"No, I was listening. Your music is wonderful, but I wish to learn." Beethoven pointed to the guitar case leaning against the wall. "I want you to teach me the guitar."

"Decided to give up the piano?" I asked, as I opened the case and laid my Gibson on the bed.

"No, Josephine. The piano, the fortepiano, the harpsichord, even the clavichord are as family to me. They are with me always. I need no lesson there."

"Then why the fascination with the guitar? You are already the master of the piano."

"Because, my love, I am here with you. And this is the instrument of this time. It is as powerful as any weapon I have ever known," Beethoven said, tracing the guitar's neck with his fingers. "Teach me; I am ready to learn."

I hooked my strap onto the Gibson's neck. "Well, then, it's time for school, and all students should report to the teacher."

Beethoven stepped in front of me and smiled.

"This is electric guitar of yours is quite colorful."

I giggled as I hooked the other end of the strap to the bottom of the guitar. "This, L.B., is a 1967 Gibson Flying V. This particular model is supposed to have been owned by Jimi Hendrix, another virtuoso. And while I was somewhat dubious of that at first, I do believe now that this was Hendrix's famed Psychedelic V, which he used in 1967 and 1968."

Beethoven ran his fingers along the strings. "You are most knowledgeable, Josephine. So this instrument was *Herr* Hendrix's?"

"Yes, I believe it was."

Slowly, a huge smile spread across Beethoven's face. "Then you must teach me to play *All Along the Watchtower*," he said. "And then, perhaps, *Purple Haze*?"

"Wow, you have a good memory for song titles." I rolled my eyes. "Something tells me you'll be playing them in no time, too. Now, hold still. Let me adjust this strap."

I tightened the guitar strap and stepped back. Beethoven looked great save for the scowl.

"You look wonderful. Why are you frowning?"

Beethoven tugged at the strap, his face growing bright red. "You have this on the wrong side. This is not right."

"Okay, okay. But that's how you hold an electric guitar."

Beethoven sighed. "But the strings . . . I cannot . . ."

"Shhhhh, let me think."

I stood silently for a moment and looked at Beethoven, then at the guitar. I was just about to say, forget it, when an idea popped into my head. I unstrapped the Flying V and took a step back and away from Beethoven.

"What are you doing?"

"You're left-handed, are you not?"

"Pardon me?"

"I said, you're left-handed." I pointed to his hand. "You favor your left hand."

"Yes. I thought you knew that."

"I know a great deal about you, LB., but I never knew that." I took the guitar and laid it on the bed. "Okay, take five while I string this bad boy in Mr. Hendrix's style."

I plopped down on the bed and started removing strings.

A few seconds later the sounds of Dave Brubeck filled the room.

Chapter 41

Wild Thing

IT HAD TAKEN ABOUT THIRTY minutes to show Beethoven how to hold the Flying V, how to play some basic chords, and how the controls worked.

"Those are the frets," I said, "and that's the whammy bar."

Beethoven scrunched his eyebrows together.

"Josephine, just how does a whammy bar make music?"

"It's a way to change the sound. I'll show you later. First you have to learn the chords. Now, try again. Show me C-7."

Beethoven arranged his fingers on the neck of the guitar.

"Like this?"

"Well, you're close. Here, let me help." I reached around his waist and moved his fingers into place. "You have to put your fingers here. How's that?"

"I think it is very good," he said quietly. "But I may need another lesson. You are a very good teacher."

I brushed my fingertips along his shoulder. I could feel the heat radiating from his body. The tension between us was so thick I was afraid the very air would ignite.

"Try it again and strum the strings a little slower," I whispered.

Beethoven nuzzled his cheek against mine.

"Perhaps we should continue this lesson in a different way," he said, taking the guitar from around his neck and leaning it back against the wall.

He pulled me onto the little bed. I rolled into his arms.

"I think my electric guitar lessons are done for the day," he said.

. . . .

Outside the snow swirled across the window pane. Inside, I found myself kissing a very young and very handsome Ludwig von Beethoven, when I really should have been worrying about the strange people who wanted to kill me. To make matters worse, I hadn't heard back from my dad and, somewhere outside in the cold, my best friend was running around and I didn't even know if he was safe.

But kissing Beethoven proved distracting.

One minute I was showing him how to form C-7 and the next moment, I was wrapped in his arms. I felt like I was going to explode, but a more steady head prevailed. And, surprise, it was mine.

I placed a hand on Beethoven's chest and gently pushed him away.

"We need to see if we can find Fa8, and we probably need to eat."

"I would be happy to brave the cold to find *Herr* Fa8," Beethoven said. "But pray don't make me eat any more Chinese food."

I laid my head against his chest. "Agreed. I'm not a fan of cold fried rice either."

Beethoven smiled. Gently, he turned my face and kissed me.

"*Ja*, a little more time together would be a nice thing, but . . ."

". . . but probably not very practical right now, Louie, my friend," Fa8 said, running into the room. "Our ge-ne-tical friends are back, and they're right around the corner a few streets over."

I jumped off the bed and ran to Fa8.

"Where have you been? I've been so worried. The Tombs has been closed for hours."

Fa8 gave me a crooked smile. "Seriously, Josie, you don't seem all that worried." He pointed to where Beethoven was still sitting. "It looks like you and me mate, Louie, are making out nicely."

I rolled my eyes but turned so he wouldn't see me blush.

I almost missed him wink.

"If you're finished analyzing my love life, why don't you tell me what's going on."

I knew something was horribly wrong when instead of matching my banter, Fa8 began to run around my room gathering clothes and my CDs and throwing them willy nilly into the plastic tubs.

"Josie, we must hurry. Those WGC goons are only a few blocks away and it appears they're going from flat to flat looking for us. They'll be here soon, and, I for one, do not intend to meet them at the door."

Enough said. I hollered at Beethoven to get his things, few as they were, and I started grabbing my own clothes and what I could of other my stuff.

"But what about the rest of our things?" I pointed to my Flying V. "I am not leaving my guitar and I am not leaving my music. Those bums will just have to shoot me."

Fa8 laughed, then cupped his hands to his mouth and shouted.

"Okay, me men. She's decent. Come on in and let's start our little movie-move, shall we?"

I watched, amazed, as the Samurai Wannabes and three or four boys I didn't recognize marched into the small apartment.

"Who are these men?" Beethoven asked, looking alarmed.

Fa8 stopped with his feet apart and his hands planted on each hip like a triumphant superhero.

"Why Louie, my friend, this is Fa8's army. And they have come to defend you and the Little Wild One."

I jerked my head around.

"Huh? Who's the Little Wild One?"

"Ahh, Josie, luv, that's the nickname they've given you."

Great. Now I have a nickname.

. . . .

With the help of the Samurai Wannabes, it took no time at all to get our stuff shoved back into boxes, carried outside, and loaded into the van. We battled slippery ice and blowing snow and winds that cut like a knife, but eventually the van was full.

It was then that I realized Fa8 seemed truly frightened.

"Josie, luv, we really should leave. I've already had one encounter with these blokes, and I'd rather not repeat it."

"Okay, okay. I'm hurrying." I jerked open one of the back doors of the van. "What happened?"

Fa8 waved me off. "Nothing, luv, no time to explainy-splain. But, seriously, dear, I don't think you're hurrying fast enough."

I shoved my guitar case in and slammed the door shut. "That's everything. Where's L.B.?"

"He's coming," Fa8 pointed over his shoulder. "He and some of the Samurai Wannabes are giving everything one last lookie see-see."

Fa8 crawled in the front seat of the van and stuck the key in the ignition and, three tries later, the motor rumbled to life.

"All right, it's started, luv," he said. "As soon as Louie gets here, we'll scram."

"What about them?" I pointed to Fa8's friends.

Fa8 smiled and nodded at a large, nondescript building at the end of the block.

"I've given them other assignments. Their job now is to help distract the WGC boys."

I held open the side door of the van, while L.B. crawled in.

"And just how are they going to do that, pray tell, Fa8?"

Beethoven touched my shoulder and placed a finger over his lips.

I watched him give Fa8 a very curious nod.

"The less you know, Josephine, the better," Beethoven said.

. . . .

This time, Beethoven picked our hideout.

That, in itself, was scary, because L.B. carries two-hundred-plus-year-old memories of Vienna inside his head, not a Rand McNally map. What made things weirder yet was that many of the places he took us to were still there.

"Turn to the left here," he said, pointing to a narrow, dark alley. "It should be there . . . at least I think that's the alley."

Fa8 slowed the van to a crawl. "Well, Louie I hope you're right because this little stretch doesn't look too terribly appealing. It's rather dark and I believe would score high on me list of 'places likely to get one's throat cut.'"

"It is a good place to hide, you will see," Beethoven said.

Fa8 inched the van down the alley. It was easy to tell this part of Vienna was much older — the streets were narrow and twisting and paved with bricks.

"I wish this snow would stop," Fa8 said. "It's making it rather hard to vis-ua-lize."

We rode along for a few moments more, until Beethoven tapped Fa8 on the shoulder. He pointed to a small door inset on the back side of an ugly brick building.

"That building, I think."

Fa8 stopped the van near the door and got out.

"All righty, then," he said, sliding open the side door. "Shall we?"

Beethoven unbuckled his seat belt. "I think I should come with you. If this place is what I think it is, well, let's just say . . . I speak their language."

Fa8 nodded. "Lead on, Louie. Lead on."

I watched them walk to the door and step inside.

They didn't return for what felt like hours.

Chapter 42

A Hard Rain's A-Gonna Fall

AS TIME PASSED, I GREW NUMB from the cold. Every so often, I started the van in a vain attempt to keep warm, but it didn't help much. I found an old tarp wedged in the back under a spare tire and a pile of rags. The tarp was dirty and stiff and smelled like oil, but it kept me from freezing.

Finally, after an eternity, Fa8's goofy face appeared at the window. I cranked the glass down and Fa8 stuck his head inside.

"Alright luv, we need to pull down about one hundred feet and park inside their little garage. Then we'll move our stuff."

I shifted the van into drive and, slowly, rolled up to a large opening in the side of the wall — the wooden door, which was broken and jagged, had been pushed up, out of the way. The whole effect was similar to a huge stone mouth with jagged teeth, waiting to consume a sacrificial virgin.

I steered the van into the garage. Behind me, Fa8 shut the door. Then I heard someone shout. The voice was angry. Furious. Whoever it was stood just outside the wooden door, yelling as if he were angry at the world.

"What are you doing here? Answer me or I will shoot."

I knelt down and peeked through a hole in the rotted, wooden door. A few feet away a huge man stood with his back to me. He was wearing a long, heavy wool coat and had a shotgun in one hand.

To his right, I could make out Fa8's skinny, shivering frame.

"Sorry, guv, we didn't mean to trespass. Me and me friend Louie here, had a meeting with the blokes inside and had just made our egress when we encountered you."

The man with the cloak leaned the shotgun against his side. "You were in there. Who did you talk to?"

"I believe his name was Axle," Beethoven said. "We were concluding a business arrangement."

The man with the shotgun took a step towards Fa8.

"So you talked to Axe, huh?"

Fa8 bobbed his head up and down like a toy dog.

"That's right. We were attempting to secure a short-term lease on some lodgings."

The man in the coat laughed. Loud. "Here? You must be insane."

Beethoven stepped into view.

"*Ja*," he said. "But, now our business is done. *Herr* Axel has agreed to our price. And we would like to move our belongings inside before the snow grows any worse."

Through the hole, I watched the large man step out of my sight. To my left, I heard a door open, a shout, and then several seconds of quickly spoken, rather harsh, German.

"Okay," the man said. "Move your crap and make it quick. There's been too much weirdness around here lately. Too many people asking too many questions."

I pulled my jacket around me and leaned my head against the door. Things were escalating. *What had we gotten ourselves into?*

The snow stopped just as we moved the last box up a long and very twisted flight of stairs. Fa8 was clapping his hands and hugging himself in an effort to stay warm. I handed him my scarf and looked around the small apartment. It was worse than the last one.

There was only one bedroom and a tiny, tiny kitchen that looked more like a converted closet. Down a short hall I spied what looked like the bathroom — it was missing a door — and I don't think it had ever been cleaned. The living area opened into the kitchen and was about half-filled with our stuff, as well as a musty couch, two small end tables, and a potbellied stove.

"I hope you didn't pay much," I said.

"Let's just say the price bought us what we desired. No one knows of this place. It is very much out of the way and, as you saw downstairs, visitors are not encouraged," said Beethoven.

I hadn't thought of that.

"Well that's good," I said. "I guess . . ."

Fa8 scurried into sight.

"I thought I saw some wood," he said. "Let's make us a cheery fire and some coffee. I do believe that would warm our spirits."

I nodded. "I could use something warm."

"As could I," Beethoven said.

Fa8 reached into a large cardboard box and pulled out a new electric coffee pot.

"Then let the festivities begin," he said.

Chapter 43

Snow

WE DRANK COFFEE (I think Fa8 added some rum) and talked long into the night. Fa8 delivered a surprisingly well-done lecture about the origins of the punk rock movement in 1970s Britain and patiently answered about seven billion of Beethoven's questions.

I scrounged for more wood and managed to keep the fire going. It was surprising how the small stove kept the place warm.

As the boys played musical trivia, I dug through the boxes until I found Fa8's laptop and dashed off another short message to Dad telling him we were all right and that we had changed hideouts.

Fa8 kept looking over my shoulder as I typed.

"Be sure you send it via the encrypted service I told you about. We don't want any nasty-wasty WGC boys reading your notes," he said.

"I did." I waved my hand in his face. "Now go away and let me finish. I'm still trying to thaw out after being left so long in the van."

Beethoven sighed. "Josephine, believe me, you would not have wanted to meet those men. They were most unpleasant."

"That's what I'm counting on," Fa8 said. "I don't think our landlord will be easily intimidated by the ge-ne-tical boys. And since we've paid them cold, hard Euros, they are somewhat likely to look after us."

"If they don't shoot us first," I muttered.

Beethoven stretched and yawned. I hadn't had the chance to talk to him since Fa8 rushed into my room and caught us kissing. And I also needed to pull Fa8 aside and take a reading on his state of mind.

The latter might warrant the most immediate action. For though I couldn't prove it, it felt like every time I moved near, or acted like I was going to speak with, L.B., Fa8's eyes were on me. It was unsettling. I started to say something when Beethoven stretched for a second time.

"There is something I do not understand, *Herr* Fa8," he said.

"And what would that be, my musical genius friend?"

"Well, I still do not understand how these musicians you speak about — earn their money. Who are their patrons? Do they use the traditional publishing houses?"

Fa8 smiled. "Well Louie, the method is similar to that of your first life. Musicians still have sponsors — only this timey-time they are large corporate giants and recording companies. For a long time, the men of means have been the ones paying the bills, but now bands often strike out on their own, too."

Beethoven looked confused. "But how does a musician build an audience other than performing in the pubs? The church?"

I pointed to Fa8's laptop. "I can answer that. It's called the Internet. And, like God and the sky, it's all around us."

"A machine?"

"Well, yes and no. The net is lots and lots of machines working together. Remember the other day when I showed you the telephone and explained how it worked."

"Yes. That was like magic. Voices from across the country."

"Or around the world," Fa8 said. "The Internet is also a global network that, quite literally, ties most of the people on the earth together."

I could tell Beethoven was trying to grasp the concept of a global network, but he didn't even have the advantage of having seen jets cut the time for getting from place to place.

"But what would be the power source of such a machine?" Beethoven asked. "The sun?"

I pointed to the electric cord snaking once again from Fa8's laptop.

"Electricity. The very same source of energy that also makes that Flying V work. Electricity, pure and simple."

"*Ja. Ja.* I must buy some of this electricity," he said. "I think it would be most helpful to me."

I set the laptop on the floor and laughed.

"Trust me, L.B. You have all the electricity you'll ever need."

The Immortal Von B.

. . . .

Three twenty-seven in the morning. Through the ice-covered window in the bedroom, Vienna looked like a frozen popsicle. The snow was an eerie, sickly hue. I tapped the face of my phone. The light of the screen filled the room, forcing me to squint. I rolled over and wrapped the blanket tighter about me. We'd only been hiding a couple of days, but it felt like we'd been on the run forever. Outside, the wind moaned and wailed.

. . . .

We spent most of the next day inside. I found some rags and an old mop and spent the morning cleaning several years' worth of grime off the bathroom. The kitchen sink was a lost cause, but wiping the counters down and having the guys dispose of several bags of trash helped immensely.

Fa8 slipped out right after noon to check in with the Samurai Wannabes. He said he'd given them several "projects" but didn't want to tell me what was going on until he knew for sure they'd finished.

"The goal is to make life very difficult for our ge-ne-tical friends," he said. "And if anyone can do it, the Samurai boys can. I shall return posthaste; keep a sharp eye out, and Josie . . ."

"Yes, Fa8?"

"You and Louie might want to pace yourselves; could be a long winter."

If he hadn't dodged, my shoe would have caught him in the head.

. . . .

Just before sundown, Fa8 returned. He was filthy, covered in grime and ice. He looked frozen solid. He stepped through the door, trying to speak but his teeth were chattering so much it was impossible to understand him.

"Jo . . . Jo . . . Jo-sie."

"Oh my God, what happened to you?"

I wrapped a blanket around him and pulled him over to the stove. I pointed to Beethoven, then the kitchen.

"Could you make some coffee? He's blue with cold."

"*Ja.* Right now."

I wiped the dirt off Fa8's face. One eye was bruised, and several scratches and scrapes creased his right cheek.

"You're bleeding. You look like you've been on the wrong end of a bar fight."

"I finally met a few of our WGC friends." He wiped a smear of blood off his forehead. "And they are not very nice."

"Are you terribly hurt?"

"No, luv, that's the joy of having Samurai Wannabes as friends, they are rather skilled at the fighting."

"Are your friends okay?"

Fa8 smiled, revealing a gap where one tooth was no longer present.

"Other than suffering a jab that'll require a little amateur dentistry, everyone is fine, as is your Fa8," he said. "However, one of our ge-ne-ti-cal friends shall find it difficult to sing bass for quite some time."

Beethoven stepped back into the room, carrying a large mug of coffee. He knelt next to Fa8 and put the mug in his hands.

"Here, my friend, drink this. It will warm you."

Fa8 threw him a weak smile, then took a long, deep gulp.

"That's rather good coffee, Louie. Bourbon or Rum?"

"Rum," Beethoven said.

Fa8 leaned his head against the wall. "Good choice."

"So, tell us what happened." I leaned so close to Fa8 our noses almost touched. "You look horrible."

"I know, luv, but it couldn't be helped. I didn't want those boys coming here. I was afraid they might hurt me friend, Louie, or even worse, they might try to hurt you. So me and a few of the Samurai Wannabes staged a rather large intervention."

I wanted to smack him upside his head.

"Fa8, how could you be so stupid? You could have been killed. I'm sure they had weapons; something you lack." I grabbed his arm. "What were going to fight them with, your red bandanna?"

"Josie, you underestimate me as always. You have to understand that I am not without some knowledge of self-defense," he said. "The Samurai Wannabes and me-self did quite well, thank you very much."

I wiped more dried blood off his face.

"It really looks that way. You do realize, Fa8, that you could have been killed."

Beethoven clicked his mug with Fa8's.

"Well, *Herr* Fa8, I think you showed remarkable courage. And I am most grateful for your intervention."

"Thank you, Louie. Unfortunately, those blokes will be back. And next time, they will bring reinforcements."

"Did they follow you here?" Beethoven asked.

"I don't think so," Fa8 said. "Nonetheless, we can't risk it. We have to get out of Vienna. We have to leave and we're going to have to do it soon. They cornered me coming out of a pub. Somehow they knew who I was and they knew I was connected to you, Josie."

Fa8 pointed to Beethoven and grimaced.

"They know what you look like, too, my friend. And they're going to find us — very soon — if we don't make a move."

"I don't understand," I said. "How are they tracking us?"

"I'm not sure," Fa8 said. "But I do believe our friends have a rather extensive network of bad-boy connections, and they do have the advantage of unlimited resources."

"What about my dad? I can't just leave him here in Vienna. They'll find him and they'll kill him."

Fa8 looked me square in the eye.

"Josie, luv, we do not have a choice. We have to get Beethoven out of Vienna. We have to get you out of Vienna. Neither of you can stay here. These blokes will never-ever-ever-ever give up. I don't think they'd give it a second thought to shoot us with their gunny-guns in broad daylight."

I swallowed hard. I had no idea how we were going to get across the border without being seen. Dad had said the WGC had friends in the Viennese government, and now that was painfully obvious. It didn't help that we were now being portrayed as terrorists. It wouldn't take long before everything got very difficult.

I wiped my hands and walked to the small end table next to the couch. I opened the laptop and signed on to Fa8's server.

I wrote Dad a short message: "Dear Dad, we're leaving Vienna now. I'm not sure how we're going to get out or where we'll go, but tonight Fa8 was beaten by some goons from the WGC. If we don't get out it's only a matter of time before they find us. Tell me what to do. I'm scared. I don't want to die. I don't want to leave you behind. I love you. Josie."

I clicked Send as the tears rolled down my cheeks.

Chapter 44

Minutes to Memories

WE STAYED OFF THE GRID as best we could. Beethoven sent a note down to our mysterious landlord and the next day several large paper bags of groceries, some soda, water and soap, and other stuff appeared outside the door.

"I don't know what you said in your note, Louie," Fa8 said. "But whatever it was worked."

Beethoven smiled.

"In my first life, I used the same method. I would send down a note, attach money, and tell the landlord to keep the change. It usually worked — and there were no questions."

Fa8 gave him a bruised smile.

"Well played, Louie. Well played."

. . . .

We spent the time we had left in Vienna talking. Beethoven listened to every CD Fa8 and I had with me, and he played my Flying V for hours. I was amazed by how quickly he mastered chording.

"Tell me, Josephine, does it sound better?" Beethoven pointed the neck of the Gibson in my direction. "I have improved? *Ja?*"

"Yes, L.B., you have. You play better than I do and I've been playing for years."

Beethoven shook his head in disbelief. "No. No. That is not correct. I am the student. You are the teacher. But I have practiced many long hours and I think I can now play *La Bamba*."

Behind me, Fa8 snorted. "Well, Louie, you may have written the Fifth, but you've still got a long way to go to play like Ritchie Valens."

"I would agree," Beethoven said. "But I am Ludwig von Beethoven. And I will master this instrument."

I tugged on Fa8's sleeve. "My money is on him," I whispered.

Fa8 gave a crooked smile. "Josie, I'm inclined to believe you."

. . . .

The snow had stopped. A little blue poked through the heavy, lead-gray clouds. No one else seemed to notice. Fa8 spent his time sleeping; L.B. had become even more obsessed with the guitar, if that was possible. If he had spent this kind of time on the piano, organ, and harpsichord, no wonder he became, well, Beethoven.

And I always thought I practiced a lot.

Beethoven practiced chords over and over — and then he practiced them some more. At the same time he started listening to Guns 'N' Roses. He still made more mistakes than Slash, but damn if he wasn't so close to Slash's style that it was borderline funny.

"Soon I shall compose for the guitar," he said. "Soon, I shall write new music."

I gave him a weak smile.

"Why the sadness," he said. "Our lives have been quiet today. This is good, *ja*?"

"It's been three days and no word from my dad. I hope he's okay."

. . . .

One fifty-three in the morning. I was wide awake and piddling about on my guitar. Beethoven was splayed across the sofa, snoring. Fa8 was stretched across the other end, his long legs draped over the back. Funny, they look so peaceful, like puppies taking a nap; I could not begin to imagine how uncomfortable they must be.

It was weird, spending so much time with the two of them. We had all become close. I knew I had developed deep feelings for Beethoven, but I was clueless as to what to do about Fa8. I mean, he was so much his own person the world didn't understand him half the time, and I had no doubt that, given the opportunity, he'd sleep with almost any girl that asked him, but he was also loyal and had always been there for me. Always.

I cared for him, I did, but I wasn't in love with him.

On top of all that, I had been existing on very cold to slightly tepid showers, and I was stuck inside a dirty, ugly dingy apartment, trapped like a rat in a cage with two boys who had very loose definitions of what constituted good hygiene.

Then there were the people who want to kill us; seriously, I was so scared I wanted to scream.

I flipped open Fa8's laptop and signed on the e-mail server.

Nothing.

Dad still hadn't responded.

The fear was almost overwhelming.

. . . .

Two forty-five. Usually playing guitar calms me, but not tonight. I know in my bones that we have to get out of here, but I don't know how. I went to put my guitar away when I noticed the blinking envelope on Fa8's laptop.

Dad!

I clicked on the envelope. His message was disquieting:

Josephine:

Use extreme caution leaving Vienna. The WGC has every exit and airport monitored. State police are working with the WGC and everyone is on full alert. Your photos have been broadcasted everywhere. Every police officer within Austria is looking for three teenagers who are supposed to be part of a terrorist organization. Please stay low and please, I beg you, be careful. I love you with all my heart and I don't want to lose you.

Do not, under any circumstances, go out in public. Avoid moving during the daytime and avoid crowds! No pubs! Be careful. These guys will stop at nothing and if they capture you, they will hurt or kill you.

I have moved out of the villa and taken precautions to ensure that my research will never fall into WGC hands, so concentrate on getting you three out of the city and across the border. Know that I, too, have friends and they will keep me safe.

I'm working on finding a place for us in America.

All my love,

Dad

P.S. Tell Fa8 the Samurai Wannabes are amazing. Watching them work reminded me of those great old Jackie Chan movies.

I touched the letters that spelled "Dad." *What I wouldn't give to have him here to tell me everything would be okay.* Silly, I told myself, that's just what he did in his message.

Slowly, I closed the laptop and stumbled down the hall and into my small cold bed. I tried to focus on what Dad had written, but the need for sleep proved overwhelming.

Outside my window, the wind howled.

I wrapped the blanket tight around me, shivering.

Somewhere out there, I thought as I closed my eyes, was a hunter and we were his prey.

Chapter 45

I Walk the Line

A FEW HOURS LATER, I awoke to the rich, wonderful smell of bacon and coffee. Fa8 was cooking breakfast.

"A good morning to you, Josie, luv." Fa8 scooped several pieces of bacon onto a plate and handed it to me. "I thought we needed some sustenance."

I grabbed a mug and poured a cup of coffee.

"Wow, it's been a long time since I've had a hot meal. And I don't remember the last time I had bacon."

Fa8 pointed a spatula at Beethoven.

"Thank him, luv. F.B.'s the one who arranged the foodie-food."

I looked across the room. Beethoven was still asleep, poured across the couch like a gallon of dark paint. I sipped my coffee and smiled. He looked so beautiful he almost took my breath away.

"He looks peaceful."

"He just nodded off. After you fell asleep, he insisted on sitting up to guard you. Sat by your side these last few hours just to make sure you were safe."

"You mean . . ."

"Yes, luv, he never left. After you finished e-mailing your father and went to bed, he stationed himself outside your door."

I felt a lump form in my throat.

"That's so sweet."

Fa8 whispered: "I do believe he's rather stuck on you."

"Yeah, right. We both know my record with boys. I'm the weird one, remember?"

"No, luv, I said you were The Wild One."

"I'm not wild, just confused."

Fa8 looked at me for several moments as if he'd never seen me before. "You don't get it, luv. There have always been people who loved you. You just didn't see it."

"Oh, stop being silly."

Fa8 gave me a tight hug.

"You never looked at what you had. You know? I've been right here for years. I love you, Josie." Fa8 leaned down and, softly, kissed me. "But I guess I'm not good enough for you. I find it rather difficult to compete with a time-traveling composer."

"Oh, Fa8, it's not like that. You know I care about you."

"But you don't love me. I know that now; I thought with time you'd change. I guess I've just wasted me time."

"I never thought spending time with you was a waste, Fa8. It's just that, well, you're my best friend. Isn't that enough?"

Stray beams of sunlight sparkled off the tears on Fa8's cheeks.

"Ouch," he said. "Never good when they invoke the *friend* word. I do understand, but it doesn't change how I feel. I know you think I'm strange and a little weirdy-weird, but that doesn't mean me feelings aren't real."

"I'm sorry, Fa8. I do love you, just not that way. But I . . ."

Fa8 cocked his head. "Yes?"

"But I always want you in my life. You are my very best friend and I, well, I don't know what I'd do without you."

The look on Fa8's face was more than I could bear. I didn't think it could get any worse. But I was wrong. He slid down the wall until he was sitting on the floor, like a sad rag doll.

"I love you, Josie, with all me heart. I've never said that to anyone. Shoot, the last time I told a girl I loved her was me granny, and that was years ago. I never supposed that you could ever love me. I just thought you should know that I loved you."

I slid down the wall beside him — what a sad pair we made.

"I never meant to hurt you, Fa8. I swear."

Fa8 nodded and wiped his face on his sleeve.

"I know, luv. Like I said, felt like I had to try. Not sure how much more time we have together what with these WGC-types running about. Never have liked this gunny-gun stuff. Somehow I guess I thought if I didn't express me feelings now, you'd never know."

I leaned my head against his shoulder.

"Dad was right then?"

"Yes, luv, as always."

Fa8 stood, offered me his hand, and pulled me up and off the floor. I stretched before heading to the kitchen for more coffee. I poured myself a second cup, took a long sip, and poured a cup for Fa8.

Then the door to the small apartment exploded and everything went dark.

Chapter 46

Turning Japanese

MY FACE WAS COVERED with a black cloth. I could barely breathe. Around me I heard crashing and grunts and the sounds of a small apartment being ripped apart. To my left I heard Fa8 grunt in pain. Someone grabbed me by the arm and twisted.

"Don't move or I'll blow your head off," a deep voice said.

A huge hand on the back of my neck pushed me against the wall. One hand searched me for a weapon.

Deep Voice barked orders in German.

"She's clean. What about the tall kid?"

"He's clean, too," a second voice said. "Where's the other one?"

"On the couch. He's not going anywhere," a third said.

I squirmed to the right. My nose hurt after being shoved against the wall. "I can't breathe."

Behind me I heard Fa8. "Let her go. It's me you want. She doesn't know anything."

Deep Voice laughed. "You're lying, skinny boy. We were told the girl would be traveling with two boys. I count one girl and two boys."

"You're not very nicey-nice," Fa8 said. "I told you she doesn't know a thing."

"*Ja!* It's me you want," Beethoven said. "Let her go."

Deep Voice jerked me around. His grip tightened on my arm.

"Stop squirming or I'll kill you right now." Deep Voice jerked the cloth off my face. "Do you understand?"

"Yes." I blinked, blinded by the sudden rush of light.

"Good." Deep Voice shoved me towards the door. I felt something poke me in the back — something like a gun.

"Any funny business and you die. Right here. Right now."

"Okay," I said, my voice shaking.

They lined us up, single file, like frightened soldiers.

The man I'd named Deep Voice stood at the door with a large gun. He was huge, with bulging arms and a long scar underneath his right eye. The others were smaller but equally menacing. One man was black with wire-like hands. The other — he was pale with ugly, rotted teeth — gripped Beethoven by the arm.

All of them had guns. And all of the guns were pointed at us.

Deep Voice waved towards the door. "Let's go," he barked.

With that, he reached in his pocket and pulled out a small cell phone. He tapped the screen then put the phone to his face.

"We have them," he said. "The girl and both punks."

The voice on the other end answered in German.

"*Ja.* Twenty-five thousand. Tonight," Deep Voice said. "We will bring them to you. Unharmed."

"What do you want with us?" I asked. "We haven't done anything. We live here. We're just students."

Deep Voice smirked. "Right. I don't care who you are, but you're not students. You're terrorists and you're worth a lot of money to me."

Deep Voice pushed me out the door.

"Now move before I break your arm."

Behind me, Beethoven spoke.

"Do not be afraid Josephine. Help will arrive shortly."

Deep Voice laughed. "I wouldn't count on it," he said.

We marched down the stairs and outside the building. I looked at the sky. The morning sun glistened over the top of the building like a giant sparkler. *This was it; we were caught. Everything was over. The guys with guns would take us somewhere and shoot us.* My stomach twisted. I was sure I would puke any second. Fa8 said nothing as he walked behind me. I tried to catch his eye, but when I turned, Deep Voice jerked me back around.

"Please," I begged. "Let my friends go. I'll do whatever you want, just let them go, please."

Deep Voice pushed the gun deeper into my back. "Sorry, missy, but we have an order for three. So shut up and walk."

He pushed me towards a black van parked a few hundred yards away. The door was open. In seconds they would shove us inside and drive us to our deaths. Silently I prayed. *I never meant for any of this to happen. All I wanted was to play my guitar and, maybe someday, find a boyfriend. How did it all go so wrong?*

Behind me, Fa8 coughed.

"Are you okay?"

"I'm fine, luv," he said. "Just the cold air."

"Fa8, I'm so sorry I got you into this. Please forgive me."

Fa8 coughed again. "No worries, luv. Won't be long now."

"But I didn't want it to end this way."

"You should know better, Josie; always trust your Fa8."

Deep Voice laughed. "*Ja!* A lot of good that will do you. Your fate is sealed."

"Please," I whimpered. "Let us go. I'll do whatever you want."

Deep Voice pulled me to him. "Really? Anything I want, eh?" He smelled of sweat and cheap beer. "I might be inclined to be nicer if you . . ."

Deep Voice never finished what he was about to say, because as he went to kiss me, his head jerked back, yanked by an invisible hand, and he fell to the ground clutching his crotch.

"Arrrrghhh," he moaned.

I tried to turn, but someone shoved me to the ground, face first into the snow. Behind me I heard shouts and yells and the sound of fists meeting flesh. I'd just pushed myself up when I felt someone grab me by the legs and drag me to the center of the street.

"No! No! Let me go!" I kicked blindly trying to get away.

"Josephine, please do not kick. It is me, Beethoven."

"Beethoven! What happened?"

"Did I not tell you that we would be okay. Does your friend Fa8 not have his own army?"

He wasn't making any sense, but I was too relieved to question anything. With Beethoven's help, I stood and brushed the snow off my clothes. In front of me, about a half-dozen of the Samurai worked over the goons who had tried to kidnap us.

"Is that? My God, is that Fa8?"

Beethoven nodded. "*Ja*! That is *Herr* Fa8. He seems to be very skilled in this street fighting."

The guy throwing bad guys to the ground didn't look like Fa8. Somehow the awkward, skinny British guy I had grown to know and love had become someone who moved with speed and efficiency. He kicked and danced and punched with the grace of a well-trained martial artist.

Moments later Fa8 and a Samurai Wannabe I didn't recognize cornered Deep Voice. Fa8 danced to the left, using his long legs to knock Deep Voice to the ground.

"Didn't like it when you slapped around me friends," he said.

Deep Voice aimed his gun at Fa8. Before he could shoot, though, the Samurai Wannabe planted a well-aimed kick on Deep Voice's arm, breaking it. Deep Voice rolled on his side, screaming in pain.

"I will kill you, you rotten bastard!"

"I don't think so," Fa8 said. "At least not this time."

With that, Fa8 jumped straight up and kicked Deep Voice in the face. Deep Voice fell backward, his gun clattering down the icy street.

He didn't move again.

Beethoven grabbed my arm and pulled me towards the van.

"Come on, Josie, we don't have much time."

"What are you doing?"

"We must leave. Hurry." He pointed to the black van, the same van that only moments ago I thought would be our death trap.

"Come on. Get in."

"Are you kidding. In there?"

Beethoven jerked the unconscious driver out of the seat and tossed him on the pavement. He stepped through the front to the middle seat. "Don't worry. *Herr* Fa8 already took care of the driver."

I smiled and slid in the passenger's side. Fa8 ran across the lot and crawled into the driver's seat.

" 'Ello luv, you look absolutely smashing. Everyone ready to go for a drivey-drive?"

I smiled, then leaned over the seat and kissed Fa8 on the cheek.

"Right now, I'd go anywhere with you. Absolutely anywhere."

Fa8 slammed the door shut and shifted the van into drive.

"Then come my friends, let us away."

I grabbed his shoulder.

"Wait! Just a second." I jerked my door open, jumped out, and ran back to the building. Less than a minute later, I slid back into the passenger's seat.

"If I'm going to be chased all over Vienna, I want my Flying V," I said. "They can kick me, they can shoot me, but this guitar was once owned by Hendrix. And if they want it they'll have to pry it from my cold, dead hands."

"Well said, luv," Fa8 said with a grin.

I tossed Beethoven a CD in a broken jewel case.

"Here, I found something you haven't listened to yet."

Beethoven cocked his head.

"What is that?"

"Zydeco. Try track five. *The Zydeco King* by Chubby Carrier."

Chapter 47

Drive

WE DROVE FOR ALMOST AN HOUR, wandering the streets of Vienna like a group of itinerant circus performers. Fa8 said we should head for the German border. Beethoven lobbied for Hungary.

"Guys, you don't get it. Remember? My dad said all the borders are being watched. We'd never get through."

Fa8 shook his head. "They can't watch every place, luv. It would be impossible."

"*Ja!*" Beethoven said. "They do not have enough men to completely seal the entire Austrian border."

"It's not just border guards. They have satellite and radar, GPS and helicopters that can pinpoint us on a road. Trust me, we'd get caught."

"Let them come," Beethoven said. "With *Herr* Fa8 and myself, these rascals do not stand a chance."

"Yes, you were both wonderful. You saved me. But now we need help. We need someone with connections."

Fa8 sighed. "You're right, luv. I feel like a ratty-rat in a cage. It's against me principles to be restricted."

I laughed. "I believe you, but I think we best keep a low profile until we can figure this out."

"Perhaps," Beethoven said, "we should go back to . . ."

Strange voices interrupted him: "Carl, this is base. Come in. Carl, this is base. Come in."

"What was that?" I asked Fa8.

Fa8 pointed to a small radio mounted on the side of the transmission well. "I believe they have two-way communication," he said. "They have people all over the city roaming around trying to find us. They appear to be communicating via radio."

"This is not good," Beethoven said.

Fa8 pulled off on a side street near the Kunsthistorisches Museum west of the Danube River.

"It's not as bad as you think, Louie. At least we can monitor them. Now we know where they are looking."

"True," Beethoven said. "But I would think they would soon come looking for their comrades."

"He's right," I said. "We have to get off the streets. It's almost noon and people will be everywhere soon. And this van screams espionage."

Beethoven slumped in his seat. "I have a memory, from my first life," he said.

I turned towards him. "What are you thinking?"

"I was remembering a time when a friend got into trouble with the authorities," he said. "He pled his case to the count and he was allowed to leave, without harm."

Fa8 smiled — weakly.

"Louie, my friend, we're fresh out of counts. And the only king close by is in London, and trust me, matie, he's somewhat of a wanker."

"I just thought . . ."

"Louie, I'm afraid that while they used to be quite popular in your time, we don't do much with them anymore. You see, after the French Revolution, the people . . ."

"That's it!"

I grabbed Fa8's arm and jumped up and down in the seat. "We don't have a count, but we do have a countess." I reached across Fa8 and started the van's motor. "Hurry, let's go."

Fa8 looked at me as if I'd gone completely insane.

"Josie luv, calm yourself. Now what, exactly, are you talking about?"

"I know what to do. For the first time in days I know exactly what to do. Go west, hurry. Go to the First District."

Fa8 turned the van around. "Alrighty, luv, but just who are we going to see? That's a rather exclusive part of town."

"Don't worry. I have a friend who lives there. She's a countess and she said if ever I needed a favor all I had to do was ask her."

Beethoven smiled. "This is good. Do you think she will help us?"

"Oh yes. The countess was a dear friend of my mom's, and," I said pointing to Beethoven, "she thinks you're a genius."

An hour later, the van rolled to a stop in front of a wrought-iron gate. Fa8 might be an excellent fighter, and he played a terrific rhythm guitar, but he could get lost in a paper bag. Twice, I almost yanked him out of the driver's seat.

"Sorry, luv, Vienna's twisty-turney streets aren't me strong point."

I smiled. "It's okay. We're finally here."

Fa8 rolled down the window. "Josie, I do believe we've arrived at a rather large palace. Indeed, it's so palace-like it makes your place, your villa, look rather small."

Fa8 was right. The countess's home was mammoth. It stood on acres and acres of land, lined with perfectly trimmed hedges, trees, and a long, winding driveway. The entire estate was surrounded by a stone wall, topped with a menacing wrought-iron fence. I slipped out of the van and walked to the gate.

Fa8 stuck his head out the window.

"Josie, luv, are you sure we're in the right place?"

"Yes, Fa8. We are."

"Then just who is this person who you say will help us?"

I pushed the button on the intercom and turned to face Fa8.

"She is the Countess Fiona von Waldstein. She knew Chuck Berry and Eric Clapton and she helped fund the Beatles and the Fallen Angels. She knew my mom."

A deep, formal voice came through the speaker.

"Yes? May I help you?"

I looked at Fa8 hard. "And she's my friend."

. . . .

It seemed strange standing in the snow, shivering, talking to a large black metal box. I felt even more stupid when I realized the countess might not even be home. We hadn't called ahead. We'd just shown up. No matter. We'd made it this far. And, let's face it, we had no other place to go. I stepped closer to the box and, sounding like a panicked first-grader, started spewing words into the intercom.

"Ahh-yes, could I-please-please-please-talk-to-Countess Fiona?"

"The countess does not speak with strangers," the voice answered. "An appointment is required. Please contact her office on Monday. Someone can assist you then."

"Please. It's very important. Tell her it's Josie. She-told-me-if-I-ever-needed-her-to-call. You see she knew my-mom-and-we-met-at-the-reception and . . ."

Silence. I stood in the cold and waited. Nothing.

I should have thought this through. Maybe I could call Theresa and have Theresa call the countess. I was tired and cold and frustrated and now I was beginning to get angry. My morning had started with a bunch of thugs trying to kidnap me and my friends and now, after we managed to escape, the woman who said I could call her any time for help won't even answer her gate.

Make an appointment. I don't think so. I turned and started back for the van. I'd taken about two steps when the speaker crackled again.

"Who again may I say is calling?"

I ran back to the gate. "I'm sorry?"

"Whom may I say is calling?"

"It's Josie, Josie Brunswick from the Beethoven retrospective."

A second later the gate swung open.

. . . .

It took ten full minutes to get to the countess's house. Seriously, I have never seen a place so big. The driveway wound through trees and gardens and fountains and miles and miles of immaculately trimmed hedges.

"Josephine, do you know where we are?" Beethoven asked.

"I'm not sure. But I'm told this is Eugene's Summer Palace."

Beethoven smiled. "*Ja.* I thought so. This is the Upper Belvedere. The home of Prince Eugene of Savoy. He began construction on it when I was a baby, during my first life in the late 1700s. He died when I was sixteen."

I gazed out the frost-tinged window. "So the countess wasn't kidding. She's related to the prince."

"It looks as if your friend is the descendant of royalty," he said. "I told you, not everything has changed in Vienna."

Fa8 rounded a long graceful curve. He slowed the van to a stop.

"Well, luv, we're here. I hope your countess friend can help us; it's a long drivey-drive back to the main road and all those nasty-wasty boys with guns."

. . . .

A tall man, dressed in a perfectly fitted gray suit, met me at the door. "Miss Brunswick, it is a pleasure to see you again. I am Terrance, the countess's personal assistant." He motioned to the door. "Please come inside and warm yourself."

I motioned to the van. "May my friends come, too? We've been driving all morning."

"But of course," he said, in a deep voice. "This way."

It was, indeed, a palace. We walked past walls covered in gilded scrollwork and huge, beautiful oil paintings of the Emperor Joseph. Beethoven stopped in front of a painting of a beautiful young woman and stood quietly for a moment.

"I have made music here," he said, touching his chest. "In the youth of my first life. I remember now."

Fa8 tapped him on the shoulder.

"Best not introduce yourself just yet, Louie. It's rather difficult to explain how you came to join us," he whispered. "We should let Josie make sure the countess is all comfy-like before we tell her your second-life story."

"A good idea," Beethoven said. "I shall remain quiet."

Terrance led us down a long white-and-gold hall, its ceiling covered in a beautiful fresco

"This is the great gallery," he said. "The ceiling is painted to illustrate war and science and the arts and agriculture of the Austrian provinces."

"Painted by Gulielmi, *ja?*" Beethoven said.

Terrance stopped and looked at Beethoven for several moments.

"Yes, young man, you are correct."

For a second I went cold. I was sure Terrance knew who Beethoven was. My fear washed away when he smiled.

"Such a pleasure to have visitors who appreciate fine art."

Fa8 slugged Beethoven on the arm and whispered. "Thought you were going to be quiet, Louie."

"Sorry, *Herr* Fa8."

We walked for several more yards, then turned left down a hallway painted a brilliant red. Terrance stopped in front of a large oak door.

"The countess is relaxing in her study," he said. "She asked me to bring you there."

Terrance pushed open the door and we stepped inside.

Beethoven gasped. Directly in front of him, across the room, stood a huge white statue of a man seated at a fortepiano. The man was older; his face twisted in pain. His hair was wild and unkempt.

It was Beethoven.

I wanted to say something, but before I could turn around, Fa8 leaned over to Beethoven and whispered. "Let it go, Louie. The past of your first life isn't your future now."

"That is true. Thank you, my friend," Beethoven said quietly.

I started to speak, but at that moment, the countess stepped through a door, smiling "Josephine, my dear, it is such a pleasure to see you."

She was dressed in a cream-colored skirt with a matching blouse. The look was elegant and simple. Her gray eyes twinkled behind her glasses.

"It's nice to see you again," I said. "I am so sorry to intrude, but, I, we did not have anyone else we could trust."

The countess took and squeezed my hands.

"Why child, you're shivering." She waved us into a room with a large fireplace and several overstuffed chairs. "Please do have seat and tell me what is troubling you."

"People . . . bad people are trying to kill me and my friends," I said.

"Trying to kill you. Who is trying to kill you? Josephine, are you in some type of trouble?"

I pointed to Fa8 and Beethoven. "We all are."

The countess took a good look at Fa8, then turned and looked at Beethoven for several moments. "Young man, you look very familiar to me. Have we met before?"

Beethoven smiled, then bowed with a slight nod.

"No ma'am. I am afraid I have not had the pleasure. I am —"

"Louie!" Fa8 interrupted.

Beethoven nodded. And I heaved a sigh of relief.

The countess smiled.

"Oh, how I love a man with old-world manners." She said to Beethoven, then giving Fa8 a little frown, she turned to me. "Now, Josephine, who might this other young man be?"

I jerked, as if I was emerging from a dream.

"Oh, I'm sorry. This is Fa . . . Frederick Bartholomew Rosenguild. He hails from Liverpool. He and I attend school together."

The countess nodded.

"A pleasure. Now, please tell me why you and your friends fear for your safety and, please, start at the beginning. I am an old woman and I would like to hear the whole story."

Chapter 48

Pastoral

WE TALKED FOR MORE THAN an hour. I told the countess about my father's research and how the WGC had turned out to be an evil company that kidnapped orphans and other children, killed them, and harvested their organs. I told her about how they had bugged Dad's lab and how they knew he had done more than just a simple tissue replication. I told her of racing across Vienna and going into hiding and how that very morning, we were almost killed.

With each word, she grew more and more agitated. I couldn't tell if she believed me or not. Finally, after talking nonstop for several minutes, I paused to take a breath; the fear and anger and pain hit me all at once.

"We have to get out of Vienna," I said. "I'm worried about my dad and how he'll manage alone, but I'm also scared to stay. I don't want to see my friends hurt and I don't want to die, either."

The countess stood and smoothed her skirt.

"Child, of course, I am happy to help you," she said softly. "I owe that much to your wonderful mother, but I cannot help you unless you tell me the whole truth."

She took her glasses off, then turned to face me.

"There is more to your story. Much more — and yet you have not told me that part. Perhaps you should do that now."

I blinked in surprise. Was I that transparent? Behind me Fa8 coughed. Beethoven remained silent, as instructed.

"It's not that we don't want to tell you or that we don't trust you," I said quickly. "It's just difficult to explain. I don't think you'll believe me, either. And, honestly, it's so outlandish a story I wouldn't blame you if you didn't."

The countess walked over to my chair. Gently, she raised my chin and looked into my eyes.

"Is it drugs. Have you broken the law? Stolen something?"

"Gosh no, ma'am. It's nothing like that."

The countess gave a little nod and returned to her seat. She sighed.

"Josephine, I can't help you if you won't trust me."

"I know," I said. I thought for a moment. "Could you promise to listen to the whole story — no matter how crazy it might sound? Promise that you'll listen to the end and then judge?"

The countess nodded.

I pointed to Beethoven.

"When we came in you asked Louie if the two of you had met before. Remember?"

"Yes, he is a very handsome young man and in a very distinct way. I could swear I have met him before."

"You have," I said. "Look around this room."

The countess looked at me then at the portraits hanging on the walls of her study. Most of the paintings were of Beethoven, mostly of an older Beethoven.

"Josephine this is my study, my own personal shrine to Beethoven. I'm not sure I follow you."

"Countess, you said Louie looked familiar. Look at your paintings; look at your statues. Then look at him."

It took a moment for what I said to sink in, but after several seconds, the countess's eyes grew large.

"But, of course, he looks exactly like Beethoven. Oh, child, you are so right. He . . . he is almost perfect."

"He is perfect," I said.

I stood and walked over to Beethoven. I took his left hand and walked him back to the Countess.

"Countess Fiona, I would like to introduce you to Ludwig von Beethoven, late of eighteenth-century Vienna and considered to be one of the world's greatest composers."

Beethoven bowed a second time.

"Madam," he said with a gallant sweep of his arm.

The countess didn't speak for the longest time. When finally she did, it was clear she was not happy at someone taking her for a fool.

"Josephine, I am hurt and astounded. You know of my love for Beethoven. Stop this charade. Tell me who this young man is and what it is that you need."

"Dear Countess Fiona, I am not joking. I would never deceive you. This is Ludwig von Beethoven. This is why we are on the run."

The countess sat silently again trying to take it all in. I could see she had made a decision when next she spoke, because her voice was cold and aloof.

"Josephine, I'm not sure what trouble you are in, but I am appalled that you would come into my home and insult me like this. I am afraid I will have to ask you to leave. I am heartbroken . . . I thought we were friends."

Tears sprang from my eyes. A blade could not have cut me anymore deeply.

"Oh I am . . . we are. You must believe me. I told you it would be hard to believe, but it's true nonetheless. This morning, I've been shot at, my friends have been brutalized, and we've been chased all over Vienna. The WGC may have my father and everything I've told you is true. A horrible, horrible nightmare, but still true."

Fa8 leaned forward. "If you have a computer I could borrow, ma'am, I can prove to you that those WGC brutes are as evil as Josie has said. And then I'll hand it over to me mate, L.B., to explain the time-traveling composer part of our tale."

The countess nodded curtly. "Follow me."

She led us into a smaller office off the study. We all squeezed in around the desk as Fa8 went to work at the computer.

"Now show me, young man," the countess said.

Fa8 pulled up a web browser. His fingers danced across the keyboard for a few moments, then the webpage of the London Times filled the screen.

"As you can see, ma'am. Our friends at the London Metropolitan Police Force have just announced an investigation of the World Genetics Council into child trafficking for organs based on information received from good sources in Syria and Lebanon."

Fa8 pointed to photos of several men in suits being handcuffed.

"The story explains how ships registered by the WGC were stopped in the Strait of Hormuz. Those ships were filled with orphans from the Balkan States."

The countess covered her mouth in horror.

"Let me see that." She turned the monitor to see the article better. "That bastard Gottlieb. I've always said he was no good."

"Theresa warned me about him the night of the reception," I said.

The countess looked at me. "Well, it does prove what you said about the threat posed by the WGC. But, as for this young man being Beethoven, that is a different matter entirely."

"The explanation is difficult," I said, "but it involves my dad's research and tissue replication and even the Beethoven retrospective."

"You mean the retrospective at the Haus der Musik?"

"Yes, ma'am. My school took a field trip there recently and to make a long story short, when Theresa realized who my mother was, she gave me a personal look at some of the never-seen-before artifacts that were going to be exhibited."

"Those are from my collection," the countess said.

I smiled. "I didn't realize that then, but that makes sense now."

The countess pointed to the walls of her study.

"As you can see, I have an extensive collection of art and personal effects from throughout *Herr* Beethoven's life."

"Even clothes?"

"For years now, I've had experts making pilgrimages to some of Vienna's lesser-known antique and thrift shops. We've found several items that, through testing, we confirmed belonged to Beethoven."

"I believe you," I said. "While I was looking at the artifacts, I handled a red scarf. A red scarf owned by a young Beethoven."

"Ah, yes. That was purchased last year," the countess said. "There were several pieces of clothing in that find, including the scarf."

I pointed to Beethoven.

"Trust me, the scarf is authentic."

The countess shook her head.

"Josephine, as much as I want to believe you, I can't. This young man can hear and, as you very well know, Beethoven was deaf. It can't be the same person. He could not even be a clone."

"But I am he," Beethoven said. "And I can prove it to you."

The countess gave a weak smile.

"And just how, young man, do you propose to do that?"

Beethoven pointed to a framed document hanging above the countess's desk. Encased behind glass in an ornate frame, it was actually a letter and a small envelope. Both looked ancient. The paper was torn and water-stained.

"I wrote this letter," he said, taking the letter off the wall.

"That's impossible to prove," the countess said. "The letter was damaged in a fire in 1878. It's impossible to make out the body of the letter. We only know that it is supposed to have been written by Beethoven because of the signature."

"That may be so," Beethoven said. "But I remember this letter. I wrote it two years ago in the autumn."

The countess smiled a slightly wicked smile.

"Then tell me, young man, to whom is the letter addressed?"

"It was written to *Herr Doktor* Schade, in Augsburg, Austria. It was a difficult time for me. My mother was dying and I had upset my friend, hence the letter."

The countess's face turned pale. Slowly, the smile faded from her face. "What did you write to *Herr Doktor* Schade?"

"The letter began 'my most esteemed friend, I can easily imagine what you must think of me, and I am afraid that I cannot deny' … and it ended, as so many of my letters did, 'in haste.' "

"But this can't be."

"Why?" I asked.

"I had that letter examined just weeks ago using a new digital analyzer. The address was to *Herr Doktor* Schade."

Beethoven picked up a small gilded music box off the desk.

"This belonged to my mother, Maria."

The countess nodded. "Yes, that is common knowledge. That particular music box has been on display in various museums off and on for several years."

"Does it still squeak?" Beethoven asked.

"Why, yes, yes it does," the countess said.

"The mechanism was not properly installed and so when it plays it also squeaks," Beethoven explained in answer to the puzzled looks on both Fa8's face and mine.

The countess gasped. "Randall from our preservation society said the very same thing. But how could you know this?"

Beethoven smiled.

"I told you. This music box belonged to my mother. If you slide off the bottom plate, you will see the inscription to her my father had the maker, Joseph Werner, inscribe when he purchased it in Hamburg."

With that, the countess collapsed on the carpet.

Chapter 49
Go Your Own Way

FOR A MOMENT, WE ALL stood there. Then, like someone yelled, "Action!" — everyone jumped at once. Beethoven reached the countess first; gently he lifted and cradled her head in his lap.

"I am a fool," he said. "I have harmed her."

Fa8 knelt beside him. "Louie, no hurt was done here. She was simply overwhelmed. The shock of actually seeing Beethoven standing before her was just too much."

I checked her pulse. "She's breathing and her pulse is normal, both good signs. We should . . ."

I heard the gasp before I saw the person.

"What have you done to her? Move! Now!"

It was Terrance; he pushed me out of the way, waved Beethoven off, then swooped the countess up in his arms and carried her to the sofa in the study.

Something about the way he held Countess Fiona gave me the feeling that there was more to their relationship than just employee-employer.

Terrance pointed to Fa8. "You. Get water now."

"I'd be happy to me friend, but not sure where to go. If you would just pointy-point me in the right . . ."

"Down the hall, left, then right," Terrance barked. "Now!"

Fa8 returned quickly with a large glass of water.

"Here, my friend. See if this helps."

Gently, Terrance tilted the countess's face. He dipped his fingers in the water and softly brushed them across her forehead.

"There, there my love. You just had a fright. Are you okay?"

For a few seconds the countess remained limp, then, slowly, she stirred. "What . . . what happened?"

"I'm not sure," Terrance said. He looked at me, then Beethoven. "What did you do to her? Tell me now before I call the police!"

"We didn't do anything," I squealed. "She was talking to Beethoven and . . . she fainted."

The countess nodded. She shooed Terrance away and sat up on the sofa. "She's telling the truth. I was simply overcome," she said.

Terrance continued to scowl. "I am not so sure, madam. Something here is not right. Perhaps I should call the authorities."

"Terrance, Terrance, I am fine. These children did nothing wrong."

Terrance reminded me of a puppy that had been scolded by its master. "As you wish, madam."

She patted his hand. "Trust me, I'm fine. Now, if you would have Agatha bring me a brandy, and perhaps some soft drinks for Josephine and her friends, I would most appreciate it."

Terrance nodded and backed out of the room.

I turned to the countess. "I am so sorry we frightened you, but like I said, all this has happened so quickly and it is overwhelming. None of this was my idea, but it's my reality now. And Beethoven has become a friend. And now both my friends are in danger, and I don't know where my dad is and you are the only person I could trust."

The countess dabbed her eyes with a small napkin.

"Child, of course, I will help you," she said. "Forgive me if it takes me awhile to get my head around the idea that Beethoven — the one and only Beethoven — is standing here in my home."

"You should have seen Dad's face when we figured it out."

The countess smiled. "Was he as surprised as I am?"

"Oh, 'surprised' doesn't begin to describe it."

. . . .

For the next hour or two Beethoven, Fa8, and I tried to explain how Beethoven came to be standing now before the countess in her

own study. When I mentioned the part about my dad trying to replicate my mom, the countess sobbed.

"I think it was an absolutely horrible and desperate deed," she said
through her tears, "but I understand your father's need. Your mother was a beautiful woman, inside and out. And your parents all but
breathed as one. I know how much I miss her. I cannot begin to imagine the pain of his loss."

"It was pretty difficult for me to hear," I said. "I accused him of
some awful things, but like you I finally realized it was an act of des-
peration. He never realized what the consequences might be."

The countess patted a spot on the sofa and motioned me to come
sit by her. I could tell she had something she needed to say.

I sat down and wait expectantly.

"Dear Josie, I apologize for not believing you, for not keeping my
word and waiting until the whole story had been told. But, like you, I
was overwhelmed."

"Believe me, I understand," I said. "And, truthfully, you're the only
other person in the world who I thought might understand — if only
because I knew Beethoven was a real person to you."

She nodded.

"In the end, I think that's what made me believe," said the countess. "Now tell me how I can help. I refuse to let you or your friends
be harmed on my watch."

"We have to get out of Vienna. I have to get Beethoven out of the
country. If those thugs from the WGC get a hold of him they will do
much worse than kill him. I'm sure of it. They almost had us once.
I'm afraid of what might happen if they found us again."

Countess Fiona patted my hand. "You and your friends are safe
here, child. For as long as you need."

"Thank you. But we can't stay here. It would put you in danger."

"But where will you go?"

"Dad has a friend, a newspaper reporter, who lives in London. If
we can get Beethoven there, he'd be safe."

"How can a journalist protect him?"

"Dad told me this reporter, Telluride, has the entire story and
friends in high places. He knows how to keep a source safe, and he
knows about Beethoven and the WGC and everything. He's the one

who wrote that story that ran in the London Times."

"But what about you?"

"I haven't thought that far yet. I want to get Beethoven out of the country first. I guess I could go back to Oklahoma. My aunt and uncle still live there in a small town off the international radar."

The countess turned to Fa8. "And what about you, young man. You're involved in this, too. Where would you go?"

Fa8 smiled a crooked smile.

"Your very highness, any place is fine. I'm pretty much on me own, but London sounds tippie-toppie — almost like going home for a Liverpool rat like me."

The countess nodded and picked up a telephone by the sofa.

"Terrance, could you please come here? I am need of your help in making some travel arrangements."

As if by magic, Terrance appeared at the door.

"Yes, madam? What do you require?"

The countess turned in her chair.

"Where is my jet? I have need of it."

Terrance squirmed. "Your Lear, madam, is in Hong Kong. You loaned it to the French ambassador."

"Oh drat, that's right," the countess said. "I shall never play poker with him again." She looked again at Terrance. "How fast can we get it back here and ready to fly to London?"

"About three days, madam. But it will be expensive and we will have to make arrangements to bring the French ambassador and his family back to Austria."

"Do what needs to be done. Spare no expense."

"As you wish." Terrance said, turning on his heels and slipping out of the room.

"Now, Josephine," the countess said. "We have a way for you to leave, but we have to get you to the jet and that, dear child, will not be easy, I'm afraid."

"What do you suggest?"

"I suggest we lie low until Friday. The Lear will be back, refueled, and ready to fly, and we'll have the perfect distraction."

I felt my face screw up with confusion. "What would that be?"

"Why child, don't you remember? The Vienna National Symphony

Orchestra will perform at the Opera House Friday evening as part of the retrospective. The entire city will be in attendance — they're bringing in huge screens so those who couldn't get a seat in the hall can watch outside."

"I thought the Opera House was damaged by fire last year."

"It was," the countess said. "And it's taken a year and several million of my Euros to restore it. Friday night is its grand reopening."

"But how does that help us?"

The countess smiled. "We shall hide you and your friends in the Opera House. Once the concert starts we'll slip you out to a waiting car, then it's off with you to London, the United States, and points beyond."

"Do you think this plan will work?" Beethoven asked.

The countess nodded. "Yes, *Herr* Beethoven, I believe it will. We have a few days before the plane arrives. That's plenty of time to make arrangements and for you children to rest and eat a good meal."

Beethoven smiled. "A good meal would be nice."

Fa8 nodded in agreement. "I could use a little washy-wash, too," he said. "Between our modest accommodations and being chased by the ge-ne-ti-cal boys, I'm down to me last pair of knickers."

Countess Fiona pulled me against her in a tight, loving hug.

"You shall all, each one of you, have whatever you need. My humble home and its staff are at your disposal."

I gave her a big hug.

"Thank you. If it weren't for you, I'm not sure what we would have done."

"Do not fret, child, everything will be fine. Your worries are over, and they shall be gone for good on Friday."

"Did you say it was the grand reopening of the Opera House?"

"Yes, I did," the countess said.

"Will there be a performance?"

"Why, of course, it's part of his retrospective," she said, pointing at Beethoven. "The national symphony is performing your Ninth Symphony — the *Ode to Joy*."

Chapter 50

Peaceful, Easy Feeling

THE NEXT TWO DAYS WERE the most peaceful I had experienced in a long time. We stayed at the Summer Palace as guests of the countess. She proved to be an amazing host (not that I had expected anything less). For forty-eight hours, we might as well have been living in a fairy tale, because our every wish was someone's command.

I used the time to take a series of long hot bubble baths in a big claw-foot tub for hours on end. After the first day, I actually felt as if I'd finally rinsed the stink of our two hideouts off my skin.

For the first time in weeks, we also had fresh clothes. I don't know how she did it, but each of us had new garments — in our size — waiting for us in our rooms. There were mountains of food and deep, soft beds with comforters as white and fluffy as clouds.

Beethoven spent all of Wednesday in conversation with the countess. Fa8 slept and I actually got to talk with my dad. I'd sent him another (encrypted) e-mail to tell him where we were and that we were safe and it actually made it through. I couldn't believe it when he called just minutes later.

"I don't know why I didn't think of Fiona before," he said. "She's quite a woman."

"I didn't realize you knew her that well."

Through the phone, Dad laughed.

"Josephine, Countess Fiona was a dear friend of your mother's — of course, I knew her. The woman practically funded your mother's early career. And even after your mother became famous, the countess was one of her most loyal patrons."

"But I don't remember you ever talking about her."

I could hear him sigh over the phone.

"Honey, there's been so much going on for so long. Your mom and I used to talk about her, but maybe you were too young to remember. Then after your mom got sick, she wasn't up to seeking out her old friends from her Vienna days, and, as you know, the countess travels constantly for her various causes. After your mom died, there was that spell when we weren't talking and, well, it's just never come up. But I'm glad you've gotten to know her."

"I'm glad she is willing to help us."

"She said she could fly us out of the country Friday. I called Aunt Jean and she said I could stay with them."

Dad didn't say anything for a few moments.

"I think that's a good idea," he finally said. "I'll feel a lot safer with you out of Europe. How are Beethoven and Fa8?"

"Beethoven is great," I said. "He's doing a huge brain dump with the countess, filling in all those early history moments, telling her things that absolutely no one knows else knows about."

Dad laughed. "I'm sure she's thrilled. It's almost like being able to go back in time. What about Fa8?"

"Fa8 has been sleeping," I said. "He'd been keeping pretty long hours and I think it all finally caught up with him."

"That doesn't surprise me," Dad said. "I'm glad he's okay."

"Dad, he saved our hides more than once. Did you know he was a black belt in karate? He and a bunch of the Samurai Wannabes left those WGC thugs in the dust."

"I thought as much." Dad said. "I may have to rethink my opinion of that young man."

"Dad, you owe Fa8 and Beethoven a big thank-you. They have both fought so hard for me."

Dad heaved a deep, soulful sigh. "They understand what I've always known. You are so worth fighting for, Josie. You always have been. I don't know what I'd do if I lost you."

"Daddy, we're fine. We're staying with the countess until her Lear arrives. Then we'll be out of the country."

"Please stay in touch with me, Josie. I don't want to worry any more. And remember just how much I love you."

I hung up the phone and smiled. *I love you, too, Dad.*

. . . .

Friday arrived and with it came more snow. I had been so busy getting ready to leave the bad guys behind me, I hadn't actually thought about leaving the two guys I loved. I sat on the edge of the bed and looked through the big window and out at the cold, gray sky. For a week now, Beethoven and Fa8 had been the sole focus of my life and now, before this day was over, they would both be gone.

I tried to push the thought of good-byes — the idea of life without Fa8's banter and Beethoven's soulfulness — from my mind.

Beethoven, gone? I had only recently come to realize I loved him. Now I didn't know if I'd ever see him again.

And Fa8? He'd been the one steady and good part of my life since my mom died. Letting go of him would be like losing my safety net.

It didn't help that I knew I had broken his heart.

After he told me he loved me and I told him I loved him but not that way, our relationship changed. Oh, I knew he still cared and that he would always protect me, but a wall separated us now.

I walked down the hall to the countess's study. She and Beethoven were talking again. I watched them from the door. For the countess, their tête-à-têtes were a dream come true. With Beethoven's permission, she had recorded every one of their conversations.

I admired her, though, for not trying to turn Beethoven into a permanent artifact. The countess seemed to realize this was a moment suspended in time, and it would not come again.

Me, I just wanted to know if Beethoven loved me back.

. . . .

By six that evening, Vienna was covered in ice. The snow had stopped, and the sky was spitting sleet. I stuffed a small backpack with clothes, CDs, and the rest of the Euros that Dad had given me.

Part of me wanted to stay. Another part of me was heartbroken about being forced to leave Beethoven, but the rest of me was excited to get out of Vienna and return to Oklahoma.

I wiped away a few tears then placed the backpack on the floor. Someone knocked on the door.

"It's open."

The countess stepped in. "Josephine, are you ready to go?"

I gave her a wan smile. "I guess so."

"I'm sure you are conflicted. This has been a difficult time for you and your friends."

"It's not something I'd want to do again."

The countess held out a hand.

"Come child, your friends are waiting. It's time to go."

The countess had spared no expense. She wore a gown and silver tiara that I'm sure cost more than the gross national product of several small countries. Terrance had the dark gray Rolls-Royce Phantom waiting out front for us.

"Miss Brunswick," he said, motioning inside. I stepped in and scooted across the dark, soft leather.

The countess slid in next to me. "Are you comfortable?"

"Yes, ma'am. Are Beethoven and Fa8 coming with us?"

"Beethoven will be here shortly. Fa8 is going by a different vehicle. I thought it safer if he went a different route."

"Is . . . is everything okay?"

Countess Fiona scowled. "I hope so, child. Terrance has noticed several rather unscrupulous types lurking about the Opera House. He was concerned that our plans might encounter some resistance."

"Everything I've tried since this nightmare began has met with resistance," I said. "These people do not want us to leave."

"Life is filled with disappointments," Beethoven said, opening the door of the Rolls and getting in. "I am afraid our new friends will just have to be disappointed."

The streets in front of the Opera House were ablaze with color. Through the window, the dark, slick pavement glistened with the glow of a million lights. The Rolls stopped at the top of the curved drive. Terrance parked in front of the grand entrance so the countess could exit. He stood to the left, blocking anyone who might accidently see Beethoven and me scrunched down on the floorboards of the car.

The countess stood and waved as strobes from hundreds of camera blinked off and on. As she took a step forward, she half-turned and whispered: "Be safe, child."

Terrance pulled away, circled the Opera House, and drove to a private parking garage four or five blocks away. He pulled inside and closed the garage door.

"You may exit now," he said, opening the back door of the Rolls.

He pointed to a small white delivery truck with a large rose painted on the side. "This will be your next ride." He handed us two white smocks with the same rose stitched on the pocket. "Countess Fiona owns this company. And there will be many, many flowers delivered tonight. Please put the smocks on and get in the back. We will arrive at the delivery entrance of the Opera House where I shall give you further instructions."

By the time we returned to the Opera House most of the crowd was inside. A few stray delivery vehicles were parked in the back. Terrance pulled the van in next to an outside door. He handed each of us a large crystal vase filled with bright pink roses.

"Take these and go inside. Walk five paces and turn to your left. You will see a small freight elevator. Take it to the top floor. Exit and go immediately right. You will see a room with the light on. Go inside and wait."

"How will we —?"

Terrance waved me silent. "Ask no questions. Speak to no one. If someone asks, your names are Ingrid and Frank. You are making a flower delivery and you are behind schedule. Do you understand?"

"*Ja!*" Beethoven said. "We will do exactly as you say."

Terrance smiled. "Good. Now go!"

We walked quietly down the hall. As we passed various doors, I heard voices speaking about schedules and timetables and why this or that employee was late. Someone touched my hand. I almost screamed until I realized it was Beethoven.

"Josephine, before this night ends, I must speak with you," he said. "There are things I must tell you."

"I suggest you hurry, then," I said, with a smile, as we stepped on the freight elevator. "Because we don't have much time left."

The elevator stopped as Terrance said it would, and we got off in a dark hallway. About ten yards ahead, a light glowed underneath a wooden door.

"This way." I pulled Beethoven towards the light.

It was a storage room filled with boxes, music stands, and stray props. Across the room, a window looked down on the street below. We followed the light, weaving around boxes and pedestals, until we came to a small table with two chairs. Someone had even thought to provide bottled water and sandwiches. There was a small note from the countess that read: "In case you get hungry. Terrance has the only key to this room. You are safe. Things will be better soon."

"Well, here we are," I said, reaching for Beethoven's hand. "You said you had something to say to me?"

He opened his mouth to answer, but never got the words out. Instead he held his hand to his ear. "Is that my music?"

"I believe they've started the Ninth."

The faint notes from his Ninth Symphony filled the room. We both strained to hear it better. I pointed to a small metal ladder. The sign next to it showed an arrow pointing up and the words "ceiling lights" in German and English.

"We could go up there," I said. "I think it connects to the rafters so the workmen can service the stage lights."

"Then come," he said, standing and reaching for my hand. "Let us find a spot closer to heaven."

"L.B., are you sure you want to do this? Remember what you said about not wanting to know your past. This music, this entire performance, is from your past. It's your most glorious work. It's your *Symphony No. 9*."

"I know this, Josephine. But over the past few days I have had many conversations with the countess. She explained how this one piece, this work, was so different. Countess Fiona told me this work, my work, had become the symbol for many of universal brotherhood."

"She's right. The Ninth. Your Ninth transcends music."

Beethoven nodded and put his hands to his ears.

"But in my first life I would never have heard the music. I know that now. The countess said I conducted this symphony only one time

— in silence. Throughout so much of my life, the world was silent. And this piece, if it is what the world says it is, is the defining moment of my first life."

"I would say it was."

"Then I must take the chance. I must listen. God has given me a second chance to learn, a second chance to listen to what he dictated to me. Who am I to deny him?"

I stepped onto the ladder and motioned for Beethoven to follow.

"You are Ludwig von Beethoven," I whispered. "And whether you believe it or not, in this life and in your past life, you will always be one of God's finest gifts to mankind."

We climbed until we came to a catwalk. Scrunching down, we kept going until we found a platform where we could sit near an opening in the middle of the large circular theater. Large, glowing spotlights surrounded us every forty feet or so. The platform wasn't big, but it was big enough that we could both sit there and not be seen.

"We must be very, very quiet," I whispered. "The acoustics in this opera house are fantastic; it would be very easy to be overheard."

In the darkness, he pulled me closer, then gently traced the curve of my face.

"You are my beloved," he whispered.

Softly, he kissed me. "You will always be my beloved."

I laid my head on his shoulder and together, we listened.

Chapter 51

Ode to Joy

THE MUSIC STARTED softly. I knew in his first life, Beethoven had marked the first passage to be played pianissimo, but already the music was building. The first movement was powerful and sensuous. Listening, I felt like I was inside a storm rolling in across the Oklahoma prairie.

Beethoven was listening intently. It was obvious even in the dark, because his whole body was rigid. He gripped a metal support with one hand and, with the other, held me. Yet the glimpses I caught of his face showed him to be peaceful, almost serene.

"You okay?" I whispered.

Silently, he squeezed my hand.

By the second movement he was unreachable. He was hearing things he would have been denied in his first life. And the second movement, with its timpani solos and triple-quadruple time, seemed to have taken him to a place far away from the physical world.

I nestled closer to him and tried to imagine what it would feel like to have bared one's soul in front of the world in a creation you thought you would never get to hear yourself, only to somehow miraculously get a second chance.

For a moment, I looked down into the dark. Somewhere hundreds of feet below, the countess listened. Somehow I knew that she, too, was hearing the voice of God this night.

The sensation of Beethoven tracing the melody in my palm as the orchestra played it below left me shaking. I had never experienced anything so intimate in my life, and I couldn't help but wonder if I would ever experience its equal again.

. . . .

The third movement brought Beethoven back to earth.

Lyrical and soft, the music of the winds and strings drifted above us like fat, slow moving clouds. Watching him, feeling him, knowing that he was hearing his own work for the first time — that moment was the most beautiful thing I had ever experienced.

I glanced at my watch. Five minutes after nine. I knew we needed to get back to the storage room. I pulled on Beethoven's sleeve and pointed at my watch face.

"No, please," he whispered. "Let me hear the entire piece."

"We're running out of time," I whispered back.

"We will find time, Josephine. But we will never be here, at this moment, again."

He was right. I sat back down and gave myself over to the fourth movement. As the chorus swelled and the voices of the choir blended with the voices of the instruments, I understood Beethoven and what he was living in that moment.

I could feel the intensity of his desire, the longing of his heart. I knew, instinctively, just how bright the fire burned within his heart for the music he composed.

This was not just his life's work . . . this was his bared soul.

And even though he had yet to compose it, he understood that this symphony was his own voice speaking to him through time and across the centuries.

And there, suspended high above the stage, as the final strains of music filled the opera house, and the last notes of the trumpets swelled to their great crescendo, Beethoven squeezed my hand.

And the tears drifted down his face.

Chapter 52

Don't You Forget About Me

IT WAS PROBABLY A GOOD IDEA that we stayed until the end. The finish brought the crowd to its feet. People were applauding and cheering, and the noise was almost deafening.

"Come, now," Beethoven said, standing. "The sound of the audience will protect us. We may move quickly back to our nest."

. . . .

The first thing I saw when we opened the door of the storage room was the face of a frantic Terrance.

"Thank God, you're here! I've looked everywhere for you two. Where did you go?"

I pointed at the dumbwaiter.

"He wanted to hear the Ninth."

Terrance's face softened.

"I understand. To wait more than two centuries to hear one's own music would be difficult, to pass up the chance to hear it for the first time after two centuries would be foolish."

I could tell Beethoven appreciated Terrance understanding why we had disobeyed our orders.

"I am a different man now," said Beethoven. "I have looked into Heaven and I have heard the voice of God."

"I believe you have, son," said Terrance as he motioned towards the door. "But now I'm afraid we must leave. Already tonight has seen one attempted break-in thwarted. Police are everywhere. Now with the crowd at its heaviest, we must move. Your driver is here. The jet is ready. We must go."

I felt my stomach sink. The only boy I'd ever loved — the only one I would probably ever love — was about to walk out of my life.

"Josephine, you must not cry, please." Beethoven said, cupping my face in his large hands. "I do not wish to part this way."

"But I may never see you again."

He took me in his arms and kissed me.

"I do not wish to go. Know that I wish to stay with you forever."

Terrance motioned again at the door.

"Please," Terrance said. "We must leave now."

We held each other until the elevator deposited us on the ground floor. Terrance stepped off first; he held his hand up, like a policeman, signaling for us to stay in the shadows. After a moment, he waved us forward.

"We want no witnesses," he whispered.

Quietly we slipped out the back of the Opera House and into the cold, icy night. Terrance started for the street and, again, motioned for us to follow.

"Softly," he said, "like little mice."

Hidden under a single overcoat, Beethoven and I scurried across the pavement. Then I stopped. There were no cars anywhere. The street was dark and empty.

"I don't understand. I thought you said we had a ride."

"You do, Josephine. Over there." He pointed to a dark limousine parked by the curb about two hundred yards away. "That's your car."

Gently, he pushed me forward.

I resisted. "But what about Beethoven? I'm not leaving until I know he is safe."

"*Fraulein*, you must have faith. *Herr* Beethoven's ride is right there, by that large bus."

I looked to where he was pointing. About seventy-five feet from me, bathed in light from a single streetlamp, a tall, slender man sat on a motorcycle He was dressed entirely in black, from helmet to boots, except for a patch in the center of his back — the Union Jack.

"Fa8? Is that Fa8 on the motorcycle?"

"*Ja.* He said he would not allow anyone else to get *Herr* Beethoven out of the country. He said he'd come too far with him to turn him over to the lackey of a countess."

"Terrance, I'm so very sorry. Sometimes, Fa8 can be a little short on manners."

Terrance smiled and waved me off.

"*Herr* Fa8 and I have become great friends," he said. "He is quite the young man."

Terrance pointed again towards Fa8.

"Now, you must say your good-byes. Keep it short. We have no more time. The jet is ready. All is in place. It would be a shame to have it all go south now."

Beethoven took my hand and walked me across the dark street until we stood next to Fa8 and his motorcycle. In the soft yellow light, he brushed his cheek against my face.

"Come Josephine, another kiss then I must leave you."

"But what will you do? Where will you go?"

Beethoven pointed to the motorcycle.

"That is up to my Fa8," he said.

"You said you wanted to tell me something. What was it? Please tell me."

Beethoven pulled me against him and kissed me again.

"There is an envelope for you in the car," he whispered. "A letter for your eyes only."

"Why can't you tell me now."

Beethoven smiled — for a moment I saw an older, wiser Beethoven.

"Patience, Josephine. Remember I am old-fashioned. Some things are meant to be written. Just remember you are my beloved, my immortal beloved. You were the love of my past life and you are again in this life. You are my beloved and I am your Beethoven, and I will always adore you."

"I will always love you, too. All this, it has changed me forever."

Beethoven nodded with understanding.

"Go now, but remember that you take my very soul with you."

I turned to walk away when I heard a voice.

"Josie." It was Fa8. He was seated on his motorcycle with his helmet in his hand, a most sorrowful look on his English face.

"Yes?"

"Remember me fondly, eh luv."

What can I say, Fa8 might not be the love of my life, but he was my friend. Only God knew when I would see him again. I ran to him and gave him a tight hug.

"You are my Fa8, too. Know that I will never forget you or what you have done for me, for my father, and for Beethoven. You are one of a kind, Frederick Bartholomew Rosenguild."

Fa8 tipped his head, but I could see he was pleased.

He slipped his helmet back on and, with a swift kick, started the motorcycle.

Beethoven climbed on behind him.

"Good-bye, my beloved, Josephine. Do not forget me."

And with that, Fa8 and Beethoven were gone, lost to the night.

Epilogue

TRIA DABBED AT HER EYES with her bandanna.

"This, all this, really happened? Seriously?"

"Yeah. It's weird. In some ways it seems like yesterday, but most days if feels like Beethoven and Fa8 have been gone forever."

Michelle's face betrayed her skepticism.

"Josie, you know I love you, but I'm sorry — it's hard to get my head around the idea that you 'replicated' a nineteen-year-old Ludwig von Beethoven. Ya know?"

This was why I never talked about my past. I knew it was so strange that no one would ever believe me.

"I'll grant you it is a pretty strange story," I said, fingering the chain at my neck.

"It's just that it's . . ."

"It's okay, Michelle. You don't have to believe me, but it did happen. For a moment I loved a boy and for a moment, he loved me back."

Michelle's eyes filled with tears. "Josie, I'm not trying to . . ."

I gave her a sad, little smile.

"He kissed me. He said I was beautiful and he shared my music."

Tria scooted closer to me. "Well, I believe you."

She pointed to my notebook, its contents now strewn all over the room, and then at the locket she knew never left my neck, though she'd never known until today what it carried.

"There's too much here not to believe," Tria said. "And no wonder you're so angry, Josie. To have found such a love, and then to have it ripped away from you before it even had a chance. I think I understand now what you're trying to do with that song . . . his song.

"Besides, why would you make up such a story and then talk about it. No one does that."

Michelle gave me a faint smile. "I . . . I guess Tria has a point."

"It was a first for me," I confided. "He said he loved me. He called me his beloved. Then he had to go and I haven't seen him since."

Michelle sobbed. "Okay, okay, I give. I want . . . heck, everyone wants to be loved like that, but what happened after Vienna? Why have you not seen Beethoven since that night?"

"You want to hear the rest?"

Both girls nodded.

"Oh, hell, yeah," said Michelle.

. . . .

We set our guitars aside. Michelle traded her drums for an armchair. Tria and I curled up on the studio couch.

I took a deep breath and hoped I could get through the rest of the story without falling apart. It wasn't going to be easy.

. . . .

The night Beethoven and Fa8 left, I found in the back seat of the countess's limo, just as Beethoven had promised, an envelope with my name scrawled across it.

I couldn't bring myself to open it; I was way too upset.

Instead, I sobbed all the way to the private airport near the Austrian-German border, and when the last tear fell it was like I lost my ability to cry. I haven't shed a tear since, until today.

Terrance didn't say anything the whole ride, until we stopped on the tarmac. And then he only pointed to a small Gulfstream jet parked on the runway and told me it belonged to a friend of the countess. It was my ride home. He told me the countess's own jet was already on its way to London with Beethoven and Fa8.

"*Herr* Beethoven is safe," he said.

I sighed with relief, thanked him, and asked him to also thank the countess for all she'd done to help me and my friends. As I turned to go, Terrance handed me a small beautiful box.

He called it "a little good-bye gift from the countess."

I climbed the stairs to the cabin of the jet and found a seat. Just as Terrance had promised, everything was on board. Blue tubs of my belongings were stacked at the back of the cabin. And across the aisle, encased in bubble wrap and belted into the seat, was my Flying V.

I unwrapped the small box from Countess Fiona and smiled. Inside, a card said simply, "Embrace your future." Underneath, the countess had placed a small locket on a silver chain. Inside the locket was a silhouette of Beethoven. I placed the locket around my neck, closed my eyes, and pushed back into the soft leather seat.

Ten hours later, we landed at Tulsa International. Because of the time change, I woke up feeling like I had gone back in time. And, maybe, in a way I had.

Though it was still winter, Tulsa was warm and sunny. I had no more stepped onto Oklahoma ground, when I noticed a parked red car and a man leaning on the hood. I recognized that ball cap, the goofy smile, the University of Tulsa sweatshirt — Dad.

I raced down the steps and threw myself into his arms.

"I was afraid I'd never see you again."

"Oh, honey, it would take more than a ring of international thugs to keep me away from my little girl." Dad held me at arm's length. "You don't look any the worse for wear."

"I'm okay," I said. "What about you? How did you get here? What happened with the WGC? Did Beethoven and Fa8 reach London?"

"Easy, Josephine. All in good time." Dad opened the door of the car — it was his old red Mustang — and slid in the driver's seat. "Get in. We'll talk on the way to Aunt Jean's."

I pointed to the airplane. "I am not leaving my guitar behind."

"Relax, we're home. Everything is in safe hands. A few of those containers are filled with my belongings, too, you know."

The Immortal Von B.

. . . .

For safety's sake, Dad decided we couldn't return to Lookout Mountain. Nor did he feel it was wise for us to locate nearby. So we said good-bye to eastern Oklahoma and headed south and west. We were going to live with my dad's sister, Aunt Jean, for a while. She lived outside Norman, the home of the University of Oklahoma.

It was nice to be around family again and back under the huge expanse of Oklahoma sky. And slowly, my life returned to a kind of normal. After a few weeks, the panic attacks subsided. I quit waking up in the middle of the night screaming for Dad.

Just as I was beginning to feel normal, all hell broke loose again — but at least this time it didn't involve me.

It was a Monday, and I walked in on Dad staring at the television. On screen a TV reporter stood outside the FBI building in Washington, D.C. Before I could ask Dad what was going on, the reporter said: "Law enforcement authorities from fourteen nations held a joint press conference today at the Federal Bureau of Investigation in Washington, D.C. A spokesman for the group said the agencies — including the CIA, Mossad, and Scotland Yard — have taken down the world's largest organ smuggling ring . . .

". . . CIA spokesman Donald Perry said undercover teams from Scotland Yard and the FBI, acting on information provided to them by a London Times reporter, arrested one hundred and thirty-seven individuals here and abroad associated with the World Genetics Council."

I looked at Dad. "Does this mean the nightmare is over?"

Dad smiled. "I believe so."

"Then why don't you look happier?"

"I'm pretty sure I'll have to fly to London and testify," he said.

He handed me a copy of the London Times.

"Read this, page seventeen, second column."

The headline was short: "Fire Destroys Historic Villa." Beneath it, a photograph showed flames engulfing Villa Theresa.

"Oh my God, does this mean everything is gone? My music? Mom's piano? Your lab?"

"No, honey. That's the funny part. Seems the villa was emptied before the fire broke out. All your belongings and your mother's piano are safe. Rumor has it some eccentric woman — claiming to be a countess — on a whim had everything moved out before the fire. As for my lab, equipment, and research, well, that's another story."

I gripped Dad's hand. "I'd say I'm sorry but part of me was never sure about the whole human replication thing."

Dad nodded, a sad look on his face. He handed me a stack of newspapers, the New York Times, the International Herald Tribune, the Washington Post. The story was everywhere.

"I can't believe I didn't realize what I was involved in," he said. "But at least I helped put a stop to it."

I put my arms around him.

"You did the right thing."

. . . .

Right after the televised news report, just as he predicted, Dad had to fly to London to testify in court. After it was over, the jury convicted everyone with the WGC, except for Hans Gottlieb. They would have convicted him, too, but he managed to slip out of the country. Seems the judge didn't appreciate what a flight risk he was. Despite a world-wide manhunt, he has yet to be found. And all these years later, that still keeps me up some nights.

Dad said good riddance — and promised me the law or karma would catch up with Mr. Gottlieb. Never one for looking back, Dad focused on rebuilding our lives. After the trial, we officially moved to Norman, where Dad went to work as a genetics professor at O.U.

Things settled down after that.

I finished high school and entered college. I chose to study — surprise, surprise — music. I should have been happy. But, honestly, I wasn't. In all this time, there had been no word from Fa8 or Beethoven — unless you counted one cryptic text message the day after I left Europe. But that didn't begin to explain the rest of the silence. Since that night in Vienna, I hadn't heard anything from Theresa or Countess Fiona or anybody else in Austria.

It was as if the Vienna nightmare had never happened.

I fluctuated from elation at being back home and safe with what remained of my family to being incredibly sad missing Beethoven and Fa8 — was it any wonder the few friends I did make at college thought I was bipolar.

I was also still scared.

I never learned for absolute certain whether Beethoven made it to London and I didn't know where Fa8 had landed either. To make matters worse, the one thing I did know for certain after all these years was that I loved Beethoven — and I loved him so much more than I had ever realized, so much that it physically hurt.

The night I left Vienna for good, he'd left a letter for me. In it he had said he loved me and that I was his immortal beloved. I have slept with that letter under my pillow every single night since. And every time I look at his spidery scrawl, my heart stops.

His letter and my locket are all I have to remind me that Vienna did happen, that it was not a figment of my imagination.

It's not that I haven't tried.

For months I sent e-mails to Fa8 but they all, eventually, bounced back, labeled "no such recipient." I tried reaching out to Theresa at the Haus der Musik, but was told she'd resigned and had left no forwarding information. I tried contacting the countess, also to no avail.

All these people had been so dear to me, and now it was as if they had never existed. I tried talking to Dad about it, with the hope he might volunteer some of his global connections or maybe Tel to help me find my friends or at least maybe learn what had happened to them, but Dad didn't want to discuss Vienna.

"That's the past, honey," he said. "Let it go."

No amount of pleading on my part would change his mind. I know he believed reaching out to anyone in Vienna would be to open the door for Gottlieb to find us, so eventually I let it go. And, as I had in the aftermath of my mother's death, I turned, once more, to my music.

And his songs.

. . . .

Michelle and Tria threw their arms around me, tears streaming down their faces. I'm not sure they believed me a hundred percent, but they seemed to know that I believed it.

"We'll get that song right for you next practice," Tria vowed.

Michelle nodded, furiously.

"It's the least we can do. Maybe it will help you feel better about him, about his being gone."

I smiled a little smile.

I was lucky to have such friends, such loyal and good bandmates.

The girls headed home, and I headed back to what was left of my life without the boy I loved . . . or my best friend.

· · · · · · · · · ·

I was late for rehearsal for The Red Dirt Vixens.

Tria needed to leave early today — boyfriend trouble — and Michelle had a study session later tonight, so we were practicing at my house, which is near campus. I should have been there an hour ago, but I had gotten hung up at this funky little bookstore in Oklahoma City and forgotten about the time.

So now I was racing down the interstate.

It was nice driving with the top down. The sun was warm and the sky filled with huge, fluffy clouds.

I turned on the radio. It was tuned to the KATT. No surprise. That station is like some kind of radio god to Dad. After we moved to Norman, he programmed every radio in the house and both cars to receive it.

"It's great music," he said. "Old stuff, new stuff. Cutting edge and bleeding edge."

"Yeah right. You just like it because late at night they play Boston and Pink Floyd."

Dad closed his eyes and sighed.

"Yeah, those were musicians."

Whatever.

I took the Robinson Street exit and turned up the volume. A song was just ending. I only caught the last twenty seconds of it, but those seconds stilled my heart. There were strings and a killer guitar riff all overlaid with some of the best piano work I'd heard in a long time.

The last seconds were particularly unusual — everything faded to a minor chord, then to white noise, then finally to a strange whisper-like hiss.

I made a mental note: that song's a keeper.

. . . .

Band practice was over. The girls were gone. I walked into the living room. Dad was snoozing on the couch. It was time to turn the television off and finish my homework — three reports due by Friday and a test next week.

I went upstairs, dropped my stuff on my desk, and plugged my headphones into my computer. It was time to get some work done. I clicked on a playlist — some old rhythm-and-blues and a piece by Bach. For some reason, none of them satisfied. And to make matters worse, I couldn't get that snippet of song I had heard that afternoon out of my head.

Great and I don't even know the name of it.

I turned on the radio. The KATT was playing *Minority*, an oldie by Green Day and not the song I was looking for. The Internet wasn't much help either, but then I didn't have much to go on. "Whisper," "white noise," and "guitar static" didn't give the Google algorithm much to work with. Then I tried *Billboard*'s website.

"The Brits are Back!" the headline screamed. "Previously unknown U.K. band talk of the music industry."

One click later, the story pulled up. Seems a new British band, Von B. and the Immortals, had released a song that, in four days, had sky-rocketed to the top of the Billboard Top 100.

My brain started spinning. I sat down at my desk and clicked on the link to the song. The page that opened was entirely black, except for a white outline of a single boy playing a guitar.

I clicked.

It was the right song. And, oh my God, it was amazing. Guitar, piano, strings, timpani; it was as if an orchestra, a county western band, and the best jazz group to ever make a record had married a rock band and this song was their only child. I put on my headphones and cranked the volume up.

It was called *Beloved*, and it was one of those rare songs that would not let you go once you heard it. Listening, I felt as if someone had reached through the airwaves, gone inside my heart, pulled out every feeling, and set them to music.

I Googled the band's name. There were hundreds of links to the song and a dozen or so to the band, but nothing anywhere said who the musicians were.

I rolled my eyes.

Why would a musician who was capable of such music not want the world to know who he or she was?

It made no sense.

I downloaded the song file to my laptop and spent the next two hours playing it over and over and over. I analyzed every word and every note. *It was so tightly written it was almost perfect.*

Almost but not quite.

The first four minutes were harmony. The ending was like a scratch on a beautiful painting. As the final guitar riff faded, it sounded like the producer had overdubbed radio static against thirty seconds of white noise.

The white noised faded in and out, then there was something that sounded to me like a whisper.

I played it several times trying to hear the words.

Nothing worked.

Finally I put the file through a sound enhancement program Fa8 had written a few years ago. I eliminated the static and the white noise, then amped up the whisper. I filtered it until I had a recognizable voice pattern, and then cranked up the volume as high as it would go.

This time I could hear the voice.

"You are my beloved," the voice said. "Continue to love me. I am yours, Josephine. And no matter where you are I'll find you . . . Josephine, I'll find you . . ."

I couldn't believe my ears. My heart raced.

I played the song again. And again.

". . . I love you, Josephine. And no matter where you are I will someday find you . . ."

My heart felt as if it would leap through my chest.

I tapped the Play button again.

It was . . .

The Immortal Von B.

It had to be . . . Beethoven.

". . . Josephine I'll find you . . ."

I hit Pause and stared at the screen of my computer.

In that moment everything became clear.

I knew Fa8 was alive, those were his bass riffs.

And I knew Beethoven was with him, because no one else could have written such magic.

And, finally, I knew all I needed to know.

My Beethoven was out there, searching and playing and writing new music . . . music just for me.

He wasn't Ludwig or Louie or L.B., he was the Immortal Von B.

And he was looking for me.

A Note from the Author

This book is a love story to music and culture and the millions of hours my friends and I spent listening to rock 'n' roll. Back when I was in college, moving into a new place always meant setting up the stereo first. This book is my attempt to acknowledge that moment — and the instant I first heard a new song and fell in love with it.

This book is also a love letter to Ludwig von Beethoven.

For more than two hundred years, his music has survived shifting time and tastes. In my case, it touched my very soul. Beethoven was a rebel and a man who wrote his music, his way. He offered no apology, but, instead, did his own thing.

This book is my nod to that independence.

This book is also a love story about a boy and a girl. First love is often the most beautiful, and the most painful. This is the story of such a love — between a boy and a girl, and a husband and a wife.

Yes, this book is a love story.

I hope you enjoy it.

There are dozens of people that I should thank for their help. But a few stand out. Mel Odom, my writing professor at the University of Oklahoma, and Jeanne Devlin, my editor at The RoadRunner Press. Both of these people believed in me when no one else did; they are at the top of the list.

But there are others: my wife, Karen; my family — including my parents, K. L. and Jean Carter; and many friends, such as Jelani Sims, Bekah Terry, Sarah Gray, and Ted Streuli, all of whom have kept me going when I did not think I could.

This book is dedicated to Paula Scheider who inspired the original idea. Yes, I remember that day and I still remember the song.

And finally, a special thank you to Stormy Jones, who walked into a classroom at the University of Oklahoma one day and brought Josephine Brunswick to life.

May each of you find your true passion.

M. Scott Carter
Oklahoma City
Winter 2012